COLLISION

COLLISION

SIEGFRIED FINSER

Library of Congress Control Number:		2016901082
ISBN:	Hardcover	978-1-5144-5256-1
	Softcover	978-1-5144-5255-4
	eBook	978-1-5144-5254-7

Print information available on the last page.

Author can be contacted at:
siegfin@gmail.com
www.finserpublications.com

Rev. date: 01/22/2016

To order additional copies of this book, contact:
Xlibris
1-888-795-4274
www.Xlibris.com
Orders@Xlibris.com
728776

CONTENTS

I dedicate this book, my first novel, to my wife, Ruth Finser. The past sixty years together have been an absolute treasure. Aside from our joys and good times together, she is a friend and colleague. Ruth has been a constant reminder that we are both still works in progress. Due to her loving efforts, I may turn out to be a good man after all.

I would also like to acknowledge the honest and gentle help of my two sons and daughter, as well as our seven grandchildren. In particular, Thomas Finser took the time to read and make valuable suggestions in the forming of this story. Armida Finser and Yohanna Finser contributed their amazing artistic and technical assistance. I feel myself surrounded and supported by the most incredible people, the members of my family. I am grateful they all chose to incarnate in our time.

CHAPTER ONE

Innocent Beginnings

In New York City, on the lower west side below Central Park, at Forty-Sixth Street, a special kind of meeting was taking place. The Premium Technical Products Incorporated was about to get together for the second time with the president and an assortment of vice presidents of its newly acquired subsidiary, Croton Green Incorporated. This small profitable company had dominated the grass seed and lawn products market for more than two decades. Its reputation for high quality and excellent service extended throughout North America and Europe. It was poised to enter the Latin American countries with an equally excellent version of its original grass seed. Competition was virtually negligible.

The owner had recently died, and the heirs were delighted to sell. Premium Technical Products Incorporated was equally delighted to buy as another step in its strategy for growth.

Facing Forty-Sixth street, the warehouse-type square brownstone building looked unimpressive. The windows were small and evenly spaced across the front. It was impossible to look through them. The glass was heavily opaque with city grime. There were no elevators but multiple flights of stairs at each corner of the building. If you were employed there, you didn't stay overweight very long. The entrance did not offer any welcome but ushered you directly into a large office that smelled of work. Stacks of papers and reports greeted the visitor.

Only one area of the entire building had been remodeled and refurbished. It was up a single flight of stairs. The entire floor was one large conference room complete with enormous wall-projection screens on three sides. Darkly stained curved tables created a large oval that encircled the entire room with just enough space outside the oval to accommodate sixty comfortable easy chairs that swiveled and tilted as desired. This room was the dream child of Armand Dillon, president and chief executive officer of the Premium Technical Products Corporation.

Twenty of the comfortable chairs around the oblong of tables were occupied. The president of Croton Green sat in the middle of the far side. On either side of his location sat the vice presidents, including Finance and Controller. Although they bent forward occasionally to exchange some words with each other, they mostly waited.

On the near side of the oval, the chairs were all empty. In the middle of the oval, a technician was fussing with the hidden projectors to make sure they worked properly for the meeting. A half hour passed uneventfully except for some mumbled annoyance, which was not tolerated by the president of Croton Green. Bending forward and with a single frown, he silenced the low murmur, and they continued to wait. The president was planning how he might register some kind of complaint at the appropriate moment. After all, he had brought his whole upper staff to this meeting at considerable cost and inconvenience. He was an old-fashioned middle-management type who liked everything to run smoothly and on time. It was now ten o'clock, an hour late for the nine o'clock meeting.

Somewhere in the atmosphere, there was a rustling of movement, hardly audible. They felt it rather than heard it. They just knew something was stirring. On the near side, doors opened into the room, and in seconds, all the seats were occupied except one, which was then promptly filled with Armand Dillon, president and CEO of the Premium Technical Products Corporation. How the newcomers all knew the meeting was about to really start was a mystery. It was like a psychic awakening felt in the entire building.

Armand was medium in size, wore an ill-fitting black suit, white shirt, and dark blue tie. Although he did not wear eyeglasses, he seemed to be peering out of deeply shadowed eyes, squinting to grasp details. His face was long for his size, gray in color, and sharply contoured. Gray crinkled hair added a touch of roundness to what otherwise was a singularly angular impression. He peered at the assembled executives, apparently checking to see if all the right people were there, and then he pulled a stack of reports and loose papers toward himself and smiled grimly at the president of Croton Green.

"I think we're ready, Russ. Go ahead. It's your show," he said. As he spoke, he glanced to the right and then to the left along his side of the oblong, nodding in what was supposed to be a friendly salute to his own staff. He never blinked. His eyes had a perpetual stare, carefully noting every detail around him and the slightest movement of any kind at all attracted his scrutiny. It was general knowledge that all employees of PTP were included in an underground betting pool to be won by the first person to identify the actual color of his eyes. They glinted darkly but did not reveal any particular color. It was even rumored, but unconfirmed, that they sometimes changed, like a mood stone devoid of feeling. No emotion found its way to be revealed in those dark, uncompromising pools of analytical intelligence.

"There should be no doubt in anyone's mind that by now we are also ready, Armand, and have been for some time!" was the Croton Green president's opening remark. He paused meaningfully while a small snicker rippled through his staff on his side of the oval. No doubt it seemed to reinstate the respect his staff had for him and he basked in their approval.

"I hope that's not your entire report today!" Armand raised an eyebrow and frowned, taking in the whole staff on the other side of the table with an icy stare. When he spoke, nothing in the structure of his face appeared to move. It seemed as though a mask were sounding out of a deep cavern, revealing nothing of his true feelings on the surface.

"Not at all. We've prepared a number of items for this meeting. If you agree, Armand, we'll start with a brief explanation of our history, our hard and soft assets, a financial report by our VP of Finance and then open it up for questions and comments. Does this seem right to you?"

Armand bent forward and spoke something in a low voice to his own controller who sat just two seats further on his right. He then rifled through some papers and finally looked up to answer the question. Some thought it was a deliberate ploy to make sure everyone understood who was in charge of the meeting, totally unnecessary given the circumstances.

"You know, Russ, we've been through a lot of this stuff in the last months while this acquisition—excuse me—merger was taking place. None of us are hearing about Croton Green for the first time. This is your show, and we'll listen, but bear in mind we already know each other." Armand leaned back in his comfortable chair, his long forehead catching the glint from the embedded ceiling lights.

"I think you'll find this interesting, what we've got prepared for you. Our staff has worked hard to share certain things you may not know, Armand," Russ answered.

"All right, get on with it. I suggest you diminish some of the history and product information and linger a bit longer on the financials. We've also got questions of our own you might find interesting."

"Certainly, Armand. We'll start with a short presentation of our history and reputation only because it gives substance to our strategy for future development. I believe you know Karl, who's been leading our development work for many years now. Take it away, Karl."

Karl painted a rosy picture of the growth of Croton Green. He described the work ethics of the original owner and his principle that hard work never exhausted, but conflict and frustration did. His whole manner of dealing with employees and customers was clearly described as a hint to Armand, who took the message with a sour, unmoved expression. His own staff glanced frequently in his direction. They had learned to read correctly every nuance of meaning from the way he tilted his head, the hunching of his shoulders, even the slight gesturing of his hands every now and then.

When Karl was finished, he offered to answer any questions. Armand's staff looked in his direction and scrutinized his face for an indication of what to do. Armand said nothing. His lips were pinched together meaningfully. Since Armand did not encourage it, no questions surfaced.

"What's next?" Armand broke the silence.

"We had a great deal more prepared, but I'd like to interrupt the flow and go directly to our strategy for the future, Armand. I know that's really what you're interested in." Russ made this split-second, on-his-feet decision.

"Hear, hear!" Armand drummed the table with his pencil signifying his approval. The staff all shifted in their seats, a little more at ease in the less tense atmosphere Armand had signaled. Russ smiled and gave a nod to the technician at the controls for the video display screens.

The video presentation appeared on all three screens simultaneously. The technician adjusted the audio volume down slightly. It began with a picture of the late founder of Croton Green. It described his devotion to the customers, some testimonials and many examples of him in the actual practice of service. The staff of Croton Green watched with a kind of reverence that appeared genuine. The PTP staff fidgeted and occasionally checked the hard copy of the presentation, which was part of their preparatory material.

Included in the presentation was a fact-filled analysis of the South American market and how Croton Green was prepared to capture it within a period of three years. When it ended, everyone shifted in the comfortable chairs and turned to look in Armand's direction.

"Thank you. I believe that all of this in no way contradicts or enhances what was already known from our previous meetings. Your staff should be congratulated on their consistency. Has anything changed in the financial presentation from the last time we met, here, I believe, in this room?"

"No. No material changes. We are still as profitable as before." The controller rose from his seat ready with his presentation.

"I'm glad to hear that. It saves a great deal of time, since we are all quite familiar with them. I suspect this means we can move on to our questions?" Armand waved his left hand in the general direction of his own staff. "Cliff, do you want to hit the highlights of your analysis?"

"Sure. Armand asked me to take a look at some of your profit margins. This meant digging a little deeper since I am not an expert in your industry. Thank God your controller is . . . an expert that is. Most of this information came from him rather than dipping into the actual minutiae. I have no reason to doubt his accuracy, as it was volunteered so openly."

Russ and the rest of his staff leaned forward slightly to check with the controller, who shrugged his shoulders.

"Enough with the credits. How about the facts?" Armand interrupted.

"The profit margins on the various products of Croton Green would surprise you. In a retail store where everything is purchased and then resold, the profit margins are easy to determine, and they generally run about the same from product to product due to a uniform markup approach. In this business, the profit per product is difficult to find due to a wide range of expense factors and markup applications. We had to use multiple allocations, differing for each product."

"All of that is no surprise! I trust your methodology. What are your findings?" Armand was tapping the table impatiently with the eraser end of his pencil. That could mean only one thing—he, Armand, had already found something he wanted to hear.

Cliff licked his lips and then wiped them with the back of his hand.

"It seems the amount of profit on each product does correlate inversely with the volume of sales in the normal way. As a rule, the higher the volume of goods sold, the lower the margin. That's also true for these products. However, we have rarely seen such a wide range in our experience. Only in the paper industry are there such low margins, and only in the defense industry are there such high margins. Croton Green has both very low margins and very high margins."

"Now we're getting somewhere. Go on." Armand sounded almost glad, but it didn't quite show up in the expression on his face.

"We know all that. You never asked for it, nor is it all that important. The overall profit margin is reasonably good, as you know from our reports." Russ rushed to clarify.

"Have you finished, Cliff?" Armand asked in clipped, dry tones.

"Almost. It seems the highest profit margins are in the accessories and machine products. Fertilizers are the very highest. Tools and mowers run a close second from the top. Most of the plants and pottery items have a low profit margin, and the profit margin on the corporate staple, namely grass seed, is almost nil," Cliff finished triumphantly.

"Now wait just a minute!" Russ exploded as he half-rose in his chair. "I have not had a chance to review his findings in detail, but I can say here and now that their accuracy is questionable. We've always been profitable, and we've always produced, distributed, and sold our special quality grass seed. There's got to be a mistake in these findings."

"Now don't get yourself in an uproar, gentlemen," Armand soothed the excited group opposite him at the table. "We'll all check and recheck our findings. Facts—true accurate facts—are the foundation of good decision-making. Most people can't tell the difference between facts and opinions. In our business, we always, without exception, build our business on quantifiable, measureable facts. One of these days, I'm going to write a paper on this. How about it, John? Can you think of a training program to hit home on this?" Armand leaned forward to look straight at a young man sitting farther along the oval on his side, who nodded his head, but didn't get a chance to answer.

"Think about it." Armand's attention was already back on grass seed. He looked across the room at Russ, who was rifling through a sheath of loose papers. He continued before Russ could answer.

"Russ, you should know, one of the chief reasons we were so interested in Croton Green was the wide diversity of products and its huge customer base. We saw you as the hub of a wide range of acquisitions and development targets. We had imagined a kind of outdoor supermarket, high quality, a sort of do-it-yourselfer nature store that included the growing numbers of people in the emerging green movement. I don't want to be following. I want to be the leader. Just so you understand how important you all are in our plans for the future."

The other side of the oval relaxed cautiously into their chairs. The immediate threat had been diverted, and they were all still alive.

"So how about going along with us and taking an objective view of this topic. We're not making a decision. At this point, we're exploring a possible issue that could help us move forward securely. All right?" Armand soothed.

"Sure, Armand. No problem!" Russ still looked wary. When he turned his eyes toward the opposite side of the oval, he saw those dark orbs of eyes focused on him. The darkly dressed figure of the Premium Technical Products Incorporated president still felt ominous to him. His clipped deep voice, without any real feeling or warmth, generally staccato like ice crystals, only thawing occasionally for effect, could not really be believed. Suspicion lingered around him like a cloud. Every time Russ came into contact with Armand, he automatically placed himself on guard.

"So, Cliff, tell us more." Armand held up his hand expectantly, palm up.

"It seems that the competition, small as it is, has a lower price and a lower quality. Nevertheless, their volume of sales was growing slowly at about two percent. Croton figured the competition's growth was primarily due to the fact they were cheaper. Did it really matter if a third of the seeds never germinated? Most of the customers are weekend gardeners. They don't really know what they are doing, generally waste most of the seed anyway. The few that come up spread rapidly.

In three months you end up with practically the same lawn as the more expensive, higher-quality Croton product.

"So it seems Croton was falling behind slightly in sales and decided, I think wisely, to lower their price to match the competition. The cost remained the same, but the margin disappeared.

"In the meantime they have been adding other products. Tools are excellent quality. The customers know this and are willing to pay more for them. They carry two lines of lawnmowers made by Deere and Farmall but sold under the Croton brand. Most of the money is made on the machines, tools, and fertilizers. The grass seed requires most of the manpower and the cost. That's where we are today."

"If they dropped the grass seed altogether, what would be the consequences?" Armand asked. A wave of shock passed along the opposite side of the oval. Apparently, even the idea was unthinkable.

"They'd increase their profits by six percent, mostly by reducing their head count and expenses. However, overall sales could be down a bit. This is still an unknown. The grass seed has been the lead product of the company. It is almost synonymous with their image. If it were dropped, many customers might no longer see an advantage to buying the other products in Croton stores. We just don't know yet what the ultimate effects might be."

Russ and the staff were nodding their heads in agreement and wanting to speak to the issue.

"Hold it!" Armand insisted. "We're still delving for facts. In other words, you're saying that the grass seed is such an integral part of the image, to drop it may affect total sales of the entire product line negatively?"

"Yes, it may. As I say we're not yet sure of the actual consequences, but it seems possible."

Russ jumped into the discussion to explain. "I can assure you from experience that most of the people get interested in the other products in the stores, but what brings them into the store is grass seed." The others nodded vehemently.

"Let me ask you this," Armand began, using an approach familiar to all his staff. "Maybe we can't drop the product without risking the loss of customers for the other products. That much I can gather from what you all are saying. So we need the product. But . . . do we need to produce it?"

"I don't get you! Are you saying we carry the product but let some other outfit produce it for us?" Russ asked.

Armand leaned forward to answer him. "Yes. It can't be rocket science to grow grass seed. We contract a couple smaller outfits with specs of our process, buy the seed we need, mark it up, and sell it under our label. Let someone else carry the labor and expense burden."

"That won't do any good. They would still have to charge us. It would certainly raise the price, and we'd have the same problem." Russ looked around for confirmation.

"You think so?"

"Of course! These smaller outfits might have less overhead, but they would still need to have a profit."

"What if we used our own subsidiary?" Armand wondered. "We could jockey the costs around to offset where we're experiencing high profits to reduce the tax bite. That would reduce your standard overhead and allow your people to work on expanding the more profitable lines."

"What about quality control? If we lose our image through faulty product, our other sales would also suffer. By doing it ourselves, we have maximum control." Russ felt himself fighting for control of the stream of thoughts.

Armand remained calm and cool as he answered. "Look, we're just blue-skying right now, but I feel we are facing a challenge. With so many bright minds in this room, I'm positive we can do better." Armand paused, tapping gently on the table with his forefinger, lips pressed together in a thin line.

Finally, he decided. "I will ask a couple of my staff to work on this with you. I know you'll cooperate since you and we are bound to benefit. See if we can come up with an approach that gives us a better total return. Cliff, do you think you can put together a small staff team to work with the Croton Green staff? I'd like some results before our next meeting here. That's in three months, I recall."

Russ and his staff looked dejected. They knew what had been decided. A team of PTP staff would descend on them. They would ask questions, demand reports, use everyone's time, and in the end, would demand the credit for whatever was decided. They would be forced to supply all the information, do all the work, and probably lose control of the company. PTP staff already had a reputation. Armand's immense power had been delegated to them.

Without understanding it fully, the staff of Croton Green felt the change in their authority and independence. All at once, something had been eroded precipitously that had been built up over years. A company culture had darkened, lost its light and vigor. Their reason for existing had been taken away and supplanted by an authority lacking in values, diminished in vision. Something crass and shadowy hovered over them as they contemplated the future.

Armand slowly looked around the room. Across from him, he felt the moods of disappointment, sorrow, and a coldness toward him. He didn't mind that. He never expected nor did he ever receive warmth. He searched for and found submissiveness, an occasional flare of animosity, some tinges of ambition, but overall, a sense of willingness to do whatever was necessary to keep whatever jobs they currently held. They would all fall into place—he felt certain of that.

Except when his eyes landed on Russ. Now there was something else. He didn't like what he sensed coming from him. He was playacting. He would try to fool Armand into thinking he was loyal, when in fact he was probably already planning how to mount resistance against him. He knew this would not work out. Russ had to be moved out one way or another. He could never trust him, no matter what he said or pretended. The coldness in Armand's eyes seemed to reach across the intervening space, matching and overcoming the coldness in the eyes of Russ.

Armand then slid his eyes along his side of the table, stopping for barely a second at each of his staff, sizing them up, feeling the effects of their character and relation to himself. In each he found what he was looking for: a submissiveness to his will covering a deeper layer of fear. He had them, every one of them. They were caught in his control. They knew it, he knew it, and they knew that he knew it. These were what he needed to achieve his aims in life: absolute obedience and loyalty.

His eyes rested a little longer on Cliff. He was something special. He was the ultimate of what he was needing and looking for in his people. He was submissive, true, but he was more than that. He was intelligent and willing to use his abilities creatively for Armand's benefit. Ultimately, Armand wanted submissive people who would willingly take up his mission and use all their forces of personality to serve him in any way he desired. He desired the ultimate human servants, ones that willingly sacrificed their freedom and all their capacities to take up his vision, his purpose, and his intentions. When he was honest with himself, he realized what he desired was dedicated slaves to do his bidding willingly and enthusiastically. Cliff came the closest to what he considered the ideal employee. He corrected himself. There was one other, even more devoted.

Naturally, he didn't want them to know that. It wasn't politically correct. But in his consciousness, he knew the truth and worked tirelessly to bring about his vision for the future of Premium Technical Products Incorporated.

After Armand had slowly circled the room with his penetrating gaze, taking in each face and figure around his table, he eased himself back into the chair. He now deliberately exhaled the overpowering psychic strength of his being, mesmerizing each in turn and sucking into his own will the loyalty and forces each of them bestowed willingly into his care. His own sense of worth and meaning increased as his eyes circled the room a second time. When he was done, the silence was growing intensely. He gathered it all to himself, like a network of reverse tentacles, rose, and left the room, the staff following him out, leaving Croton Green Incorporated leadership alone to find their way home.

*****

Horst Perla paused briefly to admire Park Avenue. He had seen it many times before, but today was special. He had already experienced sixteen interviews at the AIC Corporation. The first three were just recruiters, then psychiatrists and sessions with tests, and then various executives, including his possible future boss.

Two lanes of taxis, limousines, and cars raced south toward the Pan Am Building. The moment any light turned red at any of the intersections, the cars, braking to full stops, signaled an avalanche of pedestrians to dare the crossing. Halfway as far as the center planting of bushes was a cinch, but who could blame them for trying to make it all the way across?

Crossing all the way could be risked on the run, but the cars were merciless the moment the light turned green for them. They knew the pedestrians would run for it, so they charged forward confidently even though the crosswalk was still packed. Sure enough, by the time the cars reached the farthest crosswalk, all pedestrians had made it safely to the opposing sidewalk. It appeared to be standard protocol accepted by city drivers and daily commuters alike.

An elderly woman leaned on her cane and watched the drama for a few red and green lights. She wisely chose not to cross. Instead she grasped her cane firmly and raced lopsidedly through the cross street at Fiftieth. In all fairness, Horst noticed that one of the taxis paused ever so slightly, apparently to give the elder a fighting chance to make it. However, a man dressed in overcoat and suit had evidently signaled the cab. He hurriedly opened the back door, crumpled himself into the narrow space. It took just long enough for the elderly woman to cross safely. She didn't seem at all agitated. She was probably a resident, quite accustomed to the ordinary stress of life in the city.

Horst was glad to be already on the west side of Park Avenue, with the traffic moving downtown. From where he was, he gazed up the stacked glass building to the ninth floor. Naturally, the glass was not for looking in. It only permitted those inside to look out. Horst sheltered his eyes, but he could only see other buildings mirrored in the glass walls of the structure. The ninth floor had nothing to distinguish itself from the eighth or the tenth. The building itself had nothing to distinguish itself from the one beside it. Across Park Avenue, however, was the very voluptuous Greek Orthodox church, and beside that was the Waldorf Astoria Hotel, which looked exactly as the postcards depicted it. He temporarily had the use of a suite on the twenty-fifth floor as a guest of the Alliance for International Communications Incorporated. From his window, he had a direct view across Park Avenue to the headquarters of the Alliance for International Communications Incorporated.

He made his way through the mob in the lobby to the bank of elevators. There were six all together. He missed the first two trips, not wanting to be crushed between the front row and the closing doors. To his great relief, the third one was almost empty. He was the only one rising as high as the ninth floor. He had room enough to remove his scarf, hat, and overcoat, which he looped over his arm and carried out into the reception area on the ninth floor.

He had to pass through two glass doors with ALLIANCE FOR INTERNATIONAL COMMUNICATIONS INC. engraved on one of them along with Lucinda Brahms, President and Chief Executive Officer. He pushed through without reading the other names.

Horst knew he had an interview this morning at 9:00 a.m., but with whom wasn't clear. Several names had been mentioned yesterday, but the final choice hadn't been communicated to him at the time. Considering he already had sixteen interviews during the last two weeks, he wasn't surprised that they all began to run together as a jumbled list in his mind. His prospective boss had explained that it was a general practice of the Alliance for International Communications Incorporated to include so many interviews. The headquarters job for which he was interviewing required almost daily exposure to many of the top staff around the president. At this level, with success depending on the approval of so many important people, it made sense to get a head start on knowing them. It also gave the important top staff a chance to get to know him ahead of time and also voice their objections to him and, he guessed, their possible acceptance of him on staff. What could he say if it was normal practice?

The receptionist welcomed him with a familiar smile and took his coat and hat to the disguised closet behind her desk. She asked him to have a seat since Mr. Seiter was running a bit late. Horst made himself comfortable and chose the *Wall Street Journal* to read. At nine thirty, the receptionist apologized for Mr. Seiter and, as a substitute, offered him coffee or tea. He decided on coffee and finished the journal and then leafed through *Time*. He didn't like waiting. It tired him more than any interview or work, no matter what it was. As the time stretched out, he became increasingly tense. Was this also perhaps a test?

It was exactly ten o'clock, an hour late, when Graham Seiter bustled through the reception area, trailing an assistant carrying two briefcases and a secretary offering him his hat and coat.

"Come along." He gestured to Horst. "We can just make it in time."

"Where are we going?" asked Horst.

"We're due at the Teterboro Airport in less than thirty minutes. Don't you have a hat and coat? Hurry up."

The receptionist had already rushed to bring him his belongings as they reached the bank of elevators.

"Here you are, Mr. Perla. Have a good flight." She smiled encouragingly at him.

"A psychologist once told me that there are just two kinds of men, students and executives. You tell them apart not by what they have in their heads, but by what they have on their heads. The students are bare headed. The executives wear hats." Graham Seiter opened his mouth wide and let one huge laugh escape.

"Is that right?" Horst stifled his disagreement.

"Where are you going?" Graham motioned to his secretary. "I need you to come along in the limo to get those two memos out by noon. Come along. No, you don't need a coat. Remember, you left it on the plane this last time. Call ahead to make sure they have it ready for you."

In the basement garage, Mr. Seiter shouted angrily for the limo, which was being washed and polished. "The hell with that. I'm late as it is. We need to go."

Some credit was due the driver. He refused to become flustered. Mr. Seiter pushed and goaded him for more speed, but he knew his job. Nevertheless, they arrived at Teterboro Airport by eleven o'clock and were taking off in the company jet within minutes, leaving the secretary to ride back in the limo.

Once they were settled in the jet and Mr. Seiter had a scotch (which Horst declined), they finally had their first chance to talk. The jet was remarkably spacious and comfortable. Although there were a possible twelve seats, six were folded down and out of the way. Four of them were grouped for the two passengers to face each other. Since it was nearly lunchtime, the attendant, wearing a pleasantly cut uniform with Alliance for International Communications Incorporated embroidered on it, brought them a salad she claimed to be fresh. While they talked, she kept the food coming in shifts that included a roast beef sandwich, a selection of beers and wines, fresh fruit salad, ice cream with fudge sauce on top, and finally, coffee and a liqueur.

"So, has anyone told you yet how AIC really works?"

"No. They all told me you were going to do that!" Horst lied.

Mr. Seiter once again opened his mouth really wide and roared his amusement. Horst watched him, fascinated by the enormity of his open mouth, teeth bared, lips drawn back. Horst felt sure he caught a glimpse of his trachea, just before he snapped the entire apparatus shut again.

"You're a liar, but that was a nice touch. Somebody's been coaching you, eh?"

"Well, I have heard that you've been an important part of the Alliance for International Communications for quite a few years, and I figured you must have a thorough and perhaps unique perspective on the organization." For some reason, Horst found it easy to please this man without being too obvious.

"It's been eleven years now. For most of the time, the group was just limping along, ushering in a series of leaders and ushering them out just as easily. Nothing seemed to click. You know how that is? All good people, but they just didn't jell into a team. Maybe the time wasn't right yet," he mused.

"Then along comes this Lucinda Brahms. It was a surprise. We've always had men in the top jobs. None of us knew exactly how to behave. Most of us still don't know exactly how to behave, but there she was with ideas, energy, determination, and charm. The combination won each of us over one at a time, and here we are. Alliance for International Communications has grown from less than five hundred million to nearly a billion in assets in the last three years."

"I have not met her—yet," Horst admitted.

"Until you meet her, you won't really know what makes this organization unique."

"What's she like?"

"She is inspired, but she doesn't own any of her ideas. They are born through her, and then she works them person by person through the organization until her ideas live in everybody. Only then, not before, does she allow any major strategic decision to be made. In fact, her approach is truly remarkable."

"You sound as if she has no weaknesses or faults." Horst primed the pump a little to see if more was coming.

"Nobody is perfect." Mr. Seiter clamped his jaw together and stared at Horst. "We're not going to get anyone better, though. Anyway, AIC has a unique organizational structure. You want to know about it?" he asked.

"Very much so."

"We have the traditional pyramid and chain of command, just as you'll find in any modern organization—up to a certain point! Then comes what's unique. AIC Headquarters group is a one-of-a-kind beast that only Lucinda Brahms could manage. You'll see if and when you're in it." Mr. Seiter removed a pad from one of his briefcases and a gold pen from his shirt pocket.

"If this triangle is your typical organizational structure with everyone lower reporting to someone higher—what we all know—" He interrupted himself, putting the pad aside. "Did I ever tell you my half-serious, half-humorous advice to new folks with promise to get ahead? No, of course I haven't. Well, it's like this. The Alliance for International Communications— as well as any other modern corporate structure—in its simplest design is nothing more than a huge digestive system. Anyone joining the organization enters at the bottom of the digestive system, and we know what the bottom of a digestive system is, don't we? My advice to new recruits is to make sure they rise up in this enormous digestive system as fast as they can. You get it? You understand that the throat is the highest point in the system while the lowest point is what you sit on? Get it?"

"Of course, I get it, but that's a very cynical view, wouldn't you say?"

"Sure, it's cynical, but have you ever heard anything more true? All the work, all the blame, none of the benefits accumulate with the rank and file. In all honesty, at that level, they get all the shit! Nobody wants to be there unless they have to. Its only virtue is that it's better than nothing, and you have a fighting chance that you'll get at least as far as the stomach." Again Mr. Seiter burst open his cavernous mouth and roared.

Horst wanted to contribute something a little more learned to the conversation. "Hence, all the social revolutions around the world! Which didn't change anything except to exchange a commercial nobility for a hereditary aristocracy." Apparently, that was too much.

"Huh?" Mr. Seiter looked suspiciously at Horst. It seems he had his limitations too.

"What I mean—" Horst started, but he was interrupted by Mr. Seiter.

"Let's not get off the track. It's important that you land on your feet running in this job. All of us want you to succeed. Why do you think you've had so many interviews? We're counting on you to make a go of it. Now listen."

"Thank you. I will certainly do my very best, and I appreciate any help you can give me."

"That's the spirit!"

"Mr. Seiter—"

"How about you call me Graham?"

"Graham, tell me more about this unique organizational structure."

"I was describing the usual structure with this picture of a pyramid." Graham lifted his pad up with the drawing of a pyramid boasting an open top, which Horst assumed was open just because Graham hadn't finished it yet.

"I left the top open like this on purpose," Graham continued. "I figured you've noticed that. Because that's where the specialty of the AIC exists. It all started with Lucinda's— by the way, you'll soon learn that those closest to her call her Lucky. Short for Lucinda. Get it? Anyway, it was her idea to place a kind of egg shape at the top instead of a point."

"An egg shape? I've never heard of that." Horst was amazed. "For real?"

"I know it sounds strange, but don't forget, it works."

"How?"

"You see, even though there is a great deal of potential in an egg, the albumin is basically unorganized. It becomes organized when it is fertilized. Lucky wanted the top of our organization to be all potential, creative, a kind of deliberate chaos so that it never came to rest, always imagining and creating ahead of the reality. Open and receptive to the fertilizing idea that one way or another would surface. We never know whose idea would be the one to do the trick, nor do we know its source ahead of time. Isn't that something?" Graham looked triumphantly at Horst.

"Well, I'll be."

"She wanted nothing but the best, the most intelligent and creative people in this egg at the top. In a way, she externalized the function of leadership. The salary structure inside this egg is mayhem. In a way, each individual is a grade unto himself. No one at this level is responsible for any kind of measurable output. Their performance is evaluated on the basis of experienced influence as contributed to the corporate growth and development."

Horst didn't know what to say. This was the first time he had heard this. No inkling of this had been mentioned at any of the other sixteen interviews. He was grateful to Graham for sharing this new view of the Alliance for International Communications.

"How does this actually show up in practice?" Horst asked.

"Now listen to this." Graham smacked his lips in anticipation. "Any one of us can call a meeting, inviting anyone we wish to take part. Anyone in the egg can decide to come, nor can anyone be denied involvement. Nor can anyone be forced to attend. There are, of course, the monthly meetings with the subsidiary corporations to review results and problem-solve issues. Lucky runs those meetings in person. I'm sure you'll be expected to be present at those."

"From your comments, can I assume you'll support my candidacy for the job?"

"Your boss has the final word, but you can count on my support."

"I'm pleased. Thank you!" After a pause, Graham resumed.

"Anyway, that's how the unique structure of AIC works. It's hard to describe, equally hard to understand. It demands intelligence, good will, involvement, and dedication from everyone at the top. There's no hiding in that atmosphere, no upmanship tolerated. You either decide to contribute or you leave," Graham finished.

"I love it!" insisted Horst. "It sounds like my kind of environment."

"Good for you! I hope you'll be one of us."

"Thank you!"

Graham buried himself in a number of file folders, and before he turned over the second one, he was fast asleep. His large head, wrapped in reddish-brown curls, fell forward. Every now and then, a rasping snore escaped, and his head jerked up and back momentarily. This action did not seem to interrupt his sleep, as his head slowly migrated south again and he was gone.

Horst had a great deal to think about. Graham had been wonderfully natural, open, and candid. This seemed to signify acceptance, but perhaps also friendship. If Horst joined AIC, could he count on Graham's candor? Could he count on it in all matters? He seemed reluctant to be as candid when the subject of Lucky's character came up. He was obviously a fan. Was he part of an inner circle loyal to Lucky and ready to defend her when and if she were ever opposed or attacked? How did he fit in? How should he position himself? Horst had a great deal to think about, but first he needed to secure the trust and friendship of his boss. Where did he fit in? Was his possible boss also a fan, part of the inner circle around Lucky?

From this point on, Horst had better start doing some fact-finding of his own. They may be interviewing him, but from now on, he would also be interviewing them. Graham had given him a good start. Horst would tentatively regard him as a friendly colleague—at least until proven otherwise.

Horst began wondering what his score was right now. He had sixteen interviews, including psychiatrists and operating executives. On his fingers, he started to count the ones he thought seemed open and interested in him. Only one seemed openly antagonistic to him, but he thought maybe that was on purpose to get his reaction to opposition. Another seemed disinterested. Horst thought he was just doing his job and didn't care one way or the other what happened to him. Based on this crude analysis, he took heart in thinking he had a pretty good shot at the job.

He had to admit to himself, what Graham had described as the top of the Alliance for International Communications Incorporated interested him. It described the kind of freewheeling, unstructured environment that he himself happened to thrive in. He was excited by the possibility of demonstrating his capacity to self-motivate and generate results. He began to look forward to meeting Lucky and finding a role for himself in the exciting "egg" of the Alliance for International Communications.

*****

This was 1971, a difficult year to forget. So much happened. So much began and so much ended within those twelve months. The armed forces of the United States spilled out of the conflict in Vietnam into the colleges and universities, flooding the classrooms with a new breed of students. They had already seen too much, experienced too much to be happy with a carefree college life. The shenanigans of the normal student seemed childish; the veterans frowned on their attitudes and behaviors. There was no battle between the two; they just couldn't cope with each other. They studied apart and lived apart, meeting in classrooms where the new seriousness mingled with the confused jocularity of youth.

Neither Stu nor Robert had known each other before meeting in the third academic year at Fairmont University. Their first meeting foretold all that was to happen in this year of 1971, if they only had the eyes and ears to perceive the overtones and undercurrents.

Stu was a veteran with credit for classes and experience he had acquired in the Navy. Thus he landed successfully right into the second year with a few additional credits toward a third year. He would undoubtedly graduate in another eighteen months and advance into an engineering career with any of a dozen companies vying for his skills and knowledge. Given the character of the year 1971, his future was guaranteed, except . . . But that was not yet known to Robert.

Robert miraculously missed Vietnam entirely. It was rumored that enlisting was the best deal for young men because by enlisting they would then be offered a variety of choices. Once drafted, there were no choices. Regardless of inherent talents or interests, the placement of the draftee was made by unilateral decision of the armed forces, which often followed unknown and sometimes illogical criteria. In a mass movement to obtain the best possible fighting locations, professions, and other choices, so many young men volunteered that Robert was never drafted, and the war in Vietnam passed him by. Meeting Stu was the closest he ever came to combat.

Robert ate a sandwich at Joe's Digs. He wanted something a little tastier than the cafeteria but still within his meagre budget. The Digs was not legally a part of the university. It was hidden a block and a half, twisted off to one side street so that only those who knew about it, which was almost everybody, could find it. It filled up with students between eight and ten in the morning, again between ten minutes past noon until about three, and then one last time every day between five and eight in the evening. The students could order anything they wanted as long as it was a simple sandwich or eggs with bacon. Despite those favored possibilities, ice cream and soda were still the staples of Joe's Digs, with coffee coming in right behind them.

One of the main attractions of the Digs were the two pinball machines that were hardly ever quiet from early in the morning till closing time. One of the first customers would play a game or two with a nickel each and end up winning enough games for the university population to play the rest of the day without paying. Each one who played usually ended up adding a few free games to the accumulated winnings. Joe never adjusted the machines properly as it brought in the students all day. At the end of the day, when the lights and the electricity in the small cavity of a place were turned off, the machines reset themselves; all remaining free games were eliminated and the next morning started off again from zero. The accounting students figured the pinball machines earned about ten cents a day, gross, not counting electricity and any lease or other expenses.

"Hi, you're in my psychology class!" Stu was the first to open the conversation.

"Yeah. You're always in the front row—with all the other vets, right?"

Stu sat down on a stool beside Robert and, without looking at the one-page menu, ordered two eggs over easy, crisp bacon, and rye toast. He removed a napkin from its holder on the counter and added it to the knife, fork, and spoon that appeared at his place, still wet from washing.

"It's too restless back there in the class where you are. Most of us vets are fairly serious about learning and getting a degree." Stu reiterated what everybody already knew.

"Are you a psych major?" Robert looked Stu over and before getting an answer decided psychology was not Stu's real interest. He seemed too practical and down-to-earth to be a psychologist! His jeans were worn past the fashionable norm. He looked more blue-collar or perhaps agricultural. His hands were rough and calloused, apparently from physical work.

"No." He didn't mind denying it. "I'm in the College of Engineering."

"That's more like it. I thought maybe you might be an aggie," Robert said.

"That would have been my second choice, but the way agriculture is trending these days, an engineering or chemical degree wouldn't hurt. My parents still operate a small farm in Iowa, but I don't know how long they can keep it up. They can't afford the cost of mechanization. Besides, they're too small to make it worthwhile. Farming is becoming big business, if you know what I mean."

"What are you doing in the psych class?" Robert was curious.

"They want us engineers to be customer friendly. The idea is that technical knowhow alone doesn't bring in the moolah. You've got to have people skills. I think that really means we've got to be able to fool the customers." Stu laughed a bit ruefully, as though he didn't like his own conclusion. "Why are you in psychology?"

"About a third of business practice is psychology. I'm not talking about retail so much as corporate business. The financial is important, but in a corporate setting, they need people skills to get ahead. I know what you mean about fooling people. I sometimes get a feeling that we're learning how to take advantage of people's weaknesses. You know, catering to everyone's desires and appetites."

"Is that what you want to do? Business? Corporate business?" Stu seemed astounded.

"That's what my dad wants I should do. I'm not too sure. Haven't made up my mind."

"Well, maybe there's still some hope for you." Stu laughed. So did Robert, thoughtfully.

"You don't like business?" Robert asked.

"No!" There was no hesitation.

"You mind telling me why?" Stu turned sideways to look directly at Robert to deliver his answer.

"My synonym for corporate business is greed. It's not disguised or hidden. It's blatantly obvious. Some are worse than others, but greed lives rampant in the profession, and there's no way to survive in it without a lustful appetite for lucre!" Stu voiced his opinion without any regard for Robert's feelings. Robert didn't want to believe what he heard.

"If we want to change the world for the better, isn't that a good place to start? I mean where the need for reform may be the greatest?"

Robert's eyes were so sincere, Stu's sympathy went out to him. "Look, what's your name?"

"Robert. Robert McLane. What's yours?"

"Stu. That's short for Steward. Steward Brand." He took a quick slurp of his coffee and then went on. "Look, Robert. I've investigated this thoroughly. You'll see once you get into it, that every business starts you at the bottom. Sometimes there's six to twelve months of training. That means shaping you and retooling you so that you'll be fit for the corporate world. If you're smart, you'll learn fast, you'll adapt, you'll learn to think correctly, if you know what I mean. You'll learn to hide unsuitable thoughts. Even your feelings get purified. Nothing's forced you understand. It's just that your desire to get ahead is the driver. If you want to keep your own thoughts and feelings? Go right ahead, if that's what you want. Nobody will stop you. Except that, one by one, everyone else moves on while you remain behind, and what does this teach you? It teaches you to accept greed as an honorable desire, one that should be honorably satisfied at the expense of any other desire or person. Don't get me wrong. They might call it ambition or competition or even development. Greed is what it really is."

"That bad?" wondered Robert.

"By the time you finally make it to a place where you can do some good, you've been molded into something that has accepted greed as the ultimate good, and you've lost the desire and the capacity to change the world that feeds you."

"There are some good people in the corporation where my dad works. I've met them," Robert insisted.

"Of course. There are a few everywhere, but enough to change the world? This world is rolling around the sun, right smack to hell," Stu maintained.

"I just can't accept its being that bad. Sure there's greed, there's corruption, there are all the usual human failings, but in fact, we as people are changing, becoming more conscious and responsible. In other words, there's hope for the future. It can't be as bad as you say!"

"It's worse. I just can't find the right words to really drive it home. Others are better at that," Stu admitted.

"Others?"

"Yeah."

"Like who?"

"A teacher I know," Stu made it sound mysterious.

"Here at Fairmont?"

Stu carelessly wiped his mouth with a paper napkin before answering. "He holds a class in one of the rooms here at Fairmont. It's usually Thursday night. A few of us have been going regularly. He is a very special person—deep, I would say."

"That's very interesting. What's his name?"

"Shaman Pi."

"You're kidding!" laughed Robert.

"I'm not."

"It sounds a bit, well, far out."

"He's spiritual, if that's what you mean. Not spiritual like in a church—not religious, but spiritual." Stu was serious.

"He talks about business?"

"That and also especially about ethics and the future of humankind."

"I wonder if my dad knows about him." Robert's interest was sincere.

"Maybe. Shaman Pi is well known in some parts. Who is your dad?"

"Charles McLane. You don't know him, I would think. He works in the city, at the Alliance for International Communications Incorporated."

"Pays your tuition, room and board, as well as books, I would guess." Stu was derisive, but also a touch envious.

"Sure. Why shouldn't he? He can afford it."

"I guess so," said Stu, looking Robert up and down for the first time.

"What?" Robert didn't understand the implications of Stu's remark or his critical inspection of his appearance.

"I mean, look at you."

"What about me?"

"You're so . . . Ivy League. So well put together." Stu tried to sum it up.

"So are you!"

"No, I'm talking about the whole way you carry yourself. You're tall and straight. Why, even your pants have a crease! Whoever heard of that—having a crease even after a dozen or more washings or probably dry-cleanings. There's no doubt about it, Robert. You and I are from different worlds. Mine is poor but hardworking, full of hopes and dreams. Yours is privileged, amply sustained by greed. I can't understand why we happened to meet. I should probably despise you, but I don't. Why I actually like you is beyond me!" Stu rocked his head from side to side in mock disbelief.

Robert laughed and playfully punched Stu's shoulder as he answered him.

"You're OK, Stu. You're willing to give a fellow a chance. Besides, I have ideals too. I'm not a finished product. I'm still becoming. Don't give up on me yet. I may surprise you."

"Hey! How about that." Stu brightened. "Why don't you come along and hear Shaman Pi Thursday in a week?"

"Can I just walk in like that?"

"We can go together. I'll introduce you to the others and to Shaman. First, I have to find out which classroom he'll be using," Stu reminded himself.

"Doesn't he have the same room every time?"

"No. He's not really accepted by the other professors and certainly not by the administrative people at the university. They don't like him."

"I would think since the classrooms belong to the university, they would and should have the right to decide who uses them," Robert stated emphatically.

"You and your middle-class values," Stu chided him. "A university should be a public place. Education and all cultural matters should belong to the people, a right of the people. Somebody like the Shaman should rightfully be able to use any room where people collect to hear him. You've got a lot to catch up on."

"You don't believe in ownership?" Robert was amazed.

"Hold it! Hold it." Stu put up his hands to defend himself. "I believe I'll let the Shaman handle such questions. After all, we're fellow students. Aren't we both still exploring our values? I know the Shaman has a lot to say about this whole subject. I'll pick you up at the cafeteria in a week, Thursday, and we can go together to hear him. You still want to meet him?"

"Sure, I look forward to it."

Joe had been wiping the counters with a wet rag and busied himself in their vicinity. Gradually he worked himself closer and looked them over suspiciously.

"You fellows aren't in some sort of trouble are you?" he asked.

"No, not me," Robert answered without hesitation.

"What kind of trouble?" Stu asked.

"I don't know. I just wondered, that's all." Joe moved away, carrying their soiled plates and cutlery to the rear to be washed. When he came back, he pretended to be very busy.

"Come on, Joe. What gives?" Stu demanded.

"It's probably nothing."

"What kind of nothing are we talking about?"

"He was in here for quite a while before he finally came over to me and put the question directly to me," Joe answered him.

"Who? What question?"

"How should I know? I've never seen him before. The way he was dressed, I figured he maybe belonged to the administration."

"Administration? You mean of the university?" Stu was really puzzled.

"Yeah, some official capacity."

"What did he want?"

"He asked me if any students who were veterans had come in to the Diggs today. I told him lots of students are vets these days. He then described you pretty good. Not exact, but I figure it might have been you, Stu."

"Did he say what he wanted?"

"Yes, but I didn't believe him."

"What did he say?"

"He told a story about giving grants to deserving veterans. I could tell he was lying by the shifty way his eyes turned away from me. I didn't tell him anything, honest." Joe was adamant.

"What happened then?"

"He left, said he'd look for you around the campus. Could he be from the IRS or maybe Veterans Affairs?"

"I don't know. Can you describe him in more detail?"

"He had this really dark look about him. Dark suit, dark blue shirt, and even a dark tie. Blue striped, I think. He was really tall. Oh, and I remember his shiny black dress shoes. You don't see shoes like that around here much. That's how come I noticed them especially. What else I noticed was his pale face. I knew right away that guy must be from the city. He sure didn't get out into the sun very much. That's for sure," Joe answered.

"And you've never seen him before?"

"Never. I'd remember him if I had. Come to think of it, he looked more like an executive type. You know, the corporate image?"

"Well, I guess we'll have to wait till he comes again or finds us. Maybe we're not the people he's looking for after all. Anyway, I haven't done anything bad that I know of. We'll just have to wait and see." Stu didn't seem worried.

Both of them had finished their meal and were ready to go. They rose from the counter when Stu asked Robert, "In the meantime, how about a fast game of pinball? Are you game? I see there are at least seven free games available and no contenders at the moment."

"OK." Robert agreed. "I'm not very good yet. I may use up all the free games, and the rest of the Fairmont University undergraduates will hate me."

"You can count on me to rescue you at the pinball machine." Stu laughed confidently. "And in other matters," he muttered softly under his breath. Robert did not hear the last comment. The pinball machine had already been resuscitated and was clanging and banging away as the ball hit one cushion after another, accumulating points by the millions.

This first meeting seemed innocent enough. As far as they knew, the two of them just ran into each other accidentally, chatted a bit, and then played the pinball machine for free games. How were they to know that within a few weeks they would be mutually entangled in corporate plots that had nothing to do with either of them?

CHAPTER TWO

More Meetings

Robert waited at the cafeteria until nearly 8:00 p.m., when it threatened to close. The last student had rushed out with a sandwich, a container of salad, and a bottle of juice. The white-coated attendants were watching him suspiciously, wondering why he didn't eat something, hadn't asked for anything, was not dashing out the way normal students did. He finally mentioned to one of them that he was waiting for a friend.

When Stu did arrive, he looked harried, perhaps even as if he had just rolled out of bed. His hair was uncombed, stubble shrouded his chin, and one tail of his shirt hung out lopsidedly.

"Sorry I'm late. I still don't know where the Shaman is teaching tonight."

"That's fine. I have plenty to do. I need to prepare for a lab tomorrow morning already at 8:00 a.m." Robert retrieved his satchel and was prepared to make his way through the campus and home.

"Oh, never fear. He's teaching somewhere. We just have to find him. Let's take a look in Engineering. He's often there," Stu assured him.

"OK, I'm game."

They wandered in and out of several classrooms that were empty in the College of Engineering and checked one where a group of parents were discussing various independent school options with a guidance counselor. On the second floor, all the lights were already turned out, doors closed, inhospitable.

"We can move over to the psych building. He was there once before. Don't give up. We'll find him."

"Why can't he just get permission from the university and use the same classroom each time? I don't understand." Robert felt strange hunting down someone who wasn't supposed to be there in the first place.

"The university top cats don't like what he has to say. They are dependent on corporate largesse to make ends meet. It takes a lot of money to run a place like this, and they need all they can siphon out of the economy. Just wait, you'll see. Shaman has a lot to say about that."

"Yeah, if we ever find him."

"You can go home right now if this is too much for you!" Stu was annoyed.

"Calling my bluff?" Robert asked.

Stu laughed, good-natured again, his usual self. "Yeah, I guess."

"Who's in there?" Robert wondered as they passed a classroom that had only a dim standing light, plugged into an outlet, that illuminated a small knot of shapes clustered around a bearded man wearing a long white kaftan.

"Hey, you found him! You two must have karma!"

"Or something," Robert finished the thought for him.

Stu opened the door, and the two of them groped their way into the dark interior of the classroom. All the faces turned toward them, and the Shaman smiled benignly in their direction.

"Welcome, Stu. We were just beginning with a short verse, but maybe you should introduce your friend?" he suggested.

"Of course, Shaman Pi, this is my friend, Robert McLane. He was interested to hear you teach."

"Welcome, Robert." The Shaman's smile was masked, almost as though his face had been redone with a skin transplant. It had that shiny, nonporous sheen to it, no color or life signatures to be seen. His beard thinly covered the lowest sections and then blossomed out in a gray bush.

Robert and Stu squeezed into the tight group between a dark-haired girl with black pools for eyes and a very thin young man who made room for them. The shielded bulb cast only a dim illumination around the interior of the group, leaving the outside back of each person in the dark. After everyone was settled and a short silence brought peace into the gathering, the Shaman said a few words of introduction and then read softly from a little blue book.

"The verse I am reading was given to us by someone called Rudolf Steiner. He is *the* spiritual leader of our time. He actually wrote fifty-two of these verses, one for every week of the year. What is remarkable is that they are done in mirror images, with the corresponding verse in the other half of the year. The one I am about to read, number twenty-eight, is really for October, but I thought it appropriate for this week.

I can belong now to myself
And shining spread my inner light
Into the darkness of space and time.
Toward sleep is urging all creation;
But my inmost soul must stay awake
And carry wakefully sun's glowing
Into the winter's icy flowing.

The Shaman's voice vibrated with warmth and meaning. He read it so beautifully that every word rang with meaning and importance. When he finished, he was greeted with an appreciative silence.

"That's so beautiful," sighed the dark-haired girl sitting next to Robert. She looked up at him for confirmation or agreement or some reaction. Robert didn't know what to say, but she seemed so lost and unsure of herself he finally decided to say yes.

"Tonight, I thought I might like to talk a little bit about rules," the Shaman began, and then he paused.

Right on cue, one of the students rose to the bait. "Rules for us . . . here . . . in our group? But I thought—"

"Sh!" the dark haired girl waved him silent.

"No, not for us." The Shaman smiled. "Some of you who have been here longer probably know what I think about rules, but it won't hurt to talk about them again. You will remember that rules are only there to stop or prevent you from doing what someone has already done. Imagine that you weren't all sitting quietly and listening to me. Perhaps you might be telling jokes or laughing at the antics of Gerald over here. Perhaps the discussion might be in twos and threes and really loud. Suppose no one were listening to me at all. I might get the idea that we should have a rule. The rule might be that only people allowed in this class are those who will be quiet and are willing to listen. If anyone wants to talk, they should stay outside. Inside, you remain quiet and listen.

"However, we don't need that rule because you are quiet and prepared to listen. Whenever a rule is created in a democratic society, it is to prevent something from happening or to stop something that has already happened. That's the shadow side of rulemaking.

"The sunny side of the same coin is the goodness that comes to reside in every human being. Each one of us has something in us that seeks to do what benefits all of us, what enhances our human condition and helps to develop us further. At present, most of us have not learned to operate out of the sunshine in each of us. Either we haven't found it in us yet, are too weak to use its gentler strength, or are possessed by forces whose real intent we are not yet able to resist.

"Given these truths, here are my conclusions. Since rules, the law, are basically control mechanisms, they tend to protect the few from the many at the expense of the individual. They also propound a value structure that favors those who have, those who lead, those who benefit from the status quo. It also keeps under control those who have not, those who are followers, those who might benefit from change. In other words, the law divides people and creates classes. It keeps a few at an adult stage and the many in a childlike condition.

"What the world needs is a structure that allows every single person over the age of twenty-one to develop and keep developing to realize their full potential for the benefit of society as a whole. In other words, a sunshine structure. One that banks on the inherent yearning for good in each of us. One that nourishes and grows us, not controls and keeps us backward. I am advocating ethical individualism as a way of living together in community.

"I have said a mouthful and would like to pause here to listen to your thoughts." Shaman closed his mouth, although nobody could see that due to his full beard. At least, no further sound came from under his beard.

"That is so beautiful," breathed the dark-eyed girl, and she looked up at Robert for confirmation. He had a deep frown on his face as he puzzled over the terse statements of the Shaman.

"I take it"—the thin student cleared his throat and launched further into his question—"since we are not all perfect yet, we still need the law and rules in order to protect the weak, the elderly, women, children, and any who are wronged!"

"Those are the very people the law cannot protect," Shaman insisted. "It can only punish those who are strong, young, men and those who victimize others. There is no law that can make you be good!" The Shaman was vehement in his delivery. Excitement welled up and colored the part of his face that was visible.

"But to operate without any laws leaves everyone vulnerable. Won't we all be victimized by the strong, the bad, and the greedy?" The thin student was radiant with good will!

"Aren't you victimized now by these same persons? True, some are punished and separated from society along with the many who have regretted their actions, are changed and matured. The prisons don't recognize the capacity to develop in each of us. I recall a police chief in the state of Florida, I believe, who advocated releasing almost all prisoners who had been incarcerated as youths once they reached the age of thirty-five. Why? You see, we are capable of change, of improvement, of maturing. The law isn't structured to recognize that. If it were, prisons would have a different form and substance. Punishment can be developmental, but not when it is meted out as vengeance. Yes, there is an enormous difference to calling and thinking of a person as a thief or as a person who happened to steal something. We have to separate the person from a particular act he or she may have committed. As long as a particular act committed at one point in time is considered part of the inherent character of the person, we wrong him or her. Inside each person, there is an inherent yearning for good. Our prisons should become institutions of development, educational organizations that help those in need to ever increasing self-knowledge and self-determination." The Shaman lapsed into silence, which hung in the air as students digested these additional thoughts.

"I wonder if we would all think a little differently if we had a more long-term view of everything. We might be more patient with each other while at the same time take actions that have better long-term effects?" Robert wondered out loud. He was deeply stirred by the conversation. He was immensely bothered by it, worried about the implications of the ideas, but still drawn to them. This was a different sort of concern than he was accustomed to hear at home or in the classroom.

"Take this classroom." Shaman was on a roll, and he had all their attention. "It belongs to the university. It is a resource to all the teaching and education that goes on here—at least some of it." Shaman's smile was like a beacon through the bush of a beard thrusting out from his chin. The students nodded to each other knowingly, as if to say "Here it comes."

"It actually belongs to the university. Who paid for this building? That's a rhetorical question. We all did—through our tuitions and our tax exemptions and taxes. All students pay partly for its maintenance through their tuitions and fees. If you like, the building exists one hundred percent due to the citizens of this country and a little bit due to foreign students and foreign donors. The university is, in fact, a public institution paid for by the world and administered on behalf of the citizenry of the world by a pretty big and powerful office in another building around the corner." Shaman was warming up to this favorite topic of his.

"What makes this room meaningful is not the university's ownership of it. In a way, you could say the people of the world have asked the university to take custody of it and make sure it is used for educational purposes. Now if I were conducting a business in this room, one that primarily benefited me, I would say that would be a betrayal of its purpose and its reason for existing. In that sense, the university is charged to make sure it adheres to its purposes and does not just benefit a single person. To me, the rights of use connected with this room should belong to its purpose, not to its steward. Therefore I feel free to use it, and you must agree or you wouldn't be here, right?"

Robert wasn't too sure about that view, and he dared to speak up. "But who is to decide whether something is educational or just personal opinion, or even worse, propaganda?" he challenged.

"You're right," the Shaman said thoughtfully, "that's an important question. Any particular view, no matter how right it may seem, if it is foisted on another human being, can no longer be educational. Education, therefore, can only occur in an atmosphere of freedom. I am not here speaking about children with whom a certain degree of certainty has to be present, but even with children, we have to guard against forcing personal opinions on them. Of course, what is accepted as knowledge does change remarkably over time. I wouldn't be surprised if the inhabitants of the world in the year 3000 AD would laugh uproariously at what we consider to be true today. Perhaps I could venture to say that what makes anything educational may not be any particular opinion or statement so much as the manner by which it is offered and also the intent in offering it. If it is meant to challenge the mind and the soul and it rests solely on inner or outer experience, I would accept it as possibly being educational. Anything else can only be interesting in that it reveals the soul condition and consciousness of the person teaching."

"Shaman Pi," Stu spoke up next to Robert, "you spoke a great deal about the role of business in our society last time we met. Would you be willing to tell us a little about that again? My friend Robert, who has joined us for the first time this evening, is majoring in business. I enticed him to join us, and I don't want him to feel I did so under false pretenses."

"Are you really?" The Shaman looked unbelievingly at Robert.

"I am interested in business, but I haven't completely made up my mind yet," Robert insisted.

"I would have thought you'd be more inclined toward one of the arts or perhaps education. Look at his hands. The long artistic fingers. See his ears, how they have a slightly elongated upper portion indicating more creativity than analysis. His whole facial structure shows a level of sensitivity that might very well go under in what I know of the general business environment." All the faces were turned to Robert, inspecting his features.

The dark-haired girl next to him traced the edge of his ear with her forefinger. "How beautiful and sensitive," she breathed over him.

Robert felt the need to explain himself. "I like most early classical music and enjoy painting. I sing in a chorus, but there is also something about business. Everything in business seems so definite, you know? It either works or it doesn't. You either have a customer and you continue to exist, or you run into debt and fold. With everything else, you seem to need forever, and even then, you might still not know if you're any good. Even if you're successful, you still don't know if you're any good. Besides, once you are successful—I mean really successful—you automatically become a business. It seems to me that the only real success in life has to become a business just because that's how it is. The way of the world . . . ?" Robert petered off.

"You're on the right track." The Shaman seemed pleased with Robert's thoughts. "Let me tell you my experience with business, but first I have to tell you about certain shadowy beasts that roam the human landscape." He had their attention.

"Every business I have known started up with a single person or a group of people having an idea, an impulse to be helpful in some way to humanity. The idea helped to provide either a service or a product that could support people in their work, their pleasure, their problems, or their sustenance or improvement. In the beginning, the idea always had an altruistic motive in it. The beast saw its chance, and either after two seconds or several years, it pounced and overcame the initial impulse and took its place in the heart of the founders. In this world, that beast always seemed to win out. It transformed hearts so they became consumed by this beast that eventually revealed itself as greed. Yes, dear friends, every business seemed to be a fitting home for greed to prosper. I don't know why this is so. I only see it taking hold relentlessly of the humans caught in it.

"The initial feeling in the heart of every founder is that 'What is good for the world will also eventually be good for me.' Gradually that thought is changed to 'What is good for me must inevitably be good for the world' and that subtle transformation opens wide the door for the beast of our time to slither in. It never quite has the power to work directly in the world. It can only get in through us, the humans struggling to make something of their lives. Almost every human wants not only to survive but also to make a difference in the world. The dark, slimy beast hankers for the best in us and uses it. It takes our finest forces, which are there to move outward and transform the world for the good, the beautiful, and the true and reverses this current so they become centrifugal, work from the periphery into the 'me.' I, the 'me,' becomes insatiable. In no time, we are servants of greed, the beast in our time."

The Shaman paused to let the thought echo and reecho in the feelings around him. Robert was at first stunned. Then he caught all the implications of what the Shaman was saying and rebelled.

"That's a very cynical view of business!" He couldn't help himself. He felt it necessary to reject what the Shaman seemed to want them all to believe. "I'm sure there are many who think and act very much like you describe. I also know there are some good people in business who have entirely different motives. I know some of them myself. My father, for example!"

The silence was charged. The students' faces wore shock and disbelief. They were speechless to begin with, and then it all bubbled to the surface.

"Your father?"

"I don't believe it." The dark-haired girl was upset. She inched away from Robert, giving him a little breathing room for the first time that evening. He felt the loss of her warmth and inclusion.

"What will you do?"

"Robert is one of us. We mustn't confuse him with his father," Stu defended Robert.

The Shaman did not display the displeasure the students were voicing. He seemed to be more sympathetic to Robert.

"Don't misunderstand me, Robert. There are good people everywhere, and there are probably some that are well on their way to be intentionally bad. Whether they are good or bad, they all have to deal with this beast in our time. Whether we are good or bad, we—and I really mean *we*—that includes you and also I—we all must deal with this beast in our current lifetimes. The best of us, even in business, are those that know it and are struggling to master it, to find the right relationship to it. I might say it is the real challenge of our time!"

He waited a moment before going on.

"I notice it is getting late. Perhaps we should all think about what we have explored this evening and next time bring our questions and thoughts for further exploration. Answers are useful, but not as useful as searching for them. The answer at one point in life or at any point in time may be fleeting. By the next time we meet, I will be a different person, and so will you. In the meantime, live well, and by all means, continue to become."

"Thank you, Shaman Pi. That is so beautiful! I will treasure it." The dark-haired girl next to Robert was overcome with emotion and wept into Robert's available shoulder.

Shaman Pi bowed slightly, acknowledging their appreciation and moved off toward the door of the classroom. Two maintenance men were there to greet him somewhat belligerently.

"Pi?" they accosted him.

"Yes, I am Shaman Pi."

"We've been instructed to tell you once again that if you are caught illegally using these classrooms for your own private purposes, we have obtained the authority to have you removed forcibly. This is just another warning. Do not come back, or we will be forced to call Security. You may even be arrested for trespassing."

"Do you understand?" the other man shoved his chin close to the Shaman's bushy beard and used his chest to move him back a little.

The students pushed forward to defend him, but the Shaman silenced them, saying, "Never mind. They are too late. The good has already been done. Good night to you all.

Have a good sleep. You too!" he nodded in the direction of the two maintenance men and moved down the hall toward the exit. The dark-haired girl and two other girls went with him as they disappeared out into the night.

"Are they going with him?" Robert asked Stu.

"I guess."

"Do they belong with him?"

"They all three seem to be wherever he is. I have never seen him alone. I haven't asked any questions about that. I figure it is none of my business."

"Rightfully so . . . but . . . well, it does make you think."

"Think what?"

"Well . . . I don't know . . . it just opens another window on the Shaman . . . I guess."

"Night, Robert. We need to talk some more."

"Yes, Stu. Another day!"

"Another day."

*****

When Horst arrived home that evening, his wife, Esmeralda, was worried. She heard the car drive up and hurried to the front door to meet him. He looked tired, but his eyes were triumphant.

"Where have you been?" She wanted to know. "It's after eleven o'clock. Did you have anything to eat?"

"I'm glad to see you too." Horst laughed, took her in his arms, and kissed her warmly.

"Oh, I'm sorry, Horst, but I have been so worried. It's not like you. No phone call, no message. What was I to think?"

"Well, I was first in Manhattan, then in a limousine to Tetterboro Airport. I had my 9:00 a.m. interview with Graham at around noon in a company jet—over lunch on board—at thirty-two thousand feet. Then I was briefly at the Memphis airport to catch another plane back to LaGuardia. Graham had arranged for a limo to take me to the garage where my car was parked while I was gone. Now I'm home, and I'm so glad to see you."

"Oh, darling, can I get you something to drink and or eat?"

"Will you sit with me?"

"Of course! I want to hear all about it."

Esmeralda made him a thin sandwich with Schaller and Weber liverwurst and a hot cup of decaffeinated herbal tea, and they both sat down at the table to talk.

"Who is Graham?" Esmeralda asked.

"You know, I'm not sure. I think he might be the telecommunications group VP, but I'm not sure. He's such an interesting man with lots of experience in the Alliance for International Communications Incorporated."

"Haven't you already had a number of interviews with them? I thought—"

"Yes, would you believe sixteen not counting today? I'm being considered for a job at a fairly high level. I'll be interacting with most of the top people. That's why all the interviews. They want to be sure I know how to get along with different types of personalities and levels of executives."

"And do you—I mean did you?"

"Well, I'm a little worried. Maybe I can only get along with people at thirty-two thousand feet." He laughed and Esmeralda enjoyed the joke with him. "This Graham was special though.

He was so open and candid about the Alliance for International Communications, how it runs, and what skills are needed to succeed. I think we might end up being friends. Who knows! Time will tell!"

"I am so glad. Do you think you'll take the job?"

"If and when it's offered I think I might. I'd have to know all the details of course."

"What happens next?"

"I don't know." Just then the phone rang.

"Who could that be at this hour? I always worry that it might be bad news when it rings after midnight. Maybe you should answer it," Esmeralda suggested.

Horst took the phone in the kitchen while Esmeralda cleared everything away for the night.

"Isn't this kind of late for you to be working still? Oh, I see. All right, I'll be there." He hung up. "That's strange. That was Stanley Benning's secretary," Horst said.

"What did she want?"

"It was a he, and he wanted to be sure I was in the office tomorrow morning just before noon to have lunch with Mr. Benning."

"Who's Mr. Benning?"

"My immediate boss at Alliance for International Communications Incorporated if I get the job."

"That's a good sign, don't you think?"

"I do think, but I can't help feeling sorry for him. Can you imagine calling me at midnight for his boss? Do they all work such long hours? When does the day end for them? He claimed to be home, but he just found a message from Mr. Benning and thought he better call me to make sure I could make it tomorrow."

"That was very considerate of him." Esmeralda was pleased.

"We'd better get to bed. I want to be awake and fresh as a bullfrog."

"I think you mean fresh as a daisy, dear. Bullfrogs go with some other cliché, I think. Anyway, you're not much of a daisy either."

Whether he looked like a daisy or a bullfrog, Horst was back on the ninth floor of the Alliance for International Communications the next morning shortly before noon. The receptionist smiled to see him again.

"I believe I've seen more of you than my own husband. Welcome! Can I get you something to drink?"

"How long do you think it will be before Mr. Benning shows up?"

"He's usually prompt, but you never know. All of them are very responsive to any summons from on high." She laughed at her own insight.

"I think I'll take a chance and skip coffee this morning. Benning and I are supposed to have lunch pretty soon."

"Yes, I know. I made the reservation for him in the executive dining room for noon today."

Just then a tall, dark-haired man came through the doorway of the elevator and moved in their direction with a friendly expression on his face. He had an interesting way of walking, his head slightly tilted forward, while his feet arrived ahead of him to catch up with his head. He wore a charcoal-gray suit, a pale-blue shirt, and a blue tie with vertical red stripes making him look even taller.

"Horst?" he enquired.

"Yes, you must be Mr. Benning!"

"Stanley. Good to see you. Do you mind if we go right up? I learned through my secretary that the dining room is a little crowded today. I want to be sure we have a table to ourselves so we can talk."

"Not at all. I'm interested to see the executive dining room. Is it available to all of us?"

"Anyone at your grade level twenty-one and above can reserve a place. It is generally acknowledged that if you are just wanting to eat, it might be better to use the cafeteria, leaving the dining room for business conversations and to entertain guests. There is one long table reserved for single diners to have a quick lunch if necessary."

"I see."

"Shall we?" Stanley indicated the elevators.

The executive dining room was on the eighteenth floor. The windows along three sides allowed a wide view up Park Avenue and a broad section of the east side, even a glimpse of the East River between buildings. The white tablecloths offset by silver settings contrasted sharply with the dark blue carpeting. The waiters wore simple white linen and dark trousers. Horst immediately noticed the muted voices. Any loud laughing or boisterous behavior simply did not fit in. Maybe you would be allowed to stay, but Horst imagined the next time you needed a reservation, none might be available.

Stanley had arranged for a table by a window with a view straight up Park Avenue. When they were seated and had ordered drinks (iced tea for both of them), Stanley looked across at Horst with a slight smile on his face.

"I understand you had the pleasure of meeting Graham on your way to Memphis," he said.

"Yes. Graham had a lot to say. He was very helpful. I'm beginning to know a little more about the Alliance for International Communications Incorporated."

"Yes, he's been around. I believe he was here before Lucky took over. He may actually have been a contender for her job at one point."

"What happened?"

"He didn't have enough friends on the board!"

The waiter brought them both small glass dishes of fresh fruit cut into little chunks no more than a half inch square. Horst was glad to see mostly berries, apples, and some nuts and raisins. He never liked melon mixed in with other fruit.

"What did you and Graham talk about all that time together on the plane?"

"There were a lot of little topics about people and various departments of AIC, but what I remember the most is his description of the AIC corporate structure. I was fascinated by the picture he drew of the leadership and how it worked. Of course, what he described may not be the official organizational chart but only his opinion. However, I had the feeling he was being truthful."

"Graham? Graham is always straight. You can count on it. He may be wrong on occasion, but he will always give you a straight answer. Whenever I need some information or am trying to understand something of what's going on, I go to Graham. He's never lied to me." Stanley obviously believed in Graham.

"Then is it true?"

"Is what true?"

"His picture of the pyramid with an egg balanced on the top?"

"He told you that?"

"Yes."

"He must like you. He doesn't normally share that unless he knows you for a long time and trusts you."

"But is it true?"

Stanley ate his fruit salad, downed it with a large dose of iced tea, and brought his napkin to wipe his lips. He seemed to be thinking or else giving himself time to frame an answer.

"There is a normal organization chart that has all the direct reporting relationships clarified, as well as the dotted-line ones. As far as the world is considered, everybody reports to somebody officially. What Graham was describing is the unofficial, hidden organization consisting of trust relationships. These are underlying lines of confidence and trust by which the organization really works. The people who trust one another support each other. You might say the Alliance for International Communications Incorporated functions through a conglomeration of trust groups." Stanley stopped and watched Horst's face for signs of his reaction.

"Let me try to understand . . ." Horst turned his puzzled face off to the left as he struggled for the right words. "There is an official public organization chart with all the reporting relationships clearly specified, which everybody knows. Then there is an unofficial inner network of trust groups composed of people who trust and support each other that really decides matters."

"Almost right." Stanley leaned forward. "The official corporate decisions are brought about by the official organization. The hidden networks are influence organs. Every decision has a factual content, but the qualitative element is always subject to influence. I've noticed that when these groups do not reach some form of understanding or agreement, the decision lingers and falters. When the influence groups are in agreement, the decisions not only get made, but they are actually implemented successfully." Stanley seemed pleased with his explanation. Horst had the feeling this was a new way of describing it, even for Stanley.

The two sat quietly, digesting the ideas and the food. Stanley was satisfied with a very green salad sprinkled with small vegetable bits. Horst enjoyed a turkey club without the bacon.

"So what do you think?" Stanley asked.

"I'm surprised and don't know exactly what to think. I know one thing, I already like and trust you and Graham, so in a way, I'm feeling the truth of what you're telling me. I just hope I can connect myself with people like you both."

Stanley laughed his approval but didn't confirm anything at this point. "There is one thing I haven't figured out yet. Who did you report to at your last job? You headed up the division, but who got the credit for your good work?"

"Aha, I see what you mean. His name was Marty Olinder. He headed up the group after the reorganization following the acquisition."

"So, you reported to Marty directly."

"Yes. I didn't use him as a reference because I only reported to him for a short time."

"I understand." Stanley hesitated briefly before going on. "You worked for Marty long enough to get to know him?"

"Yes. What are you getting at?" Horst had a feeling he knew what was coming next.

"What did you think of him?"

"Marty?"

"That's who we're talking about."

"Well . . . I worked for Marty for about three months . . ." Horst paused, not quite sure what to say. "You want to know what I thought of him while I worked for him."

"Yes, what do you think of him?" Stanley repeated. He watched Horst carefully, trying to read the series of expressions that registered on his face. "I'd like to know the truth!"

"The truth? You want the truth?" Horst wondered whether to be honest with his potential boss. He wanted this job very much. It was a big step up for him, and it would add considerably to his already impressive resume. All along in his life so far, well-meaning advisors had cautioned him against expressing his opinions too freely. Better to catch the drift of the wind first before committing yourself to any course of action.

Horst took a deep breath and looked Stanley right in the eyes. "Marty . . . I didn't like Marty. His attention was entirely on pleasing the people above him. If we really carried out his orders, our performance would have been mediocre. That's what he was, mediocre. I didn't like him." Horst ended abruptly.

"Anything else?"

Although Horst had only worked for Marty a short time, they had known each other for years. They had never been friends. They had clashed a few times over strategic moves and some semiethical issues, but since Marty was at a higher level, he often felt obliged to go along with his decisions. He took a deep breath and then tossed all caution aside.

"Marty is ambitious and always looking up to snare any advantage he can. As a result, he does not manage his people very well, encourages the same kind of behavior below him, and I don't know how far I could trust him. That's what I think!"

Stanley cast a piercing glance at Horst and then laughed. "Why do you do that?" he asked.

"Do what?"

"Take such a big risk. For all you know, Marty and I are close friends and I think very highly of him."

"You do?" Horst couldn't believe his ears. How could he have misjudged Stanley so badly? He must be slipping, to be that wrong!

"I only said how do you know. It just happens to be that I can't stand Marty and wouldn't have him working for me under any circumstances, but you didn't know that. You didn't even try to find out what our relationship might have been before rendering your opinion. You took a huge risk—unnecessarily!"

"Well, now at least you know one thing." Horst ventured.

"And that is?"

"When you ask me something, you'll get the truth."

"Eventually," Stanley corrected.

Horst nodded his agreement and admitted his reluctance.

"In that case, what do you think of me?" Stanley wanted to know.

"I think I will be able to get a lot of good stuff done with you as my boss! But fair is fair. What do you think of me?"

"I think we are going to enjoy working together," Stanley conceded.

The two smiled at each other, well underway to a solid friendship. One moment, Horst thought maybe he blew the interview; the next moment, the sun was shining and not a cloud in the sky.

CHAPTER THREE

Behind the Scenes

Just above the second-floor conference room, Armand Dillon had his small working office. He had arranged it so only four other chairs could be placed in the room, around a low coffee table and a cadenza behind his desk. Although this gave a somewhat cramped impression when he had everyone meeting with him, it also made for intimacy. He liked the feeling that in such an atmosphere and space, it was possible to discuss important and confidential matters.

Armand never removed his jacket or his tie while at work. As a matter of fact, none of his staff had ever seen him except formally attired. He consistently gave a dark, forbidding impression, as though whatever he might say or decide was serious, not to be taken lightly. Whatever it was, he wanted it to be done, carried out without question. The staff knew without a doubt that he would always follow up in a timely way. They knew he never forgot anything. Never!

Armand consulted notes he had hand written in his black book. To most people the notes would simply seem like black scratches with an extremely thin pen, having no special meaning, almost illegible. No letters could be distinguished. For Armand they were simply reminders—hieroglyphics, little signs for later recall. Each little scratch indicated a subject matter, a whole impression he wanted to remember—perhaps of something that occurred in a meeting or an idea he had in the middle of a discussion with other people.

At the top of a page in his notebook, he had seven black scratches, all meaningful, placed there during the conference meeting with Russ and his staff from Croton Green. He peered at them now through the dim light in his office. Each scratch awakened remembered images and impressions, even the actual sound of certain voices. He lived intensely from scratch to scratch, recalling the reality and underlying meanings and messages. They guided his thinking, and gradually inspiration gripped him, and he closed the little black book.

"Come in, Calder. I don't know who opened the door." Armand invited whoever knocked on the door frame from the other side. "Sit. No, not there, closer. That's good. Did you bring any of the paperwork on Croton Green and especially Russ?"

"I've got it all here," Calder Tebbit answered. He was a tall, lean man with a sallow-complexioned face, hair prematurely whitening. Spider lines crinkled at the outside corners of his eyes when he tensed, but they disappeared immediately when his face relaxed. He carried a manner eternally at attention that expressed itself in his stiff-legged walk, quick hand and arm gestures, and a face never joyful. Many people thought he somewhat resembled Armand Dillon in his appearance and manner. He was someone who knew a lot of the secrets, especially those connected with Human Resources. Armand leaned heavily on him to carry out some of the more delicate decisions.

"Did you watch Russ at the meeting?" Armand asked.

"I did."

"What do you think?"

"I think he's loyal to Croton Green. He doesn't like the idea of giving up the grass seed. I think you can expect many delays and a heap of ifs, ands, and buts." Calder rendered his opinion in a gruff, matter-of-fact tone.

"Yes, I believe you're right. What about his staff?"

"There's not a single one there with any independent backbone. I wouldn't look for any help there. How important are your plans for the grass seed? After all, the whole operation is still showing a steady profit. We could leave it alone."

"Not on your life. It galls me to see us giving money away without making a deliberate donation and no benefit, either PR or otherwise. Not only don't we get any benefit—nobody even knows we're doing it. Remind me of our contract with Russ!"

"We pay him a fixed amount for five years plus a salary for the time he actually holds the top job to our satisfaction, no bonus. Of course he is also getting one PTP share for every five of his Green shares."

"How do we break the contract?"

"His attorneys have removed all escape clauses in the final that Russ and we signed."

"How do we break the contract?"

"We don't."

"I didn't ask you whether we could break the contract. I asked how we break the contract." Armand made the distinction clear in a brittle voice.

Calder was silent. For a moment, he wondered whether Armand was serious. One look at his face, and Calder knew he was dead serious. He opened a folder and went down the page line for line with his pencil, his eyes following the movement. He snapped the folder shut.

"Getting out of the salary is no problem. You just fire him. All you need is cause. The purchase agreement is pretty well fixed. I don't think you can renege on any of that. Except maybe the mix of cash versus shares. There may be a little wiggle room there."

"You mentioned cause?" Armand stared pointedly at Calder.

"What about it?"

"I wonder if cause would give us some kind of edge." Armand did not take his eyes off Calder's face.

"What are you saying?"

"There are causes, and then there are causes!"

Calder was quiet. He thought about all the steps they had gone through with the merger. They had looked into every conceivable element of Croton Green's business affairs. It had been immaculate. The original founder had been a man with the strictest ethical standards. Even the auditors came up clean. Calder was certain the only way they would find any cause was to create one.

"Are you asking me . . . ?"

"Find a cause! One that we can use if we need it." Armand didn't want to be involved. He just wanted the result. Calder found himself again in a situation he could hardly bear, and yet if he wanted to keep his job, bear it he must.

"Now about Russ. Are you telling me he can be fired given reasonable cause, without negative financial implications, without the danger of a suit?"

"According to the contract, yes. You realize he can still contest it, and then it would be up to a court of law to interpret the contract," Calder warned.

"In your opinion, he can't win that case?"

"In a court of law, almost anything can happen both in the courtroom and outside of it. However, I find it unlikely the court can honestly interpret the contract in any other way than it is blatantly written. Right here in paragraph—"

"It seems like your advising me to fire him and be done with it."

"Now wait a minute. You only asked for my opinion."

"As I recall"—Armand consulted two scratch marks at the top of a page in his little black book—"he remains loyal to Croton Green. Doesn't want to give up the seed. Will fire a load of ifs, ands, and buts at us while he drags his feet. That sounds to me like a clear recommendation to fire him. Doesn't it?"

"Those are obstacles to overcome. They mean you can probably fire him, but if you want to keep him, they can probably be dealt with by a skillful HR professional."

"Like you? You're as skillful an HR professional as I know."

"So, you want to keep him. Is that what I hear? You want me to talk him into submission."

"I won't tell you what to do! I just don't want him around. Croton Green is important. I've got plans for it. I don't want to deal with your so-called obstacles. Follow whatever HR procedures are both effective and the least risky for us, but get the job done. I need a free hand in Croton Green, and I need it now."

"This might take a little time."

"I don't have time. Just do it! High priority!"

Calder shifted his weight uncomfortably in his chair, spilling some of the loose papers from his lap to the floor. He picked them up and added them to one of the folders littering the coffee table.

"Let me think this through. I'll get back to you and tell you what we should do."

"Goddammit, Calder." Armand's face flushed red with anger and then went a dead white as he snarled back. "The reason I pay you six figures plus bonuses and all kinds of perks is to act, not think. I need you to get this done, however you see fit. After you've done it, you can go down to Boca Raton or wherever you want to do your thinking."

"If I could be just a bit clearer on what you want me to do, I would—"

Calder looked askance at Armand's ice-cold expression, dead white skin, dark eyes piercing the distance between them. He felt paralyzed, trapped in psychological chains, powerless to resist, the sheer force of the angry hatred overcoming him, and the fear gripping his insides. It wasn't just the job he might lose, he felt torn apart inside by the force of this man's ego.

In another moment, the dynamic changed. The blood eased back into Armand's face. His eyes lost their belligerence, and a grim smile brought a little warmth into his countenance.

"It's a good thing we know each other so well and have been friends for so many years, Calder. I have complete confidence in you, and I know you will do well what has to be done, right?"

Calder imitated his smile, his wan cheeks blossoming into a semblance of cheerfulness. "I've always done the best I could, Armand, you know that."

"I do. When you get through the door there, ask Esmeralda to come in here, will you?"

"Sure, Armand. Can do!"

"And close the door!" Armand called after him.

*****

Robert decided to walk home after the meeting with Shaman Pi even though it was more than two miles and would certainly take about forty-five minutes. His route from Fairmont University took him directly through town and out the other end into the burgeoning suburbs. The shops gradually gave way first to apartment buildings and then gas stations, lumberyards, a walk-in emergency clinic, and then the first tree-lined streets and single-family homes. The streetlights thinned out to one in each block and two at every intersection.

His house resembled many of the others, split-level combination brick and wood siding. The entrance was squarely in the middle of the front facade. The entrance light was on, even though the deep dark of night encroached as shadows closed in to where the streetlights stretched their glow. He could only see clearly the entrance way and two of the steps. The rest required groping in shadow, feeling his way with the tips of his shoes. He noticed that one of the bulbs was still missing, maybe even on purpose. His dad was a miser and saved pennies wherever he could.

His dad must be home even though many a night at this time he was still at work, sometimes even taking a hotel room when late meetings kept him in the city. The dark blue Mercedes in the driveway was a sure sign that he was there. He probably left the light on for him.

The image of his mother flashed into his consciousness and then was gone. She had died already three years ago. The old pain of his father struggling with all the issues around his mother's emphysema visited him briefly. He recalled his father spending the evenings attending her while the nurse stood by. She didn't mind the nurse changing linens and clothes and fiddling with the equipment around the bed, but she always preferred his gentle touch in dressing the bed sores and wounds. It still pained Robert to recall his father's patient suffering with her. They both managed to shield him as much as possible from the realities, but he felt it all around him. The potent mixture of suffering, caring, loving and knowing was everywhere throughout the house.

From the street he couldn't see any lights in the house. It was sheltered by high rhododendron and azalea bushes that hid all the downstairs windows. Only a faint glimmer occasionally escaped when the thick foliage was stirred by a passing breeze. He made his way to the front door, pushed it open, and entered.

"Dad?"

"Out here," Charles McLane answered from the back patio.

"Hey." Robert thought his father looked tired.

"It's kind of late, don't you think? Where have you been?"

"Oh, just around with friends. I wanted to audit a late class."

"Oh? What kind of class?"

"Ethics and business and self-development, I guess."

"How did they ever squeeze all that together?" Charles laughed. So did Robert.

"It wasn't easy."

"How is it going in your international management course?"

"That's going well, Dad. I think I'm enjoying that immensely."

"Good. You'll need that regardless of where you end up."

There was a long, comfortable silence between father and son. Neither of them seemed to feel the need to talk. They often sat like this on the screened-in back patio. Sometimes they were both reading and didn't exchange more than a dozen words the whole evening.

"Why are you working for Alliance for International Communications Incorporated?" Robert asked without any preamble.

"Why?"

"Yes. You've been working for them since I can remember. You know, I don't even know what you do for them. We never talked about it."

"Well, there never seemed to be a need as long as we had our heads above water."

"I mean, are you there because you like the work or because you believe in what they are doing?"

"You know, Robert, they pay me a darn good salary with all the benefits anyone could want. I even get to own quite a few shares over time."

"So it's because of the money, mostly. No other reason?"

"Listen, do you have any idea what your tuition runs as well as your other expenses? If it weren't for AIC, we couldn't afford it. Be glad I do have that job."

"What do you actually do?"

"I do special projects for the groups and also, sometimes, for the president and CEO. You remember the times I was gone for several months at a time? Those were all special assignments in South America or in Europe. For some reason, I never had anything in Africa. Probably because AIC doesn't have much business there yet. Your mother used to hate it when I was gone for such long periods. Haven't done much of that lately, although I was in New Orleans for about a month last year. Remember?"

"Do you build anything or make something people need?"

"No, I fix problems. Or also, I am good at negotiating deals for the company. A group exec will call me in and assign a project or problem to me, and I deal with it as best I can."

Charles returned to his *Time* magazine article, and Robert mulled over this new information. It sounded like an important job his father had. Solving problems seemed like a good thing to be doing.

"In one of my classes, there seemed to be a problem with corporation ethics," he calmly stated.

"Oh? How so?"

"They were saying the only reason they exist is to make money, and they'll do anything for a buck."

"I wonder who says that." Charles paid attention.

"Oh, a lot of people, even some of the other students."

"Probably the ones on scholarship," Charles suggested.

"Maybe. They say the major motivation in business is greed. They go so far as to call it an evil presence in society."

"There are always some bad apples around. I'll bet you there are even a couple in a holy place like Fairmont University."

"I s'pose so."

They let the subject rest, but Robert couldn't leave it alone.

"Dad, if you found out that Alliance for International Communications Incorporated was really a bad influence on life, you wouldn't work there anymore, would you? I mean if they were doing evil things, hurting people and taking advantage, you would stop working for them, wouldn't you?"

"Robert, you listen to me. The whole of human life rests on business. Without it, there wouldn't be any jobs, no food, no housing, not even any books. Fairmont University wouldn't exist without the massive donations and grants and tax money. Business is like the bedrock of all our lives. It is Atlas supporting the world on his shoulders. True, we need governments to regulate and protect us from errant persons and groups. As I said, there will always be a few bad apples, but don't throw the whole basket out because of those few."

"I know that, Dad, but it can't seem right that anything should exist just to make money. You have to make money, but the real reason for existing should be to contribute something of real value to the quality of life. Like a farm, for instance. Farmer's don't do their work just to make money. They have to make some in order to live and support themselves and their families. But their real reason is to feed people, to nourish them so they can live. Basically, a farmer contributes sustenance to human life. I guess I'm trying to get at motive as different from means. Money as means, not as motive. It seems to me most corporations have money as motive and ends, while what they make or create is the byproduct, and I don't think that's right. It shouldn't be that way!"

"So that's what they're teaching you at Fairmont? That's what they're doing with my tuition payments?"

"You see? That's what I mean. Money, money, money. You understand everything through the lens of money."

"Well, somebody's got to earn it. We can't all be studying!"

"You want me to quit? I can get a job."

"Oh no, you don't. Not after I've already invested three years of—" Charles stopped abruptly before finishing his sentence. "Look, we're both tired. It's late and we shouldn't be arguing anyway. We only have each other since your mother died, and you know how much I care about you and love you. So let's not quarrel. I'm going to bed. See you in the morning. Do you have an early class?"

"Yes," Robert said in a low, subdued voice. He wasn't happy. Something wasn't right. He didn't know what, but there was something in the background that bothered him. Maybe it was just the late hour. He too decided to turn in for the night.

Charles tidied up the loose sheets of newspaper and parts of the morning mail still floating around. He sat down again and rubbed his chin. His thoughts weighed heavily on his consciousness. *It's a good thing he doesn't actually know what I have had to do in the past,* he thought. He continued thinking to himself about his wonderful wife and how they shared everything. She knew! She also knew how he struggled with his job, his talents, and his feelings of obligation to family. They had a good marriage. They shared everything—although he had one big secret he never dared to share with her.

With the cancer and her earlier illness, it didn't seem right to upset her with that kind of secret. He had a feeling that if she had known, it would have upset her terribly—maybe even worsened her illness or hastened her death. Far better that he kept it to himself.

As for Robert? Well, he supposed someday he would have to tell him the truth. Not now! Definitely not now! Someday, he would have to tell him, especially if his real mother ever admitted it. Charles wondered if his real mother still had any feelings for him. It was such a long time ago.

He never dared to tell Robert more details of his work. He was too young to understand that he had to do what he was doing to meet his responsibilities as the head of the household, as a husband and as a father. He didn't think he was doing anything really bad. He couldn't say it was really good either.

Again he mulled over the idea to leave AIC and find another job. His skills would probably guide him into the same kind of work somewhere else, so what would that accomplish? Besides, Lucinda needed him. Already twice he had saved her some serious embarrassment, maybe even prevented her losing the presidency of the Alliance for International Communications Incorporated. If the board knew how close the issue came to finding its way into their meeting! He wondered why he cared so much about Lucinda that he continued working there. After all, their relationship had been such a long time ago. Well, he hated to admit it—what he had to do really didn't feel right. They say it, and he knew there was no other way to do business in South America, but did he try? Should he try? Should he have tried to persuade Lucinda to take the risk of losing all their contracts down there if they didn't . . . ?

Charles felt weary. His thoughts were going around and around, making him tired since there was no resolution. He was caught in his own net. If he wanted any sleep tonight, he should stop the cycle, get off, think about it some other time. He stood up briskly, convincing himself he had made a decision—of sorts—and climbed the stair to the second floor and the bedroom. He eventually did sleep, but not until nearly two in the morning. The weight of the world still hung on him and kept him too close to the surface in his sleep.

*****

Even the employees at the Alliance for International Communications Incorporated talked about the president and chief executive's office on the twelfth floor. Some alluded to it with pride while others considered it over the top, although none actually said that out loud. "That's just the way it is when you have a woman as president" was whispered around, quietly, especially by men. Women employees considered it delightfully refreshing and beautiful.

The moment a visitor left the elevator bank on the twelfth floor, the scent of roses and lilac overpowered all other scents. No wonder—two large ceramic urns contained the living plants, growing and flowering under special lights that imitated the qualities of sunlight. The combination of the lilac color and the deep red of the roses was striking. The first time a visitor usually stopped short immediately after leaving the elevator to take in the unusual spectacle either with shock on the face or at least surprise. It was so unexpected, especially in contrast to the pale green sofas, pink cushions, and the large Chinese rug stretching past all the elevators, right up to the glass doors leading to the offices.

The reception area had a similar look about it, matching the colors in walls and paintings. There was nothing mechanical about it. All was flowing; all had the same aesthetic mood to it. One could immediately sense that someone had personally selected every detail; a single taste bound all the colors, all the furniture, all the decoration together in an overwhelmingly feminine design.

Bruce Hershberg and Katherine Salter stepped out of two adjacent elevators at the same time, nodded to each other, and moved together toward the glass doors with the familiar ALLIANCE FOR INTERNATIONAL COMMUNICATIONS INC. and Lucinda Brahms, President and Chief Executive Officer etched in the glass and shaded with translucent milky-white lettering. They immediately started ticking off to themselves all the possible subjects that involved both of them as they had been summoned together. Katherine Salter, senior vice president, Latin American Region, assumed it had something to do with one of the country projects south of Panama. Bruce Hershberg, senior vice president, Human Resources, naturally assumed it had something to do with either employees, management, or compensation. Since he had not brought with him any of the documents or recent memos, he knew there would be lots of opportunity to postpone any topic for further investigation and consideration. This would very likely be one of those discussions that ranged far out in all directions that Lucky loved to pursue.

Lucky waved them both into her office. Katherine bustled in and took one of the easy chairs around the coffee table.

Bruce took half a step back; it was always a shock for him to be assailed by the colors, the many large and small bouquets of flowers, and strong scents.

Lucinda Brahms was never alone. She loved to have people around her. She insisted that Jolene Senter have her desk, pink file cabinets, the whole small secretarial unit in a corner of her spacious office. She didn't mind the phone ringing every now and then, nor did it bother her to have people stop by just to see Jolene as the confidential assistant to the president and chief executive officer of the Alliance for International Communications Incorporated. It was Lucky's style to do most of her thinking and creating in the midst of a hubbub of activity. Everyone called her Lucky, even the cleaning woman who sometimes breezed through and into an important meeting while completing her early evening tidying up and cleaning. Occasionally, she too had something to contribute to the discussion!

No one ever asked to see Lucky. No one ever called ahead of time to find out if she was available. Everybody just took their chances, popped in to see what was going on and came back later if she was busy or just waited awhile or, even better, joined in the action, whatever it was. There was no confusion around the decision-making, even though a different crowd might be present when it occurred. It was clear to all her officers and staff that the decision would always be made by her, even though everyone might be having some influence on it. Everyone working at the Alliance for International Communications Incorporated knew how it worked, quickly learned how to contribute actively to the process of management, or else left.

Today wasn't any different. Lucky was listening to Alfred Deed, marketing specialist, Latin American Group. Graham had brought him along to do some of the explaining. Alex Durand, chief security officer, happened to be there, as well as Stanley Benning, who had been called up early that morning to listen in.

"Well, that's the short and the long of it. From everything I have heard formally and informally, we stand a very good chance of losing that contract, even though we have already created two other switching stations for them successfully and on budget. Every indication was that we were a shoo-in, and yet . . . That's just how it is." Alfred finished up.

"Who are we dealing with?" asked Lucky. Alfred and Graham laughed.

"Remember, Lucky, we're dealing with Brazil. Any of the countries down there are about the same. You don't deal with just one person. You are engaged with a long line of semi-decision-makers, never quite sure whose influence is greatest," Graham explained.

"Who pays us?" Lucky went straight to the heart of it.

"They actually have a paymaster who functions well once the contract is signed. We rarely have to renegotiate or fine them for late payment. On our other two contracts, we only once stopped work and settled payment. They want the system in. Their whole economy suffers without communications toward those emerging parts of the country," Katherine answered for Alfred, as this was the major area of her influence, and Graham guffawed again, his usual explosive intercession.

"What do you suggest?" Lucky asked Graham and then looked around at the others as though wanting their input as well. She lived inclusively at all times.

"We can wait and see if the tide changes. It often does. I recall our shipping systems contract looked grim, and yet at the end, no other bidder could offer them a better deal," Bedding said.

"I recall we lost our shirt on that deal. Am I right?" Lucky tried to remember.

"Yes, we did," answered Greg Upstein who just showed up to get involved in the meeting. He had heard they were discussing what to do about the contract in Brazil. He was the account manager for Switching Systems, but he knew a little about the other contracts AIC had in Brazil. "It turned out we were willing to lose a little in return for the other switching station deals we had for the interior. It all worked out as we planned. Our profit was great thanks to a renegotiation one of our project leaders down there managed to accomplish. I'm pretty sure that's what happened."

"Who did that deal?" Lucky asked.

"We were all involved," Graham insisted. "It was a team effort."

"But who was the point man on that?"

They all looked at each other. The name seemed to escape their consciousness.

"Wasn't it one of the Latin American specialists here at headquarters? I seem to remember there was someone on our staff who often pulled out a few chestnuts, especially in Brazil. What was his name? He hasn't been around for a while."

Benning thought hard. "I'll look in the files and let you know," he promised.

"I may be wrong, but do I understand that nobody has any suggestions about what to do?" Lucky gave them all time to respond. There were some shrugs, a great deal of looking around, and clearing of throats, but no responses.

"I think we should pull out all the stops and go after it. We're talking about a twenty-six-million-dollar contract. I can't see AIC saying good-bye to that without a fight." Lucky expressed what seemed to be on all their minds.

"I agree."

"Yes."

"Yes." There seemed to be agreement around that course of action.

"I wonder how we fight effectively since we seem already to be losing. How do we not only get back in the ring but also win?" Lucky was clear about her support. The group around her seemed galvanized. They were excited, wanting to win, especially since Lucky agreed!

"Doing business in Brazil is a little different than elsewhere in the world. It is done—how shall I say?—with money. Do you know what I mean?" Graham began reluctantly. "Maybe we should talk about this in some other context?"

Lucky looked carefully at Graham. He seemed to be hinting at something. Could it mean he wanted to take this discussion further in secret? This challenged Lucky's entire philosophy of management, her approach to leadership.

"This is as good a time and place as any!" she said.

"What I meant to say is that this whole area requires some delicacy. The rules of doing business in Brazil are not usually discussed in public." Graham spoke hesitantly, not his way at all. There was a great deal of looking around at each other and mingled surprise.

"Come on, Graham. Out with it," Lucky urged him. "You know very well how we work here. By being entirely open, we've never had a leak yet."

Graham looked around at who was present, seemed satisfied, but nevertheless slid his eyes lower to rest on the carpeted floor for a second before answering.

"To get that contract will take money," he finally said.

"Money?"

"Yes, money. Lots of it!"

"Ah!" Lucky understood. "You have an estimate?"

"Not less than a cool million."

"You're telling me, in your opinion, we will need to spread a million around in Brazil where it will do us the most good, and you think that will get us the contract?"

"I agree," Alfred chimed in now that the secret was roaming around free.

"No guarantee!" Graham added, "But it might work. It can't just be thrown around. It has to be done with knowledge of the people and the decision-making process and by the right person—somebody who knows how to do it right."

"You, maybe?" Lucky suggested.

"Hell no! I am precisely the wrong person. I am known there, often followed by their police, other department officials, and competitors. It's not only an assignment requiring a high degree of knowledge and skill but also someone who can operate without showing up in any spotlights, if you understand me."

"OK, let's find that person. Do you all agree we want this contract and are willing to absorb some cost to get it? I trust we can make it up in the pricing?" Lucky's eyes went around the little circle of nodding heads before she turned to Stanley Benning. "Find him or her!" she told him point-blank.

"It has to be a man." Graham corrected her and shrugged his shoulders. "It's South America" seemed to be enough of an explanation.

"Find him," Lucky amended her order, and the little group broke up, feeling a solution had been found with everyone contributing.

CHAPTER FOUR

Love and Rancor

Robert found himself in the university library. He wandered among the stacks, looking for corporate problem solving or something similar. He realized this was an inefficient way to find anything and returned to the library catalogs. It was hopeless, and he turned to a wizened librarian who seemed to know just about everything.

"I'm trying to find out something about corporate problem solving," he informed her.

"You want to learn how to do it?" she asked. "Or are you just curious about the subject?"

"The latter," he decided.

"I can think of two possibilities. You might want to try *consulting* or *research*. It all depends on the type of problem you're trying to solve."

"I think I'll try *consulting*." He thought what he wanted was something more hands-on, more practical than pure research, but you never know. Sometimes research has immediate solutions, but not for what he was interested in.

Sure enough, in the catalogs, he found all kinds of links, including business, corporation, financial, consulting firms . . . It went on and on. He moved over to the stacks again and picked out four books that seemed to be relevant, including one by Peter Drucker that he had heard about. He sat down at one of the long tables and began to browse. That was his technique, first to browse through the books for general orientation. He could always dig deeper once he knew he was on the right track.

He went quickly through two books that didn't offer anything interesting and then held up the one by Peter Drucker. He studied the cover as though that might give him a clue as to its contents. *The Effective Executive*. He wondered whether his father was an effective executive. He wouldn't be surprised if he was. He had the manner of someone who expected to be effective, whatever that meant.

He lifted his eyes from the book thoughtfully and found two other eyes studying him from across the table. They were light gray, expressive, alive. She nodded her head at him as if to say that he was picking the right book.

"You think so?" he whispered.

"Definitely. My boss consults it all the time. She keeps it on her desk for quick reference," she whispered, her eyebrows raised for emphasis.

Robert had no idea why, but he knew instantly that he liked this girl. She wore no makeup that he could discern. Her hair was in a pigtail, held together by what looked like a plain rubber band. She wore a dark blue cardigan over a man's white dress shirt. A simple silver watch on her wrist was the only jewelry he could see.

"Can you tell me more?" he asked.

"Sh, sh!" several people farther down along the table insisted.

"Maybe outside?" she asked in a whisper.

"Let's."

The university library had a series of wide, broad steps leading up to the entrance. They sat down about halfway up. They were not alone. It seemed that it was the thing to do if you wanted to talk with someone. Robert was surprised at the number of students who still smoked and was glad they were clustered together near the bottom of the steps and in the far corner. Still, the smoke was in the air. How far it travelled!

"Say, would you mind if we got out of this smoke? I'm not allergic or anything. I just don't like it," he told her.

"Me too. I can't stand to be in any place where they smoke. Cigars are the worst."

"Would you like to drop over at the George Washington Restaurant? We can have coffee there and all the conversation we want." He hoped she would say yes.

"How much conversation do you have in mind?" She raised one eyebrow.

He was surprised. How quickly she had picked up on his interest in her. Her eyes twinkled warmly, and it amazed him how much he was happy to be in her company. He felt pleasantly surprised all over. It was a new and wonderful feeling.

"If I am honest with you—and I hope I can and will always be honest with you—right now I don't see any end to the possibilities." He flirted unabashedly.

She laughed. How is it possible to so completely understand each other, to have so much empathy and . . . joy? Yes, joy. He felt joy in being with her, sitting on the steps of the university library with a dozen or so other students perched around them.

"So, would you like to know who I am?" she asked.

"In a way, I feel as though I already know you, but yes, I would love to know your name and who you are."

"I'm Jolene Senter, spelled *J-O-L-E-N-E*. I am a glorified secretary, sometimes known as a confidential assistant to the president of a company in New York City."

"What are you doing out here at Fairmont University?"

"I'm actually a commuter. I live out here and join a throng of henpecked husbands all working hard to support their wives and children who live in the suburbs and wonder why their husbands are coming home later and later each evening."

"Sounds to me like you've been studying the errant habits of the suburban male for a while. I hope that wasn't real sarcasm I heard."

"Not really, I was trying to be funny. I don't know why I should want to be entertaining with you. You're perhaps the one person I've met in years with whom I can just be myself and not have to make like I might lose you if you don't laugh. You probably don't know this, and maybe I shouldn't be telling you this, but we girls actually practice smiling and laughing. It's important to look good while doing it. Otherwise, men think you don't like them. That would be a disaster. Nothing turns away a man faster than a girl who doesn't laugh and smile at their every comment."

"Are you just teasing me?"

"No, I'm serious. You didn't know that?"

"No, I never thought about it, although I know girls smile even when they are saying something serious. I always thought maybe the smile was like punctuation. You know, comma . . . smile, don't you know? Question mark . . . smile! Like that. Period . . . smile."

"That's very good. You are something. I have a feeling you know us better than you're letting on."

"Not really. That was just a guess. So did you practice a lot before we met?"

"Not any more. I used to sit in front of the mirror, sometimes with a girlfriend and we'd try different smiles. We'd try to do it very broadly, like this, and then we'd try tilting our heads one way or another. We needed to know how much of our teeth should show and when do we start looking ferocious if they stuck out too far."

Robert laughed out loud as Jolene twisted her face about and tried to show different smiles.

"Now that's a good laugh! I bet you practiced that a lot before settling on that particular version."

"I did not!" Robert was adamant. "I never even thought of such a thing. If something was funny, the way you just were, I go right ahead and just laugh without thinking about it." Robert laughed and then stopped self-consciously, no longer sure exactly how to do it.

"You see? You need more practice." Jolene teased him, digging her elbow into his side. "You have no idea how we girls struggle to get just the right laugh, one that is careless, but exactly the way we want it. We have to consider the tilt of the head, what happens to the hair when we do it, should the mouth be wide open or slightly turned to the side, should the lower jaw be dropped or the upper lip raised, baring more teeth. Then the sound that comes out. Heaven forbid if it is raucous or grates on people's nerves. You don't want it to tinkle either or resemble the neighing of a horse. There's an awful lot to consider and work out if you want a really attractive laugh, one that will attract all the men for miles around."

"I had no idea it was so difficult to be a girl." Robert was amazed. "Here I thought they just naturally became beautiful and adorable like you. That's what always attracted me. I mean, the way a girl is so marvelously put together and the way you speak and the sound of your voice. It's all so incredibly wonderful!"

Robert and Jolene then sat quietly, just glad to be together. For a moment, there wasn't any need for more talk, explanations, discussion. It just seemed natural to be together, like two sides of a coin, the two halves of a walnut, the completed symmetry of an oak leaf. It was just as it should be and was.

"Do you still want me to tell you about Peter Drucker?" Jolene asked quietly, not wanting to dispel the mood around them.

"You said your boss had it on her desk and consulted it all the time."

"Yes, she had. I only remember one quote. Let's see . . . It went . . . 'The best way to predict your future is to create it.' Yes, that's it. My boss would use that all the time."

"Isn't that a bit arrogant? I mean not all matters are predictable or creatable. I would rather say, 'The best way to understand the future is to live it.'"

"That's very good . . . what's-your-name. I told you my name, and you left me in the dark. You also invited me to the George Washington Restaurant for coffee, and here we still sit in front of the university library. I'm beginning to wonder about you." They both laughed happily.

"I have a class in a few minutes, but can we make it another time? Very soon, I mean? Why are you here? I mean, I thought you worked in the city?" Robert rose from his seat on the steps.

"I'm doing a bit of research for my boss. I think I'll be here another day."

"Great. Why don't we meet at the George Washington Restaurant tomorrow at half past noon? You know where it is, don't you?" Robert began to look forward to the next day.

"Oh yes. It's right at the foot of the hill, no?"

"Yes. See you then! I've got to hurry!" he called back to her over his shoulder.

Robert attended the class—at least he placed his body in a chair, made his ears listen to the subject matter and his eyes focus on the blackboard, but an hour later, he already couldn't remember a thing the professor had said. He groaned, knowing this meant he had to read the three chapters in the text to make up for his inattention in class. It seemed this professor made it very clear that either you listened to him or you read the text. For top grades, you did both. It was wonderful how he laid out all the rules of learning so clearly. It was so efficient! You didn't have to learn anything unnecessarily. He wondered what Peter

Drucker would think of this kind of learning. Maybe in reality we only bother to learn what is really necessary, anyway.

*****

Lucky arrived early at the office. She knew an unpleasant task lay before her. Evans, a relatively new employee, had been caught sneaking a highly confidential report out of the office in a disguised manila envelope addressed to himself. Accidentally, one of the office boys had stumbled upon it fallen to the floor next to his desk. Evans wasn't around at the moment. Since it was open, he thought it was intended for the trash, and he looked inside before noticing the address. Although the dark red CONFIDENTIAL notice stamped on it was now black, indicating it to be a copy, it was still clear that it was not to be removed from the office.

The office boy happened to know Evans, but they were not friends. He took it with him, wondering what to do. Eventually, as he passed Benning's office a little further down the line, he decided to collect some gold stars for himself and turned it in to Benning personally. Benning knew exactly what to do.

He called Evans into his office and held up the manila envelope for him to see.

"Why are you mailing this envelope to yourself at your home address?"

"I never saw it before. What is it?"

"It's a highly confidential report concerning contracts entered into by this company. You have no business holding it at all and are certainly breaking all company rules by mailing it to yourself at home."

"I told you, I never saw it before. Somebody's trying to frame me."

"It was found by your desk."

"You can't prove anything."

"Were you going to sell this list? I wonder to whom?"

"Even if I did, you can't blame a fellow for making a little on the side."

"So you did steal it?"

"I never saw it before. How did you come by it?"

"It was lying on the floor next to your desk. The address label with your address on it was typed at your desk using your old Remington. See the upper case letters with blurred tops? That's your typewriter. It has been annoying me for years, and I've been meaning to have it cleaned for you. Now I'm glad I didn't do it."

"Doesn't prove I typed it. I wouldn't be surprised if you'd typed it yourself. You've been wanting to get rid of me for weeks. Just waiting for something like this, I bet."

"Evans, you're fired. Pack up your own personal stuff—and only your own things—and check out with the security guard on the main floor. I don't want you in here a second longer than necessary. As a matter of fact, I'll call down and have the security guard come up and check you out personally."

"You ain't firin' me! I'll lodge a complaint against you. The boss ain't gonna like what I have to say to her."

That's how Lucky got pulled into this minor matter. Lucky had a way of smoothing feathers, no matter how ruffled. When Lucky heard about the incident, she also had a few questions of her own. Evans was ushered into her office by the security guard, who obviously intended to stick with him.

"Thank you." Lucky nodded to the guard. "I'd like to have a few words with him. Would you please wait for him out in reception? I'll buzz you when he's ready to go."

"Now then"—Lucky smiled at the surly culprit standing in front of her desk—"please sit down."

"I didn't do it!" he said, and he slouched his body into the eighteenth century easy chair next to her desk.

"I hear you didn't steal the document, you didn't type the address, and as a matter of fact, you never saw any of it and don't know what it's all about. Is that right?"

"That's right. Mr. Benning's had it in for me ever since I started. I feel discriminated against, if you know what I mean."

"Sure, I know what you mean," Lucky said pleasantly enough. "So what are we going to do? I guess what we need is proof. Either that you did do it or, on the other hand, that you didn't do it. Proof! Absolute, irrefutable proof one way or the other. You agree?"

"Damn right!"

"I wonder what kind of proof would do it," Lucky mused.

"You ain't got any. That's a fact."

"The trouble with proof is that it happens to be a two-edged sword."

"Huh? What you mean?"

Lucky chuckled and then smiled broadly at Evans. He was obviously only semieducated. His English was poor, his upbringing probably scanty. He must have some intelligence, or else how did he get a job? It was a desk job to be sure, but still requiring a degree of some kind. Lucky was not familiar with his file, but she guessed he might have a two-year degree, maybe from a community college.

"Here's the situation. Listen carefully. We can submit the document to the fingerprint experts at police headquarters, where they would do an objective analysis. They would also come to take your fingerprints for comparison. If you are innocent, all's well. The sun will shine on all of us, and we will be happy. Do you see?"

Lucky was not surprised to see the darkening expression on Evan's face. His eyebrows knotted, almost hiding his eyes, and his head was tilted ominously to the right as he mulled over what Lucky had said and began to get worried.

"On the other hand, if your fingerprints actually matched the ones on the document, they would prove that you had touched that document, had handled it in some way, proving you a liar and proving you a thief!"

Evans didn't say a word. For some reason, he was speechless for the first time, but he listened, and he was thinking at his own sluggish rate.

"If that is so, we will not be able to stop any and all legal processes from kicking in. It may mean fines, but probably prison. It may also mean more investigation by the police, and who knows what else they may uncover. Well, you know, police being what they are." Lucky hunched her shoulders sympathetically toward the hapless Evans. She leaned forward in his direction and asked him.

"Wouldn't it be a lot easier if we just fired you? You could collect unemployment insurance for a while, maybe look for another job. Maybe even—which I personally like and recommend for you—mend your ways?" Lucky emphasized the last few words.

Evans started to rise from his chair. He was angry. He felt defeated, but also cheated in some way. From having an upper hand, he had fallen to victim status, and he didn't like it.

"You people!" he snarled. "You're all alike. Smart and nasty."

"I take it that means you would love to be fired?" Lucky was no longer smiling. "Just for my sake, who were you working for?"

"Why should I tell you anything? I don't work here anymore! You can't make me! But I can tell you one thing!" Evans had jumped up. "You think you know everything. Man, if you only knew what I know. You'd be shaking in your little girl boots. If you only knew. But I ain't goin' to tell you nothing!" he answered smugly.

"I can guess, Evans," Lucky said. "It's probably a middleman who shells out a few cents for you, turns around, and makes the real money on selling it abroad. You're not smart enough to be a real criminal."

"That's what you think!" Evans shouted triumphantly. "You ain't getting it out of me, but I can tell you this. I'm right at the top. You have no idea who's out to get you. If you knew, it would shake you to bits, if you just knew. They don't come much higher. No small fry! No sirree! One of the biggest businesses around, and he's dealing right with little ole me! Just you wait!" Evans spurted it all out gleefully.

"I doubt if he'll pay you much for your failure to deliver," Lucky answered quietly and pushed a small button at her desk, which summoned the security guard.

That thought then came home to Evans, but he buttoned up tight and went quietly. The security guard tried to take his arm, but Evans jerked it away from him and marched out, pretending to be defiant.

After Evans was gone, Benning came in along with Graham. They both stood quietly by for a moment, waiting to see if Lucky had anything to say. She didn't even look up.

"Anything?" Benning asked.

"Not much, but something." Lucky was speaking just slightly above a whisper. "Such people in the world." She marveled.

"Yeah. I'm glad we got him before he did any real damage."

"You think he didn't?"

"I don't think so," answered Benning. "Did you find out differently?"

"He seemed to think he was stealing for someone high up in another corporation."

"Did he mention any names?" Graham was right there, close, fully awake to the threat.

"No, he said we would be surprised at who it was. He mentioned a large corporation but no names."

"It might be worth something to us if we could find out who. Should we offer to grease his palm for information? He seemed like the type who would betray his own friend for money. I think even a couple of thousand dollars would be a bargain to know who's behind this." Graham seemed willing.

"I suppose you could try, Graham, but he's probably gone by now. I hate to give the guy even a penny, especially if it encourages him to go right on with his dirty business. No, Graham. I don't like it. I also don't want the person behind it to know more about us."

"You think Evans would go back empty-handed?"

"He's got to. They'd find him no matter where he is. They probably gave him a down payment. Besides, maybe he's on a retainer, so to speak, and will try something else for them."

"I tell you what," Benning suggested, "why don't I ask around, query the people in the department, find out what I can about Evans? He might have connections, might have bragged to someone, maybe frequents a particular bar. Let's see what we can learn without actually enlisting his services."

"Yes, that's a good move. Keep me informed." Lucky approved.

"Keep me in the picture, too, Benning," Graham asked.

"Sure. I've got a new man who seems to be skilled at finding out things. You've met him, Graham. Horst? You took him all the way to Memphis to confuse him."

They both laughed, remembering the incident. Graham's laugh was so loud, Lucky made an involuntary gesture to shield her ears.

"Sorry," said Graham.

The two men moved toward the door and out to the elevators. Benning nodded to Jolene, Lucky's administrative assistant, and disappeared down one of the hallways. Graham pressed an elevator button, and when it came, he took it down to his floor.

This incident was carefully investigated without any meaningful results. It slowly faded into the busy, busy days of a large corporation until it was completely forgotten. However, it remained as an undercurrent, a kind of memory that lingers deep down and then one day surfaces again. They would all remember it then and perhaps regret that none of them had vigorously followed up and identified what—or who—was really behind it.

*****

The next day Robert collected his books and papers, stuffed them into his knapsack, and evacuated his classroom even while the last words of the professor still hung in the air. He couldn't wait to meet Jolene at the George Washington Restaurant.

The moment they were seated at a table, Jolene put up both hands, palms facing Robert.

"Wait!" she said, smiling. "Don't start anything until you tell me who you are."

"All right. I'm Robert McLane. I am a third year student at Fairmont University, majoring in business. Next year, I will graduate, get a good job, and marry you. We will have at least three children and at least one father-in-law."

"Do I have anything to say about that?" Jolene asked.

"Oh sure. You can agree to all of it one at a time or all at once in one swoop. That's the extent of your authority on the matter." Robert laughed joyfully. "Aren't you glad I am so good at predicting the future? I took seriously Peter Drucker's wise admonition, and I'm even following it to the tee. I'm not just predicting, I expect to create it—together with you, of course."

"I would laugh, Robert, if I didn't think you really meant it. But you do, don't you, really mean it. You sound serious— overjoyed, but serious."

"I am." Robert took her hand across the table. It felt warm. The touch of her skin felt familiar, as though it belonged in his hand. Stranger's hands sometimes feel really foreign, but these hands belonged in his. He was sure. "I'd ask you to marry me, but I know it's too soon. But mark my words, we belong together. I'm absolutely certain of that. Let's drink to that!" Robert raised his water glass to meet Jolene's. The clink of their two glasses sounded affirmative.

"Wouldn't it be more certain if we did it with wine?" Jolene joked.

"Waiter!"

"I was only joking, Robert. I'm all excited about what's going on, but I'm also feeling cautious, as though we need more time to grow together and not just fall together into a bucket of champagne—sort of. You know what I mean?"

"Of course. Never fear. I'm not the type to propose at the drop of a hat. I have never done it before, and I may never do it again—except with you."

"That's just it, Robert. I am a very responsible person. I have a very responsible job. I am not known to be frivolous. And yet, here I am, having just met you yesterday, talking about marriage. That's just not me! We are either crazy or besotted. Aha! Maybe you are a magician and have cast a terrible spell over me to have your evil way with my person. Shame on you, Robert."

"I'll admit it. If I could, I would, and you couldn't do a thing to resist me. So there."

Jolene folded her hands sedately on the table in front of her and quietly murmured, "Who are you?"

"I love you."

"You are even younger than I am. Why you are still in school, for heaven's sake?"

"Yes, but I didn't enroll in college right away. I traveled here and abroad, worked on farms and other jobs for more than two years, and then finally decided to attend Fairmont University. My dad had kittens waiting for me to show some sense. Poor Dad."

"Well, so you're how old?"

"I'm twenty-five next month."

"I'm twenty-six. Do you feel all right marrying an old woman like me?"

"So we are getting married! I'm so glad. I can't wait. Are you religious?" Robert was ecstatic.

"Sort of!"

"Me too—sort of. I guess you could say I'm spiritually inclined. Not really religious like belonging to a particular church."

"I've been studying Rudolf Steiner, and that really interests me, and I don't go to church either." Jolene explained.

"That's the second time I've heard that name. I went to one of Shaman Pi's classes the other night, and he mentioned Rudolf Steiner as one of his teachers."

"Who's Shaman Pi?" Jolene was interested.

The waitress brought their food and set it down carefully in front of them.

"Is there anything else you'd like?" the waitress asked.

Robert raised his eyebrows questioningly, and Jolene shook her head. "No, thank you."

"The best I can do is tell you he's someone full of ideas. Some are sensible while others seem far out and not really appropriate for someone living in the reality," Robert explained.

They quietly munched away at their food. Robert was pleased to see that Jolene tasted everything first before spilling a small amount of salt into the palm of her left hand and then on to her food using two fingers of her right hand. He liked that. It always seemed incongruous when people poured the salt and pepper all over everything before even tasting it. He liked her more and more. Everything she did agreed with him. He was convinced they were made for each other.

"Is he spiritual?" she asked.

"You could say that. Yes, I guess he is. Although it may be hard to talk about business and be spiritual at the same time."

"He talks about business?"

"Among other things. Some of his ideas seem to come from this Rudolf Steiner. I haven't had a chance to look him up yet," said Robert.

"When you do and after you do, let me know. I've been studying him already for a number of years. He's quite amazing. When I read him, it almost feels like I hear his voice. It sounds familiar, like I've heard it before, but I haven't. He died in 1925 in Switzerland."

"Did we change the subject?"

"Several times."

"Are people in love allowed to do that?" Robert wondered.

"We can do anything we want. Love is all-permissive."

"Are you sure you can handle that? I might be very demanding the way I feel."

"We'll see," she said. Robert loved her coy expression. It made him laugh.

"Tell me more about you. You work in the city, I know that," Robert urged her.

"Yes. I am the confidential assistant to the president of a large corporation with subsidiaries all over the world, but mostly in North and South America and Europe."

"That must be fascinating. You make his appointments, do research for him, and—"

"It's a she. My boss is a she."

"Even more interesting. There aren't too many female corporate presidents yet."

"I know, but she's a rare one, she is. I don't know anyone quite like her. Most of the other presidents who are female seem to take refuge in a mock machoism, but she is overwhelmingly feminine. You can't mistake it. The whole corporation swims in femininity. I don't know how the men stand it."

"Is it a cosmetic company, like Revlon or one of those?"

"That's the funny thing. No, it isn't. It is involved heavily in telecommunications, technology, and transportation. You've probably heard of it—the Alliance for International Communications Incorporated? You'd think it would be more dominated by men, and actually it is, but there she is, at the top. And she really does run it in her own way. What's the matter?"

"Oh," Robert said. "Nothing, really. No, that's not true. My father works for AIC."

"Your father? McLane. Of course. Is Charles McLane your father?"

"Yes."

"What a coincidence."

"I don't know what to think. I am actually shocked. The students think badly of Alliance for International Communications Incorporated. Or maybe it's any corporation. Or perhaps it is just any business."

"I know. I hear some of the talk. They seem to enjoy knocking the institution. Maybe it's the function of the young to kick the establishment regardless of the truth," Jolene said.

"Are they consumed by greed and are they willing to do anything, right or wrong, for the sake of profit?" Robert inspected her eyes and saw no hesitation in them.

"My boss is pretty clear about that. Without a profit, you cease to exist. The stockholders see to that. The stockholders are everybody, including you and me. That's just a given. It's the way it is. The whole world relies on business to nourish it and sustain it—"

"I know, the Atlas of life on earth. This Shaman Pi says that greed is the overwhelming motive that creeps through corporate life, like a beast, consuming the souls of anyone trapped in it. What do you think?"

"From what I have seen, there is a little bit of truth in that, but it would be wrong to paint everybody with that one brush. The Alliance for International Communications Incorporated even has a charitable foundation. Some of its profit is donated to that foundation by the president and CEO depending on the operating results of a given year. Many of the executives are leaders in their own communities and often volunteer their services to the Red Cross, home kitchens for the poor, and the like. To tell you the truth, looking at the whole question very narrowly, if AIC didn't exist, I wouldn't have a job, and I couldn't treat you to this lunch." Jolene laughed, her eyes twinkling with mischief.

"Oh no, you don't!" Robert was adamant. "I invited you, remember?"

"Let's go dutch until we're married, shall we? After all, I earn a good salary, and you are still a schoolkid. I'm even older than you. I owe it to your generation to treat you well."

"My father takes care of that."

"I am sure he does. He is well paid."

"How do you know that?"

"Remember, I am a confidential secretary or assistant to the president and chief executive officer. It seems your father has a very special, highly confidential function in the organization. It happens that I know he is highly regarded, almost affectionately so by my boss. I probably know even more than she does about the inner workings of AIC. Of course I can't tell you any of that. It's confidential."

"You just did!"

"I did not. What I told you is not confidential."

"You told me what my dad earns. That should be confidential."

"No, I just told you he earns enough. Everybody knows that. I'm very careful about disclosing anything of a confidential nature. So there!"

"Do you know what my dad does?"

"Not really," Jolene answered cautiously. "He does projects and deals with issues that are generally not talked about. Lucky knows, of course. Maybe a few others. But they have never discussed it with me, and no memoranda or file notes are lying around for me to see, nor have I recorded any."

"Sounds mysterious."

"It does rather, come to think of it. Most of the other people have job descriptions that describe a little about what they actually do, but Charles McLane has a job description that sounds a little as though he did nothing but meet with people and travel. I have no idea what he does. I think I better shut up about your dad. Suggest another subject while we share a dessert?"

"Yes, let's. Do you like fudge? Have you ever had a dusty road sundae?"

"No, but I'm willing to try one."

"Half a one?"

"Will you settle for half?"

"It's a deal. Miss . . . er . . . ma'am, can we have a dusty road with two spoons?"

The waitress was back in three minutes with the sundae and two spoons. Based on many years of experience, she also presented them with two additional napkins. She also added the check which Jolene grabbed from her to prevent Robert from taking it. They argued about it momentarily and then shared it evenly.

"When will I see you again?" asked Robert.

"For the rest of the week, I need to be in the city. Maybe on the weekend or some evening next week?" suggested Jolene.

"You're not my confidential secretary," Robert reminded her.

"Not yet, but maybe when you get that super job." Jolene laughed. "In the meantime, I can manage your social calendar for you, if you like. I'm excellent at keeping you on track, not forgetting important appointments, like with me. Making sure you don't cut any classes and do show up for your graduation. You know, such things."

"Oh boy. I can just see what life is going to be like with you. You're so efficient I won't even need a job. You can manage our whole life while I sit on the porch drinking apple juice."

"Forget it, if that's your dream! Besides, have you forgotten about the three children?"

"That's right. I did forget about them. Oh well, I guess I'll have to do some work after all."

"You betcha!"

"Back to the other subject. How about Sunday afternoon? We could do some hiking."

"Great. Will you pick me up? Here's my address."

CHAPTER FIVE

Worlds Apart

Horst spent his first morning on the job filling out forms and reading informational documents about the history of Alliance for International Communications Incorporated, a biography of Lucinda Brahms, an assortment of corporate policy manuals, and a variety of newsletters and a few press releases from the past month. By eleven, his eyes were bleary, and he was thinking of taking a walk when Charles McLane appeared in the doorway of his office.

"There's nobody out here at the desk and your door's open."

"She's getting me something from the stockroom. Come on in, Charles. I was hoping we would get to see each other again. Yours was one of the more interesting interviews I had last week."

"Welcome to AIC. I'm glad you made it. I heard about your interview with Graham." They both laughed.

"Would you like something to drink, coffee maybe?" Horst offered.

"That would be nice."

Horst had a carafe and four AIC monogrammed mugs on the credenza behind his desk. He poured a mug for Charles and offered him cream and sugar. Charles took neither. He sipped his coffee.

"Um. Hot!"

"Sorry. A little cream will cool it down a touch."

"No, thanks. I like to nurse my coffee along—throughout the morning usually. As a result, I end up drinking most of it cold." He sipped a little more of it. "Do you have children, Horst?"

"Yes. Two. A boy and an older girl. You?"

"One. A boy in college."

Another thoughtful sip of coffee and then one more.

"I sometimes wonder what they teach in colleges these days," Charles said.

"How so?"

"I mean, from what I hear from my son. They don't give them the whole truth, especially about business. My son doesn't seem to be too happy about my working in business."

"You mean your particular job or just business in general?" Horst asked.

"He picked up the idea that all business is driven by greed and a disregard for any values except money. He thinks we step all over each other in the pursuit of money. I believe he considers us to be evil, the enemy."

Horst knew enough to be quiet and wait for Charles to gather his thoughts. When he continued, they tumbled out almost randomly.

"There he is, in his third year in college," he said. "I don't believe he has any idea what it costs in the way of tuition, other fees, and books, not to mention his bills at the cafeteria and what he charges on his credit card. If I didn't have the job with AIC, I wouldn't be able to pay it all every month. Mind you, it's worth it if he got a good education, one that gave him a good head start in business with some first-class company. Lord, how that would please me. I mean, for him to do well and able to fulfill his ambitions for a good life. Of course, there are many ways to do that, but a college degree is one of the best."

"Do you think he can't have a good life unless he goes into business?"

"Hell no. I don't care what he chooses, as long as he has a choice. I figure once he has a college degree in business, it will always at least give him the option. You know, he didn't go right into college after high school. He needed a couple of years off before sitting down in a classroom again. I figure that was OK. If that's what he needed, I didn't mind."

"I'm not sure what the problem is. It sounds like he's a lucky kid with an understanding dad. What more—?"

"In one of his classes—I think about business and ethics— he's being told that business is all about greed, making money, and . . . well, that business is bad. He thinks I should quit my job, put on long robes and a string of beads . . . I guess that's what he thinks."

"Maybe" said Horst, "it's a phase all kids go through? I imagine there are bad apples in every basket. In a way, money is kind of important in business, wouldn't you say?" Horst was trying to understand what was bothering Charles so much and why he wanted to talk with Horst about it.

"Sure, it is. I don't know why kids think having money is so bad. It seems to me not having it is worse. He doesn't seem to mind spending my money. Actually, I don't mind either if it's for a good reason. Don't get me wrong. I'm not a miser, and I love him enough to wish him the best. And I'm glad to pay for it."

"It's the labels that get you? *Bad, greedy, willingness to do anything for the sake of money*? Is that what you mean?" Horst asked.

"Yes, and also that the very people whom I pay are knocking what I'm doing to earn enough to pay them. That's what really galls me. They sit in their classrooms, having read all kinds of books, being full of ideas, and foisting them on a captive audience. I don't think a single one of them has ever made it in business, and yet they spout their opinions. I think maybe they do it in order to get some excitement into their lives. You understanding what I'm getting at, Horst?"

"I think I do," Horst answered thoughtfully. "Charles, let me ask you a couple of things."

"Go ahead."

"Do you enjoy your work?"

"Enjoy my work? What do you mean? I don't come to work every day just for my pleasure. I do it to earn a living and also because I'm good at it, and yes, I enjoy it."

"Do you think you're doing anything bad?"

"No, I think I'm doing well. I'm successful, and many problems and issues I've had to deal with have been resolved successfully. I'm not an evil person. I'm not anyone's enemy, although a few of our competitors may not like me." Charles laughed and Horst joined him.

"So I've heard." Horst leaned over and eyed him directly. "What's really bothering you, Charles? You seem satisfied that you're doing the right things. What more could you do? Why does your son's opinion or the professors' opinions at Fairmont University bother you so much?"

"I'd like them at least to understand my motives, to respect me for what I do. I don't deserve their bad opinions of what we do to make their lives possible. Yeah, I guess that's it."

"You and I know that. All of your colleagues here at AIC know that. There are a lot of us, and I think maybe not too many of them. It's not bad for us to have a few folks challenging our ethics, I think. It should help keep us sharp and on our toes."

"Well, that's a thought. You know, I haven't said this before, but I sometimes wonder if maybe our single-minded quest for the almighty dollar isn't always the noblest of our qualities. I mean, for us business leaders."

"That doesn't sound like your motivation at all!"

"No, it's not, but in meetings here, and in many conversations with other AIC executives and also with other company executives, I sometimes get the feeling that maybe, just maybe, we could improve or clean up our motives a bit. Especially, I think, the folks around the stock markets, the fund and pension advisors, even charitable foundation asset managers—all those essentially driving the monetary trading around the world—might change a little some of their attitudes."

"Now that's a whole new subject, my friend. I have the feeling that folks involved in business are often being mixed in with that crowd," Horst admitted.

"I have to go. Thanks for listening to me. I'm expecting a meeting in my office. Actually, it's a technician to work on my phone and fax connections right about now. Good chatting with you, Horst, and again, welcome to the AIC headquarters!"

"Thanks. Anytime—" Charles was already gone.

*****

Armand arrived at his headquarters building already at 6:00 a.m. and expressed his annoyance to his secretary when she informed him that Cliff had not yet arrived.

"Who knows what opportunities we may be missing?"

"I understand the traffic in from Connecticut is terrible this morning. One of the trains broke down between Cos Cob and Greenwich. He lives in Stamford and will be caught in the middle of it."

"The minute he comes in, I want to see him. Put a note on his desk or tell his girl I want him!" Armand was always annoyed when he couldn't get on with something he planned to do. "There's no time like the present" was one of his favorite clichés.

Instead, he attacked a small pile of files on his desk. They were the financials of a company PTP had just acquired in Germany. He was particularly proud of this one. He thought they made TV monitors and similar consumer electronic devices. Whatever they made, it produced a steady, reliable profit year in and year out. PTP needed the cash for the plans he had. Yesterday, he had met with the controller, and they devised a way of buying their own parts through Sweden by the Spanish supplier, enabling a lenient way of freeing the profits and siphoning them off through Portugal to the United

States. He wanted that cash. He had big plans and needed a good supply so as not to dilute the shares in PTP.

By the time Cliff arrived and hurried up to Armand's office, he was deep into the financials and was primed with purpose. "Have you looked at these financial reports of the last three years from that TV company in Pforzheim?" he demanded.

"Well, sure. I was involved in the acquisition last month. I remember that dandy profit record. Is that what you mean?"

"Yes. I appreciate that, and I think we made a good deal there. What I want to know is whether you looked a little deeper, down below the summaries."

"Of course. What do you want to know?"

"Did you notice anything special?"

"I saw profit at every level of accounting. You remember we were after cash, and they seemed to be generating it at a steady clip." Cliff was trying to understand what Armand was hinting at.

"I want you to know, I now think that profit was actually a smoke screen."

"Profit as a smoke screen? What's the advantage of that?" Now Cliff was really puzzled.

"The advantage? The advantage is that it hides a bigger profit they are not declaring."

"I don't know what you're looking at. We went all through the numbers. Not just me, but every single member of the acquisition team—auditors, accountants, product specialists, you name it. That sizable profit is the real thing, and that's why we bought them." Cliff was adamant.

"Take a look," Armand commanded, "a long hard look at last year's audited financial report, focusing especially on level three, page eighty-nine, line two-oh-two and start explaining."

"I see it. So what's the problem? Line two-oh-two of the expense accounts covers the company training costs. The reason they are higher than you normally see is that they include the apprentice program. Pforzheim is in Germany. They do things differently over there. There's nothing inappropriate in that account. Before the acquisition, we actually reviewed every single item and found them entirely justified, right down to the actual transaction paper."

"You are going to have to explain it to me," insisted Armand. "All I know is that there, on line two-oh-two, are fifteen million dollars that belong in our pocket, and instead they are spending it. As far as I can tell, there is no recognizable return on that money. Am I wrong?"

"It's overhead, Armand. There's never a hard return on training dollars. You still have to have it. They get a quality product by training workers with a quality work ethic. It's the way they do it in Germany, Switzerland, Austria. Even Great Britain, France, and a little bit in Italy. The EEC countries all uniformly take this approach."

"Explain it to me, Cliff. I mean slowly and thoroughly justify my annual losses of fifteen million dollars, not deutsche marks, dollars!"

"OK, here goes. Students complete their secondary education in the eleventh grade, some go on for a twelfth and thirteenth year before going to university, which is a whole different deal that doesn't concern us here. Those students who are only fit for a vocational career are diverted in the eleventh grade into separate programs, where they learn trades. At some point in their education, companies step in and select certain ones, the ones especially having skills the particular company values, and enroll them in an apprentice program. All sizeable companies in Europe have apprentice programs. The apprentices are in the program for three years maximum. They are paid in a sliding scale upward during the three years, as they are actually more and more productive. They learn in classrooms, and they learn on the job. At the end of three years, the company has produced outstanding workers with great skills. That's how it works. That's the reason they have an abundance of good workers."

"How many good workers do they turn out annually? Tell me that."

"I have that number here somewhere. Just a minute. Here it is. One hundred thirty-two. Yes, that's right. Each year, they graduate one hundred thirty-two skilled workers."

"OK. Now tell me how many they add to the payroll each year? Have you got that number?"

"That number includes new employees at every level. I guess what you are looking for are the number of graduated apprentices they then hire. As far as I can recall, I remember them telling me that every single apprentice gets hired immediately after graduation. However, they only hire about 30% of their own graduates. The rest are hired by other companies."

"By my calculations, we are paying to train about ninety-two skilled workers for other companies. Is that what you're trying to explain to me?" Armand finally arrived at his goal.

"You don't understand their system. They hire some of the best from the apprentice programs of other companies in

Germany, not just their own. It's the way they do it over there. It happens their program is one of the best. Their graduates are sought after by other companies. They are proud of their excellence. It has a sterling reputation."

"But it's not our business!" Armand said. "We are not a school. Schools don't make money, they just spend it. Everybody knows that. Our job is to make money so they can spend as much as they can. That's another thing! Why does it take three years to train somebody how to run a machine? I could see maybe a month or even four or possibly six months, but three years? There's something fishy in all of this."

Cliff was feeling weary. He had been all over this point during the acquisition. He had actually visited the program, even interviewed a number of the apprentices and instructors. How could he possibly explain the complicated steps in the program?

"They don't just learn how to switch the machine on and off." He tried once more to explain. "They actually understand the machines inside out by taking them apart and rebuilding them. They know every part and screw and how it all fits together and works. Many of them can repair and service them even though they have other employees who do that regularly, but they can substitute for each other. As a result, their machines have a longer life since the operators know more and treat them better."

"That's not all." Cliff went on. "Try to understand that these are still kids when they enter the program. They are still learning math and physics, even psychology on a rudimentary hands-on level. What they are especially proud of is their work ethic. They are trained in manners and mutual respect for each other, for their bosses, for the machines, the raw materials, as well as the company in which they work. There is nothing like it in the US, believe me!"

"All right, you've convinced me that it might take a year, or maybe even a little longer. I am also convinced they can streamline the whole process a bit more."

Armand drummed the desktop with his knuckles while he thought. It galled him no end to see fifteen million dollars of profit escape him. He had to find a way to use it profitably. It was too much a part of him to let it go by without an attempt.

"Do you happen to know if the government gives them any break for running these educational programs?" he asked.

"I think they do, but it is not openly declared. It seems like it is under the table. I think they look the other way in regards to certain taxable gains. I also believe the government looks the other way when it comes to the amount the government foregoes when the apprentices are actually working productively at a 'less than minimum wage' type of compensation. That's hard to identify, and they don't like to talk about it."

"What would happen," Armand wondered out loud, "if we insisted they separate their educational work from their business operations? You know what I mean? A 501 designation, purely an accounting mechanism that pulls all the apprenticeship functions out of operational activity. That might be the first step in cleaning up the act. Separate the learning from the earning, so to speak. Wouldn't that make sense?"

"The same cost would be there under a different account. Oh—you mean a separate not-for-profit incorporation. The fifteen million would then be a charitable contribution? Is that what you mean? It would increase the profit, but it would also reduce your taxes."

"Not only that, we might be able to charge tuition and solicit grants from the companies benefiting from the program. You want X number of graduates, contribute Y dollars to his training. I don't know, but look into it, Cliff. One way or another, I want that fifteen million where it belongs."

"I'll look into it Armand, but I have my doubts. We are talking about national institutions and cultural givens that have a long history. It would be like ripping the heart out of long-established and deeply cherished customs. We have to consider our reputation abroad. The negative impact may actually reduce our overall profitability in the longer run."

"I'm interested in the ultimate return. I will not sanction anything that reduces our return, only what increases it. That's my mandate from the board. Look into it, Cliff."

"I will." Cliff agreed, but there was no enthusiasm in his acceptance. The more he dealt with foreign subsidiaries, the more he ran up against intangible factors other than money and profit. Especially in Europe, there seemed to be underlying values distinct from money that were often surfacing in their relations with US-based companies. On the other hand, he knew Armand would not forget about this item. He had maybe a week or two before Armand followed up. He turned to leave.

"There's one other thing I wanted to check with you, Cliff, before you go."

"Yes?"

"What do you know about the Alliance for International Communications Incorporated?"

"AIC?"

"Yes, AIC."

"Not very much. They are not one of our targets. They are bigger than we are—a lot bigger, with operations mostly in South America and Asia. Their strength is in communications, telecommunications, and technology, I believe. I don't think they have anything in consumer electronics, retail, insurance, or any of our areas. Why are you asking?"

"We've been picking up bits and pieces. That's a hard way to grow. Maybe we need to look at acquisitions that have already picked up the bits and pieces to save us the trouble. What do you think?"

"AIC is very different from us. Their fields of expertise are ones we have always steered away from. I happen to know they have enormous projects out in New Jersey that live 100% on government contracts and subsidies. I always figured you deliberately stayed away from that, preferring more consumer-oriented businesses."

"Mind you, I am only thinking about this. My idea is to have a foothold in every single industry and nationality. That way, no matter where problems arise, no matter what industry gets into trouble, we are still positioned to profit by it with our other holdings. It's a little like having chips on the black and the red to win every turn of the wheel."

"I always figured that's a good strategy to break even, but you're in this for more than breaking even."

"Along with that strategy, we need another which has to do with executive forces. I say we get the best brains aboard so we can skew our breakeven strategy a little more cleverly to break clear into the profit margin. A whole country may be in trouble, but you'll always find a few companies that are floating on the advantages to be had. Same with industries! I have charged our HR department to load our staff with the best brains in the world. Those will be our mutually supportive two strategies for maximum corporate growth and profitability."

"Maximum growth is generally at the expense of profitability. Growth usually costs money either produced or borrowed," Cliff reminded him.

"Yes. It will take brains at every level to make sure we gain in profit, grow in assets, and increase in share price without the concomitant increase in manpower, real estate, and expenses. That's my job! I plan to provide that dynamic balance so that PTP becomes a world power to be reckoned with." Armand paused thoughtfully. "I want our top executives to be outstanding managers. I would like to be able to parachute any one of them into any company in any industry in any country and have them land on their feet, functioning effectively. In other words, they have to be first-class generalists, working purely with fundamentals inherent in any business situation."

"What do you want me to do?" asked Cliff.

"Look into Alliance for International Communications Incorporated. I want to know everything about them. Look especially into the directors. I want to know everything about them, their business and financial situations, as well as their personal biographies, weaknesses, and any past mistakes or skeletons. I also want you to find a few vulnerable links in their top staff. Anybody with business in South America has got to have some dirty laundry. Start digging, Cliff, and give me some useful stuff. I don't want a proxy fight. I want to win before I make a move."

"Why don't I dig a bit and feed it to you a little at a time so we can devise a good, painless possible approach and then decide?" Cliff recognized the importance of this project and began to warm up to the challenge.

"I'm counting on you. And let's not make any undue noise either here or there. The less said, the better. And the fewer people know anything, the better I like it."

"I agree."

Cliff left the office, charged with ideas of what to do, how to do it, and with a certain determined walk that always possessed him when he was excited about the future. This could mean a lot for PTP and even more for him, personally.

*****

Charles closed the door to Horst's office and then stood there holding the doorknob as he recalled parts of the conversation. Maybe he was being a little too hard on Robert. At his age, shouldn't he be questioning everything around him, testing his own judgements and decisions? He felt a little better and was glad he had this chance to think aloud with friendly ears in attendance.

Then he remembered his appointment and glanced at his watch. It was only with a technician to clean up and speed up his connections with the internal switchboards, not really very important. For some reason, he nevertheless felt some urgency to get up there, back to his office. In some peculiar way, he felt impelled forward, and he hurried out to the bank of elevators. He pushed the Up button, and then he stood there, waiting for the elevator.

It made sense that at the age of twenty-five, his son should be looking for values in his own studies and also in the various professions all around him. What better chance to explore the world before he became saddled with family, children, mortgages, and grocery bills, insurance options and, oh yes, debt. Everybody gets into debt. Debt is the sign of increasing maturity.

The elevator arrived while he still was thinking of his son and the wonderful age in which he currently reveled. He wondered whether Robert really fully appreciated his position in a lifetime. It'll not come again. This was his one chance to be twenty-five. *What about me? Isn't this my one chance to be forty-seven?*

He jumped into the elevator just as the doors were closing and turned to push the button up to the tenth floor, where his office was located. By mistake, his fingers blundered over the wrong buttons and landed on the one to the twelfth floor.

The twelfth floor contained the various offices of the president and chief executive officer as well as those of the treasurer and controller and the suites of two other members of the office of the president. It also housed the boardroom and secretary of the board.

"Damn!" he said to himself. "What a stupid thing to do. Just when I was in a hurry! I'll be late, maybe even miss the technician. Why did I do such a dumb thing?" It couldn't be helped. The elevator rose past his floor and on up to the twelfth. When it stopped and the doors slid open, he stepped out, thinking he might be able to catch another elevator that could be going down sooner.

Just then, Lucky entered the reception room on that floor, attended by the controller, Stanley Benning, and Jolene running alongside for her last signature. Lucky paused, signed, and then looked up, standing right in front of Charles. They had nearly collided.

"Sorry," Charles apologized.

"Charles, how very nice to see you," she said.

"Yes, thank you. I mistakenly got off the elevator at this floor." Charles seemed almost apologetic.

Lucky touched his arm and turned her special smile on him, the smile that was known in every corner of the company and in all the media. It was as bright as any smile could be.

"How are you?"

"I'm fine, thank you. And you?"

"Doing well. And your son? Is he well?"

Charles turned as the elevator doors opened, put his hand in to keep them open for Lucky, but stood aside to let her in first. She didn't move. She stood there staring at him.

"Are you going down?" Charles asked as the doors began to jiggle his hand in attempts to close.

"Wait just a minute, Charles."

He let the doors close and turned to face her. There was a puzzled expression on her face, as though trying to recall some distant memory.

"Was it you that secured us the contract to build the first switching station in Argentina?"

"Yes, also the one south of Rio. We had a number of problems with that one. I recall going down there almost every month for a while."

"What kind of problems?"

"You may recall that the original contract was renegotiated fifty-seven times. Because of local complications, delays, and technical changes—even work stoppages—the final cost was three times what the original contract quoted."

"I had forgotten all that. Did we come out all right? I mean, with continually rising costs, what was the end result after all the dust settled?"

"We made a sizeable profit." Charles smiled his satisfaction.

Lucky glanced sideways at Benning and Graham, who had just turned up halfway through the conversation. They both nodded, indicating their agreement.

"Who do you know in Brazil? Have the people changed a great deal?"

"The power shifts periodically, but for some reason, it's predictable. It's like a dance! For a while, one crowd is prospering. And then another shifts over, and it's their turn. I know most of them. What's more important most of them know me."

"Are you aware of the fact that we are bidding on the large switching operation west of Rio, where massive residential development is right now taking place?"

"No. Graham, you haven't been telling me the news. I know I did not want to be involved so much anymore, but I'd still like to know what's going on."

"I'm sorry, Charles," Graham said. "Nothing on purpose! We've just been so busy trying to get the contract, I forgot how much involved you had been in the past. Bad oversight!"

Lucky took Charles by the elbow and moved him along the corridor back to her office. The others trailed along behind.

"The thing is, we want that contract. We've got manpower and equipment already positioned down there, which puts us in a very good bargaining situation. However, we seem to be losing the battle, and I think our competitors are being more persuasive than we are."

"You mean money? They're spreading it around, and we're falling behind?"

"I don't know for sure. Graham thinks that's the case. We think they might be willing to actually lose the profit on this one just to get their feet through the door. How much did the last project down there end up costing us in . . . well, extra expenses?"

"Over a million, but we got it all back through the renegotiations. It's a private way for the government to add to the pay of a good number of their favorite people without disclosure. There isn't anyone doing business down there who hasn't accepted this practice and is paying for it. The companies that are frozen out are the ones who object. If you want that contract, we will have to invest in advance anywhere up to two million dollars is my guess."

Graham agreed by nodding his head, but Benning shrugged. He didn't know enough about doing business in South America to have an opinion, but he didn't like it.

"All I know is that we want that contract. That's all I want to know. You fellows work out the details, but I have a feeling Charles is our man. Give him whatever budget he needs. I don't want to hear later that we lost the contract because we held back on . . . expenses," Lucky decided, and then added, "You agree?"

"Are we saying unlimited funding?" Benning was quick to get to the point.

"I said no such thing. Funding is always limited. I said get the contract no matter what it takes. That calls for judgement—judgement by everyone involved at every step of the way—but get the contract."

"Could we here agree that anywhere up to two—?"

"I don't want to fix anything. Do what you have to do." Lucky moved off to the elevators, and as luck would have it, the doors opened immediately when she pushed the down button. She entered quickly and turned. Charles followed her with his eyes. She was as beautiful as ever. Memories of a time gone by crowded in on him. He stood there, awkwardly staring after her. The elevator doors closed, and she was gone.

"I guess that constitutes approval," Graham said. "Meet me in the dining room for lunch, Charles. Let's talk this over."

"I've got just one quick thing to do in my office, and then I'll see you there," Charles agreed.

"Same here. Twenty minutes?"

"Agreed."

CHAPTER SIX

Seduction

Calder was waiting for Stu when he moved out of the classroom and into the quad. He approached him from the side without being noticed.

"Hello." Calder used his friendliest tone of voice. "Are you Steward Brand?"

"Yes."

"Can I have a word with you? Nothing dramatic, just a friendly conversation."

"What about?"

"You. And whether you are doing all right and if there is anything we can do to be of help to you in your studies."

"Are you from the dean's office?"

"No, I represent a small group of local business leaders interested in helping our veterans in any way we can."

"Were you asking for me at the Diggs?" Stu asked.

"That was me. So he told you?"

"Yes. Why do you want to help me?"

"Do you have to ask? Most of us realize what you have done and sacrificed for our sake. We also know the government only does so much, and then you're left on your own. That's where we come in." Calder paused and shifted his case to his right arm. "Can we sit down and talk somewhere?"

"How about right here?" Stu suggested, pointing to a vacant bench along the side of the quad.

"Why not." They sat down on the empty bench, and Calder opened one of the folders he was carrying in the case. "We don't necessarily talk to every veteran, just the ones picked out with the helpful advice of the Veterans Affairs people. You have an excellent record. Lots of decorations, good reports, one promotion, honorable discharge. Here at the university, I see good grades, a serious student, good behavior, et cetera, et cetera. Just the kind of person we'd love to extend a helping hand to."

"You know all that? Somebody has been working hard. You're not from the Alliance for International Communications Incorporated, are you?"

"No, I'm not. What makes you say that?"

"I know someone whose dad works there."

"I see. He doesn't happen to be Robert McLane, does he?" Calder acted surprised.

"Why, yes. I just met him the other day."

"Is he a vet too?"

"No, no. Nothing could be further from the truth."

"Then he probably wouldn't qualify for any of the help we provide."

"I guess not," Stu laughed out loud. "His dad pays for everything. He can afford it. Alliance for International Communications Incorporated makes sure of that."

"I wonder how he got on my list. Oh, I see. Evidently, his mother died just three years ago. Maybe that's the reason. Also, his dad is away a great deal. In South America. Well, he's not a vet so he wouldn't qualify anyway."

"His mother died three years ago?" Stu asked to make sure.

"Yes. Are you a good friend of his?"

"Not really. We just met recently, but I like him."

"It might not be remiss if you looked out for him a bit, his mother gone and his father away so much."

"Yeah."

"Maybe you and I could stay in touch a bit. I would be counting on you telling me whatever you see or hear from him."

"What for? He's not a vet."

"Let's just say we care about him and want to be sure he's not the casualty of a rough life." Calder picked his words carefully.

"You want me to spy on him?" Stu asked suspiciously.

"Frankly, yes. It wouldn't be espionage. Just friendly oversight. Any information you can give us on him, how he's feeling, where his dad is and what he is doing . . ." Calder stopped there and inspected Stu's face.

"That's very nice of you," Stu said. He was pleasantly surprised by this opportunity to do for someone else what his own intentions were. He and the Shaman had already agreed that Stu was to keep a watchful eye on Robert.

Calder gave Stu a business card. It said Local Business Cares and listed a box number and a phone but no address. It had a nice little picture of two outstretched hands, palms up supportively but not very generously—perhaps accidentally suggesting receiving rather than giving.

"You can reach me there any time of day or night—within reason. It is a dedicated line, so feel free to leave messages. Now as to my original intent. How well is the government covering your needs while you finish your study?"

"The government pays my tuition, I think. At least I do not get billed for that. I have to cover my food and lodging, books, such things. That I cover out of my salary in the reserve."

"You have any idea of what that comes to, let's say, in a month?" Calder asked. He removed an index card from his pocket and lifted a gold pen from his shirt pocket. He was poised to write down the information.

"Rough guess, I'd say probably around twelve hundred dollars. Some months, a little more, and other months, a little less. I can afford that if I watch my spending. I have been thinking of supplementing my income a little with a part-time job of sorts."

"But why should you? This is a time you should feel free to devote yourself one hundred percent to your studies. Heaven only knows when you'll get another chance. If I can get you a regular stipend at least for the next twelve months of, let's say, six hundred dollars, would you accept it?"

"Sure. Would it be a loan or—?"

"No, no, it would be a kind of grant."

"Would I have to do anything to earn it? I mean, like a paper or report or something?"

"If you like, you could consider it your part-time job. You would be receiving a monthly stipend in exchange for staying in touch with Robert and letting us know what he and his father are up to." Calder laughed loudly at his own jolly translation of the gift.

Stu laughed too. It seemed too good to be true. How could this be happening to him? He needed the funds, no doubt of that. But to receive it so easily, without any effort of any kind. It was just falling into his lap without his even asking or searching for it. It came to him, unbidden, out of the blue. It almost could be called a miracle. He wondered what Shaman Pi would make of it.

"I accept. Do I send a thank-you letter or what? And to whom?"

"Don't you dare! We prefer to work quietly in the background, if you like. No attention, no muss—just results. That's our way."

"Thank you," Stu said sincerely.

"You're welcome. I'll let the others know. You won't even receive a letter from us confirming the arrangement. Shall we say, you will phone me at that number once a week, perhaps every Wednesday noon?"

"OK. Mind you, I might not have anything to say."

"Call anyway. I might have something to say to you." Calder ordered, his voice suddenly quite authoritative, as though addressing an employee.

They shook hands, and Calder moved off toward the center of town. Stu wondered where he would be going next on his mission. For the first time, he took into his consciousness the well-tailored suit, the polished shoes, hat. It all looked expensive and cared for, as though appearance were terribly important. Stu would not have been surprised to see him in

Manhattan, perhaps around Madison Avenue or Park Avenue or even Fifth Avenue. He seemed a little out of place here at Fairmont University in New Jersey.

Oh well, he thought, *why look a gift horse in the mouth?* Then he laughed happily but quietly to himself.

*****

Cliff was not surprised to hear that Armand wanted to see him. He had been expecting it for several days. Armand never forgot to follow up on his assignments. As far as Cliff could tell, Armand never took notes. Occasionally, he scribbled a few marks in a little book he carried in his vest pocket. Once in a while, he consulted its contents.

Most of the time, he seemed to carry it all in his head, which was large enough at that to contain a world of material. His forehead arched back on the great dome of his head, which usually seemed like it was a little too heavy for his neck muscles to carry upright. His shoulders bent a little forward, tilting his head aggressively outward. Cliff picked up his materials and lists and made his way up to Armand's office.

"What have you got?" Armand asked.

"I have a list of the directors. I also included a few of the key people, those whose opinions might matter. Here it is." Cliff handed the list to Armand but went right on with his report.

"You'll notice I have added stars after some of the names. Although I have run background checks on all of them, the stars indicate that I have uncovered at least one area of vulnerability. So far, I have no really hard data, only rumors and innuendoes, but strong enough to investigate further."

"What sort of information are we talking about?"

"All kinds, surprisingly enough. Nobody is pure anymore. They've all got something hiding behind their pristine reputation. That shouldn't surprise us. After all, look at us. Any clever investigator could easily expose any one of us."

Armand looked coldly at him, knowing exactly what he meant. He didn't pursue the topic but returned to the lists in front of him.

"What about this one," asked Armand, "with a star next to his name, Allen Fullington III? He's the chief financial officer, and a director on the board. He must know a lot. He must also be deeply invested in AIC and have a lot to lose."

"Yes, he does. It seems he was involved in creating a number of transactions, approved by the auditors, securing for the corporation a series of payouts in South America not directly linked to the work performed there by AIC but nevertheless coincident in time and place."

"Are we talking about bribes?" Armand was interested.

"They don't call it that down there. They mention inducements, facilitating payments, and local favors. I have a man trying to obtain whatever copies he can dig up."

"That's good, Cliff," said Armand, carelessly rubbing his hands together in anticipation. "That's the kind of material we need. Have you got anything like that on these others?"

"Two of them have one or more skeletons in the closet, one of them had a careless night out on the town, and three of them had minor offenses that were squashed before any court appearances. They're a typical group of upstanding citizens." Cliff laughed, but Armand didn't.

Cliff wondered whether Armand knew how to laugh. He had never seen him even crack a smile that didn't look grim. Maybe his cheek and jaw muscles were not formed right for such merriment. It could also be that he hadn't done it for so long, they had lost the necessary flexibility.

"Anything else?"

"Based on what I learned so far, I took a look at this one at the bottom of the page, Charles McLane."

"He's not on the board."

"No, but he does special projects for the president and CEO. He's been in South America a great deal over the years, knows everybody and his uncle, and is highly skilled in what is called problem solving."

"I see. Like bribing people at every level of government?"

"Like bribing people at every level of government!"

"Good, Cliff. Good work." Armand almost smiled his satisfaction, but not quite. It never got to the surface. At best, a thin crack appeared in the cheek near the right side of his mouth. "See if you can follow up on that."

"I've enlisted the help of Calder in obtaining more intimate knowledge directly from people connected to Charles. We'll see what comes of it."

"Good. What about these others?"

"You want to move on them now?"

"The sooner the better. By the end of the year, I'd like to see us in control of the Alliance for International Communications Incorporated—quietly, efficiently, completely!"

"The end of the year? This will take time. It's not like our other acquisitions. We're dealing with a corporation already twice our size, well connected with the government, and having outstanding leadership, I think."

"Who's the president or CEO?"

"A woman. Lucinda Brahms. She is a people person, does almost everything with a kind of consensus. Up until the last second of a decision, everything's up for grabs, and anybody can throw in an opinion. She then makes the decision and, surprisingly enough, everybody together makes it happen. Interesting, don't you think?" Armand scowled. "Well, I thought so, anyway."

"Have you got anything on her?"

"Here's the remarkable thing. Although it is hard to pinpoint an actual decision, because everybody seems to own it, she still is remarkably responsible for everything. That's the consequence of her approach. However, she is smart, has the loyalty of staff and board to a person. I think whatever we find as any kind of corporate vulnerability—or, shall we say, misdeed—can ultimately be pinned to her tail, which I might add is a very nice one."

"Is she married?"

"No. As far as I can tell, her only affair is with the corporation. It's her sole love, her baby, and occupies her mind and body twenty-four hours of the day."

"Anybody close to her?"

"Maybe Jolene, her very, very loyal administrative assistant."

"Anybody working that angle?"

"Not yet. But we're keeping an eye on it. She was recently seen with Charles McLane's son, Robert. That looks promising, and we're working on it."

"Here's what we're going to do." Armand looked up and kept his eyes on Cliff's face as he spoke. "Let's take the board apart one by one, compromise each of them and promise to sweeten their deal if we move in. Secondly, Lucinda Brahms has to be discredited. We want it to appear that she either directly did or personally allowed something shady, if not criminal. We'll get nowhere unless the board members lose faith in her. It's an age-old device, but it works."

Cliff shifted his weight on the chair across from Armand. This was not his favorite kind of work. He often wondered why he was always asked to do this sort of thing. He must be exceptionally good at it, even if he didn't like it. There must be something in his demeanor, his character, or whatever that gave Armand confidence that this was what he would and could do. And, of course, he can and will do—exceptionally well, to boot.

"And don't waste a lot of your good time feeling guilty or by acting reluctantly," Armand admonished him. "Get right to it. Put your whole self into the task like a good boy! I'll be checking on your progress, never fear."

Shame crept over Cliff to be found out and manipulated so easily. As he left Armand's office, he was thinking, *What does he know about me? He has an unerring instinct to find my weak spot, that certain softness in my armor when it comes to dealing with authority. How many times have I thought of quitting, but I don't? Why can't I quit? I could easily get another job, probably one that pays more, maybe double what I am getting here. And yet I don't. Something ties me to him and his need for me and my talent for problem solving on the shady side of action. I hate it, but I'm thrilled to do it. How divided can I be?*

Cliff returned to his own office. His mind was already working on the next steps. He knew instinctively to begin with the most vulnerable persons, the ones easily corruptible and then working up the spectrum to the tougher variety. He loved the demand on his creativity, a certain twist of the mind that takes advantage of vulnerability and weakness in others. He knew how to do this so well. It came so naturally! Was he born with it?

Pride! That's right. He was proud of his ability to manipulate others. Cliff felt it set him a notch above others. Head held high, he picked up the phone and dialed a secret number—someone whom he held firmly under his thumb.

*****

Robert began looking for Shaman on Thursday evening. He retraced the steps he had taken on the first evening when they met. The first scan was through the engineering building. No luck there. As a matter of fact, the building was dark, not a single light in any of the offices and classrooms.

He then moved over to the psychology building and went directly to the second floor where Shaman had been last time. A security man was standing outside the door to the classroom. Robert tried to look past him into the classroom, but he shifted to block his view.

"Is he in there?" Robert asked.

"Nope. I doubt if you'll see him again."

"Too bad. He was an interesting guy."

"I suppose so, but rules are rules, you know."

Robert didn't bother to answer. He left the building and looked around, wondering if Shaman could be in another place. He noticed two shadowy figures under one of the short Japanese cherry trees and moved over closer before he caught sight of Shaman as one of them. The other turned out to be Stu.

"Robert, here we are." Stu motioned to him. "Shaman Pi wanted to talk with us tonight without the others."

"I didn't know where you were," Robert explained.

"It's OK. We would have found you one way or another."

Shaman Pi reached out and took Robert by the elbow in friendly fashion.

"I think I was a little harsh on you the other night, and I felt the need to apologize."

"That's all right, I didn't really mind. I was interested in what you had to say."

"Nevertheless, we were talking about your father, and I realized I had just lumped him together with all my memories of others. I didn't give him a chance. For all I know, he might very well be that rare activist working deep within the dragon's maw. I'm sorry for my lack of sensitivity."

"It's OK. No matter what anyone thinks, he is what he is."

Stu pushed himself a little forward into the conversation. "Shaman was asking me about your father, and I had to admit I know nothing at all about him or what he does," Stu admitted.

"It's not important," Robert said.

"Why not? We have this image of him that might very well be all wrong."

"Do we have to talk about him?"

"No," Shaman said sympathetically.

"It's important to me," insisted Stu. "You're my friend, and I don't want to harbor thoughts that may be totally wrong. Robert, do tell us a little about what he does."

"He's kind of a problem solver for the president of Alliance for International Communications Incorporated. Whenever a sticky situation comes up, he gets called in and asked to work it out. That's all I know."

"Is he working on a problem right now?" Stu asked.

"I think yes."

"Where is he?"

"I think in Brazil. Around Rio de Janeiro . . . but I'm not sure."

"Is there a problem there? What's he doing?" Stu was pushing, and Robert felt uncomfortable.

"I don't know. I'm sure whatever he's doing, it must be confidential."

"Aha!" Stu seemed triumphant. "How do you know he isn't a spy doing industrial espionage?"

"Don't be nasty. This is my father you are talking about. Maybe we should change the subject entirely. What say?"

"No, really! I'm very interested. I have never worked for a corporation and have no idea what it's like. How powerful is the president? Does he decide everything? If someone like your father takes action in, well, solving a problem, does he have a free hand? I'm really curious." Stu seemed to really want to know.

"You know, you should really ask my father. I would only be guessing. I know my dad, but I don't really know anything about the Alliance for International Communications Incorporated or how it works."

Stu's disappointment showed on his face. Or maybe it was disbelief. His eyebrows were hunched over his eyes, which were fastened, almost hungrily, on the changing expressions of Robert's face.

Shaman felt the need to break into the conversation. "If you don't want to talk about it, I think we should let you off the hook. If you ever find that we can be of help to you, just give us a ring. Right, Stu?"

"Sure. Oh, sure!" Stu caught himself and grinned awkwardly.

"Robert," Shaman drew his attention, "do you think your father might be interested in meeting with us? I mean with the group of us to talk about corporation values and such topics?"

"I don't know. He's in Brazil right now, but I can ask him when he comes back. He doesn't really lecture, you know, but he might want to hear questions and answer the ones he can."

"I think that would be great, Robert. We would all love that." Stu perked up and was all smiles.

"No promises, I'll just ask him, and we'll see."

"Great."

"That would be an interesting evening." Shaman smiled warmly at Robert.

"When will he be back?" Stu asked eagerly.

"He originally said next Tuesday, but the truth is I don't know for sure."

"Let us know, Robert. We can set up a meeting at very short notice. You'll be there too, won't you?"

"Of course!"

The two friends moved off toward Joe's Digs for a snack, leaving Shaman looking after them. He was thoughtful. There was something in the behavior of Stu that was giving him warning signals, but the two of them walking along seemed normal and friendly. Perhaps he was being too sensitive. Nevertheless, he thought he might keep an eye on them in the future.

CHAPTER SEVEN

Love

Jolene arrived at Robert's house exactly at seven. She was looking forward to seeing him again. She had been fortunate to find a seat on the bus from Port Authority even though it was in the middle of rush hour. It was the strangest thing. There was a long line waiting to get on, and the first bus filled up completely. As a rule, she would now have to wait about fifteen minutes for the next one, but there it was, right behind the one she was in. They were nearly full when yet another bus pulled in right behind this one, and the waiting passengers rushed over to get the best seats on it. Even though there were still some empty seats on her bus, it pulled out, and she enjoyed the luxury of having the seat all to herself.

This was the first time she was invited to Robert's house. He had warned her of two things. One, his father was away, they would be alone, and she would be entirely at his mercy. That was a funny, but she was thinking about it now on the bus. She knew very little about him, but enough to love him and trust him. Also enough to want to know much more about him. They talked a lot whenever they were together, but it was light conversation, nothing serious like what were his beliefs, what were his hobbies, his taste in music, art, even plants and animals. They had taken a beautiful walk in the park adjoining the university, and she had learned a little. Dogs liked him, and he liked dogs, but not enough to want to own one and take him out for poops twice a day. He especially enjoyed cats. He liked how they curled themselves into a ball, kneading the cushion before they settled into place. He was always noticing birds and seemed to know their names. As for walking, she could hardly keep up with him. He didn't walk; he marched. However, when she begged him to slow down, he sauntered along beside her quite happily.

It just takes time to know a person. Does it also take time to love a person? Why was she so drawn to him so quickly, so effortlessly? She felt deserted when not with him and couldn't wait to be beside him again. They were always touching—hands and shoulders and hips as they moved together, walking. It was reassuring to feel him close, to know he enjoyed her touch. She sighed and decided this evening was a good thing. They needed to be together—whatever.

Robert had also warned her that he could only make omelets, but they were very good omelets with cheeses, spinach, and herbs—lots and lots of herbs. Again, something to look forward to. She preferred light meals in the evening. Especially, no heavy meats. "Fish is OK, but please, no red meat." He had agreed affably.

As she approached the house, there he was at the door, waiting for her. He was wrapped in an apron, and in his right hand was a spatula, ready to use on the omelet. As she came close to him, they immediately touched. It was gentle—a soft greeting at the hips, a curling together of the thumb and forefingers, even a gentle caress of cheeks. Nothing really serious, but oh so sweet and so familiar.

"I've been waiting all afternoon for you," he said.

"I'm so glad to be here," she said, and impulsively, she lifted her face to his and gently brushed his lips with hers. It was the first. It took them both by surprise and left them awkwardly breathless.

"Are you hungry, or do you want to socialize for a bit first?" Robert asked.

"Yes," was her mischievous reply.

Robert laughed. What he liked about Jolene was the easy, abundant life in her. Her eyes always seemed to twinkle, and her lips enjoyed smiling, curving gracefully up at the corners. Robert thought her lips demanded to be kissed whenever he gazed on her. They looked as though they were soft, pliable, and tender. He rejoiced that she wore no lipstick and none of the cosmetic masks so many women hid behind. She was right there with exactly who she was for everyone, but especially for him to see and appreciate.

"Thank you for inviting me," she added. "I am entirely in your hands. In short, I could eat."

Robert laughed again. "Why don't you join me in the kitchen?"

"I'm already here," she pointed out. The living room, dining room, and kitchen were assembled together in an open concept that she liked very much. She noticed that Robert had already preheated the frying pan using light olive oil. The eggs were beaten in a bowl with just a splash of milk. All sorts of different colored dots and twigs and leaf fragments of herbs floated in them. In a wooden bowl, he had prepared a salad to go along with the omelet.

"Shouldn't we have some carbohydrates? It wouldn't have to be much," she suggested.

"Good idea. Would you be satisfied with a slice of bread? I have some multigrain baked fresh at the health food store."

"That would be wonderful. A little butter, you think?"

"By all means. It's in the fridge."

They worked in and out of the small space, not bumping but frequently touching, just easily gliding beside each other, getting the meal ready. In no time, it was on the plates, and they sat down at the table and looked across at each other.

"I feel like being grateful for some reason. Grateful that we can be together and grateful that we seem to like the same things, the same food, the same—I guess I'm grateful we work well together."

"You noticed."

"I'm amazed how we are together. Do you think we could manage a lifetime without getting in each other's way?"

"Wouldn't you get tired of me? I mean we're so synchronized, so perfect. How could it possibly last?"

"It can't, but with love, we'll manage the bumps, don't you think?"

They ate in a comfortable silence. It was a very light omelet, and the salad disappeared without a trace. They both simultaneously folded their hands, supported their elbows on the table, and warmed the distance between them with smiles.

"Maybe we should just leave the dishes? You know the song . . ."

They both sang it.

> Leave the dishes in the sink, Ma,
> Leave the dishes in the sink.
> Each dirty plate will have to wait.
> Tonight we're going to celebrate.
> Leave the dishes in the sink.

"You know," Jolene commented, "leaving the dishes goes against the grain. Cleaning them up really belongs to the meal. It's like the burp! It complements a good meal. The only reason I'm not burping is because it was so light it went down so easily. The burp is just superfluous. Would you mind if I just quickly did them for you? You did the cooking. I'll do the cleanup. There should be a rule that the person who does the cooking should never have to do the cleanup. Deal?"

"Deal, but tonight I want to do everything together. I'm celebrating having you with me in my home. It's not our home yet, but we're getting close."

Jolene chuckled as she rose, collecting their two plates and utensils and carrying them into the kitchen area for the cleanup. Robert assembled the salt and pepper shakers, the butter, and the used napkins and planted them each in its own proper place.

As they brushed by each other in the kitchen, Robert could contain himself no longer. He folded her gently into his arms, curved her to his left, and brought his face to melt into hers with their first real kiss.

It was a lingering kind of kiss, not artificially heated, more exploratory in its groping for feeling. All at once, Jolene felt a change in his hug, more intense. Robert was overcome with wanting. A new feeling vibrated between them. His fingers felt the top button on her blouse and slipped it open effortlessly. The next one stuck a little as his fingers trembled.

"Shall I help you?" Jolene asked, to let him know she knew what he was doing and didn't mind at all.

"No," he said, "I want all the pleasure of slowly finding you, even though I'm a little overexcited."

The second button finally surrendered, and Robert slipped the third, the fourth, and even the fifth button free. Her blouse fell open, and he leaned back a little to look at her. The breath caught in his throat. The soft smooth skin curving in at the cleavage between her breasts made him whimper. How could anything be so beautiful fill him with such pleasure and joy? He just had to kiss her again. It was too great a need. He lingered on her lips, caressing them softly with his own, searching for more connection with her, reaching out to her with his heart in his lips.

Jolene's blouse slipped easily from her shoulders, and Robert reached carefully for the three little hooks at the back of her bra and undid them. He glanced at her face to see if she was still willing him to go on, but her eyes were closed, and there was the sweetest little curl of a smile on her lips. He dared to uncover and discover more. The bra fluttered to the floor, and he sucked in his breath, absolutely overcome with awe at the beauty of her breasts.

"They're small," she whispered.

"They're beautiful. I love the wonderful roundness and smoothness of them, and the nipples are a treasure all by themselves. Do you ever touch them yourself?"

"No."

"I don't know how you can keep your hands away from them. If they were mine, I would be playing with them all day and all night."

Jolene chortled softly and sighed as he traced the curve of her left breast, lingered there, caressing the smooth skin and then touching her nipple, rubbing slightly with his fingernail and watching it stiffen.

"What a wonder you are. I will never get tired of you."

"When I'm old and gray?"

"I'll keep your breasts young by loving them every chance you'll let me."

He wasn't absolutely sure, but Robert thought he heard her purr. It encouraged him to loosen her skirt and gently slide it off her hips. It too fell to the floor beside the bra. He took her in his arms, placed his lips on hers, and slowly, slowly danced her toward his bedroom on the ground floor. It was dark in there. He eased her onto the bed without having to remove any of the blankets. For once, he was glad that he rarely made his bed. It accepted her gracefully.

Jolene leaned back against the pillows and looked up at him.

"Are you planning to stay fully dressed all evening?" she asked.

"No," he replied and sat down beside her to remove his shoes and socks. "What happened to your shoes? I don't remember taking them off."

"You weren't looking when I did it. Your attention was elsewhere," she said smugly. She watched him remove his shirt, then his undershirt, and finally, his trousers. When he was about to sit down beside her again, she said "Uh-uh" and wagged her finger at him.

"I'm shy," he said.

"Come here," she commanded.

Carefully and deftly, she slid his underpants down to the floor and then looked him over, not missing any of his parts, now prominently displayed and available. He colored but warmed all over with her attention, then slipped down beside her, and pulled the sheet over both of them.

The warmth of her beside him was intoxicating. It enveloped him. Without intending anything particular, his hands moved along her body as though on automatic drive. He just let them be themselves as they tenderly stroked her back, touching each vertebrae with intense interest. He allowed them to cup her shoulders and then trace the curvature of her neck, sensing her hair cascading around them both. He breathed in her scent, a wonderful feminine warmth that became part of him.

He just had to touch her breasts again, enveloping their gentle roundness in his hands, enjoying the curve rising to the now upward thrust in her nipple. Oh, how he enjoyed every second of contact with her. Every touch seemed to reveal deep secrets having no name, only accessible through his aching forces of heart. He wondered whether maybe he was truly alive for the first time in his life.

Robert slid his body down closer to her and stroked the gentle mound of her belly, finding the lovely indentures where her hips blossomed out. The softness of the skin just at that place opened to his fingers and led them further to the gentle mound of hair. His body ached with tension, and he slipped closer, still closer. Could he ever get close enough to her? He was overcome with the great need to be so close that he might actually be in her—and he tried.

He entered and reached inside for her. It wasn't enough. He wanted to be deeper. Every muscle in his body tensed and stretched, reaching for the ultimate connection. And then it happened. Jolene shuddered and gasped just as he felt the explosion. For a moment, they were one body, the perfect blend of a human being.

They lay together without speaking for a long time. Jolene made small purring sounds, and Robert felt so incredibly drowsy. He wasn't sleepy, just happily in between waking and gone. He was conscious of Jolene's body and how it fitted so neatly into the curve of his. How could everything about her be so right? He was overawed with the knowledge of her.

*****

Allen Fullington III was intrigued when Cliff asked to meet him in neutral territory, the Algonquin Bar and Restaurant. Whenever he was in Manhattan overnight, he always stayed at the Princeton Club. He knew about the Algonquin but had never been there. It was a little too far north for his liking. He preferred anything between the bottom of Central Park and Grand Central Station. Further north was too residential; further south was too commercial until one reached the Village.

They had mutually agreed on 3:00 p.m., a time that guaranteed some quiet moments when the lunch crowd had left and before the happy hour crowd arrived to blend into dinner time. Allen had never met Cliff before, but he recognized him nevertheless. Allen prided himself on having a sixth sense for such things. He could only sense a certain hunger in the lean face that turned in his direction as he entered. This must be Cliff.

"Mr. Fullington?"

"Yes, how are you, Cliff?"

"I'm fine, sir. And you?"

"OK. I don't think we have ever met, but my secretary was kind enough to look you up. You work for Premium Technical Products Incorporated, do you not?"

"I do."

"And what do you do?"

"I work on special projects assigned to me by Armand Dillon, president and CEO of the corporation. Although I work for him and all that I do is under his direction, I cannot speak for him. We are here together just for a nice friendly conversation."

"That doesn't sound like Armand. I can't quite see him turning to his special projects assistant and saying, 'Cliff, I want you to get together with Fullington to chat a little about the weather and such.' Can you?"

Cliff laughed pleasantly. He was glad to see that he was meeting with a man having an easy sense of humor and straightforward, intelligent manner. He had, as a result, a better chance of success. He knew how to deal with intelligence. Armand had taught him well. No one succeeded at PTP who didn't know how to mimic intelligence if they weren't endowed with it naturally.

"No, he wanted me to pump you for the truth about certain rumors he has been hearing."

"What kind of rumors?"

"Well, frankly, about Alliance for International Communications Incorporated."

"I don't know of any rumors." Allen frowned. "If I did, my advice to you is discount them. I only based two of my investments on rumors, and I can promise you I will never do it again."

"I wish Armand was concerned about that kind of rumor. No, it is something entirely different. I hardly know how to tell you this. I know rumors are very unreliable, but when they keep cropping up here and there and everywhere, there must be some truth in them. I was hoping you could get the truth out of them for me."

Allen showed a touch of impatience as he spoke. "Maybe you should just out with it and tell me what he's hearing. If I know anything, I'd be glad to share it with you, unless it is confidential, of course."

Cliff took a sip of his drink and then noticed that Fullington was without any libation. "Say," he said, "may I order you something to drink? I'm sorry. I've already been here for a while but I need a second. What will you have?"

Allen selected a dry martini but then returned with interest to the topic.

"Can you tell me what these rumors are about?"

"Mind you, rumors are just rumors. Who knows how they get started. It's something about AIC business deals in Brazil. You do have considerable business interests there, don't you?"

"You can discover that from our annual reports. AIC believes in open disclosures, and my guess is that you've been reading a few of them before meeting me."

"Quite a few. That's why the rumors seem to have some credence. There's no mention of their substance in the annual report, not even in the auditors' reports or management letters."

"How do you know that?"

"Armand has made it his business to follow Alliance for International Communications Incorporated's growth and successes over the years. He has admired the corporation, its vision, and its execution. Lucinda Brahms must be a wonder, considering all that she is rumored to have achieved, especially in South America."

"You keep mentioning South America and Brazil, as though there were something about our business there that coincides with these so-called rumors. As far as I know, there is and always has been full disclosure of all our contracts and business affairs south of the border. Are you going to tell me something useful or aren't you? I feel that you are stringing me along. If it's information you want from me, I have nothing to tell you unless you are more specific. How about it?"

"OK. But remember, these are just rumors, not facts."

"So you said—several times already." Fullington waited. It looked as if he were ready to end the meeting unless Cliff said what was really on his mind. This was exactly the point in the conversation Cliff had been working toward. He now leaned forward and looked at Fullington intently, eye to eye.

"It has to do with certain shady dealings of your president and CEO connected with the very lucrative switching station contracts in and around Rio." He paused there to see if

Fullington knew anything about his disclosure. He saw only puzzlement in Fullington's expression, no fear, no dawning flush of concern, nothing but interest and curiosity.

"Shady dealings? I can't imagine what you mean. Lucky would never be involved with anything shady. Now really!"

"Well, that's why I'm asking you. Rumors are just rumors. I wonder who starts these things going round. You know, I understand that a rumor can be just as dangerous as the truth—sometimes."

"Be more specific. What exactly do you mean by shady?"

"Bribery. I hear about a million or more in bribes have been spent on various levels of government in Brazil to secure the business you have there. I also hear that the increasing number of innuendoes and rumors are beginning to attract some attention in Washington and that there is a possibility an investigation is likely." Cliff sat back and let this information sink in. It did.

Allen was careful to hide his concern. "Well! I certainly don't know anything about it. I'd like to know why you are telling me all this and also why is Armand so interested."

"I told you he likes Alliance for International Communications Incorporated, admires its style and success. He is drawn to it in admiration. Who knows, maybe someday there can be a closer affiliation between the two of us?"

"I'm not sure what you are actually telling me."

"Look, Mr. Fullington. You take a look at Premium Technical Products Incorporated under the leadership of Armand Dillon. He has only been in control for three years. During that short time the corporation has grown from a miniscule fifty million in assets to well over three billion. That's impressive but doesn't reveal his true skill. The profitability of the corporation, while it was growing, has increased twenty-six percent. A record for the books. On top of that, my dear Fullington, the stockholders have reaped a seventeen percent increase in share price—annually." Cliff paused for emphasis before going on. "I understand, Mr. Fullington, you are not only a member of the board, but also the chief financial officer and a major stockholder. Don't tell me you wouldn't like to see that kind of track record at AIC?"

"Very impressive! I know his record and his reputation, but what are you getting at?"

"Nothing this minute—or today or even this week. Just bear in mind that you and your board may be casually coasting into some troubled waters. Also bear in mind that Armand is interested in AIC, has the skills and the staff, I may add, to help in the event you want it and need it. Just keep it in mind—confidentially, of course—if you are interested, we're prepared to help."

"In what way?"

"I'm just saying you may be in for a rough ride. If you are, we should get together and talk. If not, this has been a real pleasure meeting you, and I wish you all the best, which sentiment Armand Dillon shares and asked me to communicate to you."

Cliff took the last swallow of his drink and rose as he shook hands warmly, with Fullington and then made his exit.

Allen finished his drink slowly and thoughtfully. He didn't know anything about these so-called rumors. He was pretty sure Lucky wouldn't have anything to do with any shady deals. It just wasn't like her. That wouldn't prevent someone else trying to get away with a bit of bribery. He couldn't think of who that might be. Lucky ran a pretty open management structure. Secrets would be hard to hide. Somebody would be bound to know about it. He decided he would have a talk with Graham. He would certainly know of anything shady going on.

Allen was also suspicious of Armand's interest in AIC. He had a reputation for being a voracious acquisition hunter. He knew of two recent mergers that had more than doubled the size of PTP. He had also heard that he was good at cleaning house, operated frugally himself, and was a darling of the shareholders. He had a few hundred shares of PTP himself and was pleasantly surprised with their performance.

Could Armand actually be sniffing around to acquire AIC? Doubtful! AIC was significantly larger than PTP which had so far only gone after smaller prey. Allen wondered what such a merger might mean for his holdings in AIC. It might make AIC even more attractive to the stock market, especially if there were rumors floating around about its current leadership that negatively affected share value in the eyes of the market. He decided it would be prudent if he nosed around a bit and made sure he was not caught off guard. His significant holdings in AIC made him vulnerable to any loss of image or scandal. He left the Algonquin considerably more concerned about his role on the board of AIC and his vulnerability as a principal stockholder. He would quietly feel out some of the other board members, find out what they knew about Lucinda Brahms and also what they thought of Armand Dillon. He was in close contact with three of the other board members. Between the four of them, they wielded considerable influence on the board.

*****

Instead of sleeping, Jolene remained awake, basking in the feeling that she had been thoroughly and completely loved. Her body was glowing from all the touching and caressing. She stretched luxuriously and checked to see if Robert was awake. He was.

Robert smiled lazily, not feeling any urgency or impatience; he was totally relaxed, thought he might want to just lie there without moving for a day or two to let this new sensation of being loved sink in. Instead, he rolled over more toward Jolene and caressed her shoulder and back, not to revive any passion, but just to make sure she still wanted him close. She wriggled her shoulder lazily as a way of welcoming him nearer.

"How are you?" she asked.

"Me?"

"No, that other guy beside me." She laughed.

"I'm just . . . fine. You?"

"Ditto, only more so."

"Just as a matter of curiosity, Jolene, were you protecting yourself in any way? I mean contraceptivewise?"

"Contraceptivewise, no. Should I have?"

"No, just asking." Robert thought about that for a while and then said, "That's amazing. Our first time together, and you gave yourself all to me—for good, I mean. No wonder it was so wonderful to make love to you."

"Are you sorry? I mean . . . if I turn out to be pregnant."

"Not at all. It's a pretty good way to get you to marry me," he decided.

They lay together, each in a private cluster of thoughts, contemplating the future. It seemed quite natural to turn to other matters.

"Tell me about your boss!" Robert wanted to know a little more about her work.

"What do you want to know?"

"Is she a good person? Is she smart? Do you like her?"

"Yes, she's smart, and I like her very much. More than anything else, she is a good person. She figures everybody employed by Alliance for International Communications Incorporated has a stake in its future, so she tries to include as many people as possible in the decision-making. As a result, things get a little confusing sometimes. I've gotten in the habit of keeping track of who's present when she makes a decision, just so we know whose influence was involved. I sometimes think a few of the right people weren't present and told her she better check with them. You know what? She welcomes my ideas and suggestions. She's come a long way. Very few women get to be president of such a large corporation, but she's earned it."

"I guess so. My father seems to think highly of her. He claims he had to take a number of actions just to protect her from criticism and even downright negativity. Do you know if your boss and my father have much to do with each other?"

"No, I don't." Jolene was thoughtful. "I've only seen them together once, and they acted as though their meeting was unexpected. Your dad popped out of the elevator just as Lucky was approaching the elevator bank on her floor. He made some sort of a strange comment about having pushed the wrong button. Lucky wanted him to do something, but I don't know what. They met later that day in her office with the door closed. That was strange. In the years I have been with her, that was the only time I have ever seen her office door closed.

Do you think they were doing something secretive? Something like we might do if our door was closed?" Jolene chuckled mischievously and dug her heel into the calf of Robert's leg. "Huh? Do you think? Huh?"

"You're talking about my father," Robert said seriously. "He has nothing but profound respect for Ms. Brahms. That's what he calls her, even when at home or in company. That doesn't sound like hanky-panky, don't you think?"

Jolene turned over and looked squarely at him. "Maybe they are trying to keep their deep love for each other secret behind a formal facade. All this time, they have loved each other deeply and in secret, hiding their feelings from the world."

"You know what you are? You're a romantic! You never told me. Is that what we are going to do? Be unhappy lovers, secretly yearning for each other but not daring to let the world know? Is that what you have in store for us?"

"Now that you mention it, what are we going to do? Your father works for my boss. I am her confidential assistant. All of a sudden, I am the mistress of your father's son. A conflict of interest if I ever saw one. Either your father will have to disinherit you, disown you, or I'll have to quit my job and we'll both be destitute, eking out a meagre existence in the poor house."

"Never," Robert insisted. "Besides, they don't have poorhouses anymore. They only have homeless shelters. You *are* a romantic!"

"Robert, you know, I think I might have to tell Lucky you and I are an item."

"Will she mind?"

"I would advise her to consult the company attorney. It might be a problem. Oh well, another one night stand. It was wonderful sex. Stop by sometime and say hello if you're in the neighborhood again," she teased.

"Not on your life!" Robert grabbed her forcefully and hugged her close. "I'm never going to let you out of my sight. I'm going to hide your clothes and give your socks and shoes to the Salvation Army, tie you to this bed. I'll even call AIC and tell your president that you've been kidnapped and she might not see you for a few years. How you like them apples, huh?"

"Don't you dare!" Jolene struggled playfully as their game gradually warmed up and consumed both of them in another heat of the moment. It seemed so natural, so marvelously easy to love again and be consumed with the fire in it. For the moment, all the complications were forgotten, and the more serious issues of their relationship faded.

CHAPTER EIGHT

Secrets

Jolene arrived at her own desk in the corner of Lucky's spacious office thirty minutes before nine o'clock in the morning. She was still feeling the warmth of Robert's caresses. Her whole body was aglow from the night before as well as their loving on waking early. Robert was in no hurry. His first class wasn't until the afternoon.

Jolene had switched her gears from lover to administrative assistant. She looked the part of a professional administrator to the president of a fairly large corporation. She wore a trim blue suit, white shirt, hair pulled back tightly to the back of her head in a bun, horn-rimmed glasses, all very professional.

By the time Lucky arrived, Jolene had the *Times*, the *Wall Street Journal*, and *Barron's* along with a steaming cup of coffee ready for her at the desk.

"Morning, Jolene." Lucky always had a smile and a cheerful manner for her favorite assistant. Over the years, working closely together, sharing the same large office, Lucky's relationship with her had altered from employee to trusted assistant to friendship. They believed in each other.

"Good morning, Lucky. You may want to look at page seven in the journal. There's an interesting article about Premium Technical Products Incorporated that mentions us as well."

"Oh?" Lucky leafed through the journal and paused on page 7.

"Rumors? What rumors are they talking about?"

They're not disclosing their source. You know, the phrase 'From sources close to,' that usually means they're making it up."

"Probably. Does that mean we have an enemy at the journal? Stuff like this can be damaging even if it is fabricated."

"Don't know."

Lucky closed the paper, put it aside, and took a sip of her coffee. She liked it medium brown, a bit like milk chocolate with a single cube of sugar. Just the way Jolene made it for her every morning.

"Anything else drifting around the home front?" Lucky asked.

"Nothing I've heard—yet. You want I should dig around a bit?"

"No. Everything, no matter what it is, usually finds its way here sooner rather than later."

She hadn't finished the sentence before Fullington and Graham showed up to discuss the news.

"We just finished reading the journal," they announced together and then stopped.

Benning arrived carrying a copy in his arms. So did Alex Durand.

"What do you think, Alex?" Lucky wanted to know.

"I've been on the phone to our contacts at the journal since eight o'clock. They're mighty tight-lipped. No disclosure by anyone. I've had to be careful! Too much pushing might give them the idea there's some truth to the allegations."

"I suppose so." Lucky inspected their faces.

"Are we doing anything 'shady' in South America?" Alex asked.

"No, just all the normal business practices every other corporation does," Graham answered for Lucky.

Alex released a sigh of relief. "I'm glad you say that. I'd like to think that our reputation is above reproach. We have a great deal of business down there. My guess, about a third of our income is riding on those projects."

Lucky seemed to be distancing herself from any specific decisions or practices of the corporation. A good move, and Alex approved. He'd like her to remain blameless regardless of what it was.

"I don't know how much we can effectively hide behind what all the other corporations are doing. They're not going to let us pull them into any kind of mess we get into." Katherine Salter had just arrived and was eagerly distancing herself from anything happening in South America on her watch. "Does anyone know any details the journal might have? If so, I'd like to know about it."

"We will have to make a statement. The press is already gathering in the lobby. Let's spend our time getting a statement together," Alex suggested. "How about . . . 'The journal is not disclosing any sources, but we can say with absolute certainty that the Alliance for International Communications

Incorporated is not engaged in any shady dealings in South America and uses only the widely accepted business practices within the laws of our several countries'? How about that?"

"Sounds OK to me," Graham offered.

"Shouldn't Lucky be the one to say it?" Fullington suggested and eyed her carefully for a reaction.

"On the other hand, Katherine is our senior vice president, Latin American Affairs. Perhaps it would carry more weight coming from her," Graham thought out loud.

"Or how about you, Graham? They all know you and trust you. You've communicated with the press many times," Katherine added her suggestion.

"I think Lucky making this statement would carry the greatest weight and have the most significant acceptance by the press, the market, and the public. Who could doubt anything such a beautiful woman says?" Fullington smiled at Lucky encouragingly.

"I think it has to be me. It's my job, but thanks all of you for thinking it through with me. I'll use the statement Alex was kind enough to suggest. I will not take any questions at this time, saying that we are hoping the journal will rescind its false information and apologize."

"Nice touch, Lucky."

"I wouldn't say anything more than the statement as it stands. Anything else might be considered a challenge to the journal. I'd prefer to have the whole thing subside and die a natural death." Alex leaned on his extensive experience with the media.

"Thank you, Alex. I think you are right. That's why we have you and others looking out for us. Much appreciated."

"Are you ready for the press?"

"Let 'em in." Lucky licked her lips and went to stand behind her desk. She knew what she had to say but did not know if she could avoid the questions that were bound to arise. She was determined not to say any additional words. If necessary, she would just repeat the same statement, maybe using slightly different phrasing, but not wandering further afield in any way at all.

"No, no! This will not do," said Alex. "You have to meet them in a place that you can exit when you choose. This way, the press has you trapped in your own office. I'll have them assemble in the conference room. After you make your statement, get out as fast as you can. I'll exercise my authority as your press agent and escort you out and back here to your office. Jolene, you come along and stick close to Lucky. Help me get her out when I say so."

"Good thinking, Alex." Lucky smiled at him again, appreciative of his protective positioning of the meeting.

"This way, Lucky. I'll introduce you." Alex led the way across the hallway to a flight of stairs, avoiding the elevators, and down to the conference room just below. Jolene walked with her. As they neared the door to the conference room, Jolene stopped and turned Lucky to face her. She looked her over critically, adjusted her open blouse collar slightly and smiled encouragingly. Lucky took her hand and squeezed it gratefully.

"You are looking very presidential," Jolene assured her.

The press stood up respectfully as the little knot of people around Lucky entered. The informal clatter of conversation that always seemed to erupt whenever reporters are assembled ended abruptly. Alex stepped forward to introduce Lucky.

"Ladies and gentlemen of the press, may I present Ms. Lucinda Brahms, president and CEO of the Alliance for International Communications Incorporated. Please be seated. Ms. Brahms will make a short statement concerning the rumors many of you read about in the journal this morning. Our quick response to them is a tribute to this corporation's open and transparent posture toward the public. We'll arrange another time for a more in-depth interview with some of you."

Lucky allowed her eyes to scan the crowd briefly before releasing the warmth of her most popular smile, relaxing the crowd almost perceptibly. She knew a few. She nodded to several with wider smiles and then shook her hair slightly from side to side in little girl fashion that she knew almost always endeared her to the public.

"Gentlemen and ladies, thank you for charging in on us so early in the morning." A ripple of laughter greeted her. "I always thought reporters were night people. I had no idea you would be awake so early."

Alex frowned at her. He knew the dangers in humor, but he also understood that Lucky needed to warm them up before issuing the short statement. He hoped this would be enough of a warm-up.

"I know the reason you are here. I too have read the journal." Lucky's smile faded as she looked straight out at them, unblinking and stern. "You can imagine my shock and surprise to see what the journal has selected to print. I do not know what has prompted that esteemed publication to select us for such treatment, nor have I found out yet how they might benefit from such loose journalism, but I can tell you in complete honesty that this corporation uses only the most lawful and straightforward business practices in all and any of its foreign subsidiaries. I furthermore want to apologize on behalf of the journal to our South American neighbors who will be naturally upset by such unfounded allegations. As to what actions we might feel it necessary to take in response to them"—Lucky paused here and slowly her face warmed up a degree or two—"you'll have to wait and see. Those of you who know us well will surely understand that any such rumors are purely fabricated and without any substance. I cannot answer any questions yet, but we will undoubtedly have more to say soon. Please bear with us as we consider our further actions."

At least sixteen hands popped up, and a few voices rifled the air without being recognized.

"Ms. Brahms! Will you be considering legal action?"

"Ms. Brahms? Are you saying such rumors don't exist?" the journal representative shouted out.

"Ms. Brahms will not answer any questions at this time." Alex intervened while Jolene helped to usher Lucky toward the door amid the continued babble of questions and comments.

"I'm sorry. Ladies and gentlemen, we'll be in touch as soon as we have more to say on the subject or for any other news as a matter of fact. Please excuse us. Excuse us."

Lucky had disappeared and Jolene followed her out. Alex used his hands, palm down to urge them all to wait and now to leave quietly. He thought Lucky had spoken a bit too much but, on the whole, had done a good job. She didn't seem to be hiding anything, nor did she appear to be lying. He thanked his stars that Lucky was such a likable person. The reporters were just doing their jobs. He didn't sense any animosity, just a ferocious appetite for newsworthy material.

Alex exhaled, realizing how tense he had been. All in all, things were not as bad as he had expected. Still, what were they going to do about the rumors, if there were any? That was a thought. Suppose it really was all fabricated? Suppose there were no such rumors. Then who was inventing them? The journal? He actually doubted that. The journal was too respectable. As he recalled the article in the journal, there were quotation marks around the actual statement, as though they were quoting a source. This protected them. They were under no obligation to reveal a source unless criminal action were involved. He decided he better read the story again, maybe talk it over with the legal department.

Maybe this would be the end of the matter. Lie low and wait might be the best course of action. Wait to see what would happen next. It could just be a smoke screen. It could also be part of a plot to discredit the Alliance for International Communications Incorporated. If so, who was behind it? Who would gain from it? What would be gained by discrediting AIC?

Alex decided he would ask around a bit to see what was brewing. Graham usually knew things, and so did Benning. No need to involve Lucky at this point. She had enough to worry about without raising possibly nonexisting plots—even if they were sinister.

*****

When Russ pushed by Esmeralda into Armand's office, he was beside himself with fury. Armand looked up at him, surprise touching the mask of his face. He put down his pencil, leaned back in the chair behind his desk, and waited for what he knew was coming.

"You rat!" Russ sputtered, "I'll get you for this."

"For what?" Armand asked with a pretense at innocence.

"You know damn well what."

"Calm down, Russ. Try to pull yourself together. You're way too emotional!"

"You had me fired. That's what you wanted all along, wasn't it?" Russ shoved his jaw forward toward Armand.

"You were fired for cooking the books," Armand answered calmly. "Calder had to take action. Who knows what else you've done over the years? I tried to wait for an investigation, but Calder showed me the evidence, and I had no choice but to dismiss you. The stockholders would tar and feather me if I kept you on, given the evidence. Now I suggest you leave before I change my mind and let the lawyers prefer charges against you."

"The books were honest and straightforward until your staff borrowed them for their analysis," Russ sputtered. "After that, all sorts of strange transactions showed up. Those five thousand dollars suddenly appearing in my bank account and then withdrawn just days later that just happened to coincide with those checks and petty cash withdrawals that were not there before your staff mysteriously uncovered them. I'm telling you, Armand, you're playing dirty pool, and sooner or later someone will catch you. Maybe even me, if I can find out exactly who did it for you."

"I know nothing of the details." Armand remained frigidly calm. "That's why I have experts on my staff. I did see the evidence, and you ought to be ashamed of yourself. Considering what I would have paid you, how could a mere five thousand dollars lure you into stealing? Get out of my office, get yourself a defense lawyer if you can afford it, but don't you dare touch petty cash or the Croton Green checkbooks. I have an injunction against you, and you better keep your hands off."

"I'll get you if it's the last thing I do," Russ promised.

"You can always sell out if dealing with me is so distasteful to you."

Russ's lip curled as he spoke. "You would like that, wouldn't you, now that you and your staff have managed to drive the share price to its lowest point in ten years, despite the underlying asset value. Nobody trusts you, Armand. I should have known better than support this catastrophic merger."

"Sell out to us, and I guarantee the share price will rise again. My reputation may be a two-edged sword, but Wall Street knows what I can do to profits and the share price. I'll send Calder around to you with an offer for your shares at their current value," said Armand.

"I won't sell, although I'm tempted to wash my hands of the bunch of you once and for all."

"Up to you! Now get out, I've got work to do. You can close the door from the other side." Armand tried to smirk.

"Bastard!" Russ slammed the door behind him.

Armand did a few quick calculations and nodded to himself. He decided the share price was still a little high. He would have to get Calder to spread a few rumors that there seemed to be more corruption in the company than was first thought. Another one or two points down ought to do it. It might take a few more insults to get Russ to sell. He was so emotional about all this. He had no business being president of Groten Grass given his erratic outbursts and uncontrollable feelings. For management, all of that emotional business has to be under control.

Armand knew that's where he had the edge. He never let his feelings get in the way of a rational decision. He probably never let feelings get in the way of any decision. Even as a young student in college, he had already wiped clean the slate and made his intellect king. His thoughts briefly returned to that important decision. It was the last year of his college at Pace University. Alice still had one year to go. He was very careful to make it clear to Alice that marriage was out of the question until after he and, of course, she had their diplomas in hand. She didn't understand the reasoning. She kept bringing up love as a reason.

It was clear she had no sense for the reality of life. Of course, she didn't worry about such things since her parents were obviously protected and sheltered and wealthy already for several generations. That's what made her so attractive. And he might have been tempted, but when they began exploring the option, the grandfather of Alice brought him a complex document that basically stripped him of any legal rights or claims to any inheritance or family assets. That was a sure sign the family would never include him wholeheartedly in their affairs, and without that, what was the point of marrying Alice?

She cried a bit, but as he recalled, she accepted the weight of her family's arguments without too much resistance. Even if he had been included in all that wealth, he would have to find a way to resist being controlled by them. It was the grandfather who opposed him. Armand remembered what a bull he was. Not much intelligence, but a lot of power. Armand remembered him fondly almost as much as he envied him. Someday . . . Armand pulled himself back to the present issues he was dealing with.

He admitted to himself that he probably didn't have any feelings anymore. They weren't of much use anyway. Instincts, he could tolerate, since they sometimes got him out of trouble and often guided him accurately, but that was only because he had honed them well. Under the king—his mind—they turned out to be useful.

Armand's face gave way to a self-satisfied semblance of a grin, and he isolated a few of his calculations with a sharp pencil, surrounding them with double-sided rectangular boxes. He buzzed Esmeralda on the intercom. It was time to get Calder working on his strategy to subdue and then get rid of Russ completely. He had served his purpose and was no longer necessary or of any use in the further evolution of the rapidly growing Premium Technical Products Incorporated. Besides, he needed the shares as a possible bargaining chip in the acquisition of Alliance for International Communications Incorporated. He hated to give away any cash. He preferred to use shares. The risk was always cumulatively shared that way. With cash in any deal, you lose the value while absorbing a proportionally larger share of the risk. As long as he had enough of an assortment of shares, he felt comfortable acquiring ever more hard assets.

*****

Robert hurried into Joe's Diggs to grab himself a quick grilled cheese and tomato sandwich. He was hoping to see Jolene later and didn't want to waste any time eating. It was still an odd time for the Diggs, and he had the place almost to himself until Stu entered with a tall man in a dark suit, pale blue dress shirt, and dark blue diagonally striped tie. Stu slid into the counter seat next to Robert, and the tall stranger took the seat on his other side.

"Hi," Stu said, "haven't seen you for a while."

"I know. I've been busy. Classes, homework—well, you know how it is."

"Sure. We just missed you the other night at the meeting."

"Meeting?"

"Yeah. Shaman Pi asked about you."

"Oh, damn it. I forgot all about it. Listen, I don't think I can make it for a while. There's just too much going on in my life." Robert didn't want to launch into any explanations.

"That bad?" Stu ordered a coffee and a left over doughnut.

"It's nothing bad. Just a lot all at once."

"Your dad back home again?"

"Yes, thank God! He's been really busy too."

"I bet."

"What?"

"I said I bet he's been busy."

"Oh."

"You don't know, do you?" Stu looked at Robert meaningfully.

"Know what?"

"Your dad is mixed up in trouble. He's right in the middle of a big mess." Stu seemed almost pleased with his announcement.

"Where do you get your information? My dad only got back this Tuesday. He was tired after such a long flight from Rio, but thank goodness, it was still in the same time zone. What are you talking about, and who is this?" Robert pointed in the direction of the tall man sitting beside them.

"Oh, sorry. Robert, let me introduce you to Calder Tebbit. He is the senior vice president of Organization Projects at Premium Technical Products Incorporated. He works very closely with the president, maybe a lot like your father does, only he stays clean."

"What are you talking about? What do you mean he stays clean?" Robert bristled, ready to defend his father.

"What I mean—"

The tall man leaned forward and interrupted whatever Stu was about to say. "I guess you haven't read the *Wall Street Journal* this morning."

"No, I haven't." Robert was cautious.

"I'm sorry I don't have one with me to give you."

"What has it got to do with my father?" Robert asked.

"Nothing directly, I hope. There's a story in it about my company, Premium Technical Products Incorporated. In it, there's a small item about rumors concerning the company your dad works for. Sorry! That's a pretty good source."

"Is it a bad story? I mean, why are you sorry?"

"As I recall, it mentions rumors circulating around in the financial markets about illegal business practices in South America. In particular, the rumors seem to be focused on the Alliance for International Communications Incorporated's contracts in Brazil. There's no mention of your father, but it does mention the president and CEO, Lucinda Brahms. Do you know her?" Calder asked.

"No, I've never met her, but my father mentions her often. I always thought of her as being an especially talented and fine person, the way my dad speaks of her."

"I'm afraid this news may have dire consequences for her both personally and professionally."

"I thought you said they were just rumors," Robert said sharply.

"I did. But you know the old saying, 'Where there's smoke, there must be fire.'"

Both Stu and Calder were silent, watching Robert's face as he pondered various questions and finally looked up at the two of them.

"Are the two of you connected in some way? I mean, what's your relationship?"

"No, not me—" Stu hastened to say, while at the same time, Calder answered, "Yes. Premium Technical Products Incorporated is interested in Steward and his career. We'd like to hire him when he finishes his engineering degree."

"You?" asked Robert. "You, the big antibusiness advocate? Working for a corporation? Aren't you ashamed of yourself?" Robert mocked him, but laughing all the while.

"I haven't said yes yet," Stu hurried to defend himself, "but you know we all have to eat. Besides, it feels good to have your abilities appreciated. I'll decide next month."

"We are counting on you. Don't you forget that!" Calder was emphatic as he rose to his feet, left a ten-dollar bill on the counter, and exited the Diggs without further comment.

Robert looked Stu over with increased interest. He noticed the slight flush on his neck and ears. He was obviously embarrassed to be found out. Maybe he was fast becoming one of those divided personalities that railed against the status quo while simultaneously taking advantage of its benefits.

"What's the Shaman going to say?" chided Robert. "Whatever will he think of you, his chief disciple?"

"You'd have to be female to be a chief disciple, and in case you haven't noticed, I am not wearing any skirts today or any other day."

"I'm just kidding, Stu. I'm sure the Shaman has other concerns, like finding another empty classroom. Has something happened? You were his favorite. I think that from the way he singled you out and relied on you to help him."

"Nothing really. Anyway it's none of my business." Stu couldn't look Robert in the eye.

"What's none of your business?"

"He's entitled to do whatever he wants. If he happens to like the girls—well, so do I. There's no crime in that." Stu didn't look at Robert directly, almost as though he were hiding something.

"You caught him with one of the girls?" Robert was guessing.

"All three of them."

"Nothing spiritual going on, you think?"

"Don't make fun of me!" Stu said angily. "Go ahead, laugh! You're probably pleased that I am disillusioned."

"No, Stu. It's just I am not surprised that he turned out to be human, after all. What did you expect? What he had to say could still be valuable? What were you looking for, an angel in human clothing? Come on, Stu, you know better, you being a vet and all that."

"I don't think it is right to use one's so-called wisdom as a courtship tool. He set himself up as capable of advising and helping us, and then he seduces the girls. Besides, he's old enough to be their father."

"You don't think the girls had anything to do with it?" Robert voiced his suspicions.

"He's pretty powerful. He has a kind of psychic energy that girls would find hard to resist."

"Poor things. We should pity them." Robert was sarcastic. "There was a dark-eyed girl sitting next to me in the Shaman's class that I thought was a goner right from the start. Was she one of the three the Shaman was with?"

"Yes. I hate her. She had no business caving in to him."

"Careful, Stu. You know how quickly hate can turn to love and vice versa? Whole books are written about that."

Stu sat quietly, playing with his spoon in the coffee cup, tipping it and letting a few drops of coffee spill over and splash into the remains in the cup then doing it again. Robert said nothing. He had the feeling Stu was thinking, or maybe ruminating? He was far away in his consciousness. Maybe he had forgotten Robert was sitting right next to him?

"I have something to confess," Stu said finally.

"Confess away. I promise not to give you absolution. I'm not qualified."

"I've been given a grant to finish my degree." Stu stated it frankly.

"That's great, Stu. Congratulations!" Robert clapped him on the back enthusiastically.

"It's a grant from Premium Technical Products Incorporated."

"Wow!" Robert looked at Stu in surprise, "They must want you badly. Have they signed you up already and you're afraid to tell me? I wouldn't think badly of you if you did. Each of us has got to manage our lives as best we can. I still congratulate you!"

"There's more."

"More?"

"They wanted me to spy on you and your father," Stu said quietly.

"Why? Whatever for?"

"I don't know. They just kept asking questions and expecting me to keep tabs on you. They wanted me to find out everything your father was doing in Brazil."

"What did you tell them?"

"Nothing. That's the funny thing about this whole business. They have been paying my expenses, giving me money for books and even for food, and I haven't told them a thing, as far as I can tell." Stu seemed genuinely perplexed.

"Doesn't sound like a very profitable business deal for them," thought Robert out loud.

"Not at all."

"I wonder if what you told them has anything to do with the rumors and the article in the *Wall Street Journal*." Robert had a feeling he was on to something.

"Maybe."

"Stu, I am a little disappointed in you. You are older than I am, I thought a little stronger and wiser than I, and now this. Never mind. I cannot see any real harm you have caused. I forgive you. I don't blame you for taking the grant. It must be a godsend," Robert said sympathetically.

"You have no idea. I couldn't turn them down. Maybe I should've. But I couldn't turn them down."

"Hey, buddy! It's OK. No harm!" Robert tapped him lightly on the shoulder. Then he stood up, left Stu sitting there still brooding over the remains of his coffee, and left.

CHAPTER NINE

Contact

Lucky sat quietly behind her desk. Jolene was still at her typewriter. She had just mentioned to Lucky the other day about the new chips and word processing, which would revolutionize office work and also how people acquired information and managed decisions. Lucky listened to the sound of the typewriter and wondered if she would miss it.

"Jolene? I think you should go home. There's nothing on your desk that can't wait till tomorrow."

"How about you?"

"I need a few quiet moments to review the day and think."

"It's been quite a day. I wonder if the rumor matter is settled and we can go on with our lives."

"I doubt it. There's something behind all this. It isn't as if we're doing something new or different. It's business as usual. Somebody or something is pushing this from behind. What are they after? You know, it can all backfire on them. The way of doing business in Brazil is very different from what we consider appropriate here in the United States. All companies working in that country have to follow suit. If this gets to be too much of a hubbub, it will pull all the other companies into the problem."

"Maybe that would not be too bad. Things change and sometimes even for the better."

"I suppose so." Lucky pushed back her chair, stood up and then walked over to the window overlooking Park Avenue with a view toward Saint Bartholomew Church with its graceful dome. It didn't quite belong with the speeding traffic, honking of horns, and hundreds of small dots imitating pedestrians rushing in every which direction. It belonged in Venice or Constantinople.

"I am getting ready to go," said Jolene. "Ms. Brahms?"

"What's with this 'Ms. Brahms' business?"

"Lucky, I think I ought to inform you of something."

"You're not leaving me, are you?"

"No, it's not that."

"OK. Anything's good news compared to that." Lucky sighed, and Jolene laughed lightly.

"You know I wouldn't do that—unless it was absolutely necessary."

"Then what is it?"

"I found a man."

"I'm not surprised."

"Oh?"

Lucky hugged Jolene before speaking. "You're a wonderful person. I'm surprised you haven't found one sooner. He better be a good man! You better let me look him over to see whether I think he's good enough for you."

"He has a father."

"I should hope so."

"His father works for Alliance for International Communications Incorporated."

"Do I know him?"

"Yes."

"Who is he?"

"Charles McLane."

"Our Charles McLane?"

"Our Charles McLane."

"The son, you say?"

"Yes."

"He must be about twenty-five years old."

"Exactly twenty-five, but he is still going to Fairmont University in New Jersey. I think he has one more year."

"Tell me more."

"He's tall, quite good-looking. But then I guess when you're in love, what else would he be? He has light brown hair, hazel eyes, and he's quite strong in his arms—" Jolene laughed when she realized what she had said, and so did Lucky. "He's especially fine. I mean, he's so considerate, mindful of my feelings, a gentle soul. I love him."

Lucky smiled at Jolene and hugged her again. "I am so happy for you. Love is really the most precious of all feelings. I hope I get to meet him. Bring him by some time."

"Thank you, Lucky." Jolene kept her eyes on Lucky's face as she turned away. There was something a bit stilted about Lucky's response. She was hiding something. Was she already thinking of the complications, his being Charles McLane's son and Jolene being Lucky's confidential secretary? Was that worrying her? She decided to take the matter right out of the dark corner and into the daylight for both of them to see.

"I think you ought to consult our legal department. This might change matters, our relationship. After all, how confidential can I be, objectively speaking, if I am in love with the son of one of your top executives? Talk to Legal, Lucky, and then let's see what we should do."

"I'm very proud of you." Lucky admired Jolene's honesty and ethics. She eased herself into the chair behind her desk as she spoke. "What a straightforward person you are. How I trust you. No, more than that. How precious you are to me—a real honest-to-goodness friend. I'll consult with Legal, and we will consider the matter from all sides."

"Are you still staying here longer? I can stay if you need me," Jolene offered.

"No, you go. I'll be leaving soon myself."

Jolene covered her typewriter, put away some clips and pencils, closed the narrow top drawer in her desk and locked the whole desk using the key that she then tucked under her typewriter. It was magnetized and adhered with a little click to the metallic frame.

"Good night, Lucky."

"Night," Lucky said absentmindedly. She was deep in thought as Jolene picked up her briefcase, slung a handbag over her shoulder, and walked toward the reception area on her floor to the elevators.

Lucky did not move for several minutes, but then she slowly reached for the phone. She hated to do this. It had been years, but this was important. He would be—what would he be?

Would he be angry? She fondled the phone and then took her hand away again.

They had promised each other not to maintain any contact. He was married, happily so, she thought. She had seen him only from a distance. They had never talked—really talked—about more personal things. There had always been business matters, of course, but nothing about their relationship—or about their feelings. She wondered about that. What did he feel? Did he feel anything for her? It had been so long. Suddenly she had to know! What did he feel?

Her hand went again to the phone. She cradled it in her hand and then dialed the number from memory. Some other memories flooded back while she waited for an answer.

"Hello?" It sounded like a young voice at the other end.

"Hello," Lucky said. "May I speak with Charles McLane?"

*****

Allen Fullington had picked the Algonquin's restaurant for the informal, mostly social meeting even though it was far from his usual haunts. His meeting there with Cliff was still on his mind and influenced him to want this meeting with his director friends at AIC to get together here. He picked a time that was between crowds and sat at a table close to the bar, reading the *Times* and waiting.

Ralph Ballister was the first to appear. He was one of the oldest directors of the Alliance for International Communications Incorporated, had a modest holding of stock, and was fiercely loyal to Lucinda Brahms. He inspected the interior of the Algonquin, his curled gray hair picking up various highlights from the different neon-colored lights around the bar. He saw Fullington, nodded his acquaintanceship, and joined him at the table.

"What an inspiration to meet here. I haven't been at the Algonquin for . . . well, maybe fifteen years? How are you Allen?"

"Sit down, Ralph. Good to see you. What are you drinking?"

"Scotch, thanks."

Fullington ordered for Ralph, acknowledging that he was calling them together and would pick up the tab. Just then, Simon Elliot stormed in, thinking he was late.

"Sorry to keep you waiting," he apologized.

"Not at all. I just arrived myself," Ralph explained.

"That's all right then. The pedestrian traffic was so heavy on the cross streets—even at this time, could you believe it! I was afraid you'd be under the table before I got here." Simon laughed awkwardly at his own joke. He was the only one who did so. Every time Simon arrived anywhere, he was always late and always out of breath. The traffic was always his excuse. Fullington wondered whether it ever occurred to Simon that his excuse never varied and that all his friends knew it and never believed it any more.

"What made you pick the Algonquin?" Simon wondered. "I didn't know they were still in business. Is it the first hotel and restaurant on Manhattan or the second? I can't remember. I think my grandfather first mentioned it to me. Good beer though!" He ordered beer and sat back, waiting for something interesting to happen.

"I picked the Algonquin because that's where I first met Cliff."

"Cliff who?"

"I don't know his surname. Everyone calls him Cliff, and that's all I know."

"Who is he? Are we here to meet him? Why?"

"No, no. This is just for us chickens, old friends at an old dive having a quiet drink together," Fullington hurried to explain.

"Who's Cliff? Are you putting him up for the board?" asked Ralph suspiciously.

"Nothing like that at all. I never met him before in my life. It seems he does little odd jobs for Armand Dillon." Fullington answered, taking a sip of his scotch and then setting the glass back down on its coaster.

"Not that bastard. What did he want?"

"At first I thought maybe he was pumping me for information about AIC. Then I found out he was just passing along a bit of information about AIC I didn't know."

"Hey, I thought you knew everything about AIC. You talked me into buying!" Ralph laughed.

Simon showed some interest. "What information?" he asked Fullington.

"It was very strange, how he tried not to tell me. I think he really wanted to know if it was true."

"If what was true?"

"Some rumors—stories about acts of bribery in Brazil. He claimed everybody was talking about it and that the feds were starting to take notice and looking into it."

"What nonsense!" exploded Simon. "Lucky isn't the type. She has always been open and transparent with us. I don't care what bad-mouthing is going on. Someone's jealous, that's what it is."

"The *Wall Street Journal*?" Fullington asked. "I guess you haven't read the journal the other day."

"I didn't see any slander about Lucky in it. They wouldn't dare."

"Actually, they printed a story about PTP Corp. Buried in there was a simple, inoffensive statement about rumors involving Lucky's dealings in Brazil. That's all there was. From unimpeachable sources! That's what it said."

"I don't believe it."

"So Cliff just wanted to tell you about those so-called rumors? What business was it of his?" Ralph asked, detecting something peculiar in what he was hearing.

"There was more to it than that. He told me Armand Dillon had an interest in us and wanted me to know they are willing to help out if we get into trouble with Lucky."

"You don't say!"

"How is he going to help us?" Ralph asked. "We're twice his size. Maybe he wants us to help him out. That would be more like it. I don't trust that guy. He's meaner than hell!"

"Have you checked to see how your shares in AIC are doing?"

"Yeah, I know. They are down again. I don't go with the usual ups and downs. Anybody investing these days knows not to panic when shares are off by a few cents."

"It's more than a few cents. In the last two weeks, we are off the high by a good ten percent."

"We are the three biggest shareholders in the company. We stand to lose the most if there's a scandal that pulls the price down. We can ride it out, or we might want to do something about it," Fullington offered the two possibilities.

"Like what?" Simon was skeptical.

"Are you saying get rid of her?" Ralph was incredulous. "That's a bit harsh, wouldn't you say?"

"Look, we all love her, but this is business. Love and business don't mix. If I lose money every day on my shares, love is not going to make me feel any better. These rumors don't seem to be going away. On the contrary, they're growing by the hour as one analyst after another picks up on it and passes it on to a friend. Why else would the share price be tumbling like it is? Our operations are as profitable as they ever have been, and we're growing at a good clip." Fullington warmed up to his own reasoning.

Simon put his hand on Fullington's arm to calm him down before he asked, "You say Dillon wants to help? That makes me suspicious. How do you think he wants to help? Did Cliff say anything specific?"

"No, he didn't. He talked a great deal about PTP performance over the last three years since Dillon took over the leadership. I have to admit the numbers are impressive, including the share price. The guy may be ruthless, a cold son of a bitch, but he seems to get results." Fullington rubbed his chin and looked around at the other two. "Maybe you two can afford to lose on your investment, but I can't."

"So you're thinking merger or acquisition?" Ralph was curious.

"Dillon would never be interested in merger. He's acquisition-hungry. He's got plans to take over the whole world." Fullington laughed and then choked it off as he realized what he had jokingly said.

"You think we should talk with him?" Simon asked.

"I don't think he'll meet. He never does. Cliff and a guy named Calder do all the dirty work. He pulls the strings in the background. Why don't we quietly arrange a little meeting with the two of them?" Fullington suggested.

"What about Lucky? What about Graham, Benning? This might all turn unfriendly, if you know what I mean."

"If I lose any more money, it's going to be even more unfriendly on my side." Fullington said grimly.

"All right, Fullington, we're with you. You take the lead on this and keep us informed," Ralph decided.

"You traitor," Simon chided him.

"I can't afford to do otherwise. I suppose you're independently wealthy and don't mind throwing it away after someone else's scandal!" Ralph flushed in anger.

"The hell you say. I've family trusts watching my every move, even some unfriendly family members who don't give a shit about anything except a continuous stream of income that feeds them. Some of them haven't done a stitch of work in a whole lifetime. I sometimes think it might be good if they were penniless—maybe for a few days at least," Simon admitted.

"Are you in or not?" Ralph wanted to know.

Simon licked his lips nervously. The fingers on his right hand twitched uncontrollably in the palm of his left hand. Perspiration beaded his upper lip. "I'm in. But let's keep it quiet till the deal is done."

"Agreed. At this point, we're just talking," Fullington said.

"I need to be sure there's no dilution. I'd just as soon his shares were the ones getting absorbed," Ralph warned. Even as he spoke, he realized he didn't trust Armand Dillon one iota. Wall Street resounded with anecdotal stories of Armand Dillon's tactics and his incredible singly focused brain power. Few people had actually met him, but it was rumored that he was ugly to look at. He wasn't really shy. He just didn't want to be seen. He preferred to work through carefully selected proxies who feared him and dared not resist him.

Ralph wondered whether Fullington had any idea what he was steering them into. Had he heard all the stories? Would any of them really benefit, or in the end, would it be only Armand Dillon that benefitted? Better he should keep a watchful eye out. Armand Dillon could just as easily destroy them rather than save them. He just didn't trust him!

*****

Robert left the Diggs. It was surprisingly empty. Where was everyone? He realized his mind was on Jolene, and he may have missed all events at the university. For all he knew, there might have been a dance, a concert, maybe even a game. He felt far away from anything going on at the university. He might just as well not be a student at all.

As he turned the corner in the direction of his home, he felt people silently walking behind him in the same direction.

"Robert?" It was Shaman Pi. "Wait up."

"Hi, Shaman. What are you doing over here in this part of town?"

"I've been looking for you."

"Oh?"

"I wanted to talk something over."

"I'm sorry. I've been preoccupied with my own questions. Sorry I didn't make it to your classes," Robert apologized.

"No problem. Things have been ominously quiet in the atmosphere lately. You know how it is in the quiet before a storm? All of a sudden, the birds stop twittering and chirping, even the wind dies down, a feeling of expectancy lies heavy in the air? That's what I've been feeling lately," the Shaman confessed.

"You have? Me too. I feel I'm being warned . . . of something, but I don't know what. It could be something personal."

"Could be. It could also be something ripening in the karmic knot in which we are all entangled."

"You think so?"

"I do. When you and Stu first met, I listened to his description of you and thought right away there are underground currents of meanings and connections unraveling inside and outside of us. At the time, I felt it very strongly but paid no attention to it. Now I'd like to warn you. Stu is being drawn into some kind of plot in which you are involved. He's not a bad person. It's just he isn't as strong as the forces closing in on him."

"I know all about it, Shaman. He's better than you suspect. He told me he accepted a full grant for the expense of all his books and room and board from a corporation despite his concerns about the ethics of business. I think he was a little ashamed, but couldn't refuse the bait. Besides, it wasn't so bad what he had to do for it," Robert generously admitted.

"What did he have to do for it?"

"Tattletale on me and anything I happened to know about my father. I knew very little, so no real harm was done. It occurred to me that they were working with a headhunter. Perhaps they were thinking of offering my dad a job. I doubt if PTP considered the cost to them to be worth what he told them."

Shaman was benevolent in his reply. "Well, I'm glad he told you. In a way, it is understandable. It seems like a small thing to do for a pretty large benefit."

"It depends how valuable friendship happens to be. I'm not sure I can count on him anymore. I guess money is his Achilles' heel," Robert said a little sadly.

"And what's yours, do you think?" Shaman asked, smiling.

"Maybe love, maybe loyalty. I don't know. You probably don't have one," Robert thought out loud.

"Not at all," Shaman admitted. "I think it is ignorance. As long as I don't have the courage to take my consciousness all the way, I'll be prone to error and deceit. I think we're all still on the way. Maybe getting there is not as important as being on the way and not giving up."

"Maybe you're right. Are you still holding classes at the university?"

"Yes. It seems a professor has taken an interest in me. I'm being invited to a special meeting of the faculty ethics committee. They want to hear what I have to say."

"Congratulations! I'm so glad for you. If you end up giving a legitimate course, I might want to take it. Do you think you'll pass me?" Robert laughed.

Shaman answered pleasantly, "I'll have to make it tough on you. After all, there are rules, you know." He smiled. "You know I don't believe in grades. I believe in commentary about progress. That way, the message is clear. We're all only on the way. To deserve an A, the learning has to be measurable—in other words, meaningless."

"I think if I were a faculty member, I would not vote for you," Robert chided Shaman. "You'd endanger the whole university edifice. All the learning mythology would crumble in a heap, and the poor professors would have to start being creative. They'd have to join the human race and develop themselves further. Unless you're somebody different the next day, how can you have something new to say?"

"Have you been scanning my mind?" Shaman asked.

"No, Shaman, just thinking. Thanks for getting me started." Robert paused for a moment as a new thought urged in on him. "I think I need to have a good talk with my father first chance I get."

"Nothing like meeting your elders. Don't be surprised if you discover you are older than he is."

"Wouldn't that be a laugh and a half?"

"Good-bye, Robert, and good luck. I wish you well."

"You too, Shaman. Let me know what happens when you meet with the ethics committee. You've piqued my curiosity!"

"I will."

Robert looked after him as he walked away toward the university campus. He had the feeling everyone seemed at the edge of an emotional crisis, being tested in some way. It seemed like life no longer followed from previous events without challenging the psyche for something creative. It used to be you decided something and then you carried it out. Now no matter what you decide, life places an alternative before you. Maybe it was to find out whether you really knew where you were going or maybe how enlightened your will was to carry you securely toward unknown ends.

Robert started for home. He hoped his father would be in this evening. The only honest thing to do was tell him exactly what he had been hearing and asking for the truth. Is it possible to love someone when you find out they have faults? Does the mind love? Can the heart love and know the truth?

Chapter Ten

The Plot

Lucky wondered whether the voice that answered the phone was Robert. She had never heard it before, at least not as a grown man. She could still hear the youth in it when he spoke.

"One moment, please."

"Are you his—?" she started to say, but he was gone.

"Hello?" a familiar voice from at least twenty-five years ago answered.

"Hello, Charles. This is Lucinda. I think we should have a talk."

"Yes." Charles thought this would be a good idea. He guessed the reason Lucky was calling was about the *Wall Street Journal* article. Hearing her voice—it sounded so close. He suddenly realized how glad he was that she wanted to talk with him. He even thought maybe they could speak of other things besides business. He dared to hope. "You name it, and I'll be there."

"No public place. How about I pick you up and we talk in the car? If we need more time, we can always arrange something better."

"Yes, I understand."

"If I come by in a half hour, will you come out to the car?"

"Yes. I'll watch for you. See you soon."

"Bye."

Lucky dismissed her driver and climbed into her own car parked in the downstairs garage. There didn't seem to be anyone around this late in the day. Most people lived either way uptown and needed public transportation, or they occupied houses or apartments either in New Jersey across the Hudson or in Long Island across the East River. A few were beginning to commute from Staten Island. Anyway, there were many empty parking places in the garage, and Lucky couldn't see anyone moving around.

She left the garage, waving a friendly good-bye to the security guard, and edged into Fifty-Third Street. As she made a left-hand turn, some car lights flashed on to her right. At the time, she paid no attention to them. There were lights everywhere in the city. Half the time, she was partially blinded by streetlights, car lights, neon lights, store lights, you name it. City lights chased the night out of town till morning.

The streets were still crowded and noisy. Many commuters were fighting to get home. A crowd was fighting to get into the city for shows and restaurants. The buses moved fearlessly into the traffic from every stop, picking up more and more tired and irritable people. Every now and then, there was a cacophony of horns and a sudden babble of voices, usually in anger.

Lucky made her way through town and inched onto the uptown traffic on Riverside Drive. It was slow going for about fifteen minutes, but then it eased up, and at least she was able to keep moving at about twenty miles an hour. It was nearly 8:00 p.m. when she finally crossed the George Washington Bridge and sped north along the Palisades Parkway. By 8:30 p.m., she pulled up alongside Charles's house, shut off the lights, and waited.

Another car carefully exited a driveway two houses farther on. Then she noticed a car coming from behind her, edging in close to the sidewalk a little distance behind her and then shutting off its lights. She guessed there would be people coming home in these suburbs all evening long. She waited patiently, knowing that Charles would be looking out for her.

He appeared at the doorway, opened it all the way, and looked around. When he saw her car, he closed the door carefully behind him, saying good-bye to another figure partially hidden in the shadow of the door. He arrived at the car, opened the door, and slid in beside her. The other figure, a younger, more slender-looking man opened the house door again, waved good-bye, and went inside, shutting off the outside light and closing the door in one motion.

"Is that Robert?" Lucky asked.

"Yes."

"He seems wonderfully put together, handsome like his father."

"We're quite different. At the moment, he seems to have it in for businessmen like me!"

"Oh?"

"Fairmont University is apparently a hotbed of far-left professors concerned with business ethics, environmental protectionism—the works."

Lucky laughed. "What do you expect from such an activist father as Charles McLane? I seem to remember when you were standing on street corners handing out pamphlets fighting for women's rights. I was so proud of you, Charles!"

"Lucinda, I will never forget your smiling face beside me, cheering until your voice was hoarse. We were going to change the world. What happened? What transformed us into sensible folks?"

"For one thing, you decided to have a sensible marriage! Was I not good enough for you? I take that back, I know she was pregnant, but did you have to be so honorable?"

"I'm sorry, Lucinda. It all turned out differently than I thought. You know she was already ill when the baby came. She needed me to be beside her. For all those years she still lived, I couldn't believe the strength she showed and the determination to be a good mother."

"You never told her?"

"Never."

"Did she believe Robert was her child?"

"She did! You know, it was a cesarean birth. She was struggling with her consciousness the whole time after the birth. I doubt if she ever noticed any difference when they brought your child in to her. She loved Robert from the moment she first saw him."

Lucky was silent.

"It must have been very hard for you," Charles said. "We loved each other, Lucinda, but it would have been impossible. I couldn't leave her at that time. You couldn't have acknowledged Robert, kept him, nor raised him alone. What a mess. What a mess."

"I would have given up everything if you would have divorced and married me. I would have been satisfied as a housewife, a stay-at-home wife in the suburbs. But I understand, Charles. It was good of you to take my child and care for him as well as you have. I guess I should be grateful to your wife too. But there is this knot—this knot right here in my gut. It's been there for twenty-five years, Charles."

"I'm sorry, Lucinda!" Charles took her in his arms to comfort her, but was surprised that he ended up kissing her on the lips. The years unraveled in him, and he was suddenly a young man again, full of idealism and love. It was a shock, a kind of time warp to be back in his youth, feeling the strength in him. He kept kissing her, and she didn't resist. The kiss felt like the continuation of one that started long ago and still had not ended.

Just then, a car pulled out from the edge of the sidewalk behind them. The car lights flooded their car through the back window and sent blinding flashes reflected in the windshield mirror. It moved very slowly alongside, and when it was exactly abreast of them, there was the flash of a camera. They both shot upright, startled by the suddenness of it. A second flash caught both their startled faces. The car raced away, turned the next corner, and was gone.

"Were you followed?" Charles asked.

"No, I don't think so."

"It looked deliberate. I can't imagine what they were after. You're not married. I'm not married. It can't be blackmail."

"What about if they are from the *Wall Street Journal*? You know, a little more scandal to add to what they printed the other day? Could it be that?"

"That's not what the *Wall Street Journal* does. It's not the kind of news that interests them."

"Maybe it's a freelancer who hopes to make a killing?"

"Why don't we move from here? Right in front of my house might have additional complications. Let's take the Palisades Parkway and stop in one of the side parking areas. I'll keep an eye out to make sure we're not followed."

They drove in silence. Why would they be followed? Who would want to take their picture, and what did they plan to do with it? There didn't seem to be any point to it. They could do whatever they wanted with the picture. If they demanded blackmail money, he would call the police. Lucky could probably do the same. It seemed like a pointless exercise. The only reason he and Lucky were meeting out of the public eye was because of her very public position at the Alliance for International Communications Incorporated and because they simply had not been meeting for so many years. Why else? Something bothered him, nagged at the back of his head. It wasn't a memory. It was more like a warning signal in an unknown code.

They pulled over into a parking spot in a side area of the Palisades Parkway. Lucky switched off the motor and turned toward him.

"I have so many questions I'd like to ask you, but first, I have to know a bit more about what you have been doing in Rio de Janeiro, because of the article in the journal the other day."

"Are you sure you don't know? We are not in public right now, nor are we meeting the press or the stockholders."

"I know you were given a very large budget to entertain royally in Brazil. Weren't you always wining and dining and entertaining royally whenever you were courting large government and corporate customers? I don't think there is anything illegal about that, Charles."

"Lucinda, you were there when I accidentally came out of the elevator on your floor. I think Graham was there as well. The subject was our contract in Rio and the fact that we were in danger of losing it to the competition. I mentioned that it would take quite a bit of money to counter what the competition was spending there to steal the contract away from us."

"I remember that. I decided we should do whatever it takes to keep the contract, and you assured me that no matter what we spent, we would make it up in the performance of the contract. Evidently, the same thing has been happening with our other contracts, and we always made a tidy profit. We didn't do anything illegal there, did we?"

"It all depends on what is legal where we work. We are talking about a basic underground economy in Brazil unacknowledged by the government or the courts but clearly understood by all businesses providing services and products in the country. In other words, without payoffs to the right people at the right time, you don't get the business. That's just how it is. If we had to do that in this country, it would be illegal. If it leaped out into the open in Brazil, everybody, including those accepting the payoffs, would cry foul, make a public spectacle of someone, and then go right on accepting payoffs."

"So we are vulnerable after all?" Lucky began to understand the truth.

"Yes. Things are changing—slowly—and we have to watch our step and not end up being the one used as a scapegoat for the whole system. In the meantime, the country needs our switching stations, and we need the business. It's a delicate matter, and I have no doubt it will have to change. It may go even deeper into the underground, or it may burst out into the public. Whoever does the bursting is just as likely to get burned as anyone else."

"Oh, Charles. What should we be doing?"

"What I don't get is why now."

"Why now?"

"Yes, why now. We've been doing this for many years. Even the very first contract we ever landed there cost us a bundle, and we made a profit. Everybody else has been doing it for years too. Why now?" Charles asked, not expecting an answer.

"Is it possible that something political is going on either in Brazil or here that involves this way of doing business? Maybe it has nothing to do with us. Maybe it's on somebody's agenda, and we're being used?"

"By whom?"

"I don't know." Lucky put her elbow on the steering wheel and rested her chin in the cup of her hand. "Can you nose around in Brazil and see what you can pick up? I understand you know everybody down there."

"Almost everybody. Yes, I can do some quiet research, but I suspect it's not down there. Too many people are benefitting from the current practice to want to make changes. I'll bet you it's someone right here in the metropolitan area. The journal is here, but I don't think it's them. They have too much to lose from a soiled reputation. Don't forget, the item was embedded in a legitimate article about the phenomenal performance of Premium Technical Products Incorporated. Maybe it's someone there that's been leaking the rumors picked up by the journal."

"You think so?"

"Do we know anyone in that company?" asked Charles.

"We can ask around. They have a reputation for being pretty ruthless."

"Is that right?"

"Yes. Don't you remember the article in *Time* magazine about the chaos over at Croton Green after they were acquired by PTP? I understand their president was forced out and two or three of the VPs left voluntarily. They were bad-mouthing the president and CEO of PTP," Lucky replied. She read the papers every morning and had an excellent memory, especially for the business news.

"Yes, I remember now. Maybe we could get one of our people to talk with one of them," Charles suggested. "Do we have any connections over there?"

"I'll find out." Lucky made a mental note for herself to follow up on this suggested action. "Maybe one of our directors. It would be easier for one of them to strike up a conversation than it would be for staff. If I remember correctly, the directors all submitted Conflict of Interest Statements listing possible conflict identities. I seem to remember Allen Fullington owned some shares of PTP. Perhaps he could do some digging for us."

They both fell silent. The night was refreshingly cool. Although they could hear the cars whizzing by on the parkway, there were enough intervening leafy trees to shield them from all the headlights. There was only one other car parked near them, and it was empty. Perhaps someone stretching their legs before the final push into the city.

"Charles?"

"Yes, Lucinda."

"Would you object if we talked about some other things?"

"You mean Robert, I suppose. It was foolish of us to wait so long. You would be proud of him. He's a fine-looking young man, gentle and intelligent." Charles explained.

"What about his social life? Does he have a girlfriend?"

"Not that I know of. He was hard hit when his mother—his other mother died just three years ago. Lucinda? Are we ever going to tell him who his real mother is?"

"How would he take that? He might not respect me—or you, for that matter. He might wonder why we substituted him for the dead baby taken from your wife. We had to do a great deal of finagling and underhanded maneuvers to make that happen. As a matter of fact, would he believe us?" Lucinda had her doubts.

"Maybe a bigger question has to do with you and me, Lucinda. Are we going to go on living like this—apart, so secretive?"

"I've thought about that many times. Every time I think maybe the time is right for us to make a clean breast of our relationship, something comes up that makes me feel we really must wait. Right now, I don't know if there will ever be a right time. What do you think, Charles?"

Charles inched over a little closer to Lucky and took her hand in his, caressing her long, artistic fingers. Two bracelets on her arm jingled with the motion. Charles looked up into her eyes glowing softly in the semidarkness of the park when he tried to explain his feelings.

"I never stopped loving you, Lucinda, even though I had much affection for my wife. After they took away her stillborn, her pain, and then her joy in receiving Robert as if it were her own, I didn't have the heart to leave her, and we did have a good, kind relationship while she still lived. I cared a great deal for her, you know. Whatever caregivers we could find needed to be relieved and managed all the time. Many a time, I had to do it all. I didn't mind, you understand. She was a good person!"

"I know, Charles," Lucky said softly. "But that was three years ago that she died. What are your feelings now? I think what I want to know is, would this be a one-of-a-kind meeting, or would we try to meet again?"

"You know what I want, Lucinda. You must know!" Charles took her hand, caressed it gently, then he pulled her into his arms and approached with another kiss. Lucky hesitated and Charles backed away. "There's something else?" he asked.

"Yes. Complications. My confidential assistant, who's been with me for three years—who knows just about everything I'm involved in—is in love with Robert." Lucky stopped and watched Charles's eyes.

"My—I mean our Robert?"

"Yes."

"He never said a word to me about any girl. Of course I've been away a great deal lately. What do you think about it?" asked Charles.

"Jolene is a wonderful girl, intelligent and lovely. I couldn't wish for anyone better for Robert." Lucky was definite.

"But—?" Charles picked up a small signal only people who care about each other would have noticed.

"She knows about all my business affairs. She doesn't know that Robert is really my son, as well as yours. She knows everything else, and what she doesn't know, she can probably guess."

"You think it very likely that if she knows, Robert will know sooner or later."

"Does Robert know what you do in your job?" Lucky asked.

"Not really. He knows that I solve problems for AIC, especially in South America."

"Don't be surprised if he finds out one day. Jolene keeps confidential all of my affairs, but she might accidentally let something out knowing Robert is your son. She might think he already knows."

"I don't want to tell him everything—unless I have to. I have never gossiped about my work with him, and I don't want to start now," Charles said.

"Don't you think he's curious? After all, you're his father. Sooner or later, he would want to know more about what you do. It might be better to hear it from you than from someone else—like the *Wall Street Journal*."

"You've a point, I'll grant you. Maybe I should start working up to it, see how curious he really is. I can't just sort of blurt it out when he isn't asking," Charles decided.

"No, I agree."

"What happened to the other question? You know, the one about you and me?" Charles asked.

"I'm sure you know I love being with you. You and I always fitted together so beautifully. I am never tense with you, never feel I'd rather be somewhere else. It's just twenty-five years have passed. I need to find my way back—or forward."

"You are the one who called us together this time." Charles touched her hand. "What's past cannot be retrieved. I think all that happened had to happen, but this could be a new chapter rather than any sort of continuation, if you know what I mean?"

"Yes, I know what you mean. I'd like that. We could sort of start up as though we had never met before. Spend some time getting to know each other. How about coming with me to my meetings in Greenwich next week? We could talk again in the car, pretend it was just business. Get my chauffeur used to the idea that I sometimes have a man in my life. Risky, but he's very loyal."

"When is that?"

"Wednesday. I'll leave early—let's say three o'clock. You could meet me in the garage or come to the office."

"Isn't that a bit of a problem? As president and CEO, you should maybe distance yourself from me. I might be blacklisted by next Wednesday." Charles showed his worry. Lines creased his forehead.

"It wouldn't help. Don't forget, you work for me. We are joined at the hip if this thing, whatever it is, blows up."

"We are almost at my house, Lucinda. When we arrive, I will get out immediately, and you should leave at once. Remember, we might still be followed."

"Yes, I will. Oh, Charles, could there still be hope for us?"

"There's always hope. Let's try to make it happen." As they stopped for a red light, Charles leaned over and kissed her, not knowing if he ever got the chance again. At this point, everything seemed fluid—uncertain, but in motion. Change was bubbling to the surface all around them.

At the house, Charles squeezed her hand one last time, opened the door wide, and leaped out and up the sidewalk to his house. The car pulled away from the curb immediately without so much as a blinking of lights or the beep of a horn. She was gone even before Charles reached the front door. Nevertheless, he stood there for a moment, savoring this new excitement in his life, wondering how it would all end. Was it possible after twenty-five years to rekindle a love that had cooled in such a complicated manner so long ago? He had an innate aversion to going backward. Whenever he walked, he always returned by another route. Retracing his steps made him feel like the first movement was a mistake, which of course it wasn't. He would rather take a new direction than double back.

This couldn't possibly be taking up where they had left off. Too much had happened in the intervening twenty-five years. Nor could it be a revival of any kind. The only way it would work for him—and for Lucinda, he thought—would be if it were something really new. They would together have to create something new—a new relationship of some kind. What a challenge! But who knows, if anybody could do it, he and Lucinda could!

*****

Charles closed and locked the front door behind him, hung his coat in the hall closet, and went to the sideboard in the dining room to pour himself a drink. He wasn't in the mood for anything strong. He felt high enough from his meeting with Lucky without any additional stimulation. He settled for a glass of white wine from the opened bottle in the refrigerator.

"Robert?" he called, hearing a slight noise from his bedroom on the ground floor of the house. "Are you here?"

"Yes, I'm here," he called out.

"Have you eaten?"

"Yes."

"I'll make myself a sandwich in the kitchen. Do you want anything?"

"I'll settle for a glass of apple juice. I'll be right out."

Charles glanced at the mail, threw out some catalogs without even looking into them, and made his way to the kitchen. He found half a loaf of whole grain bread, cut off two slices, and then put the bread knife back in the drawer. He returned the loaf to the refrigerator, found the butter, some cheese, and a heritage tomato. One slice of tomato, one slice of Swiss cheese, a little butter on the bread and he was ready to put it all together. Adding a red radish, two thin slices of cucumber, one leaf of lettuce, and a dab of mayonnaise, and he was ready to eat. Putting it all on a plate, he made his way with it to the living room, turned on the TV, leaving it on the same news station as the night before, and settled himself in the easy chair. He knew Robert preferred the sofa, although he admitted it was hard to climb out of once he settled in it.

Robert came over through the kitchen, where he found a beer instead of the apple juice, and joined his father in the living room.

"I hear you've found a girl you like," Charles announced even before Robert managed a single gulp of his beer.

"She's more than a girlfriend. I'm going to marry her pretty soon. I was going to tell you tonight, but you went out, so I waited. How did you find out?"

"Lucinda told me."

"Ah. Jolene works for Lucinda. Only she calls her Lucky. Do you know her?"

"Of course. But I don't usually find myself around her. That is, I see her almost every day, but since she's Lucinda's confidential secretary, I don't really get to know her on a daily basis. Lucinda seems to think highly of her."

"What does she say?"

"That she's nice-looking, very competent, and intelligent. That's high praise, if you ask me. How did you happen to meet?"

"Jolene had to do some research for Lucky, and since she lives out here, she decided to do it at the Fairmont University library. I went there to try to find out a little more about what you do and ran into her. She advised me to read Peter Drucker. It turned out to be good advice. Evidently, Lucky has his book on the corner of her desk and consults it frequently."

"Yes, she does." Charles bit into his sandwich, and Robert took a long gulp of his beer. It tickled his nose, and he ended up having a short sneezing fit.

"Did you find out any more about my work in the library?" Charles asked.

"Frankly, no! I already knew you solved problems. You told me that much. I did find out solving problems could mean many things. Probably different things to different people. The problem solvers in the Mafia are the assassins for the mob, and

I know that's not what you do. Is it?" Robert finished with a short laugh.

"No, never been asked to do that. I work for a pretty straight bunch of people."

"Well, I've heard different things—about your work in South America. Some of it is obviously gossip, and I don't care about that. I met someone today who's pretty high up in Premium Technical Products Incorporated—at least he says he is—who gives scholarships and grants to students. One of my friends was lucky enough to be awarded one of those grants. In return, he agreed to spy on me and you. Of course, the corporate guy never admitted that, and he would probably deny it if I asked. Nevertheless, it makes you think, wouldn't you say?"

"I certainly would say. Did you get his name?"

"I'm not sure. I thought it was something like Caldwell, but I'm not at all sure."

"That's very interesting. I'm beginning to see the light— perhaps more appropriate would be to smell a rat. Robert, did you by any chance read the *Wall Street Journal* last week? I think it was Wednesday?"

"No, Dad, you know I never read the journal."

"If you had, you would begin to see what this is all about."

"Tell me."

"The journal did a factual report on the Premium Technical Products Incorporated, highlighting its phenomenal growth and profitability. Just facts, you understand. It attributed this great track record to the leadership of one Armand Dillon. Buried in the report was a single item suggesting that Armand was tough and single-minded in his determination to reap profits, but it said there was no hint of any corruption or underhanded dealings. It went on to indicate that no hint of any misdealing was found, unlike the many rumors circulating about Lucinda Brahms and the Alliance for International Communications Incorporated. That's all it said. No further clarification!"

"Whoa! Dad! That's nasty. Is it true?"

"No, of course not! But the whole deal is pretty clever. You know why? You know what they did?"

"What?"

"They took something that is true and twisted it around in order to discredit the Alliance for International Communications Incorporated for some sinister reason of their own—which I don't know and haven't figured out yet. If I know anything about Armand, there's profit for him hiding somewhere in this maneuver."

"Can you stop him?" Robert was ready to fight.

"That's what's remarkable. They are only pointing at something called a rumor. They don't say it is true. Even if it is a bald lie, the damage is done just by mentioning it. Other media is perking up, some even misquoting the original item. Lucinda has had to call a press conference to deny the allegations."

"What did she actually do that they are twisting around?"

"Not she, Robert, me."

"Are you mentioned too?"

"No, thank God. But my involvement is sure to surface at some point. Any good reporter will be able to dig that up."

"What did you do, Dad?"

"It's a long explanation. Do you want to hear it?"

"You bet I do. If I'm going to defend you with my friends and acquaintances, I better know the truth." Robert's face was full of sympathy for his father.

"You know, Robert. I think I've underestimated what a good person you are. I mean, you're my son and I naturally love and appreciate you, but objectively viewed, even if you weren't my son, you're a really good person. I'm proud to be your father."

"Thanks, Dad."

"Well, here goes."

"Take it slow, Dad. I really want to understand."

"You probably know that AIC does a great deal of business in Latin American countries. Our largest single product is to construct, upgrade, maintain, and repair telephone switching stations, many times in developing countries but also in established current-century cultures. These are complicated projects. We generally get them operating, train local technicians, and then turn them over to the nationals, whoever it was agreed upon by contract. We call them turnkey installations. Understand?"

"Of course."

"All the work is done under a comprehensive contract with exact specifications spelled out. Part of the process includes renegotiation points when the client either selects new or different options or alters options originally selected. At every point along the way, all during construction, we have teams of contract negotiators restructuring the contract and amending the pricing and payment terms. All of that is standard practice. Everyone in the industry does that."

"Then why is there a problem?"

"There's no problem there. The problem originates much earlier in the process. It appears in the very earliest stages. At the marketing and sales procedures—getting the contract in the first place."

"OK."

"Every country in which we do business has its own culture, its own norms—its own way of doing business. When we want to do something in any country, we first have to find out how one gets something done, how one sells something. What are the local practices that may have originated decades ago and are taken for granted now? Who are the right people to contact and persuade?" Charles cleared his throat, leading up to his main point.

"I understand. Makes sense!"

"Take Brazil, for example, since we have many contracts completed and under progress there. In order to secure a contract, we have to meet with dozens of different department heads. Even to get an appointment, we need to get past a gatekeeper. I won't mention any names. You don't need to know."

Charles paused. He took another bite of his sandwich. Robert took another beer out of the refrigerator, opened it, and reseated himself at the coffee table. He was obviously very interested and listened intently to every word.

"One of my many jobs is to make sure that the gatekeeper and every single official in the chain of decision-makers is favorably inclined toward our company. We present all sorts of credentials, contract process documents and assurances both written and spoken or recorded. That's all natural and done everywhere by anyone wanting to do business in that country.

In Brazil, we find it is customary to do a monetary contribution as a way of gaining favor. It has to be done with finesse. It is considered to be illegal, but unless we do it, someone else gets the contract who does it. This puts us in a quandary. In the US, we would be prosecuted for illegal practices. In Brazil, we either do it or we don't get the business. The funny thing is that every competitor also does it, and I don't think the amount determines who gets the contract. The successful bidder is probably the one who does it with the greatest skill."

"Dad, what you're telling me is that we're bribing the officials to get the business."

"*Bribing* is the word we use in our culture, and I think it is an accurate description. In other cultures that word *bribery* does not have the same moral coloring. They, in some countries, consider it normal to secure favorable responses. It is always a moral dilemma to decide whether one fits into the reality or whether one tries to force one's own morality on another culture. Governments often try to force their reality on others. Oftentimes, individual groups try the same approach. Businesses, generally speaking, are not ideology-driven. They tend to accept local ideology and stick to business, selling goods and services."

"So it all kind of happens under the table?"

"Way under."

"I won't ask you for details, but is that what this rumor business is all about?

"Yes."

"But who is releasing the rumors?" Robert asked.

"That's the sixty-four-dollar question. Who indeed."

"Is it somebody that hopes to gain from your disgrace? I mean, public embarrassment?"

"We think it must be. But until you told me of the grant made by PTP to your friend, we had no idea who it might be. Now it looks as if PTP might be behind the rumors."

"Can they do that?"

"There is nothing illegal about stating a fact."

"Even if it is untrue?"

"No matter what it is. All they are saying is that there are rumors. We can only claim that the rumors are false. We can't deny their existence. The act of denying them also contributes to their spread. In no time, the rumors are everywhere being denied and yet taken seriously nevertheless," Charles explained.

"I think that's dirty pool, Dad. What can we do?"

"We? We do nothing. You stay out of it." Charles was adamant.

"But I may have inadvertently given substance to the rumor without knowing what they would do with it. How about if we counter with another rumor that contains the truth? Wouldn't that be a possible strategy?" asked Robert.

"Possibly. Right now we think it would be better not to add to the noise. Sometimes, such rumors run their course and then peter out or are eclipsed by other news. Of course, if the feds decide to get involved, that would be more serious, and we would have to try to defend ourselves for doing something that is basically indefensible. We'd be in a battle we couldn't win. That's why we're staying quiet at the moment."

"OK. You know best. I'd be inclined to fight back, but maybe that's because I don't know enough or don't have anything to lose—which you do."

"You do too."

"Me? How so?"

"You're forgetting two things. First, you are attending Fairmont University, and we'd both like to see you graduate. Secondly, your girlfriend is the confidential secretary for the president and chief executive officer of AIC. Given your relationship with her, it would be difficult to prove she didn't know anything about all this. It would also be difficult to prove Lucinda didn't know anything about it. It looks like the four of us are entangled whether we like it or not."

"What do we do?"

"Right now? Sit tight. Don't say or do anything. Let our legal department and strategic advisors deal with it. Whatever you do, don't say anything to the press or PTP people."

"I certainly will say something." Robert leaned forward on the sofa.

"What? And why?"

"I feel obligated to say that you're my father and you would never do anything unlawful or unethical. That's all I would say, but that's what I have to say!"

"You're a good man, Robert McLane. I hope none of this splashes onto your doorstep."

"Thanks, Dad. I'm glad we had this conversation. I think I understand it all much better as a result."

"Robert, I've let you in on some confidential stuff. I hope I've done the right thing. I know it's already been quite a lot to swallow, but I am afraid there's more."

"More? More you haven't told me?"

"More I am very reluctant to tell you, but I'm afraid given what is going on, you better know it from me rather than from someone else."

"Now you're scaring me, Dad. What is it?"

"It's about your mother."

Just then something crashed through the living room window facing the street. Glass splinters spattered the walls and furniture. A small shard landed in the back of Robert's neck. Blood immediately trickled down into his collar, leaving it red and wet. Robert slapped his hand over the spot and inadvertently pushed the glass shard deeper into the wound and cut his hand.

Charles jumped to his feet, saw the damage on Robert's neck, ran into the kitchen to find a towel, and rushed back. He placed the towel on Robert's neck and wiped the area around the glass splinter so he could see it better.

"How do you feel?" he asked.

"I'm all right. Mostly surprised, I guess. How does it look?"

"Like a damn flesh wound that's going to hurt but not kill you. Hold still while I pull out the piece of glass sticking in your neck."

"OK."

"Here goes." Charles got a firm grip on the end with his fingernails and yanked it out, immediately pressing the towel back on to the wound. "We'll have to see a doc. You may need stitches. It looks like it missed the artery, but close—too close. I don't like it."

"What was it?"

"I hope not a bomb!" Charles moved closer to the window and began searching the floor. He recalled feeling something had crashed through the glass and landed on the floor somewhere. He discovered a large round object wrapped in cloth lying beside one of the standing lamps. Carefully, he approached and looked it over before touching it. It had an irregular shape, more like a stone rather than a box or something man-made. He picked it up and unwrapped the cloth. It was a stone and something else. A flat piece of paper. On it were cut-out letters, such as one might find in the headline of a magazine. It read simply, UNETHICAL MANIPULATOR!

Who would put together a phrase like that? It doesn't look like the usual type of activist. It wasn't a known cliché. It apparently was invented by someone unconnected with any social aberrations Charles was familiar with. He'd never heard anything like it before.

Their conversation momentarily in abeyance, Charles got Robert into the car and drove him off to Emergency for treatment. He decided not to call the police until he had a chance to talk it over with Graham and Benning. It looked very much as though matters were beginning to get rougher. Somebody was really out to get them, but why?

*****

In his office on the second floor of the brown brick warehouse that served as headquarters for the Premium Technical Products Incorporated, Armand had summoned Calder and Cliff for an update on their projects. Both had considerable progress to report.

"Let's have it already digested. I just want where we are, not all the scrambling," Armand ordered. Cliff opened a green file folder and was the first to report.

"You'll be pleased to know that Fullington and at least two other directors of the Alliance for International Communications Incorporated are leaning in our direction. They did not see enough increase in their shares and appear hungry for some improved profit."

"All right, but what about their relationships to Brahms? Are they loyal, or is profit a higher priority? Are they likely to cave in?"

"I can't tell for sure. Basically they are loyal but, I think, can be bought. Brahms has a way of nurturing loyalty. I think we might say everybody loves her," Cliff answered.

"Even with all the rumors? The article in the *Wall Street Journal*—good work on that, Cliff. That showed real finesse." Armand didn't wait for Cliff to acknowledge the complement. "As a rule, scandal drives share price down, and it has in this case too, but notice how it bounced back up to within a point of where it was last week. Loyalty may defeat us in the end. Humans are a strange mixture. It doesn't make any sense. Greed should top love every time, yet here, it is wavering."

"Brahms has collected some staunch supporters around her over the last three years. It is amazing how they stick to her even when the evidence mounts that she knew all about the bribes in Rio de Janeiro. It's going to take a lot more to break those strong ties," Cliff answered.

"What have you found out, Calder?"

"The McLane kid is in tight with his dad. In spite of the bad publicity and the efforts of his friends to discredit big business, he appears to understand what and why his dad has acted the way he did. I'm afraid the attack on his home was a mistake. It may have disclosed our hand in the whole sequence of events, and it may all backfire on us."

"So the boy knows everything and isn't in our court after all?" Armand inquired.

"That's right."

"I don't get it. He was well on his way to denouncing his dad for his dealings in Brazil, and now he's turned around. Something's not right. Are we using the wrong strategy? Something's not working, and I want results. I damn well want results. Now. Not soon, but now. We need to strike before the economy turns to work against us. All the macro conditions are correct for us to succeed. It can only be something we are not doing right." Armand had a speck of foam in the corner of his mouth, which he wiped away with the back of his left hand.

"For one thing, when Evans threw—"

"I don't want to hear anything about that."

"All right, but the boy was hurt, and that seemed to have reconciled the two. They were heading for a collision when the incident reunited them. It was a blunder on our part. We should not resort to violence," Calder exclaimed.

"I'll tell you what we should not do!" Armand shouted so loudly that the echoes rattled the window panes. He was standing behind his desk, leaning over the top, supported by his two fists, glaring at his two faithful servants. "What we shouldn't do is bungle the job. It was supposed to be a simple warning. It was only to suggest the violence that was still to come. The idea was to introduce fear, not to bundle them together against me!"

Armand sank back into his chair. His face gradually returned to its normal gray coloring. He had clamped his jaw together and was deep in thought. Slowly, a flicker of light returned to his eyes, and a grim smile made it clear he had his next steps decided.

"On top of the scandal, we now need to remove the head of this beast," Armand murmured quietly, but out loud so that both Calder and Cliff heard. They looked at each other and tried to guess at what he meant.

"What beast are you considering decapitating?" Calder was the practical one and assumed the subject had been changed and they were moving toward a new project. Cliff was more intuitive and could quickly tie the topics together.

"You're thinking it might be the last straw for the directors and also for the small knot of supporters. On top of the scandal, they have little choice, no alternative but to take up your offer of help?"

It dawned on Calder what beast they were talking about. He was shocked. "You're not thinking—"

"I believe Cliff is beginning to understand what has to happen next." Armand leaned forward to clarify his thoughts. "This time, I want Cliff to take the lead. You help him, Calder, with Evans. He's already in so deep, he should be easy to persuade. I want no tie-in to either of you or to me. This time there can be no blunders. It has to be creatively planned. Do you get me, Cliff? You see that it happens totally in the dark and without any connecting ties. Let me know when you have it all planned. Better yet, let me know when I can read about it in the paper." Armand uttered a brief cackle that took both Cliff and Calder by surprise. He had never before, ever, laughed even this little imitation of a laugh before in their entire time with him at Premium Technical Products Incorporated.

"Armand!" Calder shifted his weight in the chair and edged nearer the desk. "I don't like this. That's a beautiful and very popular woman we're harming. She has many friends, and they are incredibly loyal. I have a strong feeling that—"

"Feelings!" Armand interrupted him. "No feelings! This is modern times. Feelings don't have anything to do with it. Ever since I joined this organization, I have made it abundantly clear that we are operating on a pure, unadulterated rational basis. You may indulge in feelings all you want, Calder, but do not let them pollute your intellect. If you have something smarter to propose, something more clever, out with it."

"No, I understand the rationale. Chaos usually results when there is trouble and no leadership. Chaos is an advantage for us. I clearly see your intention. I'm not sure just how we would manage that without damaging our own cause. It would have to be done so cleverly that a slipup is almost unavoidable. The more clever something is, the more complicated it usually gets, and complications often produce error." Calder spoke from experience.

"That's where you and Cliff come in. You both have brains enough for overcoming any obstacles. It's a question of using every available brain cell to advantage. Pure intellect! Use it! Leave feelings for the lesser people." Armand set his jaw and stared them both down. They had heard his speech already many times and had not been able to fault the logic in it.

Armand took note of the uneasiness remaining in Calder's facial expression. It meant he would have to be watched, possibly corrected or supported. He'd have to keep it in mind as they progressed through this more challenging stage of the strategy he had in mind.

"One other thing, Calder. You've had the connection with Evans on this. Work closely with Cliff on the exact methodology. We don't ever want to see him again after all this is over. Get me?"

"Yes, sir."

"Yes."

"To be quite clear," Armand leaned forward even more, sending his awesome psychic power in waves over them, "I want this all to be done so that Ms. Brahms is seriously discredited and loses her grip on her remaining friends and directors. Do we understand each other?"

"Yes."

"Is everything clear?" Armand stared at them both.

"Yes."

"I believe it won't be very long," Armand began, satisfied with their acknowledgments, "before we see one of the biggest mergers in this industry—actually several industries. It will be my first step toward a new kind of prominence and acceptance. It should bring us a new horde of converts. I know I can easily triple the profitability of Alliance for International Communications Incorporated and delight the shareholders. In the end, I know all they want is profit. I can see it in the eyes of the multitude. With profit, I've got the world by the tail. Good work, boys! Get to it and give me results!" Armand leaned back in his chair and allowed a grimace to indicate his approval of the two loyal servants.

Cliff and Calder removed themselves. They met briefly in the hall before dispersing to their separate offices. Cliff felt himself to be in charge even though he was the younger of the two and Calder was twice as experienced in this field.

"What do you think we need to do to entice Evans? He'll need to do exactly what we tell him," Cliff said.

"Money, lots of it, and an escape route is my guess."

"Can we afford to let him escape? Won't he be a continuous threat to us as long as he is alive?" Cliff eyed Calder. Neither one of them wanted to answer that question.

"Let's take it one step at a time, OK?" Calder suggested.

"Yeah."

"Let me think it all over. This has to be good. How about we have breakfast together tomorrow morning?" Calder proposed.

"Right. At the Tavern? Nobody will be there then. We'll have the place to ourselves."

They agreed. This was the biggest job they had ever been assigned. It was exhilarating and also frightening. All thoughts of competing or challenging each other for the leadership disappeared. The project was so enormous—so delicate! They both knew without saying a word that it would take all their intelligence and courage, working as a team to satisfy Armand Dillon, president and CEO of Premium Technical Products Incorporated.

CHAPTER ELEVEN

The Opposition

Horst and Benning made their way together to the coffee shop. Benning had not mentioned why they were meeting. He acted very secretive. His face was serious. They didn't share much humor, so Horst was not particularly worried, but he was curious. It wasn't often that his boss just said, "Drop everything and come with me."

Both the human and vehicular traffic was so heavy on Madison Avenue, they found themselves dodging in and out and separated from each other most of the way. Even though they were walking at a good clip, Horst found a moment to ask, "What's the secrecy?"

"Wait. You'll find out," Benning called over his shoulder.

They arrived at the coffee shop. Benning looked around and saw Graham at one of the tables in the far corner. It was a table that was separated by an artificial flowering bush in a pot. It apparently provided the privacy Graham needed. Horst became even more curious about the nature and purpose of this meeting. When they were seated, they ordered coffee; Graham was already eating an English muffin and his coffee needed warming up.

"Thanks, both of you, for coming. I've got to talk with some friendly folks. You two, I know, are straight and honest and connected with Lucky. I think she's in trouble."

"I do too," said Benning before Horst could speak. "I can feel it in the air. There's something going on behind the scenes that's sending ominous vibes through the whole company."

"Well, maybe not the whole company but at least the egg." Graham sent his famous short laugh through the coffee shop, stopping all other conversation momentarily.

"I'm especially worried about the board. At the last board meeting, Bruce and I needed to discuss something with Ralph during the break. We met just briefly around the refreshment table in the lounge. We couldn't help notice how the various directors were clustered in small isolated and animated discussion groups. Some of it was heated. I couldn't hear everything, of course. I'm not a director. I kept hearing two names repeated again and again, sometimes quite loudly. That's what I want to mention here."

"Which names?"

"Lucinda Brahms was one I heard repeated. That would not be surprising. The other was Armand Dillon! That was a shocker."

"Oh?"

"Who's Armand Dillon?" Horst interrupted.

"You should know, Horst. PTP was one of the companies you interviewed for a job before you came to us."

"Oh yes. I remember the company. It was in a dingy warehouse-type building on the west side. Somebody interviewed me in a large open work space. There were machines going and people calling to each other over the noise. I never met any Armand Dillon."

"Few of us have. Most of what I know is hearsay. He is the ruthless leader of Premium Technical Products Incorporated. His main purpose, they say—no scratch that—his only purpose is to make money for himself presumably, but mostly for his stockholders. His employees are rumored to be poorly paid except for the few close to him. The stockholders love him because he gives them the kind of return they hunger for. His track record is phenomenal."

"Why are the directors talking about him? Oh no! Don't tell me. I've gone through a merger once, and it's no fun if it isn't friendly, especially for people like us that often represent additional overhead," Benning contributed his concern.

"I doubt if it's that far yet, but because of the two names being mentioned, and because I know that Armand would only consider such a merger if it involved an acquisition by him and included his escalation to top dog, I am assuming Lucky may be in for it."

"Where is Lucky, these days? She seems distracted and often out of the office. We used to meet in her office, the hallway, the elevator, or wherever at least two or three times a week. Is she OK?"

"As far as I know." Graham frowned. "Come to think of it, she has seemed a bit distant, as though her mind were on something else."

"Do you think she knows what's going on?" Benning asked.

"She has to. She's not on the board, but she's in the meetings most of the time."

"Was she at the last meeting?"

"I didn't see her during the few minutes I was in the lounge. That's not unusual, as the board has lots of business that doesn't directly involve her. Fullington is currently chair. I never liked him. He's wealthy in his own right, but still hungry for more. I think *greedy* would be a good word to describe his attitude. From what I could tell, he seemed to be leading several of the director groups and urging them to do something in a loud voice. Whatever he's after must involve more money one way or another."

"What can we do about it?" Benning wondered.

"Well, first of all, I wanted both of you to know about this and be awake to what's going on." Graham looked from one to the other.

"I'm certainly with you, Graham, on this issue. How about you, Horst?"

"I'm the new kid on the block, and my support may not matter much," Horst answered.

"Do we all realize that with someone like Armand Dillon, you are either on his side or you are an enemy and probably end up on the outside?" Benning stated his conclusion.

"We don't have to walk around with signs on our backs, nor do we have to proclaim our allegiance in loud voices. I think the main thing is to stick together, know that we can count on each other." Graham was very serious.

"Three Musketeers?" Horst laughed lightly.

"Exactly, but I think we need to be a bit more crafty. We can probably do the most good if we keep our true feelings hidden—at least for now."

"What can we do that's a little more proactive?" Benning asked.

"I think keeping our eyes and ears open and staying in touch with each other—you know, sharing what any of us might learn," Horst suggested.

"That's important! I agree." Graham thought some more while the other two watched him. "I'll try to warn Lucky. I don't want her to panic. Not at this time. It would play right into Armand Dillon's hands. I just want her to know there is a threat to be taken seriously and also that she has friends."

"Good thought!" Horst agreed. "Do we have any connections inside at PTP Corp.?"

"No, I don't. But maybe Charles can help us there. He has collided with that bunch a couple of times in Latin America."

"I know Charles!" Horst offered. "He consulted me once concerning his boy's opinions about big business and ethics."

"That's right. He's at the hub of all this difficulty. Do you both know that he was the one sent to Rio with a big petty cash budget to make sure we got the switching station contract? That item in the journal buried in the press release from PTP that accuses Lucky of misdealing in Rio seemed to be aware of what Charles was doing down there. He might actually be down there still right now."

"I'll see what I can do."

"I think you're not supposed to know anything more than what was in the journal. Any way you can dig around without giving us away for breaking the confidentiality aspect? Listen,

Horst, I think maybe you shouldn't be talking with him about it after all. I'll find him and make sure we're still friends—friends enough to count on his support. I believe he's in tight with Lucky. I've seen them clustered together in conversation, and I believe they have known each other before Lucky took over the presidency," Graham said.

"OK. Let me know if I can be of any help, and please don't leave me in the dark at any point. If I'm going to stick my neck out, I'd like it to be in broad daylight and not with my eyes closed either."

Benning reminded him that they saw each other every day and whatever he knew would be passed on immediately. For a moment, the three sat in silence. Graham had finished his english muffin, all three cups of coffee were empty except for small smears of coffee stain. Benning tilted the cup toward himself to make absolutely sure there was none left for him to drink. Graham rose first and left. Benning and Horst waited a moment, paid the check, and left to return to the office.

Madison Avenue was no different than before. How so many people and so many cars could all converge on a single geographical area was a mystery. Furthermore, moving uptown now seemed to be against the flow of traffic. Avoiding collisions while moving with some speed proved difficult. Neither of them noticed the black limousine leaving the curb and slowly inching along beside the parked cars until a few impatient beeping of horns attracted their attention. The limousine sped away uptown, crossing a yellow light in the process.

*****

"Why am I doing this? Remind me again," the scruffy looking young man requested. He had grease monkey written all over him. His fingernails were black, and his hands matched them beautifully. He wore a short ponytail tied up with a golden ribbon. The beard that scratched his face clamored for attention. He probably slept in these clothes, but certainly, nobody would want to view the condition of his sheets and blankets.

"Just do what I tell you and then forget what I said. You don't even know me. Just be sure you keep it that way. I'll pay you in cash, and I don't want you asking any questions or nosing around in this garage for information. You work while I'm here to watch you, and you go home when I leave you—or wherever you roost." Evans added as a sneering correction. "Do you understand what I'm saying? For once and for all?"

"Yeah! Yeah! I get ya!"

Evans shifted over to the corner in the garage and attached himself to a small shortwave radio using what looked like earmuffs. He monkeyed with the dials a bit and then listened intently. The boy smirked and began working on the green Buick, a late model covered in scratches, but without any dents.

Picking up an assembly of iron pipes welded together in the rough shape of a seat enclosure, he decided he better check again before installing it. He ambled over to where Evans was sitting carrying the iron contraption with him.

"Heh!" he yelled at Evans to get his attention.

Evans removed his earphones and turned around to investigate the noise.

"Now what?" he asked.

"Are you sure you want it this heavy? It will put quite a strain on the engine, to say nothing of the brakes."

"Yeah! Just do it!"

"Ya know," the kid sneered at him, "you think you're fooling me, but I know what you're up to!"

"You what?" Evans half-rose in anger from his seat.

"Don't get yourself in an uproar. I aint' gonna tell nobody."

"So, what have you figured out in that greasy brain of yours, eh?" Evans snarled at him.

"Do you have any idea how many cars I've outfitted like this? They usually don't need this kind of weight. Oh yeah! I've a dozen or more. I've even done one for my dad when he decided to use his ole car for drag racin'. You can't fool me."

Evans reached out and grabbed the boy by the shirt collar and brought his face right up to his own when he snarled again. "You tell a soul, and you can kiss your money good-bye along with most of your face."

"I ain't gonna tell. Honest. I don't care what you do with it as long as you pay me. That's all I ask."

Evans let him go but watched him slowly slink back to the car, dragging the heavy contraption with him. Then he had another idea.

"Wait a minute!" he called out and followed him to the Buick. "Why are you worried about the weight? What did you say?"

"Well, this is the heaviest piping I've seen ever used. Most of the other jobs used half the weight. I figured you must be planning something reckless. I thought maybe you were so eager to win that you're going to risk crashing into a lot of cars, and you don't want to be hurt doing it. That's what I figured. The only other thing—"

"That's enough thinking for today! I'm not used to this kind of thing. To tell the truth, I'm a little chicken. I just don't want to get hurt if I happen to end up crashing. That's all there's to it. Now just give me all the protection you can. OK?"

"Yeah, sure. Don't worry, I'll make it so tight nothing can 'appen to you, even if it's dead-on!"

"Thanks. You're a good kid, and I'll pay you well, you'll see!"

The boy worked diligently, and by evening, he called over for Evans to inspect the car. He was obviously proud of his work.

"See how snug this fits? You'll be here, and no matter how many times you roll over, these will hold. Just keep your head down—hunched so you don't ram into any of the cross braces. I've removed all the glass. You see I've substituted plexy plastic in all the windows, including the windshield. If you hit so hard that they pop out, it won't get you. I also installed this special door fixture. It will hold the door closed while you're driving, but it won't jam on you. If you gotta get out, just ram this red bar back and lift this new latch. The door should pop right open, but only when you want it to."

"Nice job, kid. Nice job."

Evans walked around the car inspecting it minutely—as though his life depended on its safety. He nodded, a satisfied look on his face. Then he turned to the boy.

"You forgot one thing," he said.

"What?"

"The license."

The boy laughed lopsidedly and hurried around the car to the rear license plate.

"Watch!" he commanded. With one swoosh of his arm, the plate came off, and underneath was a jumble of letters and numbers resembling a license.

"Oh, good job!" Evans was pleased. The boy was puzzled.

"What do you want that for? Don't you want people to know when you win?"

"Secret," he said. "If my wife finds out I'm racing, she'll kill me!"

The two laughed.

Evans gave the boy $500 in small bills and then hung on to his hand, squeezing the fingers together hard.

"Now remember, I never saw you. I don't know who you are. You were never here. You never did any of this work. I never paid you."

"Right."

"Where did you get this money?"

The kid recited his speech. "The minute I get home, I break it up in small batches and hide it in at least ten different places. Nobody will know how much I got or where I got it."

"Right. What are you then going to do with this money?"

"I thought I would buy me—"

"No, you don't! You don't buy anything for at least a month and then only a few bills at a time. These are all unmarked, used bills, but nevertheless, we're not taking any chances. Right?"

"Right."

"Here's an extra twenty you can spend right away, no risk. I got it in change from a store far from here," Evans confided in him.

"Thanks."

"Now disappear. Get lost. Vamoose!"

In a flash, the boy was gone into the night. Evans stayed with the car, inspecting every element of its construction as though his life depended on it. He sat in the driver's seat. It felt confined, but safe. All around him, the iron pipes held him in place. He might sustain some bruises and lacerations, but it would keep him alive.

He experimented with the door latch, admired how it held firm until he released it with the red iron bar. He knocked on every pane of glass with his knuckle to hear the thump of shatterproof plastic. With a deep sigh, he relinquished the seat, knowing he had done everything possible to survive the accident he had planned so tediously.

He wondered who it was at PTP that had called him and made all the arrangements. It wasn't Calder. He'd recognize that deep voice. This was a calm, even-toned voice he had never heard before. It may even have been disguised. He knew that using different types of cover on the mouthpiece of a phone gave a varied pitch to a voice. Each time there was a voice contact, it sounded just a shade differently. This was somebody very smart. He could almost hear the intelligence streaming through the clipped words.

He would be getting the final instructions this evening. He had demanded a carefully guaranteed escape route. They had agreed to his price. He was prepared to go down in the negotiations, but it wasn't necessary. Arrangements for picking up the final payment were exquisite. They obviously wanted him gone as fast as possible. What a lot of trouble to go through. He wondered what the real purpose of the accident was. They were very specific! No deaths! That's right, no deaths. So what was the purpose?

Evans shook his head, slammed shut the car door, checked around to see nothing was left that could identify him. He raised and then lowered the garage door and locked it. He was ready. When the final instructions came, he would be ready!

*****

Lucky assembled her papers, tucked them carefully into her shoulder valise, and folded her coat over her left arm. She looked around the office, fondly noticing all the special touches she had established to make it homey. She lingered, almost as though this might be the last time she ever saw it. You never know she thought smiling to herself. Who could tell what life has to offer next? In time, we are very clear about the past. Yesterday is known to us. Tomorrow is a complete mystery. She stopped herself from thinking about the future any further. It was time to go.

Just then, the door to her office opened, and Jolene hurried in, apologizing as she rushed to her desk.

"I forgot my bag," she said wonderingly. "I never forget my bag! I would never leave the office without it. I can't understand it. I don't believe I have ever done it before in all these years. Why did I do such a stupid thing?"

"It's all right, Jolene. If that's the worst thing you ever do in your life, you can consider yourself lucky and fortunate."

"I always thought of you as the lucky one!" Jolene laughed. "I'll get right out of your way."

Lucky locked her desk, using the only key to it except for the one Jolene kept in her desk. Now it was time to hurry. Her chauffeur was waiting in the downstairs garage. She was sure that Charles would be on time. At the door, she turned once more to look around when the phone rang. Instinctively, she stepped back to her desk, but Jolene got to it before her.

"It's Charles," she said.

"Thank you." Lucky took the receiver while Jolene gathered her things again and started for the door. Then she paused, wondering if Lucky might still need her for anything related to this late call.

"Hello?" a familiar voice reached Lucky through the receiver.

"Is that you, Charles? Where are you?"

"I'm just around the corner in a phone booth. I'll be there in two minutes." Charles paused as though he had more to say, and Lucky did not hang up.

"Is it all right with you if I bring Robert? He and I have had a good talk. I think it is time he met you and knew who you are in his life."

Lucky was thoughtful. How would Robert take to this new knowledge? Would he believe them? Would he be angry with what they had done? Maybe he would be angry that they never told him before. After all, he was now a grown man. Why had they kept it from him all these years? Some aspects of this secret may be difficult to explain!

"What will he think of us?" Lucky wondered.

"I don't know, but I think it is time we found out. He's a fine human being, and I believe a forgiving one at that." Charles sounded sure of that.

"What do you think we should do?" Lucky leaned on his opinion.

"I think we cannot delay any longer. I have a feeling we are going to need each other and all secrets hiding in the dark must now be brought out into the light. I feel the urgency, Lucinda."

"All right, Charles. I believe in you!" After a moment's pause and a sudden instinctive impulse she continued with this new thought. "Charles? I suddenly thought . . . maybe Jolene, who's right here with me, could come along if she doesn't mind."

"I don't know, Lucinda. This is all a bit delicate for you, for Robert, even for me."

"I have the feeling the two young people are really close and it might be a help. Maybe it's time for all of us to step out into each other's lives and explore what there is to explore."

"Sounds kind of risky to me . . . but . . . well, I don't know. I guess I started all this opening up business. Oh hell. Why not."

"I'll ask her."

Lucky returned the receiver to its cradle, hovered over it as though it were a caring thing, and then shifted her valise. She saw that Jolene was still there waiting for her.

"How would you like to accompany me to this conference in Connecticut—at least on the trip up?"

"Well, I hadn't planned on this. I didn't bring any clothes or anything. Is it important?" Jolene sounded worried. "I had a possible date with Robert this evening. I was just waiting to hear from him."

"You're in luck. He's coming along with his father. All four of us will be together in the limo."

"In that case, I'd be delighted to come."

"I thought so." Lucky smiled. "We can pick up whatever you need in Connecticut."

"Don't worry, Robert will take care of me," Jolene said with absolute confidence.

They both picked up their belongings and moved toward the door. This time Lucky did not pause but opened it and passed through in the direction of the elevators.

When the chauffeur saw them coming, he jumped out of the limo and hurried to open the door for them.

"Let's wait a minute. Charles and his son will be joining us on the ride up to Connecticut. We're becoming a crowd."

"As you wish, miss." He reached to take the valise from her, but she pulled it back.

"I'll hold on to this. I may need it on the way up."

"As you wish, miss."

After Lucky and Jolene had seated themselves in the forward-facing seat of the limo, the chauffeur closed the door and returned to the driver's side when Charles and Robert approached. He recognized Charles and assumed the young man with him was his son. Once more, he jumped out like the well-trained chauffeur that he was.

"Ev'ning, Mr. McLane. Ms. Brahms and Jolene are in the car waiting for you."

"Thank you."

Without waiting for the chauffeur, Charles and Robert each opened opposite sides of the limo and climbed in. Robert sat facing Jolene on the right side of the car while Charles took the seat opposite Lucky. As soon as they were settled in, the limo inched forward and began the ride to Connecticut.

"Robert, I'd like you to meet Lucinda Brahms," Charles said.

"I'm so glad to meet you." Lucky took his hand and held it briefly in her own. "I've heard so much about you, I feel as if I've known you for many years already."

"Yes. Dad has spoken a great deal about you too. Dad? I'd like you to meet Miss . . . Jolene, what is your family name? You never told me." They all laughed happily.

"Jolene Senter."

"I'm so glad to meet you." Charles meant it. Robert surveyed them all. He was in awe that they should suddenly be all together in a car, facing each other.

"Now that we all know each other and have been polite and all that, do all of you realize what a remarkable thing this is?" Robert said. "This was not planned! We fell together . . . kind of . . . without prior knowledge, and here we are . . . assembled as if by design." Robert sounded as if he couldn't quite believe how it happened.

Charles was more of a realist and wanted to reason it out. "Well, to begin with, I asked Robert if he could join us, and then Lucinda—"

"I know all that, Dad."

"You have to understand, Charles, that your son has intuition. He senses things," Lucky said with a touch of admiration.

"You are so right!" said Jolene. "The first time we met, he told me we were going to get married."

"The second time. You remember it was at the George Washington Restaurant that I was sure," Robert corrected her. "You still haven't accepted my proposal!"

"We agreed to wait for the right time. Now just be your patient, intuitive self, Robert," Jolene said as she held his hand.

"I hope we'll be among the first to know if you do," demanded Charles. Then, smiling, he took Jolene's hand. "I'm really glad to know you. I know that Lucinda thinks the world of you and has a great deal of affection for you. I'm looking forward to getting to know you in the time ahead of us. My son has more or less kept you as a secret to spring on his old father when he least expects it."

Lucky laughed at Robert's embarrassment, and Charles smiled and was about to cover for Robert.

"He is charming, just as you said, Charles. I'm glad you brought him along." Lucky was quick to put them all at ease. "Tell me all about yourself. You are at Fairmont University?"

The trip progressed smoothly, and so did the conversation. They covered history, biography, a considerable amount of chemistry and psychology in the process. As they neared the end of Riverside Drive, Lucky rolled down the glass partition between them and the driver and called to him.

"What do you think, Tom? Can we take the Saw Mill River Parkway instead of the New England Thruway? There might be less traffic, and it's so much the nicer ride."

"If you like," the chauffeur answered. "Do we have the time?"

"I think so."

Lucky closed the partition and eased back into her seat. She thought it might be time to enter new conversational territory.

"Your father and I, Robert, have known each other for many years," she began.

"Yes, I know," Robert said. "I think ever since you became the president of AIC."

"Oh my!" she murmured. "Even before that."

"Oh?" Robert turned toward his dad. "I didn't know that."

"Yes," Charles was ready to stab at the truth. "Lucinda and I knew each other even before I knew your mother."

"That's more than twenty-five years," exclaimed Robert.

"I knew your father when he was about your age, didn't I, Charles? Believe it or not, we loved each other before he married your mother."

Robert turned his head to look at his father. He seemed puzzled, not astonished or amazed, just puzzled. Instinctively, he reached across the aisle and held Jolene's hand as if for comfort. She was quick to respond, sensing that something important was about to happen. Charles felt it was time for him to speak.

"Society had different values at that time, Robert. I think the world has become more tolerant than it was then. It's for the better—at least in some aspects. Lucinda and I had been going together when your mother and I were expected by both our families to marry. There were complications. To do the honorable thing required that we marry quickly. Your mother was already ill. We thought she might pull through, and she did for some time—actually twenty years before she died, as you know. What you may not know is that your mother had a child that was stillborn, maybe because of her illness or maybe it was just how it was. Who knows? At any rate, I think you should know now that your mother wasn't really your mother."

"What are you telling me?" Robert leaned forward. Jolene felt his hand tighten in hers. She held firm.

"I'm telling you that your mother did have a child, but it wasn't you. Her child did not live. It was stillborn. Your mother would have been miserable if she knew. I never told her that her own child never lived. She welcomed you into her heart as if you were her own."

"I'm trying to get it straight, Dad. Are you telling me my mother's child was dead at birth, and you gave me to her as a substitute? A surrogate son . . . me?"

"Well . . . sort of . . . I mean, your mother was already ill. I was thinking mostly of her, you understand. You needed a home . . . I couldn't find a better home for you than what we could offer. We loved you!"

"But . . . then who was my . . . Oh. Now I see." Robert looked askance at Lucky. "I was your child? Didn't you want me?"

"I did, but in those days, an unwed mother was considered a tramp, unfit for proper society. I couldn't have kept you. It would have been very hard for me and even worse for you. I did the next best thing. I gave you to half of your biological family—your father. It hurt—hurt badly—but it seemed like the only thing to do, especially when your other mother's child died, and she was already feeling so poorly. It made me feel better to know that she would love you, your father would love you . . . and I . . . well. That's just how it was. I did what seemed best. I hope you are willing to forgive me."

"Why did you let me live twenty-five years without telling me?"

"I'm sorry. It was for the best. We thought many times to tell you, but the moment never seemed right, either for you or for us."

"Us?"

"Yes, us."

Lucky reached across the aisle and took his hand. "Try to understand," she said. "Your father and I were lovers. Yes. Ours was a special love that endured all kinds of obstacles and surprises. It turned out I was pregnant at a time of turmoil in my life, and your father's life and in your mother's. There is no way I could have kept you, taken care of you, and claimed you openly as my own. It was a time when what I did was considered shameful and evil. I did not consider it evil. I considered you a blessing, a treasure to be nurtured and cared for. Your father, who is your real father, would be good to you. I knew that. I knew it with absolute certainty. There was never any doubt in my mind that giving you to him and your mother was the best thing for all of us—the best thing to do in the eyes of God."

Lucky fell silent, and Charles remained quiet. The limo moved gently along the parkway, almost gracefully taking the curves, rolling over the smooth pavement. A thoughtful silence pervaded the atmosphere of the limo.

"I hardly know what to think," Robert admitted.

"What do you feel? Are you angry with me?" Lucky asked.

"Honestly?"

"Yes. We in this car all love each other. Honesty is the only way."

"I'm surprised at myself," Robert admitted. "I can't really explain it. I should be shocked or angry or something more dramatic, but I'm not. I'm just amazed. I think it might be because I've always had this feeling that my mother—well, my dad's wife was actually a wonderful, loving, and kind stranger. I heard other people talking about their mothers, and it always seemed like their mothers were . . . well, kind of part of them. I never really had that feeling. I always thought she was just part of the loving scenery in my life, but not sort of belonging to me. So this is a surprise, but it seems to fit in with what I have always felt. I can't explain it any better. Sometimes I wondered whether I had been born into the wrong family. It doesn't sound right. Oh well. Anyway, I'm OK."

"So there's some hope for me? I mean could you . . . maybe eventually accept another mother into your life?" Lucky asked him.

"Lucinda, let me live with this new situation. I'm sure you are a wonderful person . . . but you did abandon me . . . not seriously, because I was with my dad, but I have to adjust and get to know you on this new level."

"Fair enough, Robert. I can live with that. However, I want you to know I did not abandon you. I *gave* you to your father! I knew he would take good care of you!"

Again there was a thoughtful silence in the limo, broken only by the humming of the engine, until Jolene burst out.

"Do you mean to tell me that all this time I have been working for your mother?" she pretended to be shocked. "No wonder we get along so famously. Now that I know, I can see the resemblance."

"So can I," Charles agreed. "Every time I saw you at work, Lucinda, I thought how much of Robert is connected to you. Your sunshine, easy manner with people, openness, charm, and intelligence. He's got it all too. I am so glad that we are finally able to acknowledge all this - to ourselves at least."

"I agree," Lucky added. "In fact, after your mother died, the thought often crossed my mind that maybe we should, well, at least talk about the truth and what to do about it. I was afraid, Charles, that you had grown into the habit of living very comfortably without me and that I would just be a complication you no longer wanted to acknowledge."

"And I thought you were so absorbed in your corporate identity that you no longer needed a private life that had me in it." Charles reached over and caressed Lucky's face. She tilted her head into his caress.

"How foolish people can be." She smiled and then carefully brushed a tear from the corner of her eye. She sniffed and then smiled again.

"Again," Robert said, "I am so amazed—filled with awe. How all this turned out. That we stumbled into this automobile and found our real connections. It is inspiring! It makes me want to live and live and live! I feel we are nestled into a living tapestry no single one of us could have designed. Don't you all feel that something—that we are entangled in some kind of happening?" Robert looked around at the others. They returned his gaze with various shades of agreement.

They gradually became aware that the headlights of an approaching car from behind them had its high beams flooding into the back window of their car. The high beam illuminated the whole interior. Charles was the first to be annoyed by it. Since he was facing the back of the car, it bothered his eyes, and he glared back at it.

"I wish he would either pass or else keep his distance," he grumbled.

They approached a curve in the road ahead. The car behind them swerved out into the passing lane and roared abreast of them. Charles leaned forward to look, Lucky reached out as if to protect herself. Jolene wasn't really concerned about anything outside as she held Robert's hand. Robert nudged Jolene's leg with his knee and smiled at her.

Without actually being conscious of it, they were rushing toward a moment that would change all their lives. They were so content to be with each other! It was as though something precious, an aura of togetherness, embraced all of them and cushioned them momentarily from reality. That would soon change—forever.

CHAPTER TWELVE

The Accident

"She must know something about it." Fullington was excited. His face was lightly tanned, and his eyes sparkled as though an inner fire had been lit.

"I haven't seen her all day. I've been told she kept to herself in the office this morning. Only Jolene was with her. Her door was closed. Where was Graham or Benning? They're almost always around for consultation. They all love consultations!" Simon was being sarcastic. He knew it was a hallmark of her leadership style.

"All I know is that she is due at a conference in Connecticut this afternoon. When I phoned the center, they told me she had not checked in yet and wasn't expected until later this afternoon." Ralph was there too, as well as two other directors.

"Well, who's called this special meeting of the board? Was it you, Fullington? You might have given us more notice," Simon said.

"Stop complaining, Ralph, you signed the waiver of notice, did you not?" Fullington reminded him.

"Of course. I assumed you must have had an important reason."

"Do you need a reason? Have you been watching the Dow today? Do you see what's going on?" Fullington asked.

"Yes, I do, but why is the price dropping the way it is?" Simon asked.

"Rumors and more rumors. My broker tells me he is being called by clients asking if the news is true," Ralph interjected.

"What news?"

"That's what they are saying, but it isn't really news. Just rumors!"

"Will somebody kindly let me know what rumors are we talking about?" Simon demanded.

"Rumors that Lucinda Brahms, president and CEO of AIC Corporation has skipped, taking with her a sizeable petty cash box and a bank check for nearly half a million dollars," Fullington explained.

"Has it been verified?"

"Of course not. Does it matter? True or not true, the damage is done. Regardless, we are in trouble, and Lucky can't be found."

"What about missing persons?"

"No, not yet. She isn't due in Connecticut until later this afternoon," Fullington reiterated. He was a little tired of explaining things over and over.

At that point, Cliff and Calder arrived in the reception area. Security had cleared them as visitors, and they moved toward the small group of directors with smiles on their faces.

"Good to see you, sir," Cliff shook hands with Fullington. In turn, he introduced the others, and the rounds included Calder.

"We are both eager to see if we can help you gentlemen." Cliff was all smiles and friendliness. "We heard the news, of course, and understand completely your interest in turning to someone else, some objective party not internal to the organization. Can we get down to business as quickly as possible? We may not have enough time."

"What's the urgency?" one of the directors not so closely involved wanted to know.

"The way your stock is falling, Mr. Dillon may not be quite so able to help. I'm afraid anything we do is likely to cost the stockholders," Cliff said and shook his head sadly.

"It's always gone back up before when we had these little dips."

"This is no little dip," Fullington rushed in to explain. "This is a slide, and none of us know when it will stop. Right now, we are all being pushed by the press for more information, and none of us have any to give. Lucky is on her way to a conference in Connecticut. We have left messages for her to call us the minute she arrives—if she arrives, that is. The rumors are that she is in hiding."

"Damn! What do Graham and Benning have to say?" Ralph asked impatiently.

"They deny everything. They assure us that Lucky would never do anything so underhanded. However, they haven't mentioned anything about the missing money."

"We're not here to deal with that problem. I'm sure the police and your own security will get to the bottom," Cliff reminded them. "Gentlemen, can we move into your conference room and begin discussions about the possible merger? I understand from Mr. Fullington that you have enough votes to guarantee a quorum in the event we reach agreement."

"Please, this way. Let's get comfortable in there and consider the matter further." Fullington ushered the guests and directors into the boardroom, where a smaller, tighter circle had been arranged for these discussions.

"Everybody settled? If anyone wants coffee, juice, or snacks, including some fresh fruit, please help yourselves from the sideboard." Fullington felt it was his task to act as host, and he tried to take the leadership for the meeting. After all, he was chairman of the board, and he was the one who had exercised his authority to call this special, unscheduled meeting.

"Where shall we begin?" Cliff let Fullington take the lead.

"We have a possible solution for our various different perspectives on how to proceed."

"Let's hear it." Cliff leaned back in his chair.

"Yes, I'd like to hear it too!" one of the more disconnected directors agreed. He was the one who usually seconded motions brought to the board.

"Enough of us here," Fullington began, indicating the directors with a gesture of his hand, "have checked Mr. Dillon out, taking into account his track record at Premium Technical Products Incorporated and earlier responsibilities and find that his management approach, the strong focus on share price and bottom-line profitability might be just what this organization now needs. We are pleased with how Ms. Brahms has taken us this far and recognize that a change might be good for all concerned. We insist on a generous separation package for her." Fullington paused to give emphasis to his speech so far before he continued with the real meat of his proposal.

"Given the real-life situation of the Alliance for International Communications Incorporated and what has been going on in the markets, we feel we need more time to work out all the relevant details of the actual merger. At the same time, the change in leadership is what seems to be urgent. Our proposal is that we postpone the merger for one month for further clarification and negotiations, but appoint Mr. Dillon at once, at this meeting, to the position of president and chief executive officer, the one held by Ms. Brahms for the last three years. That's our proposal. What do you think?"

"Hold it! Wait just a minute. Are you saying we have already fired Lucky, that the position is open, and that we are appointing Mr. Dillon to it? Does Lucky know anything about this? Has anyone talked to her?" Simon was incensed.

"We don't have to. We are under no obligation to say or inform her of anything. She serves at the pleasure of the board of directors, who have complete authority to remove her or reappoint her. With a generous separation package—we can still work out the details, if anyone can find her—I'm sure she will not be too unhappy," Fullington said.

Simon was uneasy and expressed his concern. "It just doesn't seem right to rush into this without having even discussed this move with her. She has dealt openly and fairly with us over the years. Her style is to talk things over with all parties involved and then to make a thoroughly informed decision. That has worked well for us these last three years. This motion is a serious departure in our corporate culture."

"You bet it is! At this point, I'll go anywhere and do anything that finally gives us a better share price and a more solid profit. Gentlemen, I think it is time for a change. According to Mr. Dillon's track record, he seems to be just the one to give us what we want." Fullington became stronger in his opinion as he progressed. At the end, he sounded absolutely positive, as though any other course of action was unthinkable.

"And what does your Mr. Dillon want?" a director asked. He was the one who always came late to a meeting and needed to be updated on whatever topic was under discussion.

"We can negotiate there, but first I would like us to agree in principle that we want Lucky out and we want Armand Dillon in."

"I don't know." Ralph was hesitant.

Fullington turned in his chair and challenged Ralph directly. "Let's put it this way. How much money are you prepared to lose while we keep investigating all the issues, the pros and cons, the hidden maneuvers keeping Lucky in place? A million? Five million? How big a price are you prepared to pay for your loyalty to Lucky? I am asking you a direct question! I want you to give me a direct answer. How much?"

"Well, I don't have as many shares as you do, but then, I can't afford to lose as much as you can. How much are you willing to lose?" Ralph became defensive.

"I know the answer to that without even thinking. There isn't even a close second. Zilch! Zilch minus a million or two. I don't invest with my heart! I use my brain, and my brain is telling me let's give Armand Dillon a chance to repair the damage and make us all rich."

The directors looked around at each other, which was usually their way to make decisions under Lucinda Brahm's leadership, and nodded wisely at each other as though the logic of Fullington's reasoning was indisputably correct. Ralph and Simon looked at each other. They were feeling the intense pressure against them.

"If you put it that way, I guess I can go along." Simon was the first to cave in. "I have some uneasiness about how we are doing this, not necessarily what we are doing, but if you all think this is the right course of action, I guess I'll give you my vote."

The other nay-saying directors, including Ralph, nodded submissively.

"You can approve your motion," Cliff said, "but this option has not yet been discussed with Mr. Dillon. If you all agree, Calder and I will be glad to offer it as an option to him and get back to you as quickly as is possible. We realize the situation is serious and there is some urgency. Of course, if Ms. Brahms does show up, you are likely to change your minds?" This last item gradually rose to become a question, perhaps a tease to make sure they were really united in their suggested action.

"Not on your life." Fullington thought of himself as spokesperson for the board. "As far as we are concerned, Ms. Brahms and all the controversy around her are a separate issue in no way impinging on our decision to appoint Mr. Dillon to the position of president and chief executive officer of this corporation. The only obstacle to the action continues to be Mr. Dillon's acceptance, his terms and conditions, and our agreement to them."

"Very well, gentlemen, Calder and I will present your proposition to Mr. Dillon, and we'll see where we go from here." Cliff seemed pleased with the outcome. He knew that Armand wanted total control and a free hand. That could all be handled during the negotiations. Once he was in charge and on the inside, he would be able to maneuver everything to his advantage. Cliff knew that from experience. The trick was always to get him on the inside; the rest followed like natural law.

"Thank you, gentlemen and lady!" There actually was one. Nobody could remember whether she actually voted or not, but she must have agreed or the motion wouldn't have carried unanimously. Nobody could even remember exactly if the motion was passed unanimously or not since Fullington had never asked for any possible nays or abstentions. "This meeting is adjourned." Fullington gaveled the moment, dispensing with any possible motion for adjournment or second. He was riding high with this new wind blowing out of the north, out of the cold and frigid atmosphere surrounding the highly successful Armand Dillon.

*****

Tom didn't like the green Buick staying abreast of the limousine. He decided to pull ahead and force the car to fall in behind him. Instead, the car stayed even with him as the speedometer climbed from a gentle sixty miles an hour to hover around eighty. Then he thought another tact might shake him loose. He put his foot on the brake, gently at first so as not to hurt his precious passengers, and then harder as the car continued to stay even with them. He slowed down to just thirty-five miles an hour, but the car beside them was still exactly nose to nose.

By this time, Charles was beginning to suspect what was really happening. He understood they were all in danger. He made a split-second decision.

"Robert, take Jolene by the hand, open the door on your side and roll out of the car into the grass by the side of the road."

"But—"

"Do it now! Quickly. We're in trouble!"

Robert realized that this tactic for escape could only be done on his side, the side where the grass bordered the highway. The other side was asphalt and cement, a hard surface to land on. He didn't like leaving Charles and Lucinda in the car, but he also felt responsible for Jolene. Without further resistance, thinking or planning, he opened the door on his side as Tom began accelerating to avoid the bridge abutment straight ahead. He grabbed Jolene by the hand, then the elbow, and finally, the waist, and out she went with him following. He rolled, being the heavier of the two, more quickly, and Jolene tumbled over and on top of him, breaking her fall somewhat.

"Are you all right?" Robert asked her anxiously.

Jolene's hand was bleeding. Her blouse had been ripped along the center seam. It must have caught on the door handle on the way out. She sat up, and Robert hugged her.

"Luck of the Irish? We're both OK. Dented and bruised, but in one piece!"

Then they both turned with the sound of the crash. The limo was turning over in slow motion. It must have struck the stone wall abutment containing the bridge over a small stream that trickled in from the left. The limo tumbled ever so elegantly over and then over and ended in the stream, its entire front mashed in and collapsed into the front seat. It stopped and steam rose around it as the heat of the engine came into contact with the spray of water from the stream, which had cascaded over the entire length of the car.

Robert watched in horror, and then he and Jolene picked themselves up, still aching from the fall, and hurried in the direction of the crash. They noticed the wreck of the green Buick crumpled in a heap on the opposite side of the road. It must have forced the limo off to the right so that it crashed into the abutment and then caromed across the highway, into a stand of trees in the divide. At first he had a fleeting thought that no one could survive the condition of the green Buick, but then he saw a figure round the car, remove the license plate, and then disappear into the underbrush. Robert wasn't sure, but he thought he heard another car in the opposite lane on the other side of the divide start off and speed south.

When they reached the limo, Charles was struggling to climb through the open door on the top of the car on its side. Both doors on the top side of the capsized limo were dangling from their bent and twisted hinges. Robert helped him out.

"Are you hurt?"

"Yes, but not bad. My knee crushed against the front seat when it hit. Thank God we weren't traveling at highway speed." He limped back and looked into the car through the half off, hanging door on his side.

"Lucinda is in there. I think she is hurt bad. She's not moving. We've got to get her out."

"Shouldn't we wait until an ambulance arrives?"

"No, that was no accident. That was a deliberate crash to hurt us—probably her. She is most likely still in danger, if they come back. Check this van pulling up, make sure they're OK, and ask them to help us get her to the Westchester County Hospital." Charles felt the need to take charge and get them urgently out of there and into a safer place.

While Robert went to investigate the blue van that had stopped and the man and woman that had emerged to inspect the accident, Charles saw Jolene swaying slightly from side to side. He held her arm.

"I guess we better get you some attention too. Can you manage until we get to the hospital?"

"Yes, I think so. I'm just woozy . . . can't really think straight."

"Come, sit down here on this tree trunk. Robert and I will get Lucinda out and to the hospital, and you'll come with us for some medical help. Just rest now."

Charles had forgotten about the chauffeur. He limped back to the overturned limo and tried to move the door on the crushed driver's side out of the way. It was jammed and wouldn't budge. The window was missing except for some ragged edges protruding from the frame. He looked through the gaping hole by the front seat searching for Tom.

He was lying back low in the seat, propped against the other side of the car. The window was also missing on that side, and grass, twigs, and branches clogged the open space. At first, Charles was fooled by the relaxed position of the chauffeur, but then he noticed the body was missing a head. Instead, blood was slowly pulsing from the severed arteries of the neck. His head was sitting upright on the seat next to him with a large piece of the section-separating glass. Charles swallowed the bile rising in his throat and turned away. Poor Tom. It seemed he had been decapitated by the flying glass. Apparently, it was supposed to have been shatterproof. Instead, most of it remained in a single sheet, flying through the air, slicing him precisely at the point of his larynx hard enough to sever the entire neck. Charles paused a moment to recover his composure.

Robert returned with the man owning the van.

"What happened?" the man asked.

"That car rammed us off the road," Robert explained.

Charles interrupted, stepping forward to take charge. "We'll make a police report later, but right now we have a woman in the car seriously hurt. Can you help us get her to Emergency at the Westchester Community Hospital as quickly as possible?"

"Are you sure we should move her? It might be better to wait for the medics to arrive," the man asked.

"By then she may be dead. I'll climb back in and try to lift her out. Help me."

Charles clambered back in, avoiding the ragged edges of metal and glass that protruded at every angle. He went feet first and then disappeared inside. Gradually, Lucinda's head and shoulders emerged. Robert jumped forward and held her while the rest of her slowly appeared. She was limp and very heavy, a dead weight in his arms. Her head wobbled from side to side and both arms hung lifelessly from her shoulders. Her clothes were stained with earth and small clusters of leaves protruded from between the buttons of her blouse. Her face was smeared in mud that was speckled with blood stains. The man from the van helped to hold her.

When Charles was back out of the car and on his feet, the three of them carried her over to the van and held her half-sitting, half-lying in the backseat. Robert fetched Jolene, and they all climbed into the van and drove at first carefully but once on the road picked up speed.

Charles looked at his watch and was surprised to see first that it was still working and then that only twenty minutes had passed since the crash. To him it seemed like hours, the minutes charged with fear, horror, anxiety, and dread.

By the time they arrived at the emergency entrance of the Westchester Community Hospital, Lucinda was moaning incoherently. Her eyes were still closed. Charles had noticed her foot was bent in an odd angle, her legs were speckled with small shards of silvery blinking glass. Her dress was covered in torn cushion material and who knows what had happened to her shoes.

"I think we all need some attention, just to be sure."

"What happened?" two medics rushed over with a stretcher on wheels.

"This car—" Robert began to explain.

"It was an automobile accident. Out on the Parkway. Please take good care of her. We had to move her ourselves to get her out. She's precious to us!" Charles cut in to avoid disclosing too much unnecessary information.

They moved quickly with expert efficiency and had her on the stretcher and inside while Charles dealt with registration and paperwork. He listed her as Mrs. Charles McLane. He explained the lack of credentials and identity cards on the accident and promised to furnish them the next day.

The medics returned with the empty stretcher. Charles and Robert and then Jolene crowded around them. "Is she all right?"

"She's still unconscious. Her leg looks bad, and she has wounds and debris all over her."

"Is anybody with her?" Charles asked.

"Never you worry! We'll take good care of her. The doctor is with her now. Let's have a look at the rest of you."

Charles sat down, sagged onto a bench. He suddenly felt bone-weary, as if he had been on his feet for twenty-four hours. He knew instinctively they couldn't stay at this location. The accident had been unsuccessful so far, if the intention was to kill Lucinda, but they might still succeed if he couldn't hide her soon. Robert ended up next to him, his arm around Jolene, supporting her.

"We've got to get Lucinda out of here and into hiding," Charles explained wearily.

"You think they're going to try again?" Robert had finally caught on to the truth of what was happening to them. He didn't expect anything like this. After all, it was the twentieth century, and such things shouldn't happen anymore in real life. Nothing in his life had prepared him for this kind of deliberately vicious action. It only happened in the movies, in a virtual world, but not in this, the real world!

"I know it. That car was driven by somebody paid to do away with Lucinda. I'm sure of it. I don't know who, but sooner or later, I'll find out. Right now, the important thing is to get Lucinda, and maybe the rest of us, out of here, away from danger and into hiding."

"Where? Is there such a thing as a safe place?"

"I'll take care of all that," Charles said grimly. "You see that Jolene gets looked over for wounds and breaks. Check yourself too. I'll make arrangements—necessary arrangements. And Robert, explain that we have our own doctors and medical services and need to move everybody as soon as possible!"

"OK."

In the meantime, the man in the van that brought them to the hospital was still waiting outside in case he was needed again. He considered himself a Good Samaritan, and so he was. Not many would have done what he did. Most people today would be happy to stand by, run errands, or be generally helpful in a safe kind of way. Very few would pitch in the way this man did.

A long black limousine pulled up to the curb behind him, and a tall, black-suited man opened the door, stepped out, and stretched.

"What a nice day," he said to the driver of the van. He pulled a pack of cigarettes from his suit vest pocket and offered it.

"No, thanks. I don't smoke," the driver of the van answered.

"You waiting for a patient, too?"

"No, I just brought somebody here. They were in an accident."

"An accident, you say?"

"Yeah! A bad one. You should have seen the car. It used to be a big black limo like yours there. Not anymore. It's a pile of junk now."

"You don't say. Anybody hurt?"

"Yeah, a woman. She looked pretty bad to me. Her leg was all twisted in the wrong direction, and her clothes were covered in blood and glass. I doubt if she'll make it through."

"Sorry to hear that. Are you waiting here to find out if she makes it?"

"Nah, I just thought I'd wait a bit and then drive home. I was on my way home when all this happened. You see I'm a sales—"

"Well, nice to meet you," interrupted the tall, dark-suited man. He returned to his limousine and bent over as though he were speaking to someone in the car. He then slipped into the driver's seat and drove away.

I guess he didn't have anyone here to see after all, the driver of the van thought. He waited a little longer and then decided to go home. He already had quite a story to tell. Maybe enough for one night!

*****

Armand Dillon, newly appointed president and CEO of Alliance for International Communications Incorporated, was at work early Monday morning. He arrived on the twelfth floor of the company, stepped out of the elevators, and was shocked at what he saw.

The pale green mottled wallpaper upset his equilibrium. He stepped back a moment to recover. Then he noticed the flowering shrubs with their lush pink blossoms contrasting dramatically with the blond furniture and the flower-print cushions. The two Turner classics that had been Lucky's favorites hung, one on each side of the sitting area, leaving the center completely under the influence of the shrubs.

Armand wrinkled his nose and hurried past the area to enter through the glass doors engraved with ALLIANCE

FOR INTERNATIONAL COMMUNICATIONS INC. and LUCINDA BRAHMS, PRESIDENT and CHIEF EXECUTIVE OFFICER. He also took note of the other names displayed there. The directors were listed as well as a few of the prominent vice presidents. He knew them all, having studied their credentials meticulously before making his move. He didn't care what was written on the door. It would all be changed in due time.

His first official act was to call in the temporary secretary hurriedly employed and assigned to him over the weekend.

"Good morning, sir." She attached her finest smile to her face as part of the greeting.

He ignored her friendly approach and snapped his first command at her. "Get me Graham Seiter and Stanley Benning. See if Charles McLane is also available. I need them in here right away."

"Would you like me to bring you some coffee?" she asked hopefully.

"Just do what I ask of you, and we'll get along fine." He scowled in her general direction.

"If you need me for anything, sir, my name is Clara." This was quite brave of her, and it might have cost her the job if he had noticed. Armand was already deep into a stack of papers and reports. He then noticed that she was still there, standing squarely in front of him as though he hadn't made his demand clear.

"Do I have to repeat what I asked you to do?" He didn't shout. He really never shouted, but he might as well have. His displeasure was obvious.

"No, sir, right away." She disappeared around the corner from his office.

"Close the door!" This time, he almost did shout. It was an unusual request to hear at Alliance for International Communications Incorporated. Doors were generally left open. That way, people could wander in and out as the organizational need required. It had been Lucky's first executive order three years ago and had embedded itself deeply into the culture of the corporation. This reversal now sounded shock waves that gradually drifted from floor to floor as employees struggled to adapt.

The secretary bounced back in, shut the door, and vanished in search of Graham and Benning. They happened to be on the seventh floor, conferring together with Horst. When they heard that they were being requested so quickly, they both knew what was in store. They took their time getting up to the twelfth floor, knocked on the door, and waited. Armand was in no hurry to put them at ease. Finally, they heard his gravelly voice responding from inside. If they didn't already despise Armand, the sound of his voice would have assured it. The roughness in it was unpleasant; it grated against the eardrums, causing an irritating vibration. Graham decided on the spot what he would say if he got the chance.

"From what I understand, you two were close to Ms. Brahms. I have decided not to fire you for the time being. Only for the time being, mind you. I want you where I can keep an eye on you.

"If you do your job," he continued, "and understand how things are going to change around here, pitch in and help us achieve our objectives"—he leaned back in his chair behind Lucky's desk—"well, I'm a reasonable man. There will always be room for good performers who are loyal to me. I have tried to make myself clear. I trust you will do the same."

For a moment, neither Benning nor Graham answered. Each of them waited to hear what the other would say. They looked sheepishly at each other, and then Graham finally took the first step.

"Ms. Brahms was an incredible person and a fine leader for the corporation—" he said.

"Yes, yes, I know all that. You're exonerated completely if you decide to switch horses. What will it be?" Armand interrupted impatiently.

Graham was thinking fast. What good would it do if he left? He wasn't even sure where Lucky was at this moment. Suppose she was kidnapped or otherwise dealt with. How could he help her on the outside? Maybe on the inside, he could at least be informed as matters developed. She might actually need him right where he was. He could always quit if things got unbearable.

"I'll accept your gracious offer and do my best to serve you in any capacity you wish."

"And you?" he glared at Benning.

Benning had been watching the changes in Graham's face. He knew that Graham would remain loyal. After all the three of them had agreed together at the coffee shop. He trusted Graham.

"I also accept."

"You understand I will have you watched. Every move you make will be noticed. Any sign of disloyalty or vengeance will give me cause to change my mind. Is that understood?"

Both Graham and Benning nodded. They didn't actually say they did—they just nodded. Armand took note of their rebelliousness but let it pass.

"Good. I expect you, Graham, to report directly to Calder Tebbit."

"All right, if that's what you want."

"Cliff will be giving you supervision. We'll see how it goes." He nodded in the direction of Benning.

Graham and Benning stood before him at his desk, but he paid them no attention. He was again totally focused on the reports and papers stacked before him. They both waited, then waited a little longer, glancing at each other, and then finally turned and left the office.

"Close the door!" Armand's voice travelled after them, raising shudders up and down their spines.

"Let's get together after work at the tavern?" Graham half-whispered as they crossed the reception area.

Benning nodded. "I'll see if Horst will join us."

CHAPTER THIRTEEN

The Escape

At the Westchester Community Hospital, the excitement gradually subsided and the weariness set in. Robert and Jolene still sat hunched over each other on the wooden bench outside the ER. A nurse had looked them both over, treated a scratch here and there, and then suggested they go home and rest for two days. She advised them they were both still under shock from their accident and ought not undertake anything strenuous or mentally taxing until the next day.

Charles was the first to have his wounds treated. His knee was not broken, just bruised, but it hurt like the devil. His suit wasn't worth sending to the cleaners. Dirt and small snags and rips that could never be repaired! He also had a bad cut on the side of his head, probably from when he had climbed back into the limo to rescue Lucky. A loose bandage now covered it, but he was quite a sight with his head tilted precariously to one side and limping toward the phone in the lobby. He made a number of calls.

One of the last calls he made on a hunch was to his own home. It rang for a long time. At last, when he was just about ready to hang up, the receiver was picked up. He waited without saying a word. Nobody answered, although he was sure he heard the sound of muted breathing. Just before he hung up, he picked up the unmistakable whine of a siren and what he was sure were the loud horns of fire engines.

"I'll say this for them," he muttered to himself. "They are thorough. We better get out as fast as we can." Charles asked the doctor, "Can she be moved?"

"I wouldn't advise it. She is still dazed and in trauma. I insist you keep her here for a day or two before moving her, and then her leg has to be operated on."

"I'm sorry, doctor, we have no choice. I've ordered an ambulance, and all four of us are going to a medical facility not too far from here. She'll get all the treatment necessary there. Can you help to get her as comfortable and safe as possible for this tricky but necessary trip?"

"I don't like it."

"It can't be helped. I'm sorry."

"You'll have to sign a form. Are you related to her?"

"Yes, I'm her husband," he lied. That's her son over there. I suppose Robert can also sign the form."

Robert heard his name and raised his head to listen. Gently, he eased Jolene back down on the bench, managed the upright position for himself, and came over to sign whatever they put in front of him. In a neat penmanship, he indicated himself as Robert McLane and printed in Lucky as Lucinda McLane. He smiled knowingly at his dad.

Shortly thereafter, a sleek black hearse showed up at the emergency entrance and asked for Charles McLane. He hurried out limping from side to side and spoke briefly with the driver. The way they embraced on sight indicated clearly that a bond of friendship existed between them.

The medic was aghast. "I thought you said you had hired a private ambulance."

"That's all right," Charles explained. "I changed my mind when I heard this was available."

"What about all the equipment? You know she's on IVs and heart monitors. They have to be plugged in." The medic was probably thinking up reasons for stopping them.

"That's right. It's all arranged. Besides, it won't be very long. Honest, we'll be fine." Charles assured him and then turned away. "I hope," he added softly, eyeing Lucinda's prostrate form on the stretcher. She looked very vulnerable, but her breathing seemed normal, and he knew from the doctor that she had sustained no other damage except her leg, excessive shock, and a cut above her left temple. The doctor was only willing to let her go on the basis that she would be treated soon for her leg before the breaks healed wrong and had to be broken again.

Once Lucinda was safely in the hearse, Charles and Robert and Jolene mounted from the back without being seen and settled themselves so they could hold and stabilize the monitoring equipment. As soon as it was plugged in the rear outlet of the hearse, it omitted a steady and continuous rhythmic beep. The hearse moved slowly down the driveway, passing a parked car, which followed them for a short distance and then turned off the highway and disappeared down a side road. Charles had his eye on the car and sighed in relief when it pulled away.

"How are you, dear?" Charles took Lucinda's hand and held it firmly.

"I don't know." She tried to smile but her face hurt. "I'm at your mercy, Charles."

"Don't worry, I'll not let anything more happen to you. Besides Robert and your favorite Jolene are right here beside you."

Jolene moved closer and touched her arm, but Charles relinquished his hold on her hand and slid it over for Jolene to hold.

"Oh, dear Jolene. You're all right?"

"Yes, I'm fine. Bruised and dirty, but still in love." She laughed as Robert slid over on the bench to be in Lucky's line of sight.

"Robert" was all she could say.

"I don't know how we did it, but we are all four here, together, running away like crazy, but still alive." Jolene marveled at their good fortune.

"That was smart, Dad, getting us to jump into the grass. I've never done anything like that before. How did you come up with that idea?"

"I don't know, Robert. Where does any good idea come from? In a flash, I saw in my mind what was happening. The truth hit me with a jolt. And then flashed this idea—it just came to me. 'Get Robert and Jolene out while the car is slowed down and nearly in the grass.' I am overcome with gratitude that somehow the right idea came at just the right instant it was needed."

"Good thinking, Dad."

"I believe your father is trying to tell you—owie," Jolene winced as the car overcame a modest bump in the road.

"Here, sit back. Hold on to Robert. No more accidents! Those are my orders," Charles insisted good-humoredly.

"Where are we going, Charles?" Lucky asked in a muffled voice.

"Do you care?" he answered.

"No . . . yes!" she decided.

"I've arranged for us to be treated at a hospital in Peterborough, New Hampshire. The chief medical officer is a friend of mine. They will do everything medically necessary. I have complete confidence in them. We will then stay temporarily in a secret place I happen to know. We'll be safe there, but only for a short time. I am sure we are being watched and tailed. I hope we will lose them on the way north. Our enemies seem to have endless resources."

"Who are our enemies?" Robert was sincerely puzzled. "And what do they want? Why are they doing all this to us?"

"I don't know for sure, but I have my suspicions. If it is who I think it is, we are in great danger."

"How about letting us in?" Jolene was eager to know more.

Charles folded his hands and leaned back in the seat before answering thoughtfully. "In good time. Where we are going will be a good place to recuperate and plan together. We can't stay there long. Sooner or later, they will catch up on our location. We will need a more long-term solution while we wrestle with plans for the future. Jolene, can you take a sponge and moisten Lucinda's lips. She seems dehydrated."

"Whoever, they are," said Robert, "do you think they saw this was a hearse? I wonder if they know the three of us are here. I have a feeling they think Lucky was alone in her limo. None of us told anybody we were coming along. Charles decided in the last minute to ask me along, and I think Jolene had a date with me when Lucky asked her to come with us. You know, I believe they might actually think Lucky is dead. Hence the hearse! What do you think, Dad?" Robert was quickly seeing all the possibilities that this opened up.

"I certainly hope so. It's our only chance." Charles smiled.

"Did you arrange this on purpose?"

"I did," Charles admitted.

"Good thinking, Charles." Jolene admired him.

Lucky's eyes drooped. The doctor's sedative was obviously beginning to take effect. They fell into a respectful silence as the hearse drove calmly north through Connecticut, then Massachusetts, and finally into New Hampshire.

CHAPTER FOURTEEN

Cleaning House

Armand knew exactly what he was in for. Nobody liked him; everybody in the Alliance for International Communications Incorporated organization opposed his leadership. He caught them spying on him as he used the elevator or left the building through the lobby or to the garage for his limo. He knew very well his secretary was with him under duress; no other job was available for her if she refused this one. He tried not to use the executive dining room, but sometimes it was necessary. Most of the time, he sent someone out to the deli around the corner for a salad and roll with butter. His diet was known throughout the company, and whoever made the trip regaled the staff with stories about him.

"Today, when I set the salad in front of him with the cup of dressing beside it, he actually grunted. I'm not sure if that was supposed to be a thank-you, but I said 'You're welcome' just in case. He looked up and stared at me as if wondering what I meant. He has a very suspicious mind!"

"Did he recognize you?"

"I have no idea. After all, I've only done it five or six times. It would be a lot to expect him to know who I am."

Not only did they enjoy the humor, they retold it on every floor of the building. It was especially enjoyed in the accounting department with over two hundred accountants and bookkeepers. It sometimes took the whole morning before it completed the rounds. One could usually tell exactly how far it had gotten by the cluster of laughing men in white dress shirts and women in black jackets.

The laughter stopped abruptly as other stories began to circulate. Stories of a different kind. It seemed a decision was made and then communicated and implemented by Cliff. He explained that Mr. Dillon had made an informal study of his own and determined that the ratio of clerical help to staff was much too high. It clearly indicated a lack of efficiency on the part of the staff. He slowly and painstakingly weeded out the secretarial employees, having every other one eventually dismissed.

"In this organization," Mr. Dillion's memo explained, "sharing is an important corporate value. We want everyone to learn it and practice it. Therefore each member of our staff will share secretarial help with at least one other member of the staff. This will also send a good signal to other departments that we are planning to be lean and mean. Those are our synonyms for profit and growth."

"He doesn't even say nice things first—you know, how wonderful we all are—before getting to the point. Has he ever considered sharpening his communication skills?"

"I don't know, he's pretty clear. I don't think anyone can misunderstand him."

"That's for sure!"

Instead he established a typing pool on the third floor. It used to be a lounge for middle management personnel. The armchairs and sofas were removed. Some of the larger tables and card tables were saved to double as "supervisory stations," he called them. All the secretaries who were not assigned to serve two or more staff members had to take a typing test. They lined up on the third floor. The line was so long, some of them went out for coffee, came back a little later, and still were able to get in line.

Anyone not able to type at least one hundred words a minute with less than one mistake was awarded a pink slip and processed for departure. Those who remained, having done well on the test, were assigned a metal desk in the typing pool. They were told to wait until some work arrived. They wondered who the supervisors were going to be. They didn't have to wait long. A man they had never seen before passed among them, appointing three head clerks as he went. He then sat down at a large wooden desk at the top of the room and experimented with the telephone. It evidently worked well, because he was on it for the next thirty minutes, chatting away and laughing every now and then. This was evidently a promotion for him.

When the headquarters staff complained and threatened to rebel, they were advised that other changes were still in process. That silenced most of them. There were a few that could read signs well who began to read the newspaper more intently.

Armand then focused his attention on the accounting department. Of all the departments in the headquarters of Alliance for International Communications Incorporated, this was his favorite. He loved accounting. These were the only people that really made sense to him. He understood their way of thinking, the clarity of their thought and the directness with which they were able to communicate. Nevertheless, he couldn't in his wildest imagination defend having two hundred in the department. He wanted to give them some leeway, so he decided dismissing only about thirty, a mix of bookkeepers and clerks and accountants. This was a job for Calder. It was his kind of action.

Gradually, step-by-step, Armand cleaned house. He was looking everywhere for fat. When he located a scrap of it, he zeroed in and cut. He couldn't believe how the profit began to show up in the projections despite the various severance expenses. Then when he slowly cut back on space, reassigning whole departments to different floors, a whole floor in the headquarters building became vacant. Calder took on the job of leasing it out for a tidy additional sum on the income side.

Armand had considered moving the whole company into a leased building and selling the corporate headquarters to the highest bidder but decided the disruption would be too great, no doubt negatively affecting productivity.

He called in Cliff for a consultation at the end of a very tumultuous but satisfying day for him.

"How's everything going?" he asked, his face in shadows. He couldn't stand the light and cheerfulness of Lucky's office. He had moved the desk into the corner, turned off all of the recessed lights. On his desk, he had one light focused on his work area. Cliff looked around with astonishment.

"What an office!" he said.

"Not for long. At least ten people could work in here!"

"Who?" Cliff wondered.

"Never mind. Report!"

"You sure know how to turn a happy company into a hardworking, miserable company," Cliff dared to comment admiringly.

Armand accepted the compliment and said, "You have no idea how much fat I'm finding. This organization might as well be a government agency the way they handed out jobs. I tell you I can make an incredible recovery in this place. Do you know there were two hundred accounting clerks and bookkeepers? They had ample time to gather in little groups and laugh. On my time, they were laughing. Can you believe that?"

"I guess their laughing days are over," Cliff commented.

"You can bet on that. What do you hear from our agents on Wall Street?"

"They're spreading the word that you've taken over. Have you seen the journal? There's some nice coverage of you in this morning's paper. They are nicknaming you Mr. Profit. One of our employees has been persuaded to tell them a long story of how terrible you are. He describes in lurid detail the agony of being fired with no notice and minimal separation pay. What you would really like is his explanation when they asked what his job was. He fumbled around with a lot of words, hemming and hawing along the way. Finally the reporter said, 'In other words, you didn't do anything,' which he vehemently denied.

It is making great press. Everybody is following our progress," Cliff announced with pride.

"I see the share price is moving up sharply for the first time in months," Armand said.

"Years!" Cliff added.

"You watch. We are going to make history here. This will become a case history. Can you get in touch with Harvard University and see if they would be interested in making a case study out of our takeover? Any good PR could help us. I would like everyone to know how investor-friendly we are."

"You should be a little subdued on that, if I were you," Cliff cautioned. "There is a small but vocal underground movement advocating social responsibility that—"

"What nonsense!" Armand sputtered his indignation. "The government does enough of that without any help from us. We pay plenty of taxes for them to coddle the masses. We do our share. Without us, believe you me, there would be a lot more people needing social responsibility."

Whether Cliff agreed with him or not didn't matter. He remained quiet, waiting for more orders. Armand inspected one of the documents in front of him, littered with notes and figures in fine pencil marks. Finally, he looked up from his papers and spoke.

"I'm just beginning to look at our staff expenses. I want to keep Graham and Benning on for the time being. I want them watched. I think they will no longer be a problem. With Brahms out of the way, they might even knuckle under before long. By the way, did anyone follow that hearse? I did not get any reports of a funeral. Surely that would have leaked out into the media somehow. Look into that, will you, Cliff?"

"Yes, I know she must have been seriously hurt. The hearse came quickly. Probably it was arranged by the McLane kid. It was rumored that he was around at the Westchester Community Hospital with his girlfriend, although our people saw no sign of them. I'll check some more to see what I can find out. I know that Evans got away—"

"I don't want to know anything about Evans," Armand hurried to clarify.

"OK. If you need to know anything, check with me. I have a file on his employment."

"Destroy it."

"We need some data—"

"Destroy it right now. What I want you to keep is his identity and whereabouts. I need people who are loyal to me and will knuckle under my leadership. Even though he's just a soldier, we may just need him again."

"OK. What about Horst Perla?"

"He's the new one in Benning's HR group? Isn't he?" Armand remembered.

"Yes."

"I had hoped we could win him over, but as I recall, he seems very close to Graham and Benning. I remember a short report you sent me a while back that he apparently was willing to do errands for both of them—not necessarily nor exclusively work related," Armand said.

"Yes. Calder was working that line. It seems Horst knows little of the AIC secrets, and yet he almost seamlessly blended in with the Lucinda Brahms crowd. I think he's probably an unnecessary threat to us if we have Graham and Benning under surveillance."

"Maybe he should be one of the staff that gets terminated?" Armand questioned.

"Terminated?" Cliff was shocked.

"No, no. Fired is what I meant. Maybe he will eventually lead us to McLane."

"Wouldn't it be better to keep an eye on him here?"

"No, I think not. I don't want the opposition to gather too much strength. Best if we could isolate Graham and Benning. If they reach out . . . Outside the company, we might get a lead on McLane. Any ideas what happened to him?"

"No. The last sighting he was on his way into the city the day Ms. Brahms . . . disappeared . . . mysteriously." Cliff was being sarcastic.

"Any word from the police in Westchester County?"

"I checked that yesterday," Cliff reported. "Somebody called in an accident on the Saw Mill Parkway involving a black limousine and a green Buick. The limousine was registered to the Alliance for International Communications Incorporated normally used by Ms. Brahms. In the accident, the chauffeur was killed. No evidence of any passengers, although the Alliance for International Communications Incorporated office indicated that the chauffeur had signed out with Ms. Brahms as a passenger. No proof that she was actually in the car. The green car had been doctored for drag racing. Evidently, he had practiced a run on the parkway and crashed. From the skid marks on the highway, the green car had not turned sharply enough on a curve and forced the limousine into an abutment of a stone bridge. The car was stolen, no registered license, and there has been no record of the driver. He has disappeared completely. The records show a hit-and-run accident by unknown driver in an unlicensed car."

"It sounds like a perfectly planned and executed accident!" This was the closest Cliff ever got to receiving a complement from Armand Dillon.

"Anything else for me?" asked Cliff.

"Yes. Something very important!" Armand inched forward in his chair and claimed Cliff's undivided attention. "I want to make something very clear. Please listen carefully. I need people—ones who are intelligent, creative, and are loyal to me. I happen to know that Ms. Brahms is not dead. She is alive and will recover. It's a good thing that she is. I want her alive. What good is she to me dead? Scaring her, driving her out of the company, discrediting her before her friends and the public! All that is great! I don't want anything we do to give anyone refuge in death. I want them all—all on my side, all benefitting from my leadership. Do you understand what I am saying to you?"

"Sure. I am glad you explained that. I always thought extreme measures were unnecessary. After all, you did win over the directors of AIC and were appointed president and CEO. She had to be out of the way for that. You yourself—"

"Just listen again, Cliff." Armand was adamant. "Once a person is dead—especially an intelligent person with willpower, they can no longer be useful to me. They are simply beyond my reach. That's exactly the kind of person I need to capture alive. Getting rid of them is an extravagant waste. I won't tolerate it. I want to own them, not permit them to escape through dying. I really hope you understand me."

"Sure." Cliff looked around, wondering if maybe Armand suspected he was being recorded or his office was bugged. Why would he make such statements if it weren't for PR purposes?

Oh well, he thought, keeping his thoughts to himself. *Regardless of his reasons, I'm sure he doesn't mean it. I know him, how ruthless he can be in all regards. What possible motive would he have to keep his enemies alive? It couldn't possibly mean anything to him whether Lucinda Brahms is alive or dead, as long as she is no longer a threat to him.*

Armand was no longer looking at Cliff. Once again, his head was buried in a lengthy report about one of their European companies. When he still stood there in front of him, Armand squinted at him, evidently puzzled for a moment by his presence. He then looked around again, surveying his papers and reports, saw nothing urgent. He returned his gaze on Cliff's expectant expression, not knowing exactly what was needed. Then he had a thought. Maybe Cliff needed something inspiring to tide him over the rough work ahead.

"The thing is, I want control over all this corporation's businesses, but I don't want disruptions and tampering with the moneymaking operations. I've been looking at this report of yours in response to my request. Did you notice that on an amalgamated basis, we are manufacturing and selling, all in all, a total of two thousand ninety-six different products in fourteen subsidiaries? That makes an average of more than two hundred products per incorporated entity. Some more, others less! It bothers me!"

"I don't know, Armand." Cliff expressed his doubts, rubbing his forehead with his left hand. "Does that kind of analysis make much sense? Product-by-product analysis does make sense."

"I have redefined business for our time, and we are a forerunner for business enterprises in the future." Armand leaned back in his chair to explain. "Products—I maintain products are not what we make. Everything we manufacture are simply by-products. We don't make things. We make money. Money is our one and only product. Everything else is a means. If I could make money without any products, I would do it."

"Maybe we should start looking into insurance, banking, or perhaps this new field of electronic information transfer. Now there's a real virtual illusion for you. If it's virtual you want, there's the future of all make-believe." Cliff perked up with interest.

"Yes, I think so. Let's wait till others have scratched the surface. It's too costly to invent or create. We want nothing to do with that. The money is made in using what has already been created and distributing it throughout the universe. That's where we come in."

"I suppose so."

"Keep tabs on it, Cliff. There will come a right moment to move in on the field and make it lucrative," Armand ordered.

Cliff believed what his ears were communicating to him. For the first time in years, he began to wonder who his boss really was. He seemed consumed with a freezing passion for an abstraction. A picture of the whole natural world converted into money flashed through Cliff's mind, and he shuddered. Armand was so incredibly intelligent. His mind took in present and future as a fitting playground for his character. He seemed unbeatable. How did he always know exactly what to do when, how, and where? From where did he get his inspiration?

"I guess I am ahead of my time. I would like to see a virtual new world emerge with everything material converted into monetary value. That would be a fitting conclusion to evolution. I dream of such a new world. It would mean an end to poverty, suffering, even death. Even the masses would be eternally happy." Armand disclosed his vision.

"Boss, I've got to get down to the third floor. The typing pool is starting to get some work. I have a feeling the other departments are feeling sorry for the typists and are creating work for them to keep them on the payroll."

"Hades forbid!" Armand said. "Get on down. And, Cliff, take a look at this chart you made of our staff numbers. We've got to cut there as well. They are all scared and will do their best to create as much work as possible. We have to nip it in the bud, so to speak—if you know what I mean!"

"Yes, I'll take care of everything," Cliff promised.

Armand allowed himself the luxury of a few moments of daydreaming before catching himself and bending over to continue his work. Then he paused a moment, thinking furiously, allowing himself a rare moment of dreaming the future.

"Am I some kind of special diety that doesn't need a boss anymore? Everyone seems to need me. They all want me to succeed. Well, at least everyone who has a little money in the stock market wants me to do well. My well-wishers are the greedy ones—the ones who want more and more and more. As long as they continue to want more, I've got them in the palm of my hand. Maybe that's what I really want. People needing me—caught by me—in a world more and more shaped to my liking. If I had my way, I would turn society into an anthill— have the intellect, the intelligence be the only pure virtue. All the rest would be tolerated, but not extolled nor taught. Teachers are confused today. They should make up their minds to either develop human beings or teach brains. Colleges and schools should focus exclusively on cleverness and rational decision-making. I would be above it all, directing it, doing the only real thinking. They would probably all be happier than they are now if I had my way!"

He felt himself inspired by these thoughts. His breathing quickened; his eyes almost brightened, anticipating all he could accomplish for the world. The future seemed incredibly bright, full of potential and myriad possibilities. How glad he was to be alive on earth at this remarkable time in evolution!

CHAPTER FIFTEEN

The Hideout

Horst arrived in Keene, New Hampshire, on the noon flight. While in New York, he had made sure he was not followed. He first took several taxis, walked in between trips, even stopped at a coffee shop, but only for a quick cup before he rushed again to enter a taxi that took him directly to the Westchester Community Airport. He paid the driver handsomely.

"If you don't tell anyone where you took me—pretend that you were on your way home—this woman's husband I was telling you about will never find me way out here in the suburbs. Thanks for your help."

The taxi left, and he watched it disappear out the entrance and onto the highway used only by airport traffic. He waited a while to see if any new cars suspicious in nature entered the airport grounds. When at last he considered himself to have avoided any possible followers, he entered the terminal, worked his way through the corridors and out the back through the charter flight terminal and onto the tarmac.

"Are you Bill?" he asked a mechanic standing by a plane that was fueled and idling.

"Yes. Are you Horst Perla?"

"Yes."

"I'm ready, get in!"

They were off. Horst still had no idea where he was going. All he knew was how to get to the airport and find the right plane. He hoped he had done all that correctly and that he actually was on the right plane.

"Where are we going?" he asked the pilot.

"I'll let you know when we get there," he said and then laughed. "Charles wasn't taking any chances. I don't know what you guys are up to, but he's a good friend! Done me a lot of favors. I'm glad to do a few for him!"

When Horst emerged from the small airfield in Keene, New Hampshire, he was almost immediately hailed by a dirt-encrusted jeep that took off the minute he had thrown his knapsack into the back and jumped in.

"My name is Gus," the driver said. "I am assuming your name is Horst?"

"Yes. Where are we going?" he asked.

"I'll tell you when we get there."

"That's what the last guy said, but he never did tell me."

The driver laughed but paid attention entirely to the rutted dirt road they were traversing. Before Horst became really car sick, they seemed to have arrived.

He looked around, wondering what could be so far from civilization in the middle of a wooded setting. He was surprised when he noticed the charming entrance bordered with wild roses. The red tiled pathway was inviting. It wound gracefully up the short distance to an overhanging bougainvillea that enticed him to explore an enclosed patio leading to a large, dark wooden gate. As he stood admiring the whole appearance and charm of the setting, the gate opened, and Charles appeared. His smile was relaxed and inviting.

"Welcome, Horst. You made it."

"Thanks to your explicit instructions."

"Are you sure you were not followed?"

"Positive. Not only did I take the circuitous route you recommended, but at every point, I always paused long enough to notice any car or person trying to follow me. At the airport, I waited a long time, watching every car entering the airport circle and even the parking. When I walked through the terminals, I paused every now and then to check. It's, true, a capable tracker might have fooled me, but I doubt it very much. I didn't wait even a minute at the airplane, but climbed immediately aboard and watched through the window to see if anyone was following me. I think Bill would have noticed too, don't you?"

"His instructions were to take you to Scranton, Pennsylvania, if he observed any suspicious persons tailing you."

"Thanks a lot!" Horst laughed. "No, seriously, the arrangements have been impeccable. Now that I'm here, where am I?"

"Better you don't know. Only the pilot, the various drivers, a doctor, and a nurse know for sure."

"How is Lucky?"

"Come and see for yourself," Charles invited Horst through the gate. Horst had expected to enter the large residential building, but they circled it and joined a long red tiled walkway bordered by canopies of flowers and thriving plants that wound through the woods. Horst was surprised how far they had to walk, winding first on the tiled sidewalk and then just a narrow footpath.

"How far are we going?"

"We're trying to hide Lucinda until she is completely healed and well enough to travel."

"How is she?" Horst asked again.

"You'll see for yourself in a moment."

Without any warning, the heavily wooded terrain suddenly cleared, and they stood on the banks of a large lake. Horst looked right and then left but could see no other houses except the one straight ahead of them out in the water about forty-feet. Charles led the way onto a floating walkway that took them over the water to the front door of the house.

"How did you ever find this gem?" Horst asked.

"It belongs to a good friend of mine who uses the house out front by the road as a summer residence. I used this houseboat once for a retreat when I was going through a rough time in my life. It offered me just the complete seclusion I needed. Little did I know we would need it so desperately now."

"What a lot of connections you have, Charles."

"My whole life is built up on the basis of connecting and staying connected. That's how I have been able to be so useful to AIC."

"How does the house happen to float?"

"You see those white balloon-like projections two on each side of the house? Those are the ends of underlying pontoons, very long pontoons. It's a small house, just small enough to stay suspended by the air in those pontoons. The advantage is you can release the anchor and float the house to another spot if you like. It's a bit like the houseboats in Sausalito, California. Have you ever been there?"

"Yes, once. I walked there from the ferry starting out in San Francisco. They were actually boats with houses built onto them, weren't they?"

"I guess. This was my friend's idea. He was part of the Army Corps of Engineers that put up bridges in just a few hours during the war. They had an ingenious system of floating pontoons like these out into rivers and dumping portable roadbeds on top of them as they went. He used to tell me stories of their successful crossings."

"What a hideout! You are something!"

"It could also be a trap!" Charles explained. He took Horst around to the side of the house on a very narrow catwalk and pointed to the prow of a slender skiff wedged under the house between the two pontoons that protruded from the end. "I keep that there in case we ever need an escape."

Charles backed up to the front door, unlocked it, and held it open for Horst. The kitchen was to the right. On the left, along the hall were a series of closets and cabinets, presumably for storage. Straight ahead was a narrow hallway that passed an open doorway, revealing a bedroom.

Near the end of the hall, a fixed ladder leaned against the wall, evidently allowing access to the flat roof of the building, no doubt providing a rooftop patio for entertainment.

Further on, the hallway opened into a large living room flooded with light pouring in from an entire glass wall broken only by glass doors to a balcony outside. The view was panoramic. It provided one hundred eighty degrees of watery lakeshore views.

Sitting together around a low coffee table rough-hewn from a glazed tree trunk cut lengthwise down the middle were Lucky and Jolene. Lucky was seated in a chaise lounge chair with her eyes closed. She opened them as Horst and Charles drew near.

"Charles," she said.

"Lucinda, this is Horst Perla, one of the faithful few."

"I am so glad to meet you." Her smile was radiant.

"I am so happy to see that you are . . . recovering and smiling." Horst meant every word. He had heard rumors ranging from "She is dead. People saw the hearse" to "She has escaped, taking most of the corporate funds with her."

Although he didn't mention it, he took note of the white cast protecting her left leg. The bandages around the left side of her head covered one eye, most of a cheek and a good part of her auburn hair, which had evidently been shaved off on that side. She looked quite different from what he had expected. Lucky saw him looking her over but remained tactfully silent.

Horst turned to face Charles. "By the way, do you have a scissor or small knife?" he asked.

"Ah. Of course, we don't want to forget that." Charles produced a small silver pocketknife that he handed over to Horst. He removed his jacket, turned it inside out, and used the pocketknife to open a seam under the armpits. He pulled out a number of flat wads of small bills, mostly fifties, twenties, and tens from each armpit and lining. He handed the entire bundle over to Charles.

"Fifty thousand?" Charles asked.

"I suppose so. I didn't stop to count. That was all that I found in the petty cash box in your desk, Ms. Brahms." Horst answered.

"Since someone had spread the rumor that Lucinda had absconded with the petty cash box, I thought it only correct to make it come true. Did you do what I asked?" Charles questioned Horst.

"Yes, exactly!" Horst said. "I left a small note in the cash box with the words 'Petty cash money borrowed' with yesterday's date and your forged signature, Ms. Brahms. I kept a carbon copy, if you care to see it."

"How sweet of you," she said, smiling. "All that just for me?"

"Only borrowed," Charles reminded her. "We may have to pay it back someday."

"Please, won't you sit down and have a nice cool drink?" Lucky remembered her hospitality and gestured to a chair for Horst to take. "Now tell me—tell us what's going on in the dragon's den?"

Horst gave a short wry laugh. He hardly knew where to start. "He's turned the whole company upside-down. About twenty percent of the staff and secretarial forces have either been fired, forced into early retirement, or reassigned to lower levels at their option. Nobody has stopped him, nor does anyone really complain. It will probably take a few years before the damage shows up. He maintained the inventories in most of the subsidiaries were excessively high. In a way, it was a supersmart move. Profit margins increased dramatically, available income for headquarters has increased by a factor of three, and believe it or not, the stock price is currently almost as high as the actual asset value divided by the number of shares. Wall Street loves Armand Dillon. Stockholders love Armand Dillon. The banks love Armand Dillon and are falling all over each other to lend him money for more acquisitions. By today's standards, Armand Dillon is a high performer, darling of the financial markets even abroad, and the ideal business leader. All the business schools are extolling his tactics and superintelligence. Nobody is questioning his ethics or his personal characteristics." Horst brought his report to a sad closing.

Lucky listened intensely. Finally, she stirred in her chaise lounge and unclasped her hands. "You know, we also have something to learn from all this carnage. Maybe he wouldn't be so successful if we hadn't built up as much fat in the company. But you know, pretty soon, the fat will give out, and the lean will start hurting. That's his Achilles' heel. He shines when he can use the knife like a surgeon, but when there's no more cutting possible, he will stumble."

"Or else change his tactics," Horst added.

"That's just it," Lucky rose higher in her chaise lounge, excitement showing in the half of her face that was not bandaged. "He can't. He only knows how to destroy. It is in his character, in his psyche. I was reading in this copy of *Time* magazine a description of his appearance. Let me read it to you. 'His face is long and jagged; his complexion gray, almost ashen. He has apparently little blood circulation, for they say his hands are ice-cold to the touch. That tidbit is from a single person who was privileged to shake hands with him years ago. His outstanding feature is the high forehead. It apparently shields a brain with an intelligence beyond measurement, although no one has suggested he be tested.' Now don't you wonder who is really in there, behind that face? Who is Armand Dillon really? Does that brain have a heart? I doubt it."

"A formidable opponent to be sure," Horst agreed.

"Yes," Lucinda agreed, "without heart, without fear, without ethics. Is this our ideal for leadership? Do our schools extol this sort of person? Is smart the ruling virtue of the twenty-first century? What happened to all the other virtues such as kind, empathetic, or generous, to name a few? I think the world needs a balance in leadership. We need an education of the heart and hand as well as the intellect. Are we hopelessly at the mercy of such a man?"

"Perhaps—at least for now. Horst, tell us more. What about Graham and Benning?" Charles was eager for more news.

"I see Benning almost every day. After all, he's my boss. I share any news and information I find out with him. I think he is completely in the know. We have a good relationship," Horst was pleased to report.

"Does he share information with you?" Charles asked.

"As my boss, he's more entangled with internal affairs. I'm the one who has more time to be involved with you, so I guess I have more to report. He protects me when, for example, I am on a little trip—like to New Hampshire." Horst laughed.

"Has he ever shared any information with you?" Charles asked again.

"Well, I'm sure . . . Well, let's see . . . I can't put my finger on it, but I am sure he must've. Why? What are you getting at?" Horst asked.

"No real reason." Charles shrugged. "Just curious. He has all of HR at his disposal. I just am not sure how active he is on our behalf. Not that it matters. We each serve as best we can and as needed. What about Graham?"

"I don't know. I haven't seen him for a while. I expect to touch base with him again when I am back," Horst answered.

"Good," Charles said. "It's important that you three stay involved and keep each other informed. We are counting on you, Horst, to be the connection between all of us."

"I know. You can rely on me. You know that."

***

Robert had a long walk to the village to shop for food and various necessities. He packed most of it into a knapsack, hauled it up his back, and poked his arms through the straps. He trudged back through the main street when he saw a familiar figure coming toward him, his long white caftan fluttering around him in the breeze.

"Shaman!" he called out in surprise. "What are you doing here?"

"Robert! How nice to see you. I was hoping to be in the right place after all."

"How did you get here?"

"The same way you did, I'm sure. You've created quite a stir, missing persons and all that. The story has been in the papers. Probably the wrong story is my guess."

"What are they saying?"

"That you and your father were discovered missing yesterday when you never showed up in class. An overall-clad man was seen briefly closing your house up tight and then disappeared without a trace. The paper also indicated that your disappearance coincided with the theft of fifty thousand dollars in petty cash along with the disappearance of Ms. Lucinda Brahms, president of Alliance for International Communications Incorporated, and her confidential secretary, Ms. Jolene Senter. It was suggested by a confidential source close to the people involved that the events were linked to the abrupt change in leadership at the corporation. Are they?"

"You haven't told me what you are doing here."

"I'm not entirely sure. I had a strong intuition that something new and exciting, something meaningful for our time, was assembling up in these parts. I was drawn by the strong vibes, I guess. What's going on up here? Why are you here? Fill me in, Robert."

"Can we trust you?"

"I don't know, can you?" Shaman queried him. "Do you?"

"I guess I do, Shaman, but I'm not alone. Maybe it would be better if you came with me."

"Am I a prisoner?"

"Heck no! You're a willing guest, aren't you?"

Shaman laughed. He fell in step with Robert, and they moved along the dusty road. This was the hottest time of day. The sun burned down on them. They were thankful for the breeze that slid toward them from the mountains to the west.

"Now tell me the truth, Shaman, how do you happen to be here?" Robert asked.

"You didn't see me at the Westchester County Hospital?" asked Shaman.

"You were there?"

"Yes. I was visiting a sick friend. While she was resting, I stood at the window just gazing out at the world. All of a sudden, a hearse drove up. I thought right away some poor soul was leaving the earth. While I watched from the angle up on the upper floor, I saw you and several others climb in after the stretcher. You have to admit, anybody would be a bit curious, don't you think?" Shaman explained.

"But how did you get here?" Robert wanted it all made clear before he escorted the Shaman further to their hideout.

"Do you know the driver of the hearse?" Shaman asked.

"No. Never even noticed him." Robert admitted.

"You should have! He was in the class when Stu introduced you for the first time. He was the tall, thin fellow, intelligent and idealistic. I found out from him that he has driven for your dad on other occasions." Shaman seemed proud of himself for this bit of sleuthing.

"He told you about the Westchester Airport destination?" Robert asked.

"Well, I had a little trouble worming it out of him. I was able to put six and three together and guessed at nine." Shaman laughed. "Anyway, then I was really curious and ended up taking the flight to Keene, nosing around for any information, and wound up here, where you found me."

"Here I thought it was accidental or the result of pure intuition!" Robert sounded disappointed.

"The results of most plans are accidental. Anyway, Robert, nice to see you!" Shaman was genuinely pleased.

"How is Stu?" Robert asked.

"I don't know. I haven't seen him for more than a week. I assume he's deep in his studies. He might be graduating early."

"That's good."

"You know he felt badly about his betrayal of you."

"It wasn't a real betrayal, you now. There was nothing he ever found out that isn't common knowledge anyway. I wonder if he is still connected with that dark man in the black suit who worked for the president of Premium Technical Products Incorporated."

"I don't think so, but as far as I know, they are still paying his room and board expenses. His army support ran out, I believe."

"I have forgiven him the spying. I understood how he was tempted and don't really blame him for it, but I am not sure I could or even should trust him. You are not in contact with him, are you?"

"No. Oh, I see. You think maybe the corporate people might still use him and find out where you are?"

"Yes. It's important that we remain hidden for the time being. My father was hurt. So were several others in the escape from New York. Here they are out of danger. Are you sure you weren't followed?"

"I never thought of that. I was having enough trouble following signs without worrying about my back. However, I did not notice anything, nor did I feel anything ominous." Shaman sounded sincere. "So you are all together here, living off the stolen two hundred and fifty thousand dollars the newspapers are gossiping about?"

"I'll let my father explain things more to you. It's not what you may have read. The real story would make a best-selling movie."

"Robert?" Shaman signaled a change in subject. "You know about your house?"

"Our house? What about our house?"

"You haven't heard?"

"What?"

"Yesterday morning, somebody set fire to your house. By the time it was called in and the fire engines arrived, it was hopeless. They were able to save the houses on all sides, but yours was totally destroyed."

"How do you know it was arson?"

"That's what was said on the radio. They did an investigation. There was some form of inflammable material used in the back by the patio, evidently."

"My poor dad. Somebody really has it in for him!"

They walked along in silence. Robert grew up in that house. Then he thought of all their possessions—the furniture, clothes, dishes, and kitchen equipment. He thought of his books, his university texts . . . The more he remembered, the sadder he became. Then slowly, his sadness turned to anger.

"I wonder who is doing all this to us, what we can do to stop it! I'm feeling a terrible anger about all this. I usually do not become angry easily, but this is too much." Robert looked down as he spoke and saw that his fists were clenched.

"Unless you know who is responsible, who your enemy is, you are in the dark, unable to act coherently. You've got to identify this ruthless enemy of yours."

"Let's see what Dad has to say. He may not know either."

"Do we still have far to go?"

"We're almost there."

Another half mile through the red dust of the rutted road, and they arrived at their secluded shelter. Shaman loved the place. It certainly had charm. He couldn't have enough of the abundant blossoming bushes and trees. Mingled among the blossoms were the small brightly colored songbirds so common in summer. They popped in and out among the branches, rivaling the flowers with their extravagant bursts of color.

Charles did not seem to be surprised as Robert brought Shaman into the living room where they were all gathered.

"Hello, Shaman. Good to see you."

"You know him?" Robert asked, surprised.

"No, we've never met. However, I did have you investigated when Robert first told me about you."

"I hope I came up clean, as they say."

"You did. Somewhat a rebel, I understand, but nothing subversive. The university didn't have much good to say about you."

"No doubt. Anybody who thinks for themselves today is considered unfit to teach."

"Why are you here?"

"I was in my room near the university . . . Actually, I had company—"

"The Shaman has quite an attractive following," Robert dared to interject.

"Yes, I do. But I am here alone. As I was saying, I was meditating—surprisingly deep in meditation—when I felt these strong vibrations. Something new and different was entering the world space. I felt it to be akin to my own destiny and entered more and more into it. It remained alive in me even when I was no longer meditating. It drew me, and I responded and followed my impulse to this place, where I ran into Robert."

"As a result, you know where we are."

"Yes. I will not betray you. Besides, I don't plan to leave. I'll be here where you can have me watched. As I said, I am drawn to something happening here, and I want to be part of it."

"Do you trust him?" Charles asked Robert pointedly.

"Yes, I do," Robert answered. "Besides, if he is here, doesn't try to connect with anyone outside, he can't do us any harm even if he wanted to."

"I don't want to!" Shaman interposed.

Charles realized that he also trusted the Shaman even though they had just met for the first time. There was something in his face—the open expression that put him at ease, made him feel this was one of them, connected and belonging.

"Shaman has some sad news for us." Robert decided to open the issue.

"Oh?" They all looked at Shaman and waited.

"Yes. It has been on the news. I'm surprised you did not know. It seems your enemies have decided to make you homeless."

"Oh, that!" Charles shrugged his shoulders.

"You knew?"

"Yes. When I phoned the house from the Westchester County Airport, someone picked up the receiver but did not answer. I also did not speak. As we waited each other out, I distinctly heard police and fire sirens in the background. The phone was then quickly hung up. I assumed our house was doomed and the culprit had to run for it or be caught in the flames. We are in for it, I'm afraid to say. We have a ruthless enemy that will stop at nothing to get rid of us."

"Do you know who it is?" asked Jolene.

"I don't have enough evidence to be sure, but I think I know who is behind this. At least I don't know anyone else that it could be."

"Armand Dillon?"

"Armand Dillon!"

"But now that he has acquired AIC, why bother with us?"

"Loose ends, my friends, loose ends."

Charles looked around at this little group. There were five of them. Then he remembered Graham and Benning. That made seven, not counting Shaman. Was it enough? It was a beginning, but was it enough?

"If we include Graham and Benning, there are seven of us here and back home. It's not much, but with the Shaman here rooting for us as a kind of spiritual guide, maybe we could think of this moment as a beginning."

"Beginning, yes." Robert was curious what others thought. "But beginning of what?"

"Think of this time as an incubation period for what we'll be doing together," Lucky said.

"That's how I see it. Armand Dillon needs to be stopped, not just for our sake, but for the good of society—the world," Charles agreed.

"But is he really the problem? Think of the directors of AIC who couldn't wait to install him as leader of Alliance for International Communications Incorporated." Robert was adamant.

"Yes, and think of the media and, for that matter, the public. They are the force behind the Armand Dillons of the world," Charles added.

"If we look at it that way, I get really depressed. Is it hopeless? Are we trying to imitate Don Quixote? Will we be fencing windmills?" Robert asked sadly.

"I think," said Lucinda, "fighting Armand Dillon on his own ground is hopeless. He's got all the tools and all the resources on his side. He even has a willing public rooting for him."

"What other ground is there? You mean we shouldn't try to get Alliance for International Communications Incorporated back from him? We have some friends on the inside. I bet Armand Dillon makes some enemies along the way. Even the board might not be satisfied with his tactics. After a while, more and more money loses its luster. Well, maybe not." Horst was fishing for some new thoughts.

"Maybe what we need is something totally new—a new venture of some kind." Lucinda was obviously thinking out loud.

"One that embodies different values?" Robert asked. "Does the world want that?"

"It would have to make a profit and satisfy investors no matter what other values we work with," Charles concluded.

"This is 1971," Lucinda began thoughtfully. "It's the middle of a tumultuous century that has already experienced two disastrous wars, pitting moral evil against technological evil. No matter how many rational justifications we delude ourselves with, the dictatorship of one madman was wrong, but so was the introduction of the atom into world history. Maybe it was necessary. Maybe it saved countless lives by shortening the war. It still, in hindsight, made available to the human race a force we are still too immature to manage. Who knows what demons it will still release into our affairs?"

The group surveyed each other, seriously feeling their unique situation: at a kind of destiny crossroads, seeing both the hopelessness of the time as well as the urgent need to place something different into the stream of time—some turning point in the historical sequence.

"We have to do something, Charles. Just think, there's Robert and Jolene, and maybe they and others will have children. How can we justify ourselves to them if we permit a Mr. Dillon to capitalize on the growing greed and materialism of our generation? I have a feeling we matter after all! We matter, but only if we stand up for the alternatives," Lucinda said.

Jolene spread wide her arms to express her deep concerns. "We're caught between diminishing strength and a growing evil. What can we do? It looks like our enemy is stronger and has more support than we could ever hope to achieve."

The five plus lapsed again into silence looking at each other, not doomed but overcome with a feeling of helplessness and growing hopelessness.

"For that reason," Charles began, "I think we need a really safe place to gather strength and mostly to become clear what steps might have the greatest impact. We may not succeed, but it seems to me we are obligated to try. I am not in favor of foolish, hopeless action. I really do think we can figure out how to deal with this menace and succeed. We need time and safety for that purpose and . . . we need help."

"So what's your idea?" Robert asked, and Horst nodded his head.

"Yes, Charles, let us into your thinking," said Lucky.

Charles gazed around at them, lingered on Shaman and then came to his decision. In the end, one has to have some trust. Intelligent trust is what he believed in.

"Lucinda and I have to go into hiding, and I believe, for safety's sake, Jolene and Robert will join us. We have to keep some intelligent surveillance in New York, where the overt action is taking place. Graham and Benning will see to that. Horst, I'm afraid you are also needed there as a kind of go-between, connecting us and keeping our information accurate. If you are willing, you'll be a kind of twentieth-century pony express. Shaman, are you in? I mean actively in, which is risky and might get you into trouble? You either have to be in or out. That's clear right now."

"I'm in!" Shaman decided. "But only in my own way. I'll not cater to violence or to torture of any kind. I just am not up for anything like that."

"Neither are we," Charles reassured him.

"But how do you fight evil that enjoys violence and lies and inflicting pain? With love? Aren't we forced to fight fire with fire?" Robert was perplexed.

"No," Lucky was adamant. "I would rather fail and suffer the consequences. The minute we succumb to their methods, we are immediately lost regardless of the outcome. We'll be beaten before we start. In the long run, Armand Dillon doesn't really desire money. I'm sure of it. He wants followers. He wants his victims to collapse morally, become subject to his intellect and heartlessness."

"I agree with Lucky." Jolene reached over and took her hand.

"We all do," Charles insisted. "That's why we need time. We have to understand what we plan from an ethical point of view as well as from the practical side—that is, actually succeeding."

"Where will you four go? Is there such a safe place? Wouldn't it be safer right in New York City? You could hide there just as easily as anywhere else," Shaman spoke up.

"No, I have a special place in mind. It is not only safe but has excellent facilities both medically and also from the side of communications. I'd rather not disclose it yet until all the loose ends are tied neatly in place. Then I want to be sure the information will not find its way into the wrong hands."

"What happens next?" Shaman asked.

"Tonight, when it is dark," Charles answered, "you and Horst will be picked up by Gus, the friend in the jeep, and taken to different hotels at different airports. You'll go back and find excuses for where you've been. Horst, check in with Benning. He'll cover for you at AIC. Shaman, return to the Fairmont University area, make a little trouble so folks will know you are there. Be watchful with Steward Brand. You might find him useful, but be careful."

"He's one of my pupils. I think I can manage him," Shaman assured them.

"We will remain here until tomorrow evening when we will make our break," Charles concluded without giving much detail or revealing that the faithful Gus will again take them away in his jeep.

It felt so much better having a precise course of action laid out ahead of them. They actually felt secure, just from knowing a plan was in place. None of them liked uncertainty! All of them would be astonished to know how it really turns out.

Chapter Sixteen

Destruction

When Calder and Cliff appeared outside Armand's office, the secretary just waved them in. She didn't bother to announce them since hardly a day went by that they were not called in for a report or consultation. She just assumed Armand would want to see them.

Armand looked up from his papers and inspected each of them in turn.

"Just you, Calder. I'll see you later." He nodded in the direction of Cliff. The two exchanged glances, wondering what was up. Cliff left, and Calder stood for a minute and then eased himself in one of the hard chairs placed in front of Armand's desk.

"Well?" Armand asked without looking up.

"I found them."

"Good. Where are they?"

"In a houseboat on a lake in southern New Hampshire. It is well hidden. You were right! The Shaman met up with the

McLane kid, and the two of them led us to the hideout. We still don't know for sure how many they are. We caught sight of Charles McLane once. No sign of Ms. Brahms. However, her secretary, Jolene Senter, has been in and out. None of them are disguised. They seem to think they have escaped and are safely hidden."

"That's good. I have to tell you that Jolene being there is a good sign. It means Ms. Brahms is probably there as well. I think this means there is a good chance she is not seriously hurt."

"I'm inclined to agree. There has been no mention of any kind of funeral or religious service. That hearse was probably McLane's idea, a way to get her out of the hospital and fool our people. They only saw the driver from their vantage point. They couldn't even see any of the activity around the back of the hearse."

"Didn't you say that Ms. Brahm's secretary is dallying with the McLane kid?" asked Armand.

"Yes."

"I'll bet you he's there as well."

Calder wanted more precise instructions. "You want us to get them tonight? It would be easy. The houseboat is a neat hideaway, but it is also a foolproof trap. Once the wooden walkway is set on fire, there's no escape. It's like the wick of a candle or the fuse on explosives. The fire will speed up the walkway. Once it hits the wooden supports, it will spread sideways in both directions and engulf the entire structure."

"How will they escape?" asked Armand.

"They can't."

"They have to!" Armand got excited. "Calder, you mustn't let them die!"

"What do you mean? I don't get it. What about the accident with the limousine?"

"You still don't understand, do you?" Armand was incredulous.

"I sure don't."

Armand rose from his chair behind the desk and moved around to the front to sit next to Calder in a similar hard chair. He folded his hands together so that the tips of his fingers on one hand touched the tips of his fingers on the other hand. There was a touch of sadness in the way his eyes drooped at the corners.

"I've worked so hard to get you to understand me, my mission and purpose." Armand spoke slowly, each word distinct. "I'm only using money and profit to assemble the people I need. I am using the natural greed and all the other natural emotions attached to it as a way of enlisting my people—the ones I can count on, the ones who believe in me and trust me."

Calder was now really puzzled. He turned over in his mind all the instructions he had received from Armand over the years. Never had he been so precise. Calder just didn't understand! Armand pressed his fingertips together several times as he realized Calder's confusion.

"The masses of people are easy to get. They just follow their appetites. As long as I can continue to entice their taste buds for money and all that money can give them, I will have them at my beck and call. However, I want more than they can give me. I want people like you who are intelligent and resourceful—people who are a bit above their everyday desires, who already have the ability to think for themselves and carry values in their souls. What I like about you, Calder, is that you are a willing individual who has accepted my intentions and serves me because you want to."

Calder dropped his gaze from Armand's face and rested his eyes on the floor. He hadn't realized that Armand actually treasured him. He had always thought he was just doing his job. True, he had risen very rapidly in Premium Technical Products Incorporated these last few years. His secret was to do what Armand asked of him and to do what he thought Armand wanted him to do. That led to promotions and raises. What more was there? Did Armand want him to do something he hadn't guessed at? What would that be? What more could he do? He listened intently for more clues.

Armand continued slowly. "I want Lucinda Brahms! I want Charles McLane! I want Robert McLane and Jolene Senter. I want them all. I even want this Shaman character. These are all people with values—they're alive inside. I want that life working for me. I want them loyal to me, working with me to secure the people under my leadership."

"I'm not sure you can get them. I think they are all pretty set against you. Armand, you are talking about converting your enemies into friends!"

"Ah! You do get it."

"Yes, I do, but it won't work," Calder insisted.

"Maybe not right away. Maybe it will take a while, but I am a very patient man. I am willing to make you a bet that sooner or later I'll have them. The whole world is so configured right now that they don't have a chance to be independent beings. The media is molding everyone's feelings and thoughts for me. Their own lower instincts are bound to overcome them with enough encouragement from me. You'll see! Given enough time, I will own them."

"Armand, what do you want me to do?" Calder asked wearily. "I've arranged the little party at their hideout for tonight. I'm sure they are planning to outwit me again and find another, even safer place if I don't put an end to it tonight."

"Let them escape. Scare them out of their minds, but whatever else you do, let them live. By dying, they will be free of me, and I can't have that. I want them alive. Once they are dead, I can no longer use them, and they will have made their final escape. Don't take them from me! See that they escape, track them to wherever they go, and keep me informed of where they are. Those are my wishes. Do you understand?" asked Armand.

"This represents a change in plans. I better get up to New Hampshire as quickly as possible to make sure your wishes are carried out."

"Good, Calder! My faithful Calder. I think we now really understand one another!"

Calder was worried about his plans in New Hampshire already in motion. A slight film of perspiration veiled his forehead as he rose and made his way to the door of Armand's office. This time, he quickly closed the door behind him.

"Can I get you anything, Mr. Tebbit?" the secretary called after him. "A taxi, maybe?"

Calder never heard her. He was already half-running past the elevators and then down the stairs of the building. He hoped he was still in time to modify his intricate arrangements.

*****

In a rural farmhouse in New Hampshire, Gus assembled his few necessities in a small knapsack. He included enough drinking water for twenty-four hours. He had no idea how long this would take. Whenever Charles cashed in one of his favors, he could be sure of one thing: the unexpected. Nothing ever went routinely. There were always those unplanned interferences. On one hand, that meant excitement. On the other hand, it usually meant danger. He didn't mind. It made him sharpen his wits and create new responses. It added spice to his otherwise quite routine life.

When he had driven Horst Perla to the Manchester Airport, he was prepared for almost anything. He was almost disappointed how smoothly it all went. He didn't think he was even followed. When Horst disappeared into the terminal, he looked around and waited a few minutes to see if there was anything suspicious around him. Nothing!

"When are you taking me?" asked Shaman Pi. He had patiently gone along to the Manchester Airport, even knowing he would then have a longer ride to the Hartford International Airport.

"Right now. Charles did not want you two to travel together from the same airport for the sake of security. We'll be there for your flight in about ninety minutes." Gus was following his instructions exactly.

"I understand."

He drove back around and then to Hartford International Airport. Again, no trouble. This was unheard of. Charles must be slipping. Maybe he was getting too old for the exciting life he usually lived. Gus didn't know whether to be regretful or grateful. He decided he was probably of two minds. Either way, he was glad to help Charles.

It took him the whole afternoon, but he managed both trips without a wrinkle. For all the exciting adventures he and Charles had worked out together over the years, it was the least he could do. Besides, Charles paid him well.

He picked up his knapsack from the kitchen table, hoisted it over his shoulder, and held it in place with just one of the straps. He looked around the kitchen to make sure everything was in order. The burners on the propane gas stove were in the off position. The faucets in the sink had been turned off securely to avoid any dripping. The shades on the windows were drawn. He grunted his satisfaction that he had taken care of everything before he switched off the overhead light. Immediately, the night-light by the door blinked on.

Outside, he paused by the door and listened for any unusual sound. Charles had warned him that his enemies were ruthless and crafty. They had already engineered a car crash with serious injuries to his friends. They would stop at nothing to get what they wanted. And what did they want? That was the rub. Even Charles was not entirely sure. Everything that had been tried so far had failed to produce any ultimate results. Charles figured out that they were all a bit clumsy. They could have been executed more efficiently. So far, only the chauffeur—poor guy—had died. No guns or direct attacks had materialized. This puzzled Charles and worried Gus. Why, in this day and age, with so many intriguing weapons available, were they apparently not used?

Gus moved toward the barn, staying as much as possible in the shadows. He cautiously opened the smaller side door into the barn. He knew the inside of the barn as well as he knew the inside of the house. Without turning on a light, he moved silently toward the large barn doorway, which he had left open earlier. He carefully placed his knapsack in the backseat of his open jeep.

It was then that he realized he had made a mistake. He should not have left the jeep top off for this particular adventure. His passengers should not be visible. He didn't like it. He prided himself on planning all his activities meticulously right down to the most minute detail. What should he do now? He decided there was still time before meeting up with Charles and his passengers.

In the dark, he groped for the top of the jeep resting against the barn wall to the right of the jeep. He knew that all the latches were intact as he had inspected them himself just yesterday when he thought they might be needed.

He pulled the top closer to the jeep, scratching the ground a little as he pulled. When it was in the right position parallel to the jeep, he hoisted it up and over. This made a rumble of noise before it was exactly in the right place. He paused then and waited to see if there were any consequences. The night was calm. The tree frogs chirped and warbled, pretending to be birds but not succeeding. Other familiar sounds found his ears out of the woods nearby. He identified them all. An owl he knew well. Fluttering of those nighttime marauders, the bats! There was also a scratching sound, which he thought was probably a porcupine up in the hemlocks. He also identified the continuous soft pattering of sound made by the hemlock needles falling into their beds with other needles already at least three inches deep on the ground. He did not detect any unusual or threatening other sounds out of the night surroundings.

He deftly locked the brackets in place on his side and moved around the jeep to find the ones on the other side. When they were locked, he returned to the driver's side and was about to get in, when he felt a weight on his right shoulder.

"Don't move." The voice was close behind him. "This is a gun, which I know how to use."

Gus did not move. He was puzzled that someone could sneak up behind him in spite of all the precautions he had taken. Whoever it was had to have been in the barn already before he had arrived. Otherwise he would have heard something. That means, whoever it was knew he was planning to use the jeep. Whoever it was had some sort of connection with what Charles had planned. He realized they were ruthless, and he decided immediately he would cooperate—at least for the time being.

"Put your hands behind your back. Carefully! The gun is still on you."

"What do you want?"

"Never mind what I want. Just know that we are not out to hurt you—unless you force us. Cooperate and you will be just fine. Now I'm going to tie your hands, not just together, but behind your back. It will not be uncomfortable unless you try to break loose. If you do that, you may end up with a dislocated shoulder. If you stay quiet until morning, I know your helper will be around to release you. You understand all that? I'd appreciate to hear a simple yes!" The voice was insistent as the ropes tightened around Gus's hands and then shoulders in a firm but not terribly painful pressure. His captor seemed expert in the tying of knots—maybe a sailor?

"Why is it I have this feeling you are not going to do what I tell you?" the man said.

"I'd be a fool not to," Gus assured him.

"I think not. I betcha I will be around the corner getting into my own car, and you will already be hard at it, trying to get loose in spite of the pain!"

"I'm tired," Gus volunteered.

"Have a good rest!" the voice quietly murmured in his ear.

That was the last sound Gus heard. A loud smack blasted his eardrums as the hard object slammed into the back of his head. There appeared a flash of incredible fireworks cascading in all directions from his position in the universe, and then suddenly, black. That's all he was able to remember later when he came to—too late to help Charles.

*****

Charles and Robert assembled a change of clothes, razors, toothbrushes, pajamas, and a few items to go along with flashlights and matches. They first laid them out on one of the beds and looked them over together.

"Since I don't know where we are going, I don't really know what to take," Robert said.

"I'm sorry. I've gone through a great deal of trouble, and I figured it is safer for all of us if I kept it a secret until we actually leave. I guess I've become overly cautious. I never used to be this way," Charles added.

"At least can you tell me if we're going far away or someplace near?"

"It's far away," said Charles.

"Then why the pajamas?"

"I guess we don't really need them. We can sleep in our clothes if we have to," Charles admitted.

"It won't be the first time." Robert took them out of the knapsack and replaced them in the bureau nearby. Charles went to retrieve the little bit of laundry they had done, and Robert did the dishes and put them all back where they had found them. The leftover butter, bread, salad, and all the accessories he returned to the refrigerator.

"I guess we leave the fridge on?" he asked.

"Yes. The owner will wait a few days before returning. He doesn't want to get involved in any of my escapades. Maybe he thinks I'm here with a woman?"

"Wait till he finds out you've been here with two women." Robert laughed.

"Incidentally, where are they? It's been awful quiet."

They were going to finish their packing and then go up the ladder to the rooftop deck for a last look around.

"How do we thank your friend? This has been such a nice place, so private and yet so scenic and enjoyable." Robert seemed almost sad to leave.

"Don't worry, we're good friends and meet every now and then in different places in the world," Charles reassured him.

"I guess you've been just about everywhere on the job."

"Just about—except most of Africa is still foreign to me. We had very little business there, and others were more qualified to handle it. I've been in every country in South America, most of the large cities in the Middle East and Asia. Right now, I am in the mood to settle down a bit. Most of my life has been living out of a suitcase."

"Shall we join the ladies on the upper deck?" asked Robert.

Robert led the way down the narrow hallway to the fold-up ladder that would bring them up to the rooftop deck. He stood aside and let his father go up first. They had to move carefully among the gathering shadows to avoid the outdoor furniture, a barbecue grill, and other picnic equipment. As a rule, the furniture had to be tied down in case of a storm or off the water wind. The rope for this purpose had been neatly curled in the left-hand corner of the deck.

"Isn't this magnificent?" Lucky turned her face to Charles. The evening light of the setting sun, with its special warmed rays, blushed her features and made her smile radiant. "Charles, this has been a wonderful respite. I feel so much better. Pretty soon, I'll be myself and back in the ring." She laughed at that idea.

"No ring for you, my dear! Except for the one I will soon place on your finger," Charles promised.

"Oh, Charles! Do you mean it?"

"I do. When this is all behind us, we'll arrange it," said Charles.

"I'm so glad. It is a dream come true." Lucinda bent forward to place an arm around Charles's shoulder and kissed him.

"Aside from the ring you two are talking about," said Jolene, "the AIC ring has been taken over by monsters."

"You are so right," sighed Lucky.

"Are you both ready to go?" asked Charles.

"Yes. We've packed everything, although they are probably all the wrong things since our leader refuses to give us even a clue as to where we are going," Lucinda chided him.

"It's safer this way." Charles then smiled and said jokingly, "If you knew where we are going, you might just leave without us and go there on your own. We can't have that, can we? I would be miserable, and Robert here would die of a broken heart."

"Poor baby." Jolene cuddled up to Robert and gave him a quick kiss. "By the way, just incidentally, do you happen to still love me?"

"Oh." Robert laughed. "I forgot to mention that. There's been so much else going on, but now I remember. Are you, Jolene? I don't want to kiss the wrong girl."

"Come home to mama!" Jolene wrapped him in her arms.

The four of them sat together, watching the final minutes of light in the sky as the sun disappeared below the horizon. Darkness slowly crept forward from the east, touching everything and muting its life, closing everything that was still lingering open. The dark shadows that had grown longer and longer with the sun's setting now suddenly evaporated into an all-encompassing darkness. A cool wind gave a brief reappearance in farewell and then the calm of night settled in. In New Hampshire, this was the signal for gnats, mosquitoes, and all kinds of little buzzing creatures to come alive. The bats knew this and charged through the sky, dipping and fluttering in their excitement with the edible life around them.

"Gus should be here with the jeep any minute now. We had better get ready. Perhaps it would be wise to meet him out by the gate," Charles suggested.

Charles and Robert and Jolene and Lucky all rose with one mutual consent and turned away from the water to go inside, away from the buzzing and biting hordes.

That's when they first noticed the flames.

At first it seemed to them the fire was in the woods on land. Then it became clear the flames were licking along the wooden walkway over the water to the house. They were low along the walkway and blue-green in color as though from burning in oil or kerosene. As they watched, they had already moved some five yards closer.

"We've got to get out of here," Charles urged.

"Maybe we can all work together to put it out," Jolene suggested.

"That fire was set. Look at its color. The walkway is acting as a kind of wick. It will be here at the house in minutes. We can't get out that way any longer. We'll have to use the back door to get to the skiff!" Charles explained.

He moved them toward the ladder leading down to the main floor. In that short time, before they started down the ladder, the fire at the front was another five yards closer, and behind it, a wall of flames leapt high in the air, illuminating the entire neighborhood. It mirrored a vivid image of itself in the waters of the lake.

Robert climbed down the ladder first, ahead of Lucky, who still could only move very slowly and with help. Robert turned at the bottom of the ladder and stretched out his arms to support Lucky as she moved carefully from rung to rung. Jolene was above Lucky, reaching down to catch her hands if she slipped on the ladder rungs.

Charles was the last. He didn't bother to shut the trapdoor at the top that could be closed to protect the interior of the house in the event of rain or snow. They followed the drill exactly as they had planned it. Robert retrieved the packed knapsacks. Charles rescued a small bag and a bottle of water from the refrigerator. They began to move in a group to the back glass doors that led out and around the side to where they had the skiff stored. Jolene opened the glass door and helped Lucky out. She took one of the knapsacks from Robert, and they all three moved along the catwalk planking.

At that moment, smoke leaking into the front of the house gave way to flames. The wick had worked beautifully, and now the entire front of the house was crackling and snapping as the flames engulfed the wooden shakes that gave the house so much charm.

"Get Lucinda to the skiff," Charles asked of Robert.

"What are you going to do?" Robert asked him.

"I'll try to pour on some water with the hose we rigged for watering the shrubs and plants in pots. Maybe I can delay the fire long enough for you to get the women out."

"I think you should—"

"Robert! Please, this is no time for the democratic process. Just do it, please?"

Robert turned and inched along the planking. It was difficult to steady Jolene and Lucky from behind, but there was only room for one at a time. They both had to pass the place where the skiff was protruding from under the house between the pontoons so that Robert could start working it loose and out. None of them could get in until he had it out far enough. As he tugged on it, pushing down as they had practiced, it seemed to be caught on something underneath when it was about half way out.

Uh-oh, Robert thought.

The whole front of the house was burning. What a strange sight to see the entire front aflame and the back part still untouched. Robert felt a slight breeze on the side of his face. He knew that would affect the fire and they only had minutes more to escape.

"Hurry, Robert." Jolene's face was lit up with the light from the fire now roaring only fifteen or twenty feet away.

Robert pulled hard. He thought he heard something tear, but it gave way suddenly, and he nearly went over the side. He pulled harder on the skiff. He saw that it was more like a canoe but out of wood. At another time, he would have admired the workmanship. When he got it alongside, parallel to the planking, he held it firmly in place while Jolene first helped Lucky in and then eased herself over the side, balancing her weight so as not to tip it over. Robert held it in place, waiting for Charles.

"Charles!" he shouted for him to come. None of them could see Charles, who was still on the inside of the house with difficulties of his own.

While he was dousing the door and the entire wall at the front of the house, the pump that supplied water to the house gave out. It sprayed and then trickled and then bled a drip or two and stopped. He threw the hose down on the floor. He knew it was time to get out and fast.

Just then, the side window opposite where he was standing crashed in, and a dark figure appeared. This was the first time he saw an actual person—one of his enemies, he presumed. In the light of the fire, he took in the long face, sharp chin, and dark eyes. His nose was hooked, and his hair was tousled from his climb through the window. In his left hand, he still carried the hatchet that he had used to break down the window, frame and all.

Charles backed away from the intruder slowly while he gathered himself together on his feet. Behind him, he felt the rungs of the ladder leading up to the rooftop patio. The fire now engulfed the entire front of the house, outlining the front door in red and yellow flames. There was no escape in that direction. Charles hoisted himself up onto the ladder and climbed quickly to the roof. His last glimpse of the intruder showed him that he was not far behind.

CHAPTER SEVENTEEN

The Final Collision

When Charles reached the top of the ladder, he had to move quickly along the roof toward the rear of the house. The flames shot high as the ancient wood of the house and years of paint fed them and sent them spiraling up showering sparks in every direction with each crackle.

Charles backed up into the left-hand corner of the rooftop patio. His foot stumbled on something lying on the floor. He looked down and saw the neatly curled rope used to tie the furniture down in high winds. He tied one end to the railing and turned to check on the progress of his pursuer, who just then emerged from the top of the ladder and stepped onto the roof. His powerful frame was illuminated from behind by the wall of fire. Everywhere along the floor, little streamers of smoke leaked from cracks and pinholes in the asphalt. It couldn't be long before the fire burst through the floor from below and consumed the rest of the house.

The intruder moved in his direction, carrying the hatchet in his left hand. It hung loosely from his hand as though he had no intension to use it, but then he pointed it toward Charles as though it were just an extension of his arm.

"Jump!" he urged Charles. Puzzled by such incongruous instructions, Charles paused in the act of climbing over the railing of the roof patio.

"Jump!" the intruder urged more vehemently.

Charles clung to the outside of the railing and watched cautiously as flames broke through several places in the flooring of the roof. Where his feet touched the roof, his shoes were steaming with the heat. He saw the asphalt sealer pool as liquid and run in spider rivulets across the floor.

"Jump! Damn it! Jump!" the intruder swore at Charles.

It was getting too hot for Charles to stand. The hair on the back of his hands curled in the heat and wilted. He looked behind him, down to the water, where Robert was holding the skiff in place, waiting for him in spite of the heat and flames. He took hold of the rope and prepared to let himself down.

As he watched, the intruder's feet gave way, and he plunged down through a burning hole in the roof, blocking the flames from rising with his lower body. He screamed in agony. Then before his very eyes, Charles saw a strange look come over his face. It had elements of fear, but also, his eyes widened as though he had just realized something more than his own imminent death. Then he disappeared with a rush of smoke and fire into the inferno below. His final scream echoed among the nearby trees.

Charles rappelled himself hand over hand down to the deck and was helped into the skiff by Jolene and Lucky while

Robert pushed off, took up a paddle, and drove them out into the night and safety. They paused some fifty yards out to look back. The house had fallen in on itself, spilling sparks into a wide circle of water that hissed and sputtered wherever they landed. Only one bare two-by-four at the corner where Charles had escaped still remained upright, smoldering, but intact.

"Did you hear what I heard?" asked Robert.

"Yes," said Joleen "I heard it too. Very strange!"

"What did he scream? Did I hear it right?" asked Lucky.

"He screamed 'Free.' I know that's what he said, but I don't understand what he meant," Jolene said.

"What a strange thing to say. He was obviously caught, actually trapped in the flames. How could he think he was free?" Robert was really puzzled.

Puzzled or not as may be the case, they had plenty to concern them as they paddled across the lake to a road that ran parallel to the waterfront. A short walk down that road brought them to an all-night café with a telephone. Charles was busy at the phone while Jolene, Robert, and Lucky ordered coffee and leftover danish for all of them. Charles had just barely finished when the country style taxi drove up.

The driver was first amazed and then pleased when Charles gave him two one-hundred-dollar bills and asked him to drive south to the Westchester County Airport. Surprisingly, Charles and Lucky slept on the way. Jolene twisted and turned in a shallow sleep interrupted now and then by suddenly sitting up, eyes wide, before falling back into Robert's sheltering shoulder. Robert had too much to think about to sleep.

He wondered what would now happen to him and Jolene. Where was Charles taking Lucky? Should he and Jolene go too? Where they still in danger? Why had everything seemed so threatening and yet not ever really disastrous. So many questions. So few answers. He finally dozed until, early the next morning, they reached the Westchester County Airport.

*****

At the little Westchester County Airport, their taxi was able to drive directly to the charter plane Charles had arranged for them to fly. The pilot Charles had engaged separately obviously had done work for Charles, either at another time or perhaps many times. They shook hands enthusiastically until Charles shouted from pain in his right elbow and shoulder, where he was still nursing bruises from the crash.

The pilot climbed aboard first and spent some time getting familiar with the controls while they slowly managed to transfer Lucky from the taxi to the plane. She must have felt very secure with all her close friends about her, because she stayed mostly asleep, only lifting her eyelids for a dull look around every now and then. The sleeping pills were a godsend.

Once they had her settled in, she really did disappear into slumber. While the pilot struggled to arrange clearance for take-off, Charles lingered with Robert and Jolene. They were seriously deep in discussion.

"I don't feel right leaving her now," Jolene was saying. "I have been looking after her for nearly three years, and I am not going to abandon her now just when she needs me the most."

"Why don't you two come along?" suggested Charles.

"I have to finish my degree. You were the first to push for that, long before I really wanted to," Robert pointed out.

"And what about my job? It just occurred to me—I may not have one." Jolene sighed. "Besides my job is to take care of Lucky, and she is no longer there."

"I can assure you, going back is the worst thing you could do. Not only may PTP be after you to find out where we all are, but AIC and the press will be joining the hunt. You can't go back, not now."

"Where are we going?" Robert asked.

"Then you're going with us?"

Robert turned to face Jolene. He placed his hands on her shoulders and looked squarely at her.

"I agree with Dad," he said. "You should not go back. If you're not going back, neither am I. I can always pick up my studies later or, even better, finish up at another university, maybe one where we're going. Which reminds me, where are we going?"

"Yes, where are we going?" They both turned to Charles for an answer.

"It's a secret place. I happen to know the doctor who owns and runs the place you've never heard of. They handle two dozen patients at a time, and that's the limit. They don't advertise, nor are they in the phone book. Word of mouth! That's the only way anyone finds out about them."

"And they are . . . ? Did I miss that part?" Robert asked.

"Fifty miles outside of Rio."

"Brazil?"

"Brazil."

"Are we going to fly in this all the way to Rio?" asked Robert.

"No, we land in a private airfield outside Rio nearby our destination, where an ambulance will meet us," Charles clarified.

"Can Lucky survive that kind of a trip? It must take about ten hours?" asked Jolene.

"Look again at this charter plane. It's a BOAC Comet jet, made by de Havilland. Small but fast. We'll eat something aboard, sleep, and before you know it, we'll be there. What's really important is that it can fly at some low altitudes. Nobody—and I mean *nobody*—will know where we are."

"What about Lucky?"

Charles removed his hand from his jacket pocket. In it was a small container with capsules that clinked when he shook them. "Anti-infection pain relievers combined with sleep inducers. That nice doctor who objected so violently at our leaving the Westchester Community Hospital slipped them to me on our way out. He said no less than one capsule every eight hours. Look how Lucinda has been sleeping!"

"I'm sure it's safe where we're going," said Jolene, "but can they take care of Lucky? She was hurt pretty badly. The doctor said she needs careful watching for a number of weeks. The leg itself is supported with internal steel bars, but she also has a concussion not yet fully recovered. Out in the sticks like that, there may not even be enough equipment, and how about electricity?" Even Jolene was worried now. "We have to get her to a top-notch hospital. Her leg was twisted all out of shape. The sedative is not going to last that long," she said.

"You think I haven't thought of that?' Charles frowned. "This place has connections with the top surgeons in the world. They happen to have outstanding modern ER facilities in a service institute one half mile away that does outpatient work for the local population. That's all public knowledge. Only this hidden sanatorium, also owned by them, is deliberately unknown to protect the identity of their sometimes famous patients. Believe me, you will be amazed at what they do and how they function. We will not only be safe, we'll be well cared for. From the looks of all of us, it is just what we need right now."

"That must all cost a fortune." Robert began to understand. "Even this flight, the hearse . . . Dad, we don't have that kind of money!"

"Money is the least of my worries right now. Let's just say I'll be cashing in most of my chips—my 'good deed' chips earned along the way."

Robert put his arms around Jolene and hugged her. They rocked back and forth for a minute. Robert clarified his thoughts while holding her.

"I think we should go," he said. "It makes sense. I think they need us, anyway." He gestured toward Charles.

"Yes, I agree. Let's go." That did it for Jolene. Then she laughed softly. "We don't have a stitch of clothes, no toothbrush, no comb—nothing. What about passports?"

They both looked at Charles to see if he had thought of that wrinkle in the blanket. Neither one of them had ever travelled south of Miami and had no idea of the cultural or political atmosphere in Latin America.

"I trust both of you carry your driver's license with you at all times?" When they both nodded, Charles continued, "That's all we'll need. Don't worry. I'll get us in. I know the people where we're going. What's even more important, they know me!"

"Well," said Robert, "I guess we're all in your hands. I guess all your work in South America is paying off."

"It paid off a long time ago too. All those years I made a slew of friends. It was necessary for the job, but I enjoyed it and was well paid. By the way, Jolene, do you have a lot of money sitting in a bank account in New York City or in Jersey?"

"Dad! What a thing to ask." Robert was astounded by his father's remark.

"I only ask because they will soon find a way to trace any transactions. If I were you, I would ask the bank to transfer what you might need in the next year or so to a blind Swiss account and then draw on that as you need it. I'll show you how to do that."

"I don't have much," Jolene stated honestly.

"Then close the account. We'll do it as soon as we land in Brazil. We'd better get on board. It looks like our pilot is ready," Charles said. The pilot was waving to them from the cockpit window, urging them to climb in and hurry.

They had almost immediate clearance. Jolene checked on Lucky and found her sleeping. She made sure the seat belting around her was tight, tucked her in with the light blanket, and turned off the overhead light near her.

When Charles was aboard, he pushed the short entrance ladder clear of the plane, closed the door, and locked it securely. He obviously knew what to do, surely from prior experience. He made sure Robert and Jolene were properly seated and belted in before he picked up the intercom to let the pilot know all were safely secured. He switched off the cabin lights for takeoff.

"You've done all this before!" suggested Robert, in awe of his father's competence and experience.

"Only three times—strangely under somewhat similar conditions. Once, we cleared the runway only just in time. AIC had to pay for bullet holes in the fuselage and tail."

"One day, you will have to tell us the whole story," Jolene said and yawned. "Oh dear, I must be sleepy."

"I wonder why?" Robert chuckled and tucked the blanket around her.

"It's been quite a day." Charles reassured them both. "Let's hope all our immediate troubles are now behind us."

"You think?"

"Well, Lucinda still worries me. That leg really must heal, and I have the feeling she's still having aftereffects from the concussion. Her eyes were not focused. I wish I could have just left her at the hospital and not moved her at all. I didn't feel that was safe for her. Whoever is behind all this, and I am now positive whose sick brain is involved, is persistent and ruthless. Once we're settled, I'll continue my inquiries. I have to be careful not to reveal our whereabouts." Charles settled himself in the seat, but kept it upright for the takeoff.

"You're thinking Armand Dillon?" asked Robert.

"Armand Dillon. Who else could it be?"

"Why? What does he want?"

"Money! Everything that man does is motivated by profit. I've never known anybody so dedicated. It must be like a religion to him. He believes in it the way most people believe in God," Charles said and then yawned.

"To think I once was afraid that you might believe money to be that important! Dad, I wonder if Shaman Pi was able to return back to Fairmont University safely."

"I think so. I would have heard otherwise," Charles answered and closed his eyes.

"Your connections?" asked Robert.

"Yes. Are you asleep?"

"Close."

"Don't fight it."

"Good night."

CHAPTER EIGHTEEN

Sad Victory

To Cliff fell the job of bringing the news to Armand. He wasn't looking forward to it. He knew that Calder was the only one at PTP—and now Alliance for International Communications Incorporated—who was completely trusted by Armand. No one else actually knew what Calder's job was. He operated in a blanket of secrecy no one could penetrate. He came and went without leaving a trail nor did he connect with anyone, not even a secretary. He had a direct line to the administrative services unit in the basement of the headquarters building, which obeyed his every request without question. Nor was he ever countermanded by anyone else. He reported only to Armand, even though he, Cliff, was technically his boss.

When Cliff heard that Calder had died in a terrible fire in New Hampshire over the weekend, he assumed Armand would know what he was doing up there. Sadly, the details were sketchy. Some neighbors claimed he had entered the blazing building to save two couples who were guests of the owner. It seemed the guests all escaped while Calder ended up crashing through the roof and dying in the fire. The body was unrecognizable. Only the somewhat distant neighbors who had gathered on shore to witness the tragedy had a vague description of him to confirm his identity.

Calder had no living relatives, it seemed. There was no file on him in the human resource department. No one claimed the remains. Cliff had given orders to have them sent to the morgue in New York City in the event someone did show up to claim them. They fitted into an urn. Nothing else was left of him.

Cliff wondered how to time the news. This was a big moment in Armand's career. The chairman of the board had called an impromptu informational meeting of stockholders and the joint boards of PTP and AIC with the promise of world-shaking good news. Even some of the board members were in the dark. They called each other, demanded Fullington let them in on the secret. He required them to maintain absolute confidentiality. The news was so good, none of them objected, an unheard-of unanimous agreement and approval. Whispers began leaking to friends of friends of the press. Whispers were mysterious, nothing factual, just innuendos that immense changes to benefit the holders of shares were about to erupt.

As the stockholders picked up some false and some true inklings, the whispers spread, became slightly audible, then loud enough to be heard up and down the street. Before the impromptu meeting was in actual session, everyone was excited and knew nothing whatsoever. The press gathered in the lobby outside the hall where the stockholders were gathered. There were not enough seats, and many had to stand in the aisles and across the back behind the rows of folding chairs hurriedly assembled to meet the demand.

When Fullington gaveled the meeting to attention, the room grew quiet, and for the first time, the assembled crowd noticed Armand quietly slipping in and seating himself in a prominent chair beside Fullington. Whispers circled the room as one after another recognized who he was and shared the information. Fullington had to gavel the meeting for a second time.

"Ladies and gentlemen, fellow stockholders of both the Alliance of International Communications and the Premium Technical Products Corporation, by agreement of both boards of directors, I will call this meeting to order. Just to remind you all, this is not an official directors' meeting. It is called only as a meeting to transmit certain information that all stockholders in both corporations have a right to know. It is purely informational in character.

"This is a most historic moment, not only for our two corporations, but also for the wider business world, who will also be informed directly after the conclusion of this meeting. I am sure you will all have noticed the immense gathering of the media directly in the adjoining hall. Now to the business at hand. I know with what intense expectation you must be awaiting our announcement.

"The board of Premium Technical Products, in joint agreement with the board of Alliance for International Communication, has taken the unprecedented action of appointing the same individual to identical jobs in each of our corporations as an act of collaboration. There is no overlap in product or industry coverage between our two corporations, and therefore, no intracompetitive rivalry or conflicts of interest. The matter is pending final approval by the FTC, which often takes a considerable length of time to make its ruling. We are in no rush for approval, nor are we holding our breath and waiting for it. Our two boards have unilaterally and unanimously agreed in serving the best interests of all the stockholders.

"Dear stockholders, have any of you failed to notice what has happened to your shares just these last two days?"

There was a rustle of approval moving in waves through the hall as the crowd signified its recognition of the increasing share price in both corporations. One segment of the hall actually began a brief applause but then stopped, waiting to hear more.

"Yes," Fullington acknowledged the response, "we all are pleasantly surprised. There is nothing like an increase in share price to gladden the heart. Especially if it is based on some underlying reality that promises more and more profit, wouldn't you say?"

Now there was applause, and as it continued to rumble, many had stood up and a few shouted, "Hear! Hear!"

Fullington waited for the applause and cheers to quiet down and then went on. He seemed to relish this moment. No doubt he felt some ownership of the good results himself.

"These good things don't happen by themselves. They are not like ripe fruit that just drops from the trees into our waiting laps. No, sir. These things are caused—caused by good management and by good timing. Dear fellow owners of both corporations, I want to tell you how what you've seen these last few days and will see in weeks, months, and the years ahead are due largely to these two boards taking courageous action—unheard-of action in the history of corporations and solely and completely in the interest of all the shareholders. Fellow owners, I introduce to you someone you have all heard about, but probably never seen before, the president and CEO of PTP and, simultaneously, now the president and CEO of the Alliance for International Communications, Mr. Armand Dillon."

There was a stunned silence in the room. It wasn't just shock, it was surprise, and it was also confusion. Many wondered what the implications of such a move might be. Could anyone serve two masters and serve them equally well? How could the two corporations benefit equally? What about conflicts of interest?

In the disturbed silence of the room, Armand rose from his chair and approached the podium. Fullington shook his hand, smiling, and gave way for him to address the assembled stockholders.

"I am a man of few words," Armand's rough voice announced. "These days, words can only present a mirage. We all know this and are therefore skeptical of anything and everything we hear. I speak the universally understood language of action. Listen to my deeds and what you hear or see printed won't confuse you."

Armand paused and looked past the first few rows and up into the back of the room, taking careful note of the many upturned faces hopefully awaiting his words. He sensed in all of them an equal hunger for profit, gain, money. This was the atmosphere he could use: people greedy for material good. If anyone could satisfy them, he would do it.

"In this time of value confusion," Armand continued, "where some of us have been torn by conflicting motives, I have stood by you with uncompromising loyalty. I have made it clear who I am and what I do. I'm not a priest. I'm not an environmentalist. I don't play the piano, nor do I sing on prime time. I leave all artistic, cultural, religious, and political matters in the hands of others. My sole function in life is to serve you, the stockholders of AIC and PTP."

Armand paused again and watched the needy expressions on the sea of faces turned toward him. He continued, his voice gravelly and unpleasant to the ears, but the message eagerly awaited.

"What does this mean? How do I serve you? I steadfastly continue to build value for you, the shareholders. I generate monetary increase and abundance. Should it happen one day that you, the stockholders say to me, *'Enough! For heaven's sake, no more gain! We are sick and tired of all this money. To hell with share price. Who cares? We're fed up with success!'—*"

As his voice gathered in volume and intensity, the laughter rose to a roar.

Armand paused to wait for the laughter to subside. "When I hear you say that to me, I'll resign or change my ways. In the meantime, those shares will continue to build value, the corporations I lead will be more and more profitable, and we will all become wealthy. I will not change my ways until you change your appetite for lucre. Am I understood? Am I?"

In one massive surge, the entire assembled owners rose to their feet and applauded. Cheers broke out, and loud cries of "That a go!" supported him. It was clear to Armand that the will of the public endorsed his methods and his intentions.

He did not wait for the applause and cheering to stop. He moved quickly to take his seat, as though eager to be done with talking and get on with the action. His steps were firm and overflowing with energy.

Fullington took his place at the podium and raised his arms to request silence. He had to wait and repeat his motions several times before there was enough quiet for his voice to be heard.

"Thank you for your support and approval of our courageous move into the future for both our corporations and for you, the stockholders. This informational meeting has served its purpose, and we'll need to meet with the press in the adjoining hall. We only have time for two or three questions, but I am sure you'll be hearing more from us as Mr. Dillon takes charge and implements his intentions. I'm sure you've probably already heard rumors of his activity to date. I'll take a question. Yes, you, sir!"

A young man in a gray pin-striped suit and softly pink tie stood up and asked, "What will happen if the FTC does not approve? Aren't we moving a little too fast? After all—"

"Yes," Fullington interrupted him. "We're running a business, have checked with the best legal advice, and other than that, we do what we have to do to serve you, our owners. No matter what the FTC comes up with, it will be hard to prove we are not serving the best interests of the stockholders. It would be something if the FTC or the SEC set itself above the law, don't you think?"

Fullington basked in the ripple of laughter that met his comments and attitude. Hands flew up in all corners of the room. He pointed toward a woman he knew to be one of their larger stockholders.

"Would you please clarify the situation with Lucinda Brahms? Has she been fired?"

Fullington paused thoughtfully before answering. The room fell to an absolute silence.

"Ms. Brahms, the former president and CEO of the Alliance for International Communications Incorporated has not been heard of for the better part of a week. The circumstances around her departure are being investigated by our own internal security system and also by the police and FBI. We are not going to comment on any of that until the investigation has been completed."

"Is it true she took off with half a million of our money?" a voice shouted from the left side of the hall.

"No comment."

"Do you deny it?"

"No comment." Fullington pointed to a hand waving frantically at him from the right side of the room.

"We all love success. No complaints there! What about social responsibility? Does Mr. Dillon give a toot about that? From what we—" the waving hand was lowered as the young man started his speech.

"I'll let Mr. Dillon answer that."

Armand rose from his chair and moved to the podium unhurriedly. He preferred a calm atmosphere for anything he had to say. He knew the intellect usually does not function at its best in a cloud of emotional hysteria.

"Even though it is not our primary responsibility, we will not shirk any responsibility lawfully demanded of us or required as part of good business practice. You will read in our annual reports that a modest, but reasonable amount of our profit is given—I say, given—through the PTP and AIC Foundations to benefit education and worthy nonprofit projects. However, we fulfill our social responsibility in ways you may not have thought about. In the last six months, we have added one hundred new blue-collar jobs. We have increased our overall compensation of employees by two percent, and we have provided our system-wide customers with a total of seventeen million needed and wanted product units, which include thirteen new products developed in our R and D facility. I think we more than satisfy our social responsibility by doing business in the best way we know how. Don't you?"

"But, Mr. Dillon—" The questioner was drowned out by bursts of applause and approval.

Armand Dillon nodded his head, indicating his satisfaction with the response, and returned to his chair. He also made a gesture to Fullington resembling that of a guillotine cutting through his neck. Fullington raised his hand and waited for an uneasy quiet to settle in before speaking.

"I'm sorry, dear stockholders, we don't have time for more questions today. You'll certainly hear more from us as Mr. Dillon works his well-known magic. Thank you for attending at such short notice. Thank you!"

***

Cliff knocked at the closed door of Armand's office. After a moment of silence, Armand's gravelly voice summoned him in.

"Good morning, sir." Cliff added a slight note of sadness to his own voice. Armand looked up. His focus was on a series of organizational charts blending the two corporations.

"Any word from Calder?" he asked immediately.

"No." Cliff cleared his voice, somewhat hesitant as to how he should proceed. "I'm afraid I have some bad news."

Armand frowned instinctively, knowing the bad news had something to do with Calder's mission. "Let's have it."

Armand had complete confidence in Calder's loyalty and ability. If there was a problem, he was sure Calder would handle it effectively. If it was a cost issue, that would not have deterred Calder. The proper results always involved a variable cost, and Calder never yet bothered him with such matters. He hoped it wasn't an issue involving the secrecy of the operation. That could backfire and leave them with a public black eye. He doubted it. Calder had understood right from the very beginning that all of his activity would be covert. Armand looked sharply at Cliff. He couldn't imagine what bad news was involved.

"I have heard and understand it to be true . . . Calder perished in a disastrous fire in New Hampshire over the weekend. He must have been vacationing there, although none of us knew where he was until we were notified."

"Calder? You say Calder perished? Died?" Armand was shocked.

"Yes. He died in the fire, saving the lives of some guests of the owner."

"I can't believe it. Are you sure?"

"I'm afraid it's definite. The fire department is sending his remains to the morgue here in New York City. As far as we know there is nobody to claim them."

Armand continued to stare at Cliff, his eyes hooded and reflective. "I've spent years getting that man ready. I trained him to read balance sheets and financial reports, analyzing their connections with reality. You came to me knowing all that, but he had to be taught. What a magnificent follower he turned out to be. He had something you will probably never have. He had unequivocal loyalty. I trusted him with the most delicate assignments. And now he is gone. Escaped without so much as a thank-you. After all my trouble. I've invested years of training and special attention on him. Wasted years! Wasted attention! He is lost to me for good."

A small patch of moisture appeared on the ashen skin of his left cheek. He kept his eyes fastened on the charts lining his desk showing all the organizational connections he had envisaged for the combined two corporations.

"I'm sorry, sir." Cliff tried to be comforting.

"Not as much as I am."

"There's nobody to send flowers to. Should I do something about the remains?" Cliff asked.

"Won't the city bury them after a while?" Armand was being practical.

"I expect."

"Let them! They can afford it. They'll probably use our tax money to do it. On second thought, find a good resting place for him. AIC can afford it now," Armand decided, and then he asked, "What happened to the guests Calder attempted to save? Did they survive?"

"I believe so. There was no mention of any other death. Although it was revealed that they were to be picked up by a jeep that never showed up. Nor does anyone know what happened to the guests. You'd think they would hang around to make sure no one else was caught in the flames. Do you want me to make further inquiries?"

"No. If you should find out anything further about those guests, let me know." Armand stroked his chin thoughtfully before he went on. "Calder was using someone. Evans, I believe?"

"Yes."

"Where's he?"

"As part of the agreement for his services, Calder promised him a safe haven. Even I do not know where it is, but I am sure I can find out."

"Do that, Cliff. He's a good man?" Armand asked.

"I don't think so. He'll do anything for money. That makes him useful. It also makes us vulnerable. A higher bidder could easily get him." Cliff voiced his opinion.

"Double reasons to keep tabs on him. Is he expensive?"

"I think Calder was paying him by the job. Maybe we should keep him attached with a small stipend, shall we say a kind of retainer of sorts?" Cliff smirked his dislike of Evans.

"All right. I see it as insurance," Armand agreed.

Armand then pushed one of the charts in the direction of Cliff, indicating him to scan it.

"All of these charts are useless now. I have to rethink the future. I'm relying on you to help identify someone like Calder. It will probably take time, and even so, who knows if we'll ever find another with the same level of devotion to our cause."

"Actually"—Cliff thought he might be able to cheer him up—"we've signed up a young engineer that will graduate from Fairmount University in the spring. He was a prodigy of Calder's. Calder had been seeing him regularly as the person keeping tabs on the McLanes."

"What's his name?" Armand perked up with the news.

"Steward Brand. He's a vet. We've been paying for some of his expenses in return for his services. In a way, we've already got him partially hooked."

"Keep tabs on him, Cliff. Let's not preclude any others that might still show up on the horizon. I need creative engineers as well as devoted accountants. The world is turning in our direction. Beneath the surface of the natural world, a new world is taking shape. It will have no substance to it at all. It will be an entirely virtual world—a profitable mirage. Everyone leaning in my direction will automatically find themselves citizens of that new world. Ha!" Armand had recovered from his sadness entirely and was spinning more webs to catch followers.

"I forgot to mention there's someone outside waiting for a chance to speak with you." Cliff remembered.

"Who?"

"It's Benning. You'll remember he heads up Human Resources for AIC. He's been giving us a little resistance with some of our scaling-down operations. I wouldn't trust him if I were you. He seems to be in tight with Graham and Lucinda Brahms."

"You're not me!" Armand scowled at Cliff. "Send him in. I'd like to know what he wants."

"Anything else for me?" Cliff asked.

"Let me know when you've located Evans."

"Yes, sir. If that's what you want me to do!"

"Still need orders from me, Cliff?"

"Yes."

"For another thing, I want to meet this new fellow . . . Steward Brand? Can you arrange that?"

"I'm not sure if you should. He will be joining the company when he graduates in June. He'll be in orientation for a while, probably start as an engineer in training, way down in the organization. It's not appropriate for you to single him out at this stage," Cliff said.

"I need people who serve me with their whole soul. I want those who believe they are thinking for themselves as they serve me. They will be totally in the dark while believing themselves to be the light of the world. My followers will think they are free. Perhaps this Steward is one of them?" Armand asked hopefully.

"Perhaps. I'll do my best to train him well," Cliff assured him. "Shall I send Benning in now?"

"Yes."

Armand watched as Cliff left, leaving the door open. Benning entered and closed the door behind him. He came right up close to Armand's desk and stood waiting.

"Did you know that Calder is dead?" Armand asked him.

"Yes. I heard from Horst."

"He shared that with you?"

"I'm his boss. What do you expect? He tells me everything."

Armand shrugged his acknowledgment. "What do you want? We should keep any except the obvious business meetings to a minimum. I prefer you to remain undercover. The people here are not stupid, you know!"

"This is important, if you want my loyalty," Benning explained.

"All right, what?"

"Calder was paying me. I counted on him, and he was reliable." Benning licked his lips nervously. "Who will pay me now?"

Armand took note of Benning's nervousness. "Deep in debt, are we?" he asked.

"I took a few chances in reliance on Calder's monthly payment," Benning admitted.

Armand thoughtfully drummed his fingers on the polished top of his desk before he answered. "At first, I thought maybe it's time we cleaned up this little act of ours. I considered promoting you."

"A different job?" Benning asked hopefully.

"No, the same job, but a different title and grade. I was thinking senior vice president, Human Resources."

"As long as it gives me the same money, net after taxes."

"I've changed my mind. Promoting you would signal Graham and Horst that you've compromised yourself. I want them to consider you a friend—on their side. So instead I am going to demote you and have you report to Cliff. You'll still be responsible for Human Resources, but at a lower grade. This will signal everyone that you are not trusted by me. You will be able to serve me, unhampered by the suspicions of the Brahms contingency," Armand said.

"You're cutting my pay?" Benning asked angrily. "After all I've been doing for you? You wouldn't even be at the head of AIC if it weren't for me!"

Armand looked at Benning disdainfully before he answered. "Money, money. Don't you ever think of anything else?"

"If I had known about Calder, I would not have made certain . . . investments." Benning wondered whether Armand really appreciated the risks he was taking all along for his sake.

"Don't worry, I will double what you get under the table to make up for your cut in salary. I am paying you to stay faithful."

"Do I have to do anything additional? I mean, above and beyond my job duties?" he asked.

"Only what you've been doing all along, snitching on your friends and betraying their trust! That's all." Armand made it clear how much he despised Benning, and Benning felt it. He remained quiet. If he didn't have all his debts and other obligations, he would have quit right on the spot. However, the way things were, he better just be quiet and try to please his benefactor.

"I want you to keep pumping Horst—as a friend and his boss—for any information on the whereabouts and activities of those escapees. I want to know everything they do and plan. I want you to continue to be trusted and included in whatever plans they hatch. In particular, keep an eye on Graham. They are all too creative and entrepreneurial to lay low in South America for long. Now start earning your money."

"With Calder gone, who will pay me?" Benning asked again.

"Until further notice, I will. Once every month, I'll ask to meet with you for an update on HR matters. I'll see that you are compensated then—privately."

"Very well, sir."

"All right, Benning. You can go. See that you don't betray me! See that you reserve that for friends. I am not your friend and never will be!" With that Armand dismissed him and returned to the charts on the desk in front of him.

There was silence in the room. What consequences of this day's action would surface in the future was not clear. Armand was absorbed entirely in his charts as Benning eased himself out through the door and pulled it closed behind him.

Author Biography

Siegfried E. Finser

Siegfried is the founder of RSF Social Finance, a nonprofit financial services organization that has pioneered *associative economics* by connecting financial transactions with the highest intentions of the human spirit. He currently serves on the board and advises selected clients.

He has written children's books, plays, and books about money and destiny. His current novel features the struggle of humanity between head and heart domination. He blames the majority of our social problems worldwide on the focus of our present educational institutions on the exclusive development of the intellect.

Siegfried has been a Waldorf schoolteacher, a corporate executive, and a consultant. He has a BA from Rutgers University and an MA from New York University. His published works include *Money Can Heal*, *Footprints of an Angel*, and *A Guide to Full Enrollment*. As a young man, he traveled the country in freight trains and reefers, picked fruit, and sold bibles. All these grassroots experiences have enriched his fifty short stories!

He is appreciative of the wonderful support of his wife, Ruth; three grown children, Torin, Mark, and Angela; and seven grandchildren. They exceed his fondest wishes for them.

The battle between the unscrupulous intellect and the caring heart has never been so poignantly portrayed as in COLLISION. The president of PTP Corporation uses every trick to secure the acquisition of AIC Corporation. He is so smart and so ruthless his subordinates hardly know how to interpret his commands and often fall short. The stockholders love him, but in the final episode, he might actually be failing while achieving the greatest success.

The lovely, kindhearted Lucinda Brahms loses her job but gains what is most precious to her. Do the young couple in the story find each other in spite of the dangerous intrigues and unexpected secrets exposed? How will they escape the evil overshadowing them and survive to fight again on their own terms?

The collisions in this story are on several levels. The action moves from the boardroom, to the university campus, and on to secret hideouts. Light and dark, warm and cold intersect as the key figures collide in the struggle for power.